THE MATT DRAKE THRILLERS

"Devoted action fans will be right at home. All can benefit from Drake's insider tips: get military pepper spray if you can; the commercial stuff is powder-puff." —*Booklist*

"Bentley adds brains to the traditional brawn of yester-year in crafting a thinking man's shoot-'em-up that keeps us on the edge of our seat from beginning to end."
—*The Providence Journal*

"You can smell the cordite, hear the explosions, and feel the fight in this one. Action jumps from every page."
—Steve Berry, *New York Times* bestselling author of *The Malta Exchange*

"Weaves adrenaline and angst, intrigue and insight, onto every page. In a crowded field, Bentley just raised the bar and vaulted over it."
—Andrews & Wilson, US Navy veterans and authors of the *Wall Street Journal* bestselling Tier One series

"Destined to be the best debut of the year. Bentley writes with the precision of Lee Child and the wit of Nelson DeMille."
—Brigadier General Anthony J. Tata, US Army (ret.), national bestselling author of *Dark Winter*

"Matt Drake has to fight two wars, maybe more, and he has to save himself before he can save everyone else. An intense, deeply personal story written by someone who has been there."

—Larry Bond, bestselling author of *Arctic Gambit*

"Hold on tight. You're in for one helluva ride!"

—Mike Maden, *New York Times* bestselling author of *Tom Clancy Enemy Contact*

"I am blown away. . . . Top-notch."

—Sean Parnell, *New York Times* bestselling author of *Outlaw Platoon*

"Don Bentley has lived this life, and he writes with deep authenticity. This is one hell of a book."

—Nick Petrie, national bestselling author of *Tear It Down*

"Another supercharged, action-packed adventure that's tailor-made for fans of Mark Greaney and Brad Taylor. . . . Gritty, timely, and packed with nonstop, heart-thumping action, Don Bentley's *The Outside Man* is a must-read for fans of propulsive, unputdownable thrillers."

—Ryan Steck, The Real Book Spy

"An unflinching dive into the soul of the modern warrior that is so beautifully written and expertly executed that I cannot believe it is a debut novel."

—Joshua Hood, author of *Clear by Fire*

"A white-knuckle ride through both the Syrian battlegrounds and the innermost sanctums of DC politics, with deadly twists and turns along the way."

—Matthew Betley, bestselling author of *Rules of War* and the Logan West series

TITLES BY DON BENTLEY

THE OUTSIDE MAN

DON BENTLEY

BERKLEY
New York

BERKLEY
An imprint of Penguin Random House LLC
penguinrandomhouse.com

Copyright © 2021 by Donald Burton Bentley II
Excerpt from *Hostile Intent* copyright © 2022 by Donald Burton Bentley II
Penguin Random House supports copyright. Copyright fuels creativity, encourages
diverse voices, promotes free speech, and creates a vibrant culture. Thank you for buying
an authorized edition of this book and for complying with copyright laws by not
reproducing, scanning, or distributing any part of it in any form without permission.
You are supporting writers and allowing Penguin Random House to continue to
publish books for every reader.

BERKLEY and the BERKLEY & B colophon are registered trademarks of
Penguin Random House LLC.

ISBN: 9781984805157

Berkley hardcover edition / March 2021
Berkley premium edition / February 2022

Printed in the United States of America
1   3   5   7   9   10   8   6   4   2

Book design by Kristin del Rosario

To Will, Faith, and Kelia—
I'm so very proud of each of you
and so very thankful that God chose me to be your dad.

You come at the king, you best not miss.

—THE WIRE

It is well that war is so terrible, or we should grow too fond of it.

—ROBERT E. LEE

ONE

AUSTIN, TEXAS

Austin in February is paradise. While the rest of the country is gripped with snow, biting cold, or both, the self-professed home of the weird is in full flower. Endless blue Texas skies stretch from horizon to horizon, temperatures hover in the low sixties, and woodsmoke and slow-cooking brisket flavor the air. In February, it's hard to have a bad day in Austin.

But I was giving it a helluva try.

I stomped on the gas pedal as the traffic light changed from yellow to amber. The eight-cylinder Hemi replied with a chest-rumbling growl, sending my truck hurtling through the intersection. A split second later, I slammed on the brakes, bringing the five-thousand-pound Dodge Ram to a screeching stop. A comfortable six inches now separated my pickup and the bumper-sticker-adorned electric blue Prius ahead of me.

On the bench seat to my right, a packet of papers slid

toward the floorboard. I made a grab for them and missed, snagging the thin green tissue wrapping a bouquet of crimson roses instead.

All things considered, I'd take the flowers over the papers any day. Even with the papers scattered across the truck's floorboard, I could still read the words RADIOLOGY DEPARTMENT stamped across the tops of the pages in sterile block letters. At this distance, the spidery blue handwriting filling the margins wasn't legible, but I knew what the doctor had scribbled all the same.

The Prius driver glared in his rearview mirror, and I chuckled. Apparently the COEXIST sticker plastered to his bumper didn't extend to fellow Austinites. At least not during lunch-hour traffic anyway. Though to be fair, I wasn't in much of a *coexist* mood myself. But this had nothing to do with the angry Prius driver. No, my ire was focused on the man in the late-model Honda one intersection to my rear.

The man who wanted to kill me.

My name is Matt Drake, and I do not have a normal vocation. For the last year, I haven't had much of a vocation at all. However, before my self-imposed leave of absence began, I worked in a unique field. A field in which the ability to tell the difference between a distracted driver and a trained operative transitioning from surveillance to interdiction was a matter of life and death.

This is why I knew that the dark-complected man driving the Honda was focused on more than just traffic. At the previous stoplight, he'd cut off a white Tesla Roadster to edge in behind me, abandoning any pretense of remaining covert. He hadn't followed me through the red light, which bought me a bit of time, but not much.

As I waited for the signal in front of me to change, the Honda's driver reached above his head, adjusting the sun visor. This innocuous-seeming motion provided final confirmation. The driver was wearing gloves. Gloves in sixty-degree weather. And not just any gloves. The thin Nomex variety that stretched from his hand to midway up his forearm. The type of gloves favored by just two groups of people—pilots and shooters.

My leave of absence was officially over.

Shifting in my seat, I drew the Glock 23 tucked into my Don Hume in-the-waistband holster and press-checked the pistol. A shiny .40-caliber hollow point winked back at me. Easing the slide forward, I set the pistol on the seat between my legs and considered what to do next.

The signal turned green, and traffic heaved forward. Or at least most of it. Mr. Coexist did not. Instead, he rolled toward the intersection at a snail's pace, burning time until the light cycled yellow. Then he accelerated, surging through the juncture at the last moment. As his tiny car barreled beneath the now-red traffic signal, he bade me farewell with a one-fingered salute.

Behind me, the shooter eased through the intersection, nudging up to my bumper.

The key to defeating an ambush is actually pretty simple—don't get caught in the kill zone. I didn't know where the shooter intended to initiate, but since lead had yet to start flying, the kill zone had to be somewhere in front of me.

Which meant I needed to act. Now.

Smashing the brake with my left foot, I shifted the truck into neutral and revved the engine with my right. As the RPM crept past six thousand, I tightened my seat belt, locked the Glock under my right leg, and prepared to throw the transmission into reverse.

And that was when a woman pushing a stroller stepped into the road.

TWO

The woman was dressed in black yoga pants and a hot pink tank top that showed off toned brown arms. White earbuds accessorized her outfit—the wireless kind because Austinites are nothing if not hip. She rolled the stroller right in front of my truck's vibrating hood as if she didn't have a care in the world—again, Austin in February. Though even if she'd been the most vigilant of mommas, a gunfight on South Congress probably wouldn't have been on her radar. That just wasn't her life.

But it was mine.

Behind me, the shooter was talking on his phone. Which meant he wasn't alone. Which meant that my window was closing.

Slamming the gearshift into reverse, I wrenched the wheel to the left. The Hemi didn't disappoint, much to the chagrin of the driver of the compact Hyundai to my right. One moment, the Hyundai's driver was contemplating the perfect Austin sky. The next, the black brush guard covering my front bumper scraped along his emerald green quarter panel as I turned my truck perpendicular to the threat behind me.

Not a perfect solution, but it would do.

Grabbing the Glock, I exploded out of my truck, coming face-to-face with the woman pushing the stroller. To her credit, she went into immediate momma-bear mode. Though her eyes were as wide as saucers, she put herself between me and her precious cargo. Then she screamed out a question.

"Are you crazy?"

Books could be written in response. Still, I understood why she might ask. My current appearance was what my wife playfully called *rustic*. At least I hoped it was playfully. My hair was a bit on the shaggy side, and my face hadn't seen a razor for the better part of three days. My pearly snap shirt was ironed, my jeans clean, and my Ariat cowboy boots freshly polished. But there was still something about me that didn't sit right with the woman. Maybe it was that my broad shoulders and scarred knuckles were somehow at odds with my carefully cultivated ragamuffin appearance. Or maybe it was something else.

Something more primal.

Either way, I didn't have time for niceties. Grabbing the woman by her toned arm, I jerked her and her stroller toward the relative safety of my truck's front wheel well.

"FBI," I said, pulling her forward. "Get down!"

Now, before you get the wrong idea, I am not a law

enforcement officer of any kind. The men and women of that career field must stand before juries while swearing to tell the truth, the whole truth, and nothing but the truth, so help them God. My own relationship with the truth was a bit more problematic. For example, I have found it beneficial to impersonate an FBI agent from time to time. This is because most Americans seem preconditioned to trust FBI agents and obey their commands.

Unfortunately, my new friend was not like most Americans.

"Get your hands off me," she said, pulling away with surprising ease.

This girl worked out. Maybe Pilates or kickboxing.

I grabbed her left arm, fingers encircling her biceps, and tried to drag her back toward safety. She expressed her displeasure with a rather respectable right cross. Her knuckles connected squarely with my cheekbone, and I felt the jarring impact all the way to the base of my neck.

Definitely kickboxing.

"The man behind me has a gun," I said, sliding beneath a jab as I wrestled her and the stroller behind the truck's front tire.

"So do you," she said, attempting to stomp one of her pristinely white cross-trainers through my instep.

God bless Texas girls.

I got my foot out of the way. Barely. When this was over, I might have to pay her kickboxing instructor a congratulatory visit. I'd snatched Muslim Brotherhood members off the streets of Cairo with less fuss.

A police siren cut through the air, once again proving

Dad's adage that when it rains, a bear craps in the woods. I have no idea what that means, but Dad sure seemed certain when he said it.

The she-lion posing as a suburban mom aimed an elbow at my groin. I turned with the blow, catching it on the outside of my thigh. Ignoring the pins-and-needles sensation running the length of my leg, I edged over the truck's hood. What I saw on the other side wasn't pretty. One of Austin's finest was out of his patrol car, pistol in hand. His thick shoulders and narrow waist contrasted with his baby face and rosy cheeks. He didn't look a day over twenty, but young or not, he was running in my direction, ready to take care of business. As our eyes met, he skidded to a halt, dropping into a shooter's stance.

Right next to the Honda.

I tried to shout a warning, but wasn't fast enough. The policeman jerked like a marionette, spasms racking his body. The accompanying series of *pop*s was surprisingly soft. The shooter had a suppressed submachine gun—a Heckler & Koch variant if I had to guess. The 9mm pistol rounds didn't pack the stopping power of an assault rifle's, but the weapon was accurate, compact, and easy to suppress.

In short, the perfect tool for an assassin.

The cop collapsed to the ground in a tangle of limbs. The blood-soaked right side of his uniform meant that at least one of the slugs had found its way either through or under his vest. That distinction was important. *Through the vest* meant that the assassin was firing rounds designed to defeat body armor. This, combined with the suppressed HK, would point to a shooter who was both well financed and well trained.

As my SEAL friends liked to say, the only easy day was yesterday.

"Stay here," I said to the she-devil. For the first time in our short but turbulent relationship, she listened. Maybe it was something she saw in my face or heard in my voice. Or maybe with her mother's intuition she somehow interpreted the meaning behind the suppressed gunfire and breaking glass. Either way, she nodded, blond ponytail bobbing, as she scooped her squirming baby out of the stroller.

"Where are you going?" she said, pressing against the truck's tire.

"To end this."

THREE

The cardinal rule of surviving gunfights is simple: Avoid occupying the same space and time as a bullet. But in practice, this is often easier said than done. This was why I was running toward the rear of my truck instead of peeking around the front bumper.

During periods of intense stress, people react instinctively. Since the gunman had last seen me crouching by the hood, that was where he would instinctively remain focused. At the same time, my instincts were telling me to vault over the hood and run toward him, Glock blazing.

So I did the opposite.

As I rounded my truck's rear bumper, the scene before me came in disjointed flashes as time seemed to slow down. To my right, the cop gave a wet cough, misting his chapped lips with fat crimson droplets. To my left, the driver of a burnt orange Audi was in the process of opening his door. He paused when he saw the Glock in my hand. I rewarded his indecision by hip checking his door, slamming it shut. Then I focused on the shooter, who was still in his car, staring intently at my truck.

My firearms instructor at the Farm used to say that pistols were defensive weapons only. I couldn't have agreed more. Unfortunately, the modified M4 I'd carried in the Ranger Regiment wasn't available right now.

Neither was the option to stay defensive.

Though it fired a smaller-caliber round than my Glock, the gunman's HK sported a much longer barrel, making it inherently more accurate. This meant I didn't have the luxury of hiding behind a car and trading shots with my attacker. Instead, I had to rely on the two things that have kept infantrymen alive since the invention of the musket—speed and violence of action.

I brought the Glock to eye level. My focus narrowed and then narrowed again as I oriented on the gunman's chest. I started my trigger press as the Glock's front sight post came even with the gap framed by the rear sight.

Even height, even light.

The pistol kicked.

The front sight post drifted up, then floated down, settling again between the rear sights.

The pistol kicked.

The process repeated.

I fired another aimed pair before looking past the front sight for the first time while moving forward. My weight transferred from heel to toe in a rolling motion perfected through thousands of rounds and hundreds of hours on the range. The Honda's window spider-webbed around my shot groups, but the shooter in the front seat was still very much alive.

Killing someone in a car was tricky. Windows, doors, and countless other obstructions affected a bullet's trajectory in ways that were impossible to predict. I'd seen terrorists felled by a single shot and fighters emerge unscathed after a battery of automatic weapons fire.

In the end, there was only one way to be sure—get closer.

Vaulting onto the car's hood, I did just that, firing from the high-ready position. I no longer bothered with aimed pairs. Instead, I sent a constant stream of lead into the windshield while advancing. The driver jerked, an HK MP5 falling from his hands.

I centered the Glock's front sight post on his forehead and pulled the trigger twice more. He'd started the fight. Now was not the time for mercy. His body spasmed as my hollow points tore through the bridge of his nose and right eye socket.

Then he slid forward.

The entire engagement had lasted maybe fifteen seconds, but it had felt like fifteen years. As my brain finally recognized that the threat to my life had been eliminated, my other senses came back online. I could feel the Glock's pebbly grip beneath my fingers and smell the coppery scent of blood mixed with the acrid smell of gunpowder.

But it was my sense of hearing that really brought things into perspective. Over the gunfire-induced ringing in my ears and the gasps of the wounded cop, something else demanded my attention—squealing tires and crashing steel as a pair of SUVs battered their way through the traffic jam. One swung up on the curb to my right while the other rolled over the sidewalk to my left.

Both were heading straight at me.

FOUR

In my line of work, training is great, but nothing beats experience. As the two SUVs careened toward me, my experience in shitholes the world over allowed me to process several things at once: One, my Glock's slide had locked to the rear, revealing an empty chamber. Two, my spare magazine was in the truck's glove box, which meant, at this moment, it might as well have been on the other side of the earth. Three, the two men driving against traffic on opposing sides of the street were probably not on the side of the angels.

The assassin's help had just arrived, and I was outgunned, outmanned, and out of ammunition.

In other words, just another day at the office.

I vaulted off the Honda's hood, and landed next to the fallen police officer as squealing brakes and opening car doors announced the arrival of bad-guy reinforcements. The cop was a big 'un, probably tipping the scale north of two twenty-five with all of his gear. Dropping my pistol, I hooked both hands through the fabric loop at the top of his tactical vest and began dragging him toward my truck to the accompanying *pop*, *pop*, *pop* of multiple suppressed weapons firing on automatic.

Rounds snapped past my head like rabid hornets, but I kept pumping my legs until a ricochet slammed into my right calf muscle, causing an instant charley horse. Thanks to equal parts adrenaline and grit, I finished dragging the cop behind my truck's front tire. Then physics took over. I collapsed next to the ninja mom and her toddler, working the cramp from my leg. Once again, her eyes widened at my unexpected appearance, but this time she didn't try to punch me.

Things were looking up.

"I thought you were ending this," she said as my truck rocked under the onslaught of automatic weapons fire.

"Working on it," I said, reaching to unholster the cop's pistol.

Like many law enforcement officers, this cop seemed to believe that bigger was better. He was wearing a customized Springfield 1911. It was an extremely accurate pistol chambered in a man-stopping .45 caliber, but it held only seven rounds in its single-stack magazine, plus one in the chamber. This was a problem. In gunfights with multiple opponents, more bullets were always better.

Still, a Springfield .45 with eight rounds was a hell of a lot better than a Glock with zero. Squeezing the checkered walnut grip with both hands, I leaned against the truck's frame and popped up to have a look.

What I saw took the proverbial wind out of my sails.

Two teams of two shooters were advancing toward me with textbook precision. The gunmen were working the street from opposite sides, one member of each team advancing while his partner laid down suppressive fire in short, controlled bursts.

These guys knew their business.

Sighting down the Springfield's narrow barrel, I fired an aimed pair at the advancing shooter on the left before doing the same to the shooter on the right. The .45's cannonlike report echoed across the street, nearly drowning out the HKs' suppressed *pop*s. Both my opening volleys missed, but the advancing shooters still paused, reassessing the tactical situation.

Score one for the good guys.

Unfortunately, that single engagement had also cost me half my ammunition.

Not so good.

Ducking behind the truck's hood, I reached for the leather magazine holders attached to the cop's patrol belt and then stopped midmotion as my eyes settled on the radio on his chest. Goddamn it, but I was smarter than this.

Ripping the radio from the cop's bloody shirt, I mashed the transmit button.

"Shots fired, corner of Congress and Chavez Street. Officer down. Multiple gunshot wounds."

I released the transmit button, and the radio exploded with voices. Voices I didn't have time to answer. Instead,

I grabbed two magazines from the cop's belt, combat-reloaded the Springfield, and popped back over the hood.

The team of four shooters was now even with the gunman's Honda. As police sirens wailed, one of the men freed the dead shooter from the car. The second tossed something about the size of a Coke can into the backseat.

My sudden appearance brought another onslaught of bullets from the shooters pulling security, sending me diving to the pavement. Leaning on my side, I stretched past the front tire, edging around the bumper. My front sight post found one of the gunmen. I snapped off a shot and was in the process of firing a second when the Honda exploded.

The concussion smashed me into the ground just as a hubcap scythed past my face in a blur of steel. I grabbed onto the bumper for support, and hauled myself into a seated position as the hit team moved back in short, disciplined bounds.

The professional part of me admired the team's tactical soundness. Their break-contact maneuver was textbook, like something out of the movie *Heat*. I was still alive only because of the legion of converging police sirens. A few minutes more and the team would have flanked me. I know that some folks claim that it's better to be lucky than good, but I'll take an M4 equipped with an EOTech reflex sight and a tactical harness full of spare magazines over luck any day.

Which was exactly what the cop rounding the building on foot was carrying.

FIVE

Good cops are absolutely fearless. They charge into banks mid-robbery and run toward the sound of gunfire. The stud who careened around the building as the hit team was piling into their SUVs was no exception. His eyes found me, then my gun, then his blood-soaked brother.

He never hesitated.

The M4 came up to his shoulder in one smooth motion, and he began taking the slack out of the trigger. He didn't yell *freeze*, didn't tell me to drop my gun, and didn't call for backup. He saw a threat, and moved to eliminate it.

But he didn't see the shooter to my left hesitate as he climbed into his SUV. I might have been the target, but that was before the op had gone sideways. Now the bad guys were in break-contact mode. My hiding behind my T-boned truck wasn't going to stop that battle drill, but the cop was a different story. If he transmitted their description, there wasn't a wheelman alive who could outrun the radio waves.

Which meant that the cop had to die.

So I shot him.

Actually, the three of us fired our weapons almost simultaneously. But I shot first. My slug caught Austin's finest squarely in his chest plate, and as big as he was, the hit to the body armor still staggered him. Which meant that his round zinged across my shoulder instead of drilling me in the chest, and the burst from the shooter's HK cratered the wall above the cop instead of his forehead.

Hot damn.

Ignoring the line of fire etched on my shoulder and the throbbing in my calf, I squeezed off another series of aimed pairs at the shooter. I didn't hit him, but he got the message all the same. Rather than finishing the cop, who was on his hands and knees dry heaving, the shooter jumped into his SUV and slammed the door. The SUV reversed course, smashing over a newspaper stand before squealing down a side street, the second SUV in trail.

Now shrieking sirens seemed to be coming from everywhere. Half a dozen emergency vehicles converged on the burning Honda from all directions. A police cruiser rolled up behind me, and another hero vaulted out of the driver's side.

"Drop the gun," she said, the muzzle of her pistol rock steady, despite her adrenaline-soaked voice.

I did as I was told, placing the Springfield on the pavement in slow, exaggerated motions. After releasing the pistol, I started to get to my feet. I needn't have bothered. A sea of blue uniforms smashed into me, driving me to the ground. For once, momma bear seemed to be on my side. I could hear her screaming that I was the good guy, but the cops were having none of it. Metal bit into my wrists as someone snapped on a set of handcuffs.

Then the blows began in earnest.

I suppose that I should have been mad about taking an ass kicking after just saving a cop, but I couldn't blame them. The police officer with the tricked-out M4 and plate carrier was still alive, but the youngster who'd responded first was lying unmoving in a pool of his own blood. Someone had been trying to kill me, and one of Austin's finest had been in the way. Now a kid who looked barely old enough to shave was dead.

And the kick in the balls was that I didn't even know why.

SIX

Y"ou're like herpes. You just keep coming back."

I didn't dignify the comment with a response. At least not right away. The beatdown I'd received from the police officers had rung my bell more than I cared to admit. Consequently, I was still having trouble putting together a worthy comeback. I hoped that's what was causing the fogginess, anyway. Unbidden, the image of the doctor's report lying on my truck's floorboards came to mind.

And then the shakes began.

"Hey—what the fuck's wrong with you?"

The tremors normally started small, originating in the minor muscle groups of my extremities before progressing to the major ones in my chest, back, and arms. But not today. Today, my shoulders and hands were already jittering like a tweaker's.

"I'm just excited to see you again," I said, my teeth chattering. "Agent Rawlings, right?"

I could no longer control my hands, and the handcuffs and metal chain binding them together rattled like a Gypsy's bangles.

"Are you seizing?" Rawlings said.

"No. Maybe. It's complicated. It's either a physiological reaction to a previously experienced psychosomatic stressor or the side effects from an experimental chemical weapon. The doctor wasn't real specific."

"You need a medic?" Rawlings said.

"I need you to uncuff my fucking hands," I said, holding my manacles across the IKEA-quality table separating us.

The trembling had turned the handcuff chain into a blur of metal vibrating like a tuning fork. Still, I could see the indecision written across Agent Rawlings's face. Based on the accounts of the ninja mom and other bystanders, he had to be ninety-nine percent sure I hadn't instigated the shootout on South Congress Avenue. But that other one percent was a bitch, especially since the last time we'd been face-to-face, things had turned a wee bit physical.

Time to address the elephant in the room.

"Look, you know who I am and what I do. I'm sorry we got off on the wrong foot, but we both know you had it coming. Now, uncuff me before things become unpleasant."

Rawlings hesitated another long second, but then he

reached into his coat pocket and fished out a handcuff key, just as I knew he would.

Our history was limited to a scuffle in the Austin airport, so I didn't know him well. But I did know the type. Today, like the last time we'd met, Special Agent Rawlings was wearing a sport coat, slacks, a button-down shirt, and lace-up dress shoes. His brown hair was stylishly cut, and he had the earnest face of someone you'd trust.

Rawlings was an employee of the Federal Bureau of Investigation. This was an important distinction because the FBI was first and foremost a law enforcement organization. Unlike me, Rawlings was answerable to lawyers and judges who took a dim view of handcuffing people posing no threat. Especially people experiencing a poorly defined medical episode.

Contrary to what you might think, I love the Constitution. I just don't love it when we try to apply our founding principles to the world's scumbags. American exceptionalism is driven by America's values, and these values fundamentally differ from those held by much of the rest of the world. The sooner we quit pretending otherwise, the sooner we can get about the business of addressing the world's problems as they really are.

Grabbing the chain with nicotine-stained fingers, Rawlings inserted his key into the locking mechanism and twisted. The metal restraint opened with an audible pop. He did the same with the second handcuff, and just that quickly, I was free.

Balling my hands into fists, I closed my eyes and dropped into the first song that came to mind.

During my self-imposed sabbatical, I'd begun taking guitar lessons in earnest. As the calluses on my fingertips could attest, my skill had progressed beyond simple G-C-D chord progressions. Even so, I still heard Glenn Frey's haunting voice singing the first verse of "Take It Easy." I pictured myself strumming along, my left hand forming the chords on my battered old Gibson knockoff while the fingers on my right tapped out the strum pattern. Once I reached the chorus, I no longer felt tension gripping my shoulders and back. By the start of the bridge, the tremors had stopped altogether.

For now.

I inhaled deeply, and hung on to the breath until my lungs started to burn before exhaling in one continuous stream. Then I opened my eyes.

"What was that?" Rawlings said.

"I already told you," I said, resting my newly liberated hands on my knees. "So what's this about?"

"What's this about?" Rawlings said. "Seriously? Who were the shooters?"

"No idea."

"Bullshit."

"Are we really going to do this?" I said. "A team of military-quality gunmen just shot up Austin, and you want to play bad cop?"

"You weren't exactly an innocent bystander."

"What's that supposed to mean?"

"They were targeting you," Rawlings said.

"Agreed. But how exactly does that make me complicit?"

"A team of professionals tried to assassinate you in broad daylight. You're not a cartel member or a mafioso—I'll give you that. But you're also not a schoolteacher. You're a Defense Intelligence Agency intelligence officer. Your chosen profession probably has something to do with South Congress becoming the OK Corral. I'll bet that you might even have an idea or two as to why."

Rawlings leaned back in his chair with a self-satisfied smile, like a lawyer who'd just given his closing argument. Which he probably was, since the FBI was positively lousy with lawyers. Still, just because he'd had the poor judgment to go to law school didn't mean that Rawlings was wrong. In fact, I did have thoughts on why.

The assassination attempt hadn't been a shootout between two gangs. Those men were professional shooters targeting a single individual—me. And since I'm not a terribly interesting person, their attention probably had something to do with my line of work.

Or ex–line of work.

As of late, that distinction was becoming increasingly unclear. But since I was a spy, not a cop like Rawlings, I did what spies did best. I answered his question with a question.

"What do you know about the shooters?" I said.

"Nope," Rawlings said, shaking his head. "That's not how this is gonna work. You're in my house. I get to ask the questions. Tell me what you know, and I'll reciprocate."

"Okay. This is gonna be fast, which is good, because I'm late for a date with my wife. I don't know anything. Your turn."

For the first time, I could see the stress Rawlings was under break through his carefully cultivated blank face. What had happened on South Congress was clearly bigger than anything the FBI's tiny Austin Resident Agency had seen in a long time. Maybe ever. My shootout must have already gotten headquarters' attention. Judging by Rawlings's reaction, they weren't happy.

"Listen to me," Rawlings said, leaning across the table. "I'm the only thing standing between you and a building full of cops convinced you're responsible for a police officer's death. I say the word, and two of them give you a ride downtown to a holding cell. Trust me when I tell you that ride won't be pleasant. If you don't want to spend the next forty-eight hours making friends with MS-13 cellmates, you'd better start talking."

"Agent Rawlings, I really did think you were smarter than this. They do still teach Investigation 101 at the Academy, right? So investigate. What did I have in my hand when I was taken into custody?"

"A pistol."

"A bit more specificity, please," I said. "It was the patrolman's sidearm. Why did I have his sidearm?"

"Because yours was out of ammunition."

"Exactly. And that's because I had one magazine in my Glock and zero on my person. Please put the Bureau's legendary investigative training to work for a moment.

Do I strike you as the kind of person who would be out and about with a Glock and a single magazine if I knew a team of hitters was stalking me?"

Rawlings stared at me for a long moment, trying to come up with a scenario in which I knew more than what I was saying. Unfortunately for him, facts were stubborn things. Exhaling a sigh of defeat, he slowly shook his head.

"No, you don't," Rawlings said.

"Damn right, I don't. If I'd known about the shooters, I'd have had an M4 in the passenger seat, low-profile body armor beneath my pearly snaps, and at least three spare Glock mags. Not to mention a countersurveillance team and my own crew of shooters. But you didn't find any extra hardware in my truck, did you?"

"No."

"That's because I have no idea who those dudes were. But I think you might."

My statement wasn't exactly a question, but his body language said that Rawlings understood what I was asking all the same. He pushed back from the table as he tried to worm his way out of answering. But he wasn't the only one who'd learned his tradecraft at a federal schoolhouse.

The Farm's training course for fledgling spies was no less prestigious than the FBI's Quantico Academy. I'd learned how to recruit and run assets from the very best in the business. In the seven years since, operational experience had honed my elicitation skills the world over. I might have been on the bench for a while, but I wasn't too rusty to get information from a stressed-out FBI agent.

"Look," I said, leaning forward to bridge the gap Rawlings had created. "I've been straight with you—I don't know anything. And I'll give you something more: I'm not operational. Haven't been for the last twelve months. But you're right. This wasn't a coincidence. Tell me what you know, and I'll try to fill in the rest. If something you say pings, I'll reciprocate. What d'ya say?"

Rawlings stared at me for a long beat, his face drawn into the expressionless mask federal agents must practice in the bathroom mirror each night before bed. Inside, I was feeling positively antsy, but like Rawlings, I didn't let it show. In this game of chicken, to the winner would go the spoils.

Rawlings blinked first.

"All right," Rawlings said after exhaling through his teeth. "Here's what I've got. It isn't much. Yesterday, my squad got a lead from FBI Headquarters."

"You work CT?"

Rawlings shook his head. "No, CI."

It took every bit of my spy-craft training to keep a straight face. I'd thought that Rawlings worked counterterrorism, or CT, but that wasn't the case. Instead, my Bureau colleague worked counterintelligence. Rawlings was a spy catcher. This made no sense. But rather than reveal my ignorance and cede the initiative, I nodded my head while wearing my best bored expression.

And I listened.

"It's not unusual to get a lead from headquarters," Rawlings said. "On the CI squad, it happens all the time. Austin's become one of the country's tech hubs. Half of California has already moved here to escape the taxes, and the other half is house hunting. Apple, Google, Facebook all have downtown offices. Amazon won't be far behind. Even the straitlaced Army moved their Futures Command here to take advantage of Austin's mini–Silicon Valley vibe. With that much tech, you can bet that this place is thick with foreign agents looking to illicitly buy or straight up steal it."

"But this lead was unusual," I said.

Rawlings nodded, taking a pack of cigarettes from his pocket. He shook an unfiltered Camel loose and offered me one. I almost accepted, but didn't. Building rapport was all well and good, but I still had hopes of getting laid tonight. I was willing to sacrifice many things for my country.

Sex with my wife was not one of them.

"Yep," Rawlings said. He produced one of those futuristic-looking cigar lighters that was more blowtorch than match from his sport coat pocket, incinerated the cigarette's tip, and took a long drag. "Headquarters is working a high-priority CI investigation, and the case agent running the show in DC found a nexus in Austin."

"Wait a second," I said, feeling the beginnings of a *ping*. "That's unusual in itself, right? I mean, I thought Washington's job was to coordinate investigations, not run them."

"That's correct," Rawlings said after taking another

drag. "But this case is different. Access to the case file is restricted. I caught the lead, and even I can't read the corresponding paperwork."

"Why?"

Rawlings shrugged. "If I had to guess, I'd say it's because of the sensitivity surrounding the investigation's target. Either that or the case agent has already managed to recruit some high-level sources, and she wants to protect their identities. Anyway, the lead from headquarters tasked us to put a suspected foreign agent under surveillance."

"Without providing a reason?"

"When FBI Headquarters tasks you with a lead, you don't ask questions. If the paperwork had come from anywhere else, I'd have told the sending agent to pound sand, but flipping headquarters the bird isn't conducive to a long career. And to add insult to injury, the assistant director in charge of counterintelligence called to talk to my supervisory special agent. He wanted to make sure we understood the tasking's importance. Bullshit lead or not, we were going to play nice."

"When did it come down?" I said.

"Yesterday afternoon. We put the target under surveillance last night to start building a pattern of life. You know the deal. The lead came with all the requisite authorities. Once we established a pattern of life, the black bag team was going to hit the target's apartment and wire it for sight and sound. As of last night, the surveillance log was pretty mundane. Then again, after less than twenty-four hours, it's hard to know exactly what you're looking for."

"But you found something anyway."

Another nod. "Pure dumb luck, but sometimes that's how it goes. Surveillance team leader followed the target to a Whole Foods parking garage. The target drove in but left on foot. The team leader was stretched thin, but made a snap decision to leave an agent on the vehicle. Sure as shit, somebody got in and drove away about an hour after our target beat feet. The agent snapped a picture of the new driver. Look familiar?"

Rawlings opened the folder on the table between us, withdrew a single glossy picture, and handed it to me. The quality wasn't fantastic, but it was good enough. I have an eye for faces—most spies do. Especially faces belonging to men who've tried to kill me.

"That's my guy," I said, staring at the picture.

"You sure?" Rawlings said. "You never got to look at him face-to-face, and glares on windshields can be tricky."

"Trust me, it's him. He was about as close to me as I am to you."

"No shit?"

"No shit. I was standing on the hood of his car."

Rawlings wisely let that go, which was just as well. Something about the picture grabbed me and wouldn't let go. Then it hit me.

"You know him, don't you?" Rawlings asked the question almost nonchalantly, like we were two guys talking politics over a beer. But I knew that behind that cool outer facade, his heart was a-thumping.

"Got any more shots of him?" I said, stalling while I thought.

Rawlings nodded and slid two more glossies across the table. Rawlings was old-school—unfiltered Camels, cuff links, the works. None of that newfangled digital-image shit for him. Probably still carried a flip phone. Even so, the two additional shots he placed on the table weren't as good as the first. The surveillance agent had probably mashed down the button on her camera, snapping for all she was worth, and the pictures looked the part.

These two images had been taken in a sequence. The first showed a profile of the mystery man's face. The second revealed the back of his head as he turned away. Sucky photos, but the quality didn't matter. The first shot I saw had been enough. The resemblance was uncanny.

"Who am I seeing?" Rawlings said with the same nonchalant voice. But his fingers were tapping out a staccato on the table that would have made Lars Ulrich proud. Maybe that was why Rawlings smoked. His nervous fingers needed something to do while he interrogated wayward spies.

"I don't know," I said, sliding the pictures back across the table.

"What kind of bullshit is this? You told me if I shared, you'd do the same. So share."

"I'm telling the truth. I don't know who that guy is, but I'm pretty sure I knew his father."

"How?"

"He tried to kill me too. Maybe it runs in the family."

SEVEN

I looked at my watch as I bounded up the worn concrete steps and breathed a sigh of relief. I'd made it. Barely. After finishing with Agent Rawlings, I'd had just enough time to scrub the worst of the grime from my face in the police station's bathroom before retrieving my truck from the impound lot and flooring it across town in a desperate fight with rush hour traffic. I'd thought about asking Rawlings to sign a get-out-of-jail-free card in the likely event I blew through a speed trap or three on my wild flight, but decided against it. Even though my FBI friend was solely to blame for my time crunch, he didn't seem to be in a sympathetic mood.

Probably because our interview had ended on less-than-friendly terms.

"Can I help you?" the young woman standing behind the hostess desk asked.

"I have a dinner reservation for Drake," I said.

In true Austin style, the hostess's hair sported at least three colors, two of which I couldn't name. Her lips and nose were both pierced, and the start of a tattoo snaked from beneath her left shirtsleeve. Even so, she took one look at me and sniffed.

Audibly.

Okay, so maybe my cleanup job in the patrol station's sink hadn't been as thorough as I'd hoped.

"Your party's arrived, sir," the hostess said. "She's sitting at a table in the back."

"She looks fantastic, doesn't she?" I said.

The hostess took another long look at me, and I could see her weighing her options. Did she tell the crazy man the truth and risk her job or act politely and not ruffle his feathers? To her credit, truth won.

Again, this was Austin.

"She looks amazing," the hostess said with a pointed glance at my rumpled shirt.

My sport coat covered the bloodstained spot on my shoulder where the policeman's 5.56 round had nicked me. Luckily for my wardrobe, the ricochet that had clubbed my calf hadn't broken the skin. It hurt like hell to walk, but no permanent damage. Even so, there was nothing I could do to camouflage my rumpled shirt or the oil spots on my jeans where I'd taken a knee in the dirty streets.

On any other night, I would have changed before meeting Laila. But this was Taj's Place—one of Austin's hottest Indian restaurants. I'd made our reservation almost two months ago, and there was no way I was giving it up, blood or no blood.

Besides, tonight wasn't just any other night.

"I appreciate your honesty," I said to the hostess. "What's your name?"

"Emma."

"Emma," I said, taking my money clip from my pocket, "you're right—the woman in there is way out of my league. It's been six years, and most days I still can't believe she married me. Tonight's our anniversary, and I'm a bit unprepared. Here's a hundred bucks—would you please run to the flower shop across the street and bring back a dozen roses? I'd do it myself, but I've kept her waiting long enough. You can keep the change."

For a long moment, I thought Emma was going to refuse, but she didn't. Instead, she reached up, straightened my collar, and smoothed the front of my shirt. "Make sure you compliment her outfit," Emma said, pocketing the stack of twenties. "She's rocking that dress. I'll send out champagne."

Emma was right—Laila was rocking that dress. Though she was facing away, it wasn't hard to pick my wife out of the crowd. She was wearing a cream-colored sheath, open to the back, that accentuated the mass of midnight hair tumbling across her bare shoulders. Seeing my wife across a crowded room always stopped me in my tracks. But tonight, the sight of her profile made my stomach clench.

I walked to the table in quick, even strides and bent to kiss her almond-colored shoulder. Even after six years of sharing the same bed, the silky feeling of her bare skin sliding across my lips made me shiver.

"Hey there," Laila said, reaching up to run her fingers through my hair. "You're late."

Her comment was a statement, not an accusation, but I felt guilty all the same. As a former military officer turned spy, I had a life that revolved around timelines. I wasn't late. Not ever. But tonight, on our anniversary, I'd kept my beautiful wife waiting for the better part of thirty minutes. Not exactly a promising start.

"I'm sorry," I said, sliding around to the seat across from her, the one facing the door of course. "I ran into some trouble."

"My God," Laila said, her green eyes widening at my appearance, "baby, you look like shit. What happened?"

My wife cursed sparingly. Her Afghan mother and Pakistani father were immigrants, and while Laila wasn't a practicing Muslim, many of her parents' mannerisms had rubbed off, including an aversion to foul language. Laila using two minor curse words in the same sentence was the equivalent of a Baptist dropping the f-bomb. She didn't curse often, but when she did, it was worth noting.

"Not sure yet," I answered, reaching across the table to thread my fingers between hers. "But I think it was work related."

"Why?"

I paused, considering my response. The thought of

lying to my wife never crossed my mind. We'd begun dating while I was finishing my company command in the Ranger Regiment and married shortly before I'd reported to the Farm. She knew what I was and what I did.

But that wasn't to say I was completely transparent about the operational aspects of my professional life. My wife understood I was a spy, but there was much that she didn't know, and rightfully so. And yet I'd officially resigned my DIA position a year ago. I was no longer a part of the clandestine world.

At least that's what I kept telling myself.

"Here's what I know," I said, opting for a sterilized version of what happened. "Earlier today, a team of men tried to kill me."

"Who were they?" Laila said. To her credit, she didn't react emotionally. Instead, she applied to my problem the same intellect that had put her on the path to partnership at one of the nation's largest accounting firms.

"I don't know. But one of the shooters looked familiar."

"Like you'd met him?"

I shook my head. "Not him. Maybe his father."

"Where?"

"Syria."

The word *Syria* dropped into our conversation like a platter of three-day-old fish. Fortunately, this was the exact moment when Emma made her entrance.

"Happy anniversary," Emma said, presenting Laila with a bouquet of pink roses as a waiter placed two flutes of champagne in front of us. "Did he compliment your dress?"

"He didn't," Laila said, accepting the flowers. When my wife was angry, her eyes glittered. Right now, they were flashing like twin jade disco balls.

"I was about to," I said, enduring a death glare from Emma. I'd spoken to exactly two women in this restaurant and somehow managed to piss them both off. Maybe I had a gift.

"No," Laila said, "you weren't. You were going to tell me about Syria."

"Syria?" Emma said, giving me another appraising glance. "Have you been?"

"No," I said, just as Laila said, "Yes."

I inclined my head slightly toward Emma, trying to give Laila the *not-now* signal, but she stared back without acknowledging the gesture at all, her eyes shimmering. With a sigh, I looked at Emma and said, "It's complicated."

"Men usually are," Emma said, placing her hand on Laila's bare shoulder. "I'll tell the server to give you a couple of minutes. Let me know if you need anything, sister."

"Thank you," Laila said, never breaking eye contact with me.

After another pointed glance, Emma spun on her heel and sauntered back to the hostess station, leaving me to face my radioactive wife. Alone. To be fair, the word *Syria* carried with it a dump truck's worth of baggage. Fifteen months ago, a mission gone wrong had cost the life of my asset and his family and crippled my best friend. The damage to me had been no less substantial, just more subtle. I'd begun seeing the asset's dead wife and toddler daughter while experiencing uncontrolled seizures.

A year ago, I'd returned to Syria to rescue a captured CIA paramilitary officer held captive by an ISIS-inspired splinter cell. This time, I'd brought the person I was responsible for home alive, though my body had been broken in the process. Laila and I had agreed it would be my final mission. After returning to the States, I'd resigned my DIA position, and we'd moved to Austin, trying to put both physical and emotional space between our old life in DC and the new one we were trying to create.

Except that my old life had just decided to make an appearance in my new one. And the crazy thing was, I couldn't say I was disappointed.

"Wait," Laila said, reaching across the table to grab my arm. "Your test results. I almost forgot. Did you still see the doctor?"

"Yes."

"So?"

"He said everything was fine."

"Fine?"

"Yes."

"I'm sure he said more than that."

"He did," I said, remembering the sheaf of papers with the spidery blue handwriting. "But nothing new. MRI results are the same. The damage to my brain is visible, but not getting worse."

"So you're not in a flare-up?" Laila said, smiling as she asked the question. She gave my wrist a squeeze, and I tried to smile back.

"No."

Laila's expression turned from joy into puzzlement as she tried to make sense of my reaction.

Then it hit her.

"And now you're petrified because you can't blame your exposure for what's been happening," Laila said, withdrawing her hand from mine.

I'm sure my wife's a good accountant, but that's not really my field. What I do know is that she has an unparalleled ability to sift truth from bullshit. So instead of answering, I raised both hands shoulder level high, palms facing her. An act of surrender.

Laila was having none of it.

"Matthew Drake," Laila said, slowly shaking her head. "I love you like I've never loved anyone else, but you are not an easy man. For the past six months, I've been terrified that a chemical weapon was eating away my husband's brain. Terrified that I'd have to watch as you slowly became a vegetable. Do you know how many nights I lay awake, just to listen to you breathe? How many times I sobbed in the shower so you wouldn't hear? And then today we get the best news we could hope for. Except now you're the one who's scared. Why? Because for you, dying a slow, horrible death is preferable to admitting that your problems might be psychological rather than physical."

"Baby, I'm sorry," I said, reaching for Laila, but she leaned away and folded her arms.

"Don't *baby* me," Laila said. "If you don't want to talk about it tonight, fine. That's my anniversary gift to you. So let's talk about something that does interest you. Tell me about the man who tried to kill you."

Needless to say, this was not how I'd envisioned our anniversary dinner. I thought about trying to change the subject, but one look at Laila told me that would be a fool's errand. My wife was one of the most tenacious people I knew. Once she made up her mind, God himself couldn't change it. If she wanted to hear about the assassin, there was no talking her out of it.

"The shooter resembled a target I pursued in Syria," I said. "Like maybe his son."

"And you killed his father," Laila said, the statement matter-of-fact rather than accusatory. As I said, Laila knew who I was and what I did. For that much at least, I was grateful.

"Yes, but it was close. The target led the ambush that crippled Frodo, and he was tied into the splinter cell holding the CIA paramilitary officer. In the end, I punched his ticket, but there were still a lot of unanswered questions. Questions I didn't think were worth pursuing since you and I had both decided it was time for me to get out of the game."

"Except that you're not out of the game anymore, right? Not with the target's son hunting you."

"He isn't still hunting me," I said.

Laila stared at me for a second before slowly nodding. "What else?"

"He wasn't alone. He had a team of shooters as backup. Until I figure out who sent them, this isn't over."

"It's never been over, has it?"

I started to reply, but Laila shook her head. "No, let me finish. I knew something was different tonight the moment you sat down. Know how?"

"I can guess," I said, fingering my rumpled shirt.

"Not just that. When you sat across from me, you looked . . . alive. Do you understand? For the first time since you left DIA, you looked like the man I fell in love with. And now I know why—someone tried to kill you."

This time it wasn't anger that caused Laila's eyes to glitter. A tear rolled down her cheek, and she wiped it away with the back of her hand. "Our goddamn anniversary and I finally get my husband back. But you aren't back. Not really."

"Laila," I said, but she scooted her chair away from the table and got to her feet.

"Matt, I love you," Laila said as another tear followed the black mascara trail. "I really do. But this isn't us. It isn't you. I need the man who's sitting across from me right now, not the stranger who's been sleeping in my bed. If that means I have to share you with the DIA, so be it."

"Laila, wait."

"I mean it. Go. Figure out what you need to do. I hope to God it doesn't take someone shooting at you to feel alive, but if so, I'll manage. I just want my husband back. When you find him, please let me know."

She looked at me for another beat and then turned to leave. I didn't stop her. Not because I didn't want to, but because I was terrified. Terrified that Laila would understand that she was only half right. In that moment, I did feel alive. Vibrantly so. Winston Churchill once said that nothing in life was so exhilarating as to be shot at without result.

But what if my newfound vitality wasn't because someone had tried to kill me and failed? What if the world suddenly seemed a brighter place because it had been me who'd done the killing?

That was a thought I wasn't quite ready to face. So rather than stop the woman I loved more than life itself from walking away, I pulled out my phone and booked a flight. I didn't know why the son of a terrorist had just tried to kill me or who had whisked his dead body away.

But I knew someone who might.

EIGHT

Y ou look like shit."

The thing about good friends is that they tell you the truth, whether you want to hear it or not. A best friend does so without the obligatory sugarcoating that passes for conversation in polite society. Frodo is my best friend, and for that I am eternally grateful. Still, sometimes just a little sugarcoating goes a long way.

"You look . . . fabulous," I said, stammering over the word.

Though Frodo and I had been an operational team since I'd reported to DIA as a baby case officer straight from the Farm, things between us since Syria had been different. This was because the onetime Delta operator had been reduced to a shell of himself, and it was my fault. This was why my witty comeback about his appearance died in a pregnant pause. I prayed Frodo would miss it. I might as well have been praying for the heavy gray clouds to shed gold instead of snow. Frodo was a former special operations sniper.

He didn't miss. Not ever.

"I do not look fabulous," Frodo said, holding open his town house door with his good hand. "I look like a former door kicker who's had his arm blown off by an IED. Now, get your ass in here and tell Uncle Frodo who kicked the shit out of you this time."

Frodo was right; he didn't look fabulous. Not anymore anyway. But even before an explosively formed penetrator, or EFP, had amputated his left arm and nearly done the same to his left foot, he'd never been physically imposing. At least not at first blush. He was a soft-spoken black man with a physique skewed more toward endurance than strength. Even so, his ropy muscles and prominent tendons seemed to be crafted from steel cables and iron ingots rather than flesh and blood. He'd once fireman-carried a wounded comrade up two thousand feet of treacherous Afghan mountain to reach a helicopter landing zone.

Now those days were over.

I passed through the front door and into the living room, heading to my old spot on his overstuffed leather couch. Like most single DIA employees, Frodo preferred the convenience of a short commute to the more expansive real estate offered by a home in the suburbs of northern Virginia or southern Maryland.

But that wasn't to say that life in the District was all lattes and upwardly mobile single women. Though Frodo lived in a respectable section, crime across the failed city-state was both rampant and unpredictable. In other words, gangbangers and petty criminals didn't respect the socioeconomic boundaries that separated Frodo's neighborhood from the public housing located a scant four miles to the south.

Accordingly, Frodo was prepared.

Reaching under the couch, I found a SIG Sauer secured to the metal frame in a custom-made holster. Sliding the pistol out, I press-checked it and found a round in the chamber. I'd expected nothing less.

"What the hell?" Frodo said, easing himself into the recliner situated catty-corner to the couch. "Didn't your momma teach you that touching another man's piece is like grabbing his junk? I'd thought by now that at least some of my culture would have rubbed off on your ignorant redneck ass."

My supposed lack of culture was a common theme in our relationship. I'd grown up dirt-poor outside Salt Lake City on a stretch of rock-strewn ground my parents had optimistically termed a ranch. Frodo, on the other hand, was a product of Philly's streets. He'd managed to steer clear of the gangs infesting his neighborhood, mainly due to an Army recruiter brave enough to look for raw talent among the city's forgotten inhabitants. He'd found Frodo on a community center basketball court, to the Army's everlasting benefit.

Not to mention mine.

"Just wanted to make sure you were still taking precautions," I said, sliding the pistol back into its holster. "This neighborhood isn't getting any safer."

"Shiiiiit," Frodo said, popping the recliner's footrest. "I may only have one hand, but that's more than enough to take care of the wannabes around here. Want a beer?"

"Love one."

"Seamus—get this man a beer."

Frodo's command was directed toward the pile of fur lying midway between the living room and small kitchen. Seamus was a dog of questionable heritage. His shoulders and body bore traces of husky or German shepherd, while his square jaw spoke to some form of mastiff or pit bull. What the mutt was indisputably was large. Very large.

When he cared to stand, Seamus's shoulders brushed my waist. Frodo was convinced he was part Irish wolfhound—hence his name—but what he most definitely was not was a service dog. At Frodo's command, Seamus huffed and closed his eyes.

"I see the training sessions are going well," I said.

"He understands me. I know it. He just does things in his own time." Which was Frodo's way of saying if I wanted a beer, I needed to grab it myself.

"Don't worry, Seamus," I said, getting to my feet. "I need the exercise."

"Since you're going . . ."

"Sure," I said, pausing as I drew even with the sleeping dog.

On cue, Seamus's eyes opened. He rumbled something that sounded more like an old man's grumble than a growl. Accordingly, I reached down, and he rolled over, exposing a belly the length of an end table. I rubbed, he gave a doggy sigh of pleasure, and just like that, the path to the kitchen was clear.

I stepped over the service dog who wasn't, retrieved two beers, and passed one to Frodo as I returned. We each took a long pull from our respective bottle, and then Frodo gave me the look.

"Okay, Matty," he said, fixing me with the same stare that had caused terrorists the world over to wet their man jammies, "let's hear it."

"A team of shooters tried to take me down this afternoon," I said, beginning my tale of woe for what seemed like the hundredth time.

I spoke nonstop for the better part of ten minutes, leaving nothing out. Frodo and I had been teammates for almost as long as I'd been married to Laila. Over the course of our professional association and then friendship, he'd served as my bodyguard, driver, and point man. His skill with a long gun was unparalleled, and he was one of the best CQB, or close-quarters battle, assaulters I'd ever worked with.

But that was just the tip of the iceberg. Recruiting and running agents was more a mental than physical game. Convincing someone to become a spy took a level of mental acumen that was rare, and I'd practiced many a recruiting pitch on Frodo before trying it on my target.

Frodo was a confidant, but more than that, he was my consigliere. He understood everything about me, and for him, no question was out-of-bounds. Even so, what he asked when my narration was complete still felt like a curveball.

"How are things with Laila?" Frodo said, his stare unrelenting.

"Fine," I said, and took a swallow of beer. "Great."

"Matty."

"Shitty. The worst they've ever been, and I don't even know why."

"You must have some idea."

I opened my mouth but closed it again without speaking. Did I know why? Maybe. But not in a way I could explain.

"I thought it was the job that was tearing us apart," I said, trying to put my feelings into words. "Especially after . . ."

"Syria."

I nodded. "Yeah. I thought going back would bring me closure. Maybe it did. After my last op, I had no regrets when I turned in my creds. Zero. But the last six months . . ." I shrugged.

"What have you been doing?" Frodo asked.

"This and that. Okay, the truth? Not a lot. The first month and a half were understandable. Laila took a leave of absence from work, and I spent a ton of time in physical therapy. But after the scars healed and the bruises faded, we didn't know what to do next. Laila worked from home, and I spent my time playing guitar and filling out grad school applications."

"But?"

I took another long pull from my beer, emptying half the bottle over the course of a single swallow. Frodo was a beer connoisseur, and he was particularly proud of this batch. It had been imported from Austria and probably brewed by left-handed monks who lived in a secluded monastery and spoke only Latin. Or something like that. Anyway, it was good beer, but I knew that wasn't the reason I was sucking it down.

So did Frodo.

"There's plenty more where that came from. Finish your story. Otherwise, Seamus gets involved."

The hairball gave another grumble that made my feet vibrate. Irish wolfhound, my ass. The monstrosity was probably one of George R. R. Martin's direwolves.

"It's hard to explain," I said, picking at the bottle's label. "But it's like I went from knowing exactly who I was to seeing a stranger in the mirror. One of the things I bitched about when we were operational was time—as in I never had enough. For seven years, we were either prepping for an op, executing one, or recovering from one and planning the next. I can't tell you how many anniversaries, birthdays, and holidays that never-ending schedule consumed. And then suddenly I went from the gas pedal slammed to the floor to sitting in park."

"And you couldn't figure out how to adjust?"

"I guess. I mean, Laila's great. She was super supportive, and the first couple of weeks were fantastic, but then . . ."

"What?"

"Time started to feel like a curse. A prison sentence. I couldn't get out of bed in the morning. When I did, I surfed the Internet all day, reading stories about what was going on downrange. I started obsessing about the teams that had taken our place. I couldn't sleep, eat, or concentrate. Other than working out and playing guitar, I didn't have energy for anything."

"What'd Laila say?"

"She was afraid I was having some kind of flare-up. That my brain damage was getting worse. She begged me to get another MRI. I did. Results came back today. Everything's normal."

"Except it's not," Frodo said.

I nodded. "I don't know where I fit anymore. If I'm not carrying a rifle or recruiting assets in the back alley of another third-world country, then who am I?"

"I can dig that," Frodo said, lifting up his prosthesis. Light glittered across the metallic surface.

"Jesus, I'm sorry," I said, setting my beer on the floor.

"For what? Truth is truth, Matty. And the truth is, I dealt with a lot of the same feelings. You know what helped?"

I shook my head.

"Staying plugged into the game. My days as your shadow are over. Nothing I can do about that. But that doesn't mean that the sum of my existence has to be sitting in this chair and drinking craft beer while trying to train a dumbass dog to do tricks."

Seamus gave an exasperated canine sigh, but Frodo plowed ahead. "My body might be broken, but my mind is fine. James still needs my help, and he could use yours. Go see him with me. Tomorrow."

"What?" I said, leaning forward. In my surprise, I kicked over the beer bottle. The contents bubbled across the imitation Persian rug Frodo and I had picked up at a bazaar outside of Bagram. With an agility that belied his bulk, Seamus clambered to his feet, trotted over to the spill, and lapped it up.

"Shit," I said, "sorry about that. Let me get a towel."

"Don't sweat it," Frodo said. "That rug's seen worse. Besides, my service dog is taking care of things. Now, about the job offer."

"Look, brother," I said as Seamus's massive red tongue moved from the rapidly drying puddle to the bottle itself, "I didn't come here to get my job back. I just wanted to pick your brain about the shooters."

"Why?"

"What do you mean?"

"Why do you want to know about 'em?"

"So I can make sure they don't come at me again."

"How? Look, Matty, those men are long gone. They're professionals. When a job goes sideways, a professional doesn't stick around. Your shooters are ghosts. Fortunately, I know someone who used to be pretty damn good at finding ghosts. In fact, he just spilled half his beer on my priceless Persian rug."

"Look, Frodo, I appreciate it—"

"Where's Laila?"

"What do you mean?"

"Goddamn it, boy. That wasn't a hard question. Where is your wife at this exact moment?"

"Home, I guess."

"You guess?"

"We had dinner tonight. It didn't go well. She told me to . . ."

"What?"

I reached for the beer bottle before remembering it was empty. No help there. "She told me to go find her husband and bring him back."

"Hmm," Frodo said, burying his fingers in Seamus's thick coat. "Well, farm boy, her husband ain't here. But I've got a good idea where we might find him. And so do you. But before we go looking, you need a good night's sleep. You look like shit."

"So I've been told."

"The bedroom in the back's already made up. You know where everything is. I've got to get my ass to bed. We have an early start."

With that, Frodo climbed to his feet and began an awkward shuffle toward the steps leading to his master bedroom on the condo's second story. In a blur of fur, Seamus was at his owner's side, just when Frodo needed something to lean against as he mounted the first stair.

It occurred to me, as my friend and his dog disappeared from view, that Frodo's life would have been much easier if he'd switched bedrooms to the ground floor. But he hadn't. Men like Frodo never took the easy way out.

Neither would I.

NINE

"Who in the hell is this?"

The question, as obnoxious as it was, wasn't the worst part of the encounter. That distinction rested with the questioner himself. DIA Branch Chief James Glass was an ex–Army Special Forces team sergeant and current night terror to Islamic jihadis everywhere. He also happened to be my boss.

Or former boss. These distinctions were lost on James.

"Come on, Chief," Frodo said, looking a little like a kid caught with his hand in the cookie jar. "This is Matty."

"Matty who?" James said, a red flush creeping up his tree trunk of a neck. "I don't know any Matty. I used to know a shit-hot case officer named Matt Drake, but he was a fucking quitter, and I hate quitters. That man is dead to me. Do you hear me? Dead!"

James stabbed his desk with his index finger as he

yelled *dead*, and I had to fight back a smile. Don't get me wrong. James's rage was legendary. Before a Taliban RPG had taken his right eye and ended his operational career, he'd put more men in the dirt than cancer. But at this moment, he looked strikingly like Robert De Niro doing Al Capone in *The Untouchables*.

I want him dead. I want his family dead. I want to piss on his ashes.

"Why the fuck are you laughing?" James said. His single eye zeroed in on me like a howitzer's barrel.

Maybe I should have fought that smile a little harder.

"You like Kevin Costner, Chief?" I said, trying to keep a straight face.

"Oh shit," Frodo said. "Tell me you did not just go there."

"Go where?" James said, looking from Frodo to me and back again, his close-cropped head swiveling like a tank's turret.

"Come on, Chief," I said, "you telling me you weren't doing a De Niro impression?"

"This is funny?" James said, the flush reaching his cauliflower ears, deformed from decades of Army combatives training. "Is that what you think?"

"No," I said, finally losing my patience, "I think this is pitiful. A team of shooters made a run on me yesterday in broad daylight. I'm pretty sure they're connected to my last mission in Syria. A mission I undertook at your request. Yes, I told you I wanted out, but things have changed. I want back in. Can we dispense with this bullshit and get down to fucking business?"

The frustration building over the last twenty-four hours caught up to me, and the second half of my answer came out a little stronger than intended. Okay, a lot stronger. I was leaning over James's desk, eyeball to eyeball with a man who'd spent eighteen years sending terrorists on one-way trips to paradise.

"Everything all right in here?"

The question came from behind me, but I would have known the voice anywhere. Ann Beaumont, James's long-suffering executive assistant, had just peeked in the open door. At the sound of her Southern drawl, the testosterone-laced tension drained from the room.

"Just peachy," James said with a grin. "Matty's back."

U se a coaster," James said as he passed me a beer.

Technically, alcohol was forbidden in this, the inner sanctum of DIA headquarters, but James didn't stand much for technicalities. He might have been only a Branch Chief, but James Glass swung a big operational stick. More than that, he had the president's ear. The bureaucratic rules that governed this agency were written for mere mortals, which James had ceased being about the time he'd pulled Saddam Hussein out of his spider hole. SEAL Team Six might have been the ones to kill bin Laden, but that was only because James and his team had been weathered in. The aviators who had refused to fly James that night still lived in fear.

To be fair, even Mother Nature was expected to blink in a contest of wills with James. I half believed that if the

Chinook pilots had just taken off, the clouds would have cleared, and the winds calmed. James might not walk on water, but he came awfully close.

I dutifully selected a coaster from the dispenser located in the center of the spotless conference table and studied the image. An aerial view of a car engulfed in flames, undoubtedly taken by a loitering UAV.

"Who was this?" I said, holding the coaster.

"Zarqawi," James said without missing a beat.

"You added UAV kills to the list?"

James gave me a flat stare, the black eye patch covering one eye adding menace to his already formidable expression. "Zarqawi wasn't killed by a UAV. You can't believe everything you read, Matty."

I chuckled as I set the coaster down and placed my beer on top. In an organization that was becoming more bureaucratic by the day, James made it his mission to remind the analysts laboring in sterile cubicles that the real world was full of blood and tears. He wanted to ensure they never forgot that the life of a covert operative half a world away might depend on the quality of their work product.

In an earlier time, James might have driven his message home by wearing a necklace of ears. In today's quieter, gentler DIA, he compromised by keeping a collection of coasters imprinted with the after-action imagery of missions in which he'd had a hand. The stack loomed larger each time I visited his inner sanctum.

"Enough ass grabbing," James said once Frodo was seated. "What have you got, Matthew?"

That was the million-dollar question. I'd been working on an answer for the last twenty-four hours but still didn't feel any closer. "I'm not sure," I said, ordering my thoughts, "but I think the team of shooters is somehow connected to the ISIS splinter cell we took apart in Syria."

"Why?" James said.

"The shooter who went after me looked like a younger version of Sayid."

"His son?" James said.

I nodded. "The age would be about right."

"What about the rest of the team?" Frodo said. "They Middle Eastern too?"

"Yes," I said, "but something about them felt off."

"What's that mean?" James said.

"It means they didn't act like jihadis. Their movements were disciplined, their fire controlled. It felt like I was fighting fellow commandos."

My conclusion sounded incredibly weak, but James and Frodo shared a look as soon as the words left my mouth. I was onto something.

"What?" I said, looking from my boss to my best friend.

"Show him the tape," James commanded.

As ordered, Frodo grabbed a remote and brought the floor-to-ceiling screen that covered the far wall to life. Many DIA bureaucrats had the small flat-screens in their offices perpetually tuned to MSNBC, CNN, or Fox News, depending on their political affiliation.

Not James.

In the odd instance when his screen was tuned to programming, James had it pegged on Al Jazeera, usually with the sound up loud and the subtitles on so he could practice his Arabic. But that was only once in a blue moon. More often than not, James's TV was tuned to his own version of the news—UAV feeds.

The screen came to life, but for once, I wasn't looking down the aiming reticle of a Sentinel ghosting through Iranian airspace or a Reaper about to turn a Toyota Hilux into spare parts. This time, the quality of the footage was poor, probably because a team of analysts had lifted it from a security camera's feed. It was also familiar. Not because I'd seen the video before, but because I recognized the man in the middle of the frame.

Me.

"What the fuck, boss?" I said, pointing at the screen.

"Don't get your panties in a wad, Matthew," James said, not even having the grace to look embarrassed. "I didn't find out it was you until last night."

"How?"

This time James did register a reaction. But it was more annoyance than embarrassment. "Nothing you need to worry about. I—"

"How?" I said again.

"He's got you tagged as a Foxtrot Charlie One," Frodo said.

"You've got to be shitting me," I said.

"Get off your high horse," James said. "Did I illegally make you a target of national surveillance? Yes, and this is why." James gestured toward the screen with one of his ham-sized hands. "You might have been on the bench, pretending to be a civilian for the last four months, but pretending was all it was. I hate to break it to you, Matthew, but former Iraqi commandos don't fly halfway across the world to target civilians."

"What?" I said, not bothering to mask the confusion in my voice.

"Come on, son," James said, "get your head back in the game."

"He was almost there on his own, Chief," Frodo said.

"Almost only counts in horseshoes and hand grenades. Besides, the clock is ticking. I don't have time for this old son to get there on his own. Roll the tape, Frodo."

On the screen, the ambush was unfolding in real time. Me tussling with the momma bear. The gunfight with my would-be assassin. Me emptying the Glock through his windshield.

"Nice work there, Matty," James said as he reached beneath his desk for a tin of Copenhagen, then slapped it between his fingers as if with a rattlesnake's quivering tail. "This is where your new friends make an entrance."

On the screen, the backup team arrived in two dark-colored SUVs. Once again, the shooters broke out in two teams of two, one team bounding forward while the second laid down suppressive fire.

"Those are our tactics—," I said.

"Because US Special Forces trained them," Frodo said.

"I can't believe I didn't pick up on that," I said.

"To be fair, you were trying not to get your ass shot off," Frodo said.

"Bullshit," James said, and thumbed a fist-sized wad of dip between his lip and his gum. "Any jackass can survive an ambush. You guys get paid to think."

"I was on vacation," I said, watching the action unfold. The American influence was easy enough to spot now that I wasn't concentrating on just staying alive. But learning that my attackers were Iraqi didn't bring me clarity. If anything, this revelation made things only more confusing. "So is anybody going to tell me why Sayid's son was linked up with an Iraqi hit team? Or better yet, why they decided to turn the streets of Austin into a shooting gallery?"

"Or why they were targeting you?" Frodo suggested.

"I figured the answer to the first two questions would probably point me in the right direction," I said.

"And you would be wrong," James said, pulling a foam cup from his drawer.

"Why don't you let me be the judge of that?" I said.

"Okay, smart guy," James said, "here's what we know. The jihadi was probably related to the Syrian you waxed."

"Probably?"

"As you're well aware, we don't have a body," James said, and sent a stream of brown tobacco juice into the white cup. "In fact, you might say that the Iraqi shooters went to extraordinary lengths to retrieve the jihadi—a guy they had to know was already dead. Why?"

"Because they didn't want us to get his DNA," I said, watching as one of the shooters tossed an incendiary grenade into the car's backseat.

"Ding, ding," James said, "we have a winner. So to

cover their tracks, the team exfils the dead body and torches his car. But not all is lost. The scientists working artificial intelligence over at DARPA have made some amazing progress during the last year or so. Shit that would make your head spin."

"Like why nobody in this organization has the balls to fire you?" I said.

"Focus, dipshit," James said. "We're talking about artificial intelligence. Algorithms. The dirty web."

"Dark web, boss," Frodo said. "The dirty web is something else."

As always, Frodo delivered his jab completely deadpan. And as always, James paused for a second. His famous one-eyed stare locked on his obnoxious subordinate as James pondered whether Frodo was truly trying to help him or just jerking his chain. This time, I was the one who rescued my ex-bodyguard.

"You were saying?" I said.

"I was saying that I should have traded the two of you to the CIA a long time ago. A DARPA program manager just rolled out a new version of facial-recognition software. Instead of just identifying someone, it can also determine familial relationships between photographs."

"Like whether the dead jihadi has his dad's smile?" I said.

"Nobody likes a wiseass," James said. "Frodo?"

Frodo touched a button on the remote, and the screen changed. This time, the footage from the ambush was replaced with a series of close-ups of my would-be murderer. The images must have come from several different cameras, but the minions down in data science had done fine work.

A succession of yellow circles appeared over various aspects of the jihadi's face before materializing on a second face to the right of the jihadi's head shots. Sayid. The man who had led the ambush that had crippled Frodo. A man I had beaten to death in a rathole of a Syrian prison moments before a team of Delta Force commandos saved my bacon.

"So . . . what?" I said, staring at the spiderweb of lines joining the two pictures together. "I killed Dad and now Junior decides to settle the score? That doesn't explain the Iraqi shooters."

"No, it does not," James said. "It also doesn't explain why they came for you in broad daylight."

I looked at James in silence, dumbfounded. My boss was exactly right. I was not an assassin, but I'd hit a high-value target a time or two. Those operations were always executed at the time and place most advantageous to the assaulters. I could think of a million locations more suitable to put me down than the streets of Austin. Why hadn't the assassins triggered somewhere more discreet? Somewhere more advantageous to them?

"I've been thinking about that too," Frodo said, spinning the TV remote on the polished table. "Those guys were professionals. They must've had a reason, and I can think of just one."

"They wanted to make a statement," I said.

"Exactly," Frodo said.

"Why?" James said.

"That's the question," I said. "I don't know the answer. But I do know where to start digging."

"What do you mean?" Frodo said.

"The man who was Sayid's handler in Syria works on the other side of the Potomac," I said. "It's time I paid him a visit."

TEN

You want to do what?" James said at the same time Frodo blurted, "I don't think that's such a good idea."

Frodo and James never agreed about anything. I must have been onto something.

"Why not?" I said.

"Didn't he take out a restraining order?" Frodo said.

"That was just a misunderstanding," I said, waving away my friend's concerns.

"You broke his nose," Frodo said.

"Po-*tae*-to, po-*ta*-to," I said. "How are his confirmation hearings going?"

"Haven't started yet," James said. "You're not watching?"

"I told you," I said, "I'm retired."

"Was retired," Frodo said.

"Semantics," I said. "You think he'll be confirmed?"

"Without a doubt," James said. "Regardless of what happened in Syria, the president's senior adviser has his back."

"By *what happened in Syria*, are you referring to the time Frodo and I almost died because the Chief of Base, Charles Sinclair Robinson the Fourth, left our asses hanging in the breeze?"

"Semantics," James said. "Look, everyone knows some hinky shit went down in Syria, and that Sayid, and by extension Charles, was at the center of it. That said, you weren't exactly here to press your case over the last twelve months. For the most part, all that's blown over."

"Doesn't feel that way to me," I said, pointing to the image of the dead assassin linked by yellow lines to his equally dead father. "What else have we got on the dead shooter or the commandos? Anything?"

Frodo and James looked at each other before turning their gazes back to me.

"Nope," James said.

"Well, then, it looks like I need to make an appointment to see the future Director of the Central Intelligence Agency," I said, getting to my feet.

"Matty," James said, "one thing."

"Yeah, boss?"

"If you come at the king, you best not miss."

ELEVEN

"Your face is looking better," I said, sliding into the empty seat across from the once and future king. "The bruising's barely noticeable."

Charles had been reading from his phone and hadn't noticed my approach. Still, if my unexpected appearance upset him, he didn't show it.

"Matt, good to see you," Charles said, putting the phone into his pocket.

Charles came from old money, and he looked the part—tall and trim with wavy black hair, a square jaw, and perfect teeth. A regular blue-blood aristocrat. His suit had never graced a store rack, and a TAG Heuer aviator watch dominated his left wrist. It wasn't enough to Charles that he was loaded. He wanted everyone else to know it too.

"Nightmares still keeping you up?" Charles said. "Or

is it just the shakes? Word on the street is that you piss yourself. I'd hate for that to be true."

"Haven't had a nightmare in weeks," I said, grabbing a roll from the bread basket in the center of the table. "Since I shattered your nose, I've been sleeping like a baby. Should've decked you a long time ago."

Charles smiled, revealing teeth bleached alabaster white. "The thing about you, Drake, is that you're a has-been. A washed-up case officer who cracked under the pressure. No shame in that. Men better than either of us have done the same. The difference is they quit *before* people got killed. But not you. You just kept on trucking. How many have you lost, Drake? Let's see. Frodo's a cripple. Your Syrian asset and his entire family were butchered. Your weapons scientist had his brains blown out. Am I missing any? I'm sure there're more. With you there're always more."

I looked at Charles with a sardonic smile even as I gripped my pant leg underneath the red linen tablecloth. My index finger was trembling.

Finding Charles hadn't been hard. It was Wednesday evening in DC—the time to see and be seen. Charles wasn't the Director of the CIA yet, but everyone knew he was in the running. So where would a humble public servant who wished to increase his visibility with the senators voting on his confirmation take his dinner on Wednesday night? Sophie's—the trendiest restaurant in the District, of course. A single call to the maître d' had confirmed my suspicions. Charles had a table booked for seven o'clock.

My plan had been to show up unannounced, rattle Charles's cage, and see what shook loose. But two minutes in, he'd rattled mine. Maybe I was a bit out of practice. Fortunately, a voice off my left shoulder granted me a reprieve.

"Good evening, sir," the waiter said. "Would you like a menu?"

"I just ordered, so feel free," Charles said. "The crab cakes are amazing."

"Coffee," I said, "with cream and sugar."

"Very good," the waiter said before retreating.

Charles tracked the man's progress over my shoulder, waiting until he was out of earshot before leaning across the table.

"Listen to me, you little prick," Charles said. He was still all smiles, but his jovial expression didn't extend to his flat, cold eyes. "I came to Austin to see you in order to try to reach an understanding."

"What kind of understanding, Chuck?" I said, ripping the roll in two and buttering one of the halves. "It was hard to understand you with all that blood pouring from your nose. I remember you threatening to deport my wife's parents. After that, things got a bit hazy."

"I wasn't threatening. I was explaining. Explaining your new reality. I was afraid that you might have been operating under an incorrect assumption: that rescuing my paramilitary officer had somehow cleared your previous fuckups off the slate. But that isn't the case. After Syria, I got a promotion and the president's ear. You got nothing. But here you are, sitting in front of me, barking like a junkyard dog. Because I'm in a good mood, I'm going to try this one more time. Stay retired. Understood?"

"Sure."

"Good. Consider this closure, or making amends, or whatever trendy words they call it in whichever twelve-step program you're undoubtedly working. Go back to Austin. Grow a beard. Hang out in coffee shops. Maybe even smoke a little weed if it helps. Bottom line—forget about your old life. It no longer exists."

"Here's the thing, Charlie," I said, returning both halves of the roll to the basket uneaten. "I was happy in Austin. In fact, I'd be there right now if a team of shooters hadn't interrupted my afternoon. People who try to kill me get my attention, so now I'm here to get yours."

"You think I sent them?"

"Please. You give yourself way too much credit. You were a shitty case officer and a shitty chief of base. If not for your college buddy in the White House, your Agency career would have been over a long time ago. Do I think you've wished me dead? Maybe. But do I think you have the operational chops to hire a team of mercs and send 'em to Austin? Not a chance. No, I'm here for just one reason. You fucked up. Again. This time, I'm not gonna let it slide."

"You need help, Matt. I'm telling you this as a professional. You need to talk to someone before it's too late."

While old Charles might indeed have been a shitty case officer, he would have made an excellent used-car salesman. The sincerity in his tone took me aback. I almost rethought my entire approach.

Almost.

Except that for once I wasn't the only one with a case of the shakes. The little finger on Charles's right hand was vibrating like a tuning fork. He was scared. Terrified. His unconcerned attitude to the contrary, I'd rattled his cage. Now it was time for the coup de grâce.

"Maybe you're right, Chuck," I said. "Maybe I do need help. But the difference between you and me is that I don't have to fight my demons alone. You, on the other hand, are flying solo. Once the FBI ties the shooter who tried to kill me to you, there won't be a person in this town willing to take your calls. And that includes your supposed friend on the president's staff."

"What are you talking about?" Charles said.

"We've identified the shooter. He's the son of the asset you thought you were running in Syria. Pretty big coincidence, don't you think? Or maybe not, since I'm pretty sure your asset was the one running you."

"You're out of your mind."

"Maybe. But I'm not the one about to spend some quality time with the FBI. Good luck, Chucky. Hope you have a great lawyer."

I got up without waiting for Charles to reply. In truth, I didn't need him to. The deafening silence was answer enough.

TWELVE

The phone rang as I spun the card with my favorite special agent's contact information between my fingertips. He'd shoved it into my hands as I'd left the station to meet Laila. In my rush, I almost hadn't taken it. Now I was hoping I'd be glad I had.

"Agent Rawlings."

"Agent Rawlings, this is Matt Drake. How the hell are you?"

The valet from Sophie's eyed me across the darkened street. He didn't seem too happy that I was parked in front of his restaurant, but he wasn't doing anything about it either. Yet.

"Drake. Remember how I compared you to herpes? I was wrong. Herpes isn't fatal. You, sir, are syphilis."

"The investigation isn't going so well?" I said.

"No. The San Antonio SAC wants updates twice a day, which means the assistant director in charge of counterintelligence is probably crawling up his ass on an hourly basis. We've kept the jihadi connection out of the news for now. But it won't last. Something's got to give. Soon. Where are you?"

"DC."

"Which part of *don't leave town* did you not understand? Austin PD wants a statement."

"Austin PD can wait. I'm trying to figure out who wants me dead."

"Any progress?"

Rawlings sounded beaten down, and I understood how he felt. All things considered, he was a good guy in a shitty situation. Rawlings was the case agent in charge of the investigation. It was his career on the line, and that was what I was counting on.

"I'm close," I said. "But I need a favor."

"Jesus, Drake. I shared info with you thinking I'd get something useful in return, but so far this relationship has been entirely one-way. I don't need this shit. If I want to get jerked around, I'll call the CIA."

"That was below the belt," I said. "Say bad things about my momma if you want, but don't *ever* compare me to the CIA."

"If O.J.'s glove fits, you must acquit."

"The last time I checked, the only one dodging bullets on South Congress was me. Cut the hurt-feelings act. I'm onto something, but I can't close the loop by myself. If you've got other angles to work, knock yourself out. But if you want to bag the shooters who tore up Austin and killed a cop, I need a favor."

For several long seconds, Rawlings didn't answer. He was unhappy and wanted me to know it. More than that, he wanted me afraid that he was going to tell me to pound sand. But we both knew it was just an act. Rawlings had a boss who wanted answers and a story that would crash across the news like a tsunami once the talking heads discovered the jihadi connection. A drowning man couldn't be choosy when someone threw him a lifeline, and Rawlings was going under.

"Okay," Rawlings said, exhaling a long breath. "What do you need?"

I told him.

"Are you out of your fucking mind?" Rawlings said, spitting out the words. "I can't authorize that. Nobody can authorize that."

"If you want the rest of the shooters, you can, and you will. Get me what I need. I'll take care of the rest."

"Take care of the rest, my ass. This has serious blowback potential. Like, getting-dragged-in-front-of-Congress-to-testify kind of blowback."

"Save it. I'm certain you're a damn good investigator, but trust me when I tell you that I'm good at my job too. If there's blowback, it ends with me. Spy's honor."

Rawlings hemmed and hawed and cursed and threatened for another minute or two, but in the end, he agreed.

They always do.

THIRTEEN

I looked at the address displayed on my phone a final time, comparing it with the building in front of me. The numbers stenciled on the side of the brick facade matched the digits Rawlings had texted, but I was still a bit leery. Either Rawlings was messing with me, or I didn't know Charles as well as I thought.

Neither prospect boded well.

Shoving my cell into my back pocket, I grabbed hold of a grimy door handle framed by panes of blacked-out glass and pulled.

I'd told Charles the truth at the restaurant. I didn't believe he had the operational chops to bring a team of shooters into the country undetected. And even if he could, I had no idea why he'd want me dead. Those troubling details aside, Charles was the only link I had to Sayid's son. With that in mind, I'd done my best to shake him in the hopes that he would lead me to the next link in the chain.

While Charles wasn't the world's most stellar case officer, he was still a Farm-trained operative. The chances of my running a one-man surveillance op against him without being detected were slim. I needed another way to track him.

Enter Agent Rawlings. I'd asked Rawlings to illegally locate Charles's phone, but I must have forgotten to mention that the number in question belonged to the next Director of the Central Intelligence Agency.

Whoops.

Anyway, ten minutes after our conversation, Rawlings came through. Which was none too soon, because by then the valet had worked up his confidence. I traded Sophie's for the parking lot of a 7-Eleven, waiting for Charles to move. Once he did, I tracked the flashing icon that denoted his phone, determined to follow the CIA operative wherever he led me. Even if that happened to be a seedy strip club on the outskirts of the District.

The things I do for my country.

Stepping into the foyer, I allowed my eyes to adjust to the semidarkness as the door swung closed on shrieking hinges.

While I am not a connoisseur of gentlemen's clubs, it was clear to me that this particular establishment was not the high-priced kind of place lobbyists took congressional staffers. The carpet was threadbare, and sticky chunks of discolored concrete gaped in places like leprous flesh peeking through ragged bandages. Pounding music pummeled me, the thumping bass line reverberating in my chest. The smells of cigarettes and stale booze permeated the air, with the pungent odor of marijuana lurking beneath like exotic seasoning.

"Ready to party?"

The shouted question came from a waif of a girl dressed in an ankle-length faux-fur coat. She was standing behind a podium next to a darkened hallway.

Girl certainly seemed to be an apt description. Her hair was peroxide blond, and she gave me a sultry look, but something felt off. Even in the murky light with caked-on makeup and ridiculously high-heeled shoes, she looked young.

"I'm supposed to meet a friend," I said, walking up to her podium. "Maybe you can tell me if he's here."

Standing closer only confirmed my suspicions. I could see the teenage acne she was trying to conceal around her nose and mouth, and her skin was wrinkle free. Only her eyes seemed old. They were a dark brown that should have been pretty but looked washed-out and hard instead.

Lifeless.

"Fuck if I know," the girl said, her eyes narrowing. "If your friend's here, he's inside. If he's not, he's not. Either way, to get in, you have to pay the cover charge. What's it going to be?"

"I guess I'm ready to party," I said, reaching for my wallet. "Take plastic?"

"Sugar, we take everything," the girl said, her attitude markedly better now that she had my Visa between her fingers. Her smile warmed her face, but never reached those cold, vacant eyes.

The club's interior wasn't an improvement over the lobby. The stage with the all-important metal pole was currently empty. The platform's wooden flooring was cracked and uneven with warped boards reaching up like skeletal fingers. A series of plastic chairs and cheap tables ringed the stage and a pair of scantily clad waitresses worked the room, tottering on heels that made the stilettos on the girl manning the door look like flats.

The music didn't exactly stop when I walked in, but both waitresses keyed off my appearance like a dog hungry for table scraps. Probably because I was the only customer in the place. Rawlings and I were going to have words once I left.

The two waitresses raced from either side of the room, trying to be the first to take my order. A short redhead beat out a lanky brunette by a stride or two, but the brunette didn't look like she was ready to concede. For a moment I thought they were going to get physical, but then the brunette gave a long-suffering sigh and walked away.

"Next dancer comes out in ten," the redhead said. She was smacking a wad of chewing gum as she talked. The noise clashed with the seductive vibe she was trying to cultivate as she sidled up next to me. "What're you drinking?"

"I'm looking for a friend," I said, edging around a chair so that a flimsy table separated us.

"You can look for whoever you want. But if you want to stay here, you have to buy a drink."

"How many?"

"One every fifteen minutes unless you're tipping the dancer."

"You have bottled?"

"Bud or Bud Light." The gum popped like a rifle shot.

"Bud."

"That'll be twenty."

"For a single beer?"

The girl shrugged her narrow shoulders as the gum popped three times in rapid succession, moving from semi- to fully automatic.

"I'll take two," I said, buying myself thirty minutes. James was going to love this expense report.

I surrendered my credit card once again, and the waitress ran it through her tablet and then disappeared behind a black curtain to my left. I looked over to see the brunette eyeing me from where she was standing against the wall. I waved her over.

"Yeah?" she said.

"What's your name?"

"Tiffani. With an *i*."

Of course.

"Hi, Tiffani. I'm Matt. Can you talk?"

"If you buy me a drink."

"I'll buy you four. How's that sound?"

"You must have a lot on your mind."

Tiffani ran my card and then settled into the chair next to me. "What do you want?"

"I get nervous around pretty girls," I said, leaning forward so that she could hear me over the pounding music. "Is there somewhere else we could go? Somewhere private?"

Tiffani looked at me for a long moment before shaking her head. "I'm just a waitress. I don't do that."

"Two hundred bucks for fifteen minutes. And I mean talk—that's it."

She looked at me for another beat and then held out her hand. "Three hundred. Pay up front."

I gave her my card. She ran it, looked at the screen, and then nodded. "Okay," she said, getting to her feet, "let's *talk*."

Tiffani led the way down a narrow hall, parted a black ceiling-to-floor curtain, and waved me through. The curtain must have been made of acoustic-dampening material, because the volume of the migraine-inducing techno-pop dropped.

Recessed lighting cast writhing shadows on the threadbare carpeting. A series of alcoves branched to the left and right of the main hallway. I glanced in one and saw what I expected—a cramped room with a worn sofa that ran the length of the far wall. Large mirrors covered the other three walls, and a disco ball hung from the ceiling.

Charming.

"I told you, I don't do private dances," Tiffani said, catching me looking into the empty room. "But I can find you someone."

"Not much of a dancer," I said. "Two left feet. But I'd like to ask you some questions."

"You a cop?"

I shook my head. "The furthest thing from it. My wife's friend is going through an awful divorce. Her ex isn't paying child support. She thinks he's spending his money here."

"Why do I care?"

"You don't. But I do. I told my friend I'd try to figure out if he's a regular. What she does with that info is up to her. Being a single mother is hard enough. A deadbeat dad who doesn't pay child support just makes things harder."

The lines on Tiffani's face softened. "You have a picture?"

"On my phone. Will you take a look?"

Tiffani nodded. "I'll show it around to the other girls in the break room too. But that's it. If something happens it's my ass. I need this job."

"I understand," I said, selecting a picture of Charles and handing her the phone. "I'll wait."

Tiffani stared at the picture, using two bloodred fingernails to enlarge the image before shaking her head. "Looks familiar, but I can't be sure. I see a lot of faces. Wait there. I'll be back."

She pointed toward an unoccupied room.

I nodded, walked inside, and let Tiffani draw the curtain closed behind me. The furnishings were even less impressive up close. No part of me was touching the stained couch against the wall. Instead, I stood in the center of the room, staring at my reflection for a ten count. Then I eased back the curtain and checked the hallway.

Empty.

Edging past the curtain, I looked at the alcoves to either side and thought about what to do next.

I'd checked Charles's location once more before handing the phone to Tiffani. The coordinates hadn't changed. He was here somewhere, but I still didn't know why. Seeing who else was frequenting the club was probably the only way I was going to answer that question. The curtained room across the hall from mine seemed like as good a place to start as any.

Edging across the hallway, I crept up next to the room and grabbed a handful of velvet fabric. As I collected my thoughts, planning what to say once I unexpectedly confronted whoever was inside, I heard what the pounding music had obscured. Voices. A man and a woman arguing.

In Arabic.

FOURTEEN

leaned closer, convinced at first that I'd misheard, but Arabic wasn't a language easily mistaken for anything else. Especially once you've heard it while facing the business end of an AK-47. But I digress. The two people in the room were screaming in Arabic, and they weren't talking about the weather.

"Please, not again," a woman said.

"Quiet, whore," a man said.

The dull *thump* of flesh hitting flesh punctuated his comment, and the woman cried out. She might have said something else, but I couldn't be sure. This was because the part of my brain that had been focused on translating was now focused on something else.

I ripped open the fabric and charged inside.

Spending eight years as a DIA case officer in garden spots the world over should have prepared me for whatever was happening on the other side of that curtain.

It hadn't.

Like the previous room, this one had mirrors on the walls and a disco ball hanging from the ceiling. But that is where the similarities ended. Instead of a couch, a futon ran along the far wall. A futon occupied by a woman whose hands were secured to restraints attached to the furniture's metal frame.

A man stood in the semidarkness above her, his back to me. He was in the middle of swinging, and his right fist connected with her nose, spraying blood across the nearest mirror. He raised his left hand to follow up.

He didn't get the chance.

I closed the distance between us without conscious thought, snapping my knuckles into his right kidney. I started the punch with my toes and drove through my calves and hamstrings, picturing my fist exiting his stomach. The man collapsed like a deflated balloon, spilling across the screaming woman.

I chased the right with a left, not wanting his other kidney to miss out on all the fun.

A well-executed kidney strike will drop a man to his knees. Two in a row will take the fight out of most anyone. Though he was a good two inches taller than me, and at least fifty pounds heavier, my new friend was no exception. A high-pitched keening escaped his lips, and the smell of urine filled the air.

He was done.

I was not.

Grabbing his collar with my left hand and his shoulder with my right, I pivoted, hurling him across the room. He smashed headfirst into the far mirror, shattering it before sprawling through the black curtain into the hallway. I followed, murder in my heart and blood on my fists.

Left to my own devices, I would probably have beaten him to death. But we were no longer alone. Tiffani and a second man stood in the darkened hallway. The newcomer looked from me to the bleeding man sprawled across the floor.

Then he went for his gun.

FIFTEEN

The newcomer swept aside his sport coat with a practiced motion, right hand streaking for his waistband. And that was a mistake. I could smell his spicy cologne, which meant he was too close to draw his gun. He should have known better, but didn't.

I did.

Leaping toward him, I smashed my elbow into his chest. Then I pistoned my legs, driving him into the concrete wall behind him with a block that would have made my eighth-grade football coach proud. He grunted, the air leaving his lungs in an onion-laced cloud. My fingers found his gun hand. I compressed his wrist against his holster, preventing him from clearing the pistol.

Or so I thought.

One second I was congratulating myself for not getting shot in yet another dimly lit room. The next I was staggering backward, blinking the stars from my eyes from the kind of headbutt that would have made Jack Reacher proud. Through equal parts luck and skill, I'd turned my head to the side just before impact. I'd saved my nose, but the blow still hurt like a son of a bitch.

Doing my best to ignore the white lightning bolts exploding through my skull, I tightened my grip on his wrist and yanked him toward me. He stumbled, and I stomped on his kneecap. He grunted, tumbling downward. I kicked him in the head as he fell, picturing myself punting a football.

His neck snapped with a wet-sounding *pop*.

Clearing his sport coat, I reached for his waist, found the holster, and drew his pistol. Turning, I looked for my next target but found only Tiffani. Screaming. The man who'd started this nonsense was gone.

But I had a feeling he'd be back.

"Who's the girl in the room?" I said, pointing the pistol at Tiffani.

"I don't know. I don't know," Tiffani said, covering her face with her hands as she backed away. "They just brought her in today."

"Who?"

The door at the far end of the hallway crashed open, revealing a pair of men holding sawed-off shotguns. I dropped to one knee, firing as I went. Earsplitting shotgun blasts echoed down the hall even as I shifted the pistol's green front sight post from one dark center mass to the other, squeezing the trigger until the pistol's slide locked to the rear.

If the idiots had turned on the overhead lights, things

might have shaken out differently. But they hadn't, and it hadn't. Their eyes had needed time to adjust to the dimly lit room, while I saw just fine. Still, it was hard to miss with a shotgun in an enclosed space. A couple of the buckshot pellets had scored the top of my shoulder, making my shirt sticky with blood. I turned toward Tiffani only to find her sprawled against the wall. Fear had kept her frozen in place, and now most of her face was missing.

Swearing, I discarded the pistol and grabbed my phone from her lifeless fingers. I sprinted back to the room with the shackled girl, and found her struggling against her restraints, her face a mass of blood and tears.

"Easy, easy," I said in Arabic. "I'm here to help."

She stopped struggling, her dark eyes watching me, even as her shoulders still shook with silent sobs. Her wrists were raw and bleeding from where the metal handcuffs had bitten into her flesh, and I had to fight down the murderous rage threatening to overwhelm me. Ripping through the seam ringing my shirt cuff, I extracted the key I kept secreted there and showed it to the girl.

"I'm going to unlock these," I said, pointing to her cuffs, "okay?"

She nodded, her eyes never leaving mine. I slid the key home, twisting and then ratcheting loose the first cuff. The girl snatched her free hand toward her chest as I went to work on the second.

I should have seen what was coming next, but was too focused on freeing her before more gun-toting commandos arrived. To her credit, the girl waited for exactly the right moment. I had one hand on her wrist and was working the cuff's locking mechanism with the other. The moment metal rasped against metal, signifying the lock's release, she acted.

I caught her motion with my peripheral vision and ducked, saving my eye. But the handcuff's metal teeth still scythed into my cheek. Rearing back, the girl tore the handcuff free before whipping it back toward my face. This time I was ready. Catching the chain on my open hand, I wrapped my fingers around the metal linkage and jerked the cuffs away.

"Goddamn it," I said as blood poured down my face. "I'm trying to help. But if you want to stay here, have at it."

I pressed my left hand against my cheek, trying to hold the scrap of skin in place, while drawing my Glock with my right. Squeezing around the curtain, I cleared the hallway with the pistol's front sight post, angling through the open space like I was slicing a pie.

Empty.

For now.

"What's it gonna be?" I said, looking back at the girl crumpled on the futon. "Leaving or staying?"

She looked at me for a long time, and I couldn't imagine what she saw. Even so, I'd unlocked her handcuffs and refused to retaliate after she'd sliced open my face. That must have counted for something.

"Leaving," she said, getting to her feet on unsteady legs.

Good enough for me.

SIXTEEN

Matty," Frodo said, his deep baritone sounding somehow confined since my cell was on speakerphone, "where the hell you been?"

I was driving a rental, and I hadn't bothered to sync my phone and now I was paying the price. Though, to be fair, I hadn't envisioned a contingency where I'd be nursing a facial wound with one hand and fighting DC traffic with the other.

Then again, with my history, maybe I should have.

"Chasing a lead," I said.

"What does that mean?"

"Later. I need help. Now."

"Talk to me, Goose."

This was one reason I loved Frodo. When I needed help, he was all in, no questions asked. He'd had my back in firefights across the globe, and losing his arm had done nothing to diminish his loyalty. The world would be a better place with more Frodos.

"I need access to a safe house for me plus one."

"Is this a party line?"

I looked over at the girl before answering. She was curled in her seat, staring outside. She didn't appear to speak much English, but I wasn't assuming anything. "Affirmative."

"Current location?"

"North of the District, heading south."

"Roger—give me a couple of minutes to see what's available. I'll text you an address. I'm assuming the house needs to be fully furnished?"

"Yep. Including a med kit."

"For you or the plus one?"

"Both."

"Severity?"

"Non-life-threatening. Can you suture with one hand?"

"Like a goddamn surgeon. I'm texting you the address now. See you in fifteen."

"Roger that," I said, and ended the call.

My head throbbed where bad guy number one had headbutted me, and blood from my cheek laceration was running between my fingers and down my wrist. I had a girl who wouldn't talk in the passenger seat and a pile of dead bodies back at the strip club.

Still, somehow I already felt better.

This was partly due to the artificial high that always

accompanied someone shooting at me and missing. But only partly. This was the second time in as many days that someone had tried to kill me, and I certainly hadn't felt this happy yesterday. No, the reason I wanted to break into song was more savage. The tables had just officially turned.

Frodo was now in the mix.

The thought of my best friend joining the fray almost made me pity whoever'd been dumb enough to take a shot at me in the first place.

Almost.

SEVENTEEN

"Doesn't say much, does she?" Frodo said, gesturing toward where the mystery girl was sitting on the safe house's plush leather couch.

Budget cutbacks had hit the Department of Defense hard, and the DIA was no exception. But judging by the furnishings in this three-bedroom bolt-hole, the Agency's forced austerity hadn't applied to the network of safe houses used by senior DIA officials to debrief repatriated case officers and foreign agents.

Rank did have its privileges.

"Not so far," I said, wincing as I flushed the cut on my cheek with another squirt of hydrogen peroxide. "Though if I'd been through what she had, I'd probably be keeping my thoughts to myself too."

"True," Frodo said. "But if we're going to help her, she's got to talk."

"You want to give it a go?" I said, preparing to affix

the flap of skin back to the side of my face with a couple of butterfly bandages, "be my guest."

"Use this instead," Frodo said, handing me a tube of superglue from the med kit. "And thanks for the offer, but I don't want to talk to your girl. She isn't real keen on the male species."

As usual, Frodo had things right. After hanging up with my best friend and former bodyguard, I'd tried to engage the mystery woman, but she rebuffed my attempts with one notable exception. I'd offered to drive her to a police station, and she'd adamantly refused, becoming almost hysterical in the process. At one point, she'd clawed at the door handle, ready to leap from our moving car, until I convinced her we wouldn't go to the police.

Not involving the authorities actually made things easier. I hadn't had time to process what had happened at the strip club, let alone what Charles had to do with any of it. But I did know that showing up at a police station in my present condition would generate far more questions than I had answers for.

"Can't say I blame her," I said. "When I found her, she was chained to a wall, getting the shit beat out of her."

"Who was doing the beating?" Frodo said.

I shrugged as I pressed the flap of skin back into place, holding the cut closed as the superglue did its work. "I didn't get a chance to ask him before more men with guns showed up."

"Is he still alive?"

I nodded. "Yep. His two friends not so much."

"Damn, boy," Frodo said. "Between the shootout in Austin and this clusterfuck, you're dropping bodies faster than Ebola. Might want to pace yourself. So, what's going on?"

A buzzing from my pocket kept me from answering him, which was good, because answers were still in pretty short supply. I pulled out the phone, examined the screen, and showed it to Frodo.

"Rawlings?" Frodo said.

"Yep. I have a feeling he's not calling to shoot the shit. Can you watch her? I gotta take this in the other room."

"No worries. Uncle Frodo's got things under control."

I walked down the hallway, took the first left, and found myself in a small but tastefully furnished bedroom. Shutting the door behind me, I put the phone to my ear.

"Drake."

"What the fuck did you do?"

"Good evening, Agent Rawlings. So nice of you to call."

"You think this is fucking funny? You near a TV?"

"Nope," I said, sitting down on the bed.

"Then I'll give you the CliffsNotes version. I traced a phone to a strip club in Bethesda. For you. Now that club looks like a war zone. Three dead bodies. Three!"

"Would have been four if I'd been half a second slower," I said. "I was outgunned and outmanned and damn near bought the farm. Excuse me if I seem a little less than sympathetic."

I'd started the conversation calmly enough, but the stress of the night must have gotten to me. I'd screamed the last sentence. Now my hands were shaking.

"Okay, okay," Rawlings said, his voice dropping a register or two. "Tell me what happened."

So I did, holding the phone with one hand while I tapped out the rhythm to Journey's "Don't Stop Believin'" with the other. Yes, it might be the world's most overplayed song, but that doesn't mean it's not a masterpiece. Try humming the chorus, and see if your homicidal urges don't just evaporate. Steve Perry could give Don Henley a run for his money when it came to songwriting genius. Anyway, before I knew it, my story had run its course and so had the trembling.

"Fuck me," Rawlings said. "You've either got the worst luck or the best. I can't decide which."

"Join the club."

"The girl might have answers. I want to talk to her."

"What," I said, "on the phone?"

"No," Rawlings said. "I'm in DC."

"Why?"

"Later. Give me the address to the safe house. I'll be over with an Arabic linguist."

"She's not ready for that," I said. "When I tried to take her to the police, she almost jumped out of a moving car."

"It's a common reaction from folks from that part of the world. In many countries, the police have the authority to detain and even torture people without probable cause or a warrant. If she's been sexually assaulted, she might even be afraid that she'll be held responsible."

"So the guy who doesn't speak Arabic is giving me a lesson on Middle Eastern culture? Thanks, jackass. I clearly hadn't put that together."

"Don't get all sensitive on me. I'm just thinking out loud. But since you're such a smart guy, you must have an idea or two. Let's hear 'em."

And that was the rub, because I didn't. Or at least I didn't until that exact moment.

"The girl is the key," I said, "but she isn't talking to us. Probably not to any man. She needs someone she can trust. Someone we can trust."

"Agreed. Know anyone who fits the bill?"

"Actually, I do."

EIGHTEEN

I drove up to the redbrick building and parked in an empty visitor's spot, trying not to dwell on the absurdity of what I was about to attempt. On the surface, this made very little sense. There were plenty of people in both the DIA and FBI who specialized in Middle Eastern customs and culture. Between our two organizations, we undoubtedly had female native Arabic speakers.

But that wasn't what I'd suggested to Rawlings, or Frodo, who was back in DC playing chaperone to the mystery woman.

The espionage business was a strange one on many levels. Technology had vastly improved the tradecraft aspects of the profession, but at the end of the day, recruiting a spy was still a deeply personal endeavor. Stripped down to the basics, pitching an asset meant convincing another human being to become a traitor.

The perfect pitch was still as much art as science, and

the artist in me believed that the right spy to bond with my mystery woman wasn't a spy at all. She was a chemistry professor from East Tennessee who didn't speak a word of Arabic. As pitches went, this might just be one for the record books.

If it worked.

Locking the car behind me, I walked up the sidewalk, pulled open the door to the chemistry building, and ducked inside. The gray winter sky had faded into darkness more than an hour ago, and the biting wind that had been harassing me all day had turned positively wicked. Temperatures were plunging now that the lukewarm sun had ceased to provide even the illusion of warmth. Since joining the DIA, I'd spent a fair amount of time in the greater DC area. Other than brief interludes provided by fall and spring, the nation's most self-important city didn't offer much in the way of an appealing climate.

The building's overactive heater blasted me full in the face with a wall of moistureless air. I'd been back in DC for less than forty-eight hours, and my lips were already chapped and bleeding. Nothing like the District to make you miss tracking Taliban through the Afghan mountains.

Students pushed past in clumps of twos and threes, paying me no attention. This was good. While I was fairly certain the scientist I was coming to see wouldn't mind the intrusion, I couldn't say the same for her fellow faculty members.

George Washington University was one of the nation's most prestigious institutes of higher learning, and a factory for future government workers. Even so, there were limits to higher education's sense of patriotism. Guest lecturers from previous presidential administrations were always welcome, but a case officer hoping to recruit a faculty member was another thing altogether.

A touch screen at the far end of the lobby listed faculty members and their offices. Paging through the names, I selected one. The screen asked me if I wanted the scientist paged. I did not. It then asked if I needed directions to her office. I did. The list of names morphed into a 3-D rendering of the building with a dashed blue line directing me where to go.

Ah, the marvels of technology.

"Can I help you?"

"Nope," I said, ignoring the man standing behind me in favor of pressing the house-shaped button at the bottom of the screen. The blue line vanished and was replaced by the alphabetical listing of faculty members.

I could see the man's reflection on the touch screen— thirties, about my height and weight. No uniform, so he wasn't a security guard or campus cop. Probably just an angry postdoc looking to unleash pent-up frustration.

I'd started toward the stairwell that the blue line had indicated when the angry postdoc grabbed my shoulder, spinning me around.

"I wanna see some ID."

Now that we were face-to-face, I had to change my assessment. He was my height, but he was definitely not my build. He was bigger. Considerably. Engorged biceps and pecs bulged beneath an artfully faded shirt that was at least one size too small. His five-o'clock shadow was masculine without being scruffy, and his thick brown hair was stylishly messy.

I'm sure in a world populated by men who spent more time in a book than in a gym, he was quite the catch. But to me, he was just another pain in the ass.

"And I want a date with Dana Perino," I said, shrugging off his hand. "But sometimes we don't get what we want. Please, move out of the way."

"Dana Perino? I figured you for more of a Megyn Kelly kind of guy."

The new speaker was standing somewhere off to my right, but I couldn't see her. Then again, I didn't need to. Her East Tennessee twang was unmistakable.

"Hello, darling," Virginia Kenyon said, sliding between me and the tough guy as if he wasn't there. "I've missed you."

Before I could reply, she wrapped her arms around my neck and planted a kiss on my lips.

"God," Virginia said as she pulled away, "I've been wanting to do that all day."

"You know each other?" the tough guy said, looking from me to Virginia.

"Well, of course," Virginia said, looping her arm through mine. "This is how we say hello to our cousins in the South. Come on, cousin. Let's head to my office, where we won't be bothered."

Without waiting for a response, Virginia led me up

the stairs. I looked over my shoulder at the tough guy and waved.

He didn't wave back.

Sorry about that," Virginia said, offering me a cup of coffee freshly brewed from her Keurig. "I know it was a little over-the-top, even for me, but that jackass has been asking me out for the better part of a month."

I studied Virginia as I took the coffee, trying to figure out what was different about her. And then it hit me—this was the first time I'd seen her in anything but contractor garb. In Syria, her wardrobe had consisted of outdoors clothes: 5.11 Tactical pants, REI shirts, and a faded Yankees ball cap holding back her hair. Today, she was wearing an outfit that flattered rather than hid her athletic figure: a curve-hugging sweater paired with skinny jeans tucked into calf-length leather boots.

The change was startling.

"He did seem awfully persistent," I said, adding a generous helping of cream along with several packets of sugar.

"If it was just persistence, I might think better of him," Virginia said, settling into the small love seat across from me. "But you're giving him too much credit. For reasons known only to the Almighty, he's considered quite the catch around here. Undergrads swoon over him, and he's gone through the graduate students like shit through a goose. Now he has his sights set on me. Since I haven't responded to his overtures, he's abandoned any pretense of subtlety. Yesterday, he asked me how long it had been since I'd been laid."

"Seriously?" I said, setting down my coffee. "What did you say?"

"That I'd rip out his tongue if he ever used words like that again."

"Did you go to your department head?"

Virginia looked at me over her cup, her blue eyes glittering. "Because we're friends, I'm going to forget you said that. Daddy taught me to shoot before I could ride a bike. If that jackass can't take no for an answer, I'll put a thirty-eight-caliber slug through his man parts. Now, I know you didn't come all this way to hear about my love life. On the phone you said you needed help. Is this about another undetectable chemical weapon?"

The last question was not a demonstration of Virginia's subtle sense of humor. The sassy Southerner was a top-notch synthetic chemist. For reasons known only to her, Virginia had taken an interest in chemical weapons. Several of her papers on novel nerve agent formulation methods had made their way to the DIA's Directorate for Science & Technology. From there, it wasn't hard to guess what had happened next. We'd met while both on an operation in Syria, and Virginia had impressed me with her grit and outside-the-box thinking. Now I wanted to see just how far down the rabbit hole she was willing to go.

"No weapons, chemical or otherwise," I said, setting my empty cup on her cluttered end table. "In fact, there's no science involved at all. But I do need your brain."

"You know just how to get a girl's attention, Matty," Virginia said, tucking her auburn hair behind her ear. "If that mouth breather downstairs had your way with words, I'd have already taken him to bed. Please, tell me, how can my superior intellect be of service?"

"There's this crossword puzzle I've been working—"

"No one likes a smart-ass, Matthew."

"Sorry—couldn't resist. There's a girl—"

"There's always a girl. Ever since Eve motivated Adam to finally get his ass out of Eden, every man has been convinced that his problems revolve around a girl."

"And lack of good beer. If Adam could have kicked back with a six-pack of Yuengling, he'd never have given that apple a second glance."

"Yuengling is for savages. Is this going somewhere? I've got papers to grade."

"Not tonight. Tonight, you're going with me to a DIA safe house to meet my partner and a girl I found in a strip club."

"Matthew!"

"An Arabic-speaking girl. When I found her, she was getting the shit beat out of her by an Iraqi commando. We need to figure out her story, and I think you can help."

"Why not ask the commando?"

"He's more of the strong, silent type."

Virginia leaned forward, her eyes sparkling. "This conversation is both interesting and indecipherable. Though I appreciate your faith in me, I'm not sure it's warranted. I'm a damn good chemist, but my Arabic is mediocre. And by *mediocre* I mean I don't speak a word."

"Here's the thing," I said, shifting forward to match Virginia's intensity. "I'm not sure how you're gonna help either. But I have a feeling you will. Know why? Because when I look at you, I see me."

"Forget what I said earlier about your way with words."

"I'm serious. How long have you been back from Syria?"

"A year."

"A year?" I said.

"A year, two weeks, and four days."

"Know why the time has passed so slowly since you've been back?" I said.

"Because my freshman students were raised by helicopter parents?"

"Worse. Because you're bored. One year, two weeks, and four days ago, you were doing something that mattered. Something that lit your blood on fire. And you want it back. Two days ago, a team of foreign shooters tried to kill me. I don't know why, but I do know that their trail leads through a scared girl sitting in a safe house twenty minutes away. She won't even look at me, but you're a different story. So, what's it gonna be? Take a ride with me or spend another night grading papers?"

For the first time since I'd known her, Virginia didn't answer with a sarcastic comeback. Instead, she looked at me for a long moment before blowing out a held breath.

"Let me get my coat."

NINETEEN

rodo, this is Virginia. Virginia, Frodo."

"Did your momma not like you?" Virginia said, forgoing Frodo's offered hand in favor of pulling the former commando in for a hug. "I mean, don't get me wrong. East Tennessee has its own naming conventions. But we stick to Earls and Bubbas as opposed to mystical creatures with furry feet."

"My momma liked me just fine," Frodo said, returning Virginia's hug one-handed. "My first team leader gave me my call sign."

"Call sign?"

"It's a Unit tradition. New operators get christened with call signs. On my first trip to the range, we had some downtime. I pulled out a book, and that was that."

"*Lord of the Rings*?"

Frodo shook his head with a laugh. "Actually, it was *The Briar King* by Greg Keyes. But my team leader wasn't exactly a fantasy novel connoisseur. He saw the cover and asked if I was into hobbit porn. I've been Frodo ever since."

As war stories went, this one wasn't exactly a doozy, but I still shook my head. Frodo had been my shadow in combat zones the world over. For six years, I'd tried to get the story behind his call sign and never succeeded. Virginia had needed all of fifteen seconds.

Maybe bringing her along hadn't been so crazy after all.

"Well, I'm glad to meet you," Virginia said. "What can you tell me about our girl?"

"Not much, I'm afraid," Frodo said. "She's not catatonic, but she's close. She's in the back bedroom. I've checked on her a couple of times, but she hasn't moved since Matty left."

At the description of the girl, Virginia's smile faded, replaced by a more serious expression. "Let's see what we're dealing with."

By unspoken agreement, Frodo drifted back to the living room while I walked Virginia to the bedroom. Frodo's Arabic was worse than mine, and he thought that his presence would do more harm than good. If the girl had wanted to open up to him, she would have already. In fact, if I hadn't needed to translate, I'd have let Virginia handle the interview solo. It didn't take a genius to understand that something terrible had happened to the girl, probably at the hands of a terrible man.

I paused outside the closed bedroom door, intending to take a second to strategize, but the chemistry professor had other ideas. Virginia stopped just long enough to knock and then entered.

The girl was lying on the bed, staring at the ceiling. She flinched as the door banged open, pushing herself against the wall until she saw me. Only then did her narrow shoulders relax.

I felt a murderous rage at the thought of what she must have endured to provoke such a reaction. But just as quickly, I pushed those images aside, afraid that she might see my anger but mistake its source. Fortunately, the girl was focused on Virginia.

The chemistry professor crossed the room in three easy strides and then crouched down so that she was eye to eye with the girl.

"Hi," Virginia said, reaching out to squeeze the girl's shoulder. "I'm Virginia."

I started to translate, but the girl interrupted.

"I speak English."

Her words were halting, as if carefully chosen, but still understandable. I was shocked. Virginia was not.

"Of course you do," Virginia said, pulling a chair from the desk next to the bed without breaking eye contact. "My friend's gonna make us something to drink while you and I talk. Is that okay?"

The girl gave a hesitant nod.

"Good," Virginia said, settling into the chair. "Coffee or tea?"

"Tea."

"Perfect. We'll make that two. Matt?"

"Two teas coming up," I said, taking my cue. I ex-

cused myself and shut the door quietly behind me. Once
the latch clicked home, I leaned toward the door, listening. I couldn't make out her words, but I could hear
Virginia's voice. Her Tennessee twang sounded soothing
as she spoke with an even cadence. After a moment of
silence, the girl answered. Her words trickled out at first
and then became a torrent, as if a dam had burst.

At its core, the profession of espionage is built upon
relationships. Upon people. Judging by what was happening behind that door, Virginia was well on her way to
becoming a spy.

Ten minutes later, I knocked on the door with a TV
tray in my hand. I waited for Virginia's "Come in"
and then entered. As asked, I'd brewed two cups of tea
and then added a plateful of dates along with a box of
baklava. Though I still thought the safe house's furnishings were a bit ostentatious, the housekeepers knew their
business. The kitchen and the large pantry looked like
Costco's ethnic food section. Cuisines the world over
were represented, but the majority of delicacies were
Middle Eastern.

Go figure.

Virginia indicated the desk with a wave, but otherwise
didn't acknowledge my presence. The girl had been talking, but stopped midsentence, her lips compressing into
a thin line as she watched me with hard eyes. Again taking
my cue from the chemistry professor turned case officer,
I set the tray down and closed the door behind me.

"How's it going in there?" Frodo said as I joined him at the kitchen table.

"Hell if I know. Arabic I can comprehend, but the language of women is still beyond me."

"Truer words have never been spoken. Want some coffee?"

"Sure."

"Then get your uncrippled ass up and go make it. And sandwiches too. Salami's in the fridge."

"If you weren't missing an arm, I'd kick your ass," I said, getting to my feet.

"Cream but no sugar. I'm watching my figure."

A pot of coffee later, I heard the bedroom door open and close. Then Virginia appeared.

"Take my chair," Frodo said, springing to his feet.

"Coffee?" I said, standing as well.

"Something stronger if you've got it," Virginia said, collapsing into Frodo's offered seat.

The horrors she'd discovered in the bedroom had shaken her. Her eyes were puffy and bloodshot. For once, she didn't have a zinger on the tip of her tongue. Instead, she looked . . . drained.

"Beer, whiskey, or wine?" I said, opening the pantry door.

"Whiskey. Straight."

I found a bottle of Maker's Mark, added a pair of ice cubes, and poured three fingers into a glass. Taking the bottle and glass to the table, I handed Virginia her drink. She took a long swallow and then set the tumbler down.

"My daddy drank Maker's Mark," Virginia said, tracing patterns in the condensation dripping down the glass. "I wish he were here."

"Why?" I said.

"Because he was good at telling stories, and I'm not sure I can keep it together long enough to do this one justice."

Her name is Nazya," Virginia said, "and she's a Yazidi."

The girl's story began in Iraq. As I'd suspected, she'd been sex trafficked. But that was where my suspicions and her story diverged.

Yazidis are religious minorities in Iraq and, as such, uniquely vulnerable. While ISIS was in power, the council of men who passed for the jihadi group's theologians had decided that Yazidis were a special brand of apostates. As such, the Koran sanctioned exterminating the men and selling the women into slavery. Entire villages were destroyed in the ensuing genocide. After ISIS was beaten back, other criminal organizations moved in to fill the void, no longer relying on grotesque theology to justify what had turned into a very profitable endeavor.

In other words, sex sells.

Nazya's father and most of her brothers were killed during the ISIS occupation, and the rest of her male relatives scattered. Her small village tried to reestablish itself once the black-flag-waving crazies had been driven back west into Syria. Unfortunately, with most of the men dead or missing, the women and children who remained were easy targets. Nazya had been kidnapped in broad daylight while walking home from the market. That had been almost six weeks ago. What she'd endured since was almost unspeakable.

Virginia's telling didn't so much end as run out of momentum. One moment she was talking, relaying in clinical detail the abuse Nazya had suffered. The next, her words simply sputtered to a stop. I didn't realize until that moment how much she'd been struggling to maintain her composure. Virginia's breath hitched in her chest, and tears streamed down her cheeks.

"Goddamn it," Virginia said, wiping away the tears with the back of her hand. "I hate it when women cry."

"I don't," Frodo said, refilling her now-empty tumbler. "Besides, if that story doesn't make you cry, you're not human."

I understood what Frodo meant, but Nazya's story didn't make me want to cry. It made me want to kill. To exterminate every person who'd had a hand in what happened to the girl. But that wasn't possible. Instead, I pulled out my phone and scrolled through pictures until I found Sayid's son.

"Sorry to do this," I said, sliding the phone to Virginia, "but can you show her this? I need to know if she recognizes him."

Virginia made no move to pick up the phone. Instead,

she put the tumbler to her lips and drained the whiskey in a single long swallow.

"Damn, that burns," Virginia said, slamming down the glass. "I don't know how Daddy drank it."

Grabbing the phone, she headed toward the bedroom. I thought about following, but didn't want to risk the bond she'd formed with Nazya. Instead, I tracked her progress via sound—the bedroom door squeaking open, the low murmur of Virginia's voice, and the woman's answering words. I pictured Virginia showing the woman my phone and wondered if I should try to eavesdrop.

I needn't have bothered. The screams were answer enough.

TWENTY

I picked up the surveillance about a block from the safe house. To be fair, my tail wasn't trying to be subtle. I'd started a surveillance-detection run more out of habit than because I was worried, but practicing tradecraft was a little like wearing a motorcycle helmet—it was better to be safe than dead.

Case in point—a green Pontiac Grand Am had followed me through the last three turns.

Usually bad guys weren't something I thought about on American soil. I operated overseas as a ghost, using a series of backstopped identities that had no connection to my true name, let alone my actual address. The technological revolution that had begun with World War II and continued through the Cold War and now the War on Terror had produced a plethora of tools and gadgets. Capabilities my shadowy forefathers would have called science fiction. Even so, a spy's best weapon was still anonymity. No one could track the Gray Man because he didn't exist. In theory, I had nothing to worry about once I crossed back to my side of the ocean.

In theory.

But theories had a way of breaking down when confronted by reality. The shootout on South Congress was a perfect example. While a Pontiac tailing me through the bustling streets of Arlington wasn't normally a cause for concern, normality had ended two days ago.

I eased my Glock from its concealed holster, wedging the pistol between my leg and the seat cushion. If this nonsense kept up, I would have to switch to a shoulder rig and a sport coat. Drawing from an in-the-belt holster was a bitch while seated.

With my Glock where I could reach it, I thought through the next phase of this engagement. The phase where bullets started flying. South Congress could have gone down completely differently were it not for luck. I'd been lucky to spot the assassin before entering the kill zone, where his shooters had been presumably waiting, but Lady Luck was a fickle mistress.

If the jack wagon tailing me was intent on mixing it up, I couldn't change his mind. But I could select the time and place of the engagement. I was in the middle of trying to find terrain that would favor me rather than my opponent when the Pontiac driver flashed his high beams twice.

Then he activated his right turn signal.

Glancing to my right, I saw a local bookstore's inviting parking lot. Wrenching the wheel around, I eased over and then backed into a space. The Pontiac followed, taking the spot next to mine. I unbuckled my seat belt and moved the Glock to my lap, waiting. A second later, the Pontiac's door opened, and my favorite special agent emerged.

Hunching his shoulders against the cold drizzle, Rawlings opened my car's passenger door and climbed inside.

"Jumpy?" Rawlings said as he eyed the Glock.

"It's been that kind of a week," I said. "You're a long way from Austin."

"Tell me about it. Other than the mandatory eighteen-month TDY, good people stay as far from DC as possible. This place attracts two types of agents: lazy ones who'd rather push paper than chase bad guys and those vying for a spot in upper management."

"Which are you?" I said, clearing the rain droplets from the windshield with a touch of a knob. Just because Rawlings wasn't out to get me didn't mean that someone else wasn't. General Pershing said that there were only two types of soldiers—the quick and the dead. If you replaced *quick* with *paranoid* the same was true of spies.

"Neither. I'm a naive case agent from Austin who was stupid enough to run a joint operation with a fellow member of the intelligence community. Now I've been summoned to the ivory tower known as FBI Headquarters to atone for my sins."

"Cut the woe-is-me crap," I said. "Last I checked, you haven't been the one dodging bullets. What do you want?"

"Information. Everything you've been holding back

and then some. Headquarters has convened an emergency strategy session. They've pulled in everyone working the CI investigation, including yours truly. I've somehow forgotten to mention my involvement with you, but that's not going to fly much longer. Please, tell me you've got something more than just dead bodies. How about we start with the phone I illegally traced? Who's it belong to?"

"Who's the target of the investigation?" I said.

Rawlings reached into the pocket of his suit jacket and came out with his ever-present pack of cigarettes.

"No smoking," I said, pointing to the admonishment sticker on the rental car's windshield.

"FBI," Rawlings said, baring the gold badge clipped to his belt. Lighting a cigarette, he took a deep drag before exhaling a blue cloud toward the ceiling.

I rolled down his window, and fat raindrops began to splatter against his suit.

"Here's the thing," Rawlings said, ignoring his rapidly dampening sleeve. "My ass is already hanging way out on this. The way I see it, it's your turn to put some skin in the game. Give me something I can use. Now."

I thumbed the windshield wiper again, buying time. I'd be asking the same thing if I were him, but I wasn't. I was me. I liked the FBI agent, but this operation had ceased being business as usual the second time bad guys had tried to use me for target practice. I was now in survival mode. So rather than answer his question, I did what any good spy would do. I applied a bit of misdirection.

"The girl I found is a Yazidi. She's been sex-trafficked from Iraq."

"Jesus," Rawlings said, ashing his cigarette into a cup holder dangerously close to my fingers. "That's horrible. But what's she got to do with my case?"

"I showed her a picture of the shooter I bagged in Austin."

"She recognized him?"

"You could say that. She took one look and started screaming. Needed the better part of fifteen minutes to calm down. The shooter was one of the men who helped break her in."

"That's horrible. What's her story?"

"Her kidnappers seemed more crime syndicate than terrorists. She was part of a group of Iraqi girls smuggled to the US. I think they were all dropped off at strip clubs and massage parlors."

"How old is she?"

"Eighteen."

"Fucking animals. Look, I can't imagine what she's been through, but are you sure this is legit? I mean, what are the odds that a girl in a Bethesda strip club is somehow tied to Iraqi commandos in Austin?"

"Better than you think," I said, sending rain droplets scattering again. The windows were beginning to fog, and I didn't like the idea of not being able to keep an eye on our surroundings. I'd have to start up the car if this conversation went too much longer.

"The Austin shooters were well equipped," I said. "Body armor, suppressed MP5s, the works. Not the kind of hardware you pick up at a local gun store, even in Texas. Your boys make any progress on the weapons?"

Rawlings shook his head. "No. The serial numbers are gone. Not filed away. Gone. As if they were never there in the first place. These aren't the rust-bucket pieces ATF confiscates from gangbangers or cartel muscle. The HKs were pristine. Like they'd rolled straight off the factory line."

"Probably had. From what the Yazidi said, I think the weapons and girls arrived in-country on the same container boat. Before she was trafficked to DC, a group of men visited the warehouse where she was being held. The shooter was with them. He raped her while the men with him loaded boxes into waiting trucks."

"When?"

"About two weeks ago," I said.

"Any idea where?"

I shook my head. "She was kept in windowless rooms. She didn't even know she was in DC."

"What was she doing at the strip club?"

"Turning tricks with about ten other girls who were dropped off last week. The strip club owner must be part of the trafficking organization."

"Not anymore," Rawlings said, pulling out his phone. He scrolled through several mug shots until he found the one that he wanted. "You whack this guy too?"

I looked at the picture and mentally compared it to the two men with the shotguns along with the commando whose neck I'd broken and the man I'd found abusing Nazya. None of them matched.

"No," I said.

"You sure?"

"Positive. I'm a spy. Recognizing faces isn't a party trick for me. It's survival. I've never seen this guy before."

"That's what I was afraid of," Rawlings said, squirreling the phone back into his pocket. "He and three of his buddies were found in the club's back office with 9mm holes in their foreheads."

"Somebody's tying up loose ends," I said, keying the wipers again.

Rawlings lit another cigarette. I unrolled his window farther. The rain was coming down harder, pinging off the hood and roof.

"Couldn't you at least smoke manly cigarettes?" I said, as he exhaled another gray cloud. "That smells like old-lady perfume."

"I smoke when I'm nervous, which is damn near all the time around you. Okay, so we've got a traumatized girl who probably wouldn't hold up for shit on the witness stand, a dead assassin who's also a rapist, and three equally dead members of a sex-trafficking ring. Wonderful. Did I miss anything?"

"Yeah," I said, dreading what was about to come next. "I need to tell you about the cell phone's owner."

"The supposed terrorist I illegally tracked to the strip club you turned into a slaughterhouse? I assumed he was part of the body count."

"You know what happens when you assume," I said. "The cell phone owner isn't dead. He also isn't a terrorist."

"And the hits just keep on coming. Not only did I run

an illegal trace, but my so-called source lied to me. Fantastic. Please, tell me the phone's owner isn't a senator or congressman."

"Nope," I said. "His name is Charles Sinclair Robinson the Fourth. In spite of that impressive-sounding name, he's not a politician. But he may be the next Director of the Central Intelligence Agency."

"Are you insane?" Rawlings said, choking on clove-laced smoke. "You had me ping a federal officer? Oh Jesus. And to think I was only worried about losing my pension. At this point, I'll be lucky to stay out of prison."

"You said you wanted to know everything. This is everything."

"I didn't want to know *that* part of everything. Unlike you Agency cowboys, I have to take a polygraph every five years. This is shaping up to be a shit storm of biblical proportions."

"That's why I want to know the CI investigation's target," I said. "The Arab shooter I bagged in Austin was the son of an asset Charles ran in Syria. Now, I'm not an FBI-trained investigator, but I doubt that's a coincidence."

"So you rattled Charles's cage and then had me trace his phone so you could see where he went next?" Rawlings shook his head. "You don't do anything by half, do you?"

"You're welcome," I said. "So, what now?"

"Do you have *anything* that will stand up in court? Anything at all? Because an illegal phone trace sure as hell won't."

"I'm a spy, not a cop," I said. "My people don't do court."

"Which is why my instructors at Quantico told us to *never* run a joint op with your people. How about the Yazidi girl? Do I get a crack at her?"

I thought for a moment and then slowly nodded. "Yes. Maybe you can recover some of the other girls she was trafficked with. But my colleague Virginia stays present for the questioning."

"Deal."

"So we're good?" I said.

"Hell no, we're not good. I'm still seriously exposed. I'm opening you as a confidential human source to cover my ass. Consider yourself so admonished."

"I can't be your source."

"You sure as shit can. You're my get-out-of-jail-free card. I'm feeding everything you gave me into a source report. It's still not enough to predicate a phone trace, but I'm getting closer."

"Then at least tell me if Charles is the CI investigation's target," I said.

Rawlings shook his head. "First, give me evidence I can use. Then we'll talk. Otherwise you are an admonished confidential human source working for the Federal Bureau of Investigation. There's a bunch of things I'm supposed to tell you that go along with that statement, but we both know I'd be wasting my breath. Here's what I will do—I'll type this up, but I won't enter it into the database unless headquarters forces my hand.

You've still got time to make something happen. But not much."

Without waiting for a reply, Rawlings opened the passenger door and dashed to his car. The cloud of smoke trailing behind him dissipated in the driving rain, just like my thoughts on what to do next.

TWENTY-ONE

There was a time when you two caused mayhem on the *other* side of the ocean," James said, working a small X-Acto knife around the mug shot situated on his desk. "Don't get me wrong. I like body counts as much as the next guy. But when you boys kill shit bags here, it causes me no small amount of ass pain."

"Chief, can we dispense with the *you boys*?" Frodo said. "Matty's done all the killing."

"Oh, no," James said, rotating the picture as he slid the knife around the edges, "you two are a package. I can never tell where one of you ends and the other begins. You're like a pair of hemorrhoids."

"Can we stop with the ass imagery?" I said. "I just ate lunch."

James laughed, and that was a mistake. When James laughed, his whole body got into the act. Normally, it was kind of funny watching a steely-eyed killer give a belly laugh reminiscent of Santa Claus. Today, his mirth came with a price. James clapped his hands together, inadvertently plunging the X-Acto knife into his index finger.

"Jesus, Mary, and Joseph," James said as blood streamed down his swollen knuckle in thick crimson rivulets. "Ann—get in here. And bring the med kit."

A second later Ann burst through the door, a tactical-trauma kit clutched between her manicured fingers. Unlike her boss, Ann wore her age well. Her shoulder-length brown hair was still gracefully transitioning to silver, and her forehead's lines had yet to deepen into true wrinkles. Once upon a time, I might have wondered why a secretary in the Defense Intelligence Agency would keep a level-one med kit in her desk drawer, but that was before I'd met Ann Beaumont.

"I told you to let the photography folks take care of that," Ann said, sounding more like a scolding mother than a concerned employee. "You're bleeding all over the rug."

"I wouldn't be if you'd hand me the ever-loving med kit," James said. "Besides, the imagery people always crop the pictures wrong. If you can't see their faces, it ruins the effect."

While James riffled through the kit in search of a bandage, I took a look at the offending picture. I shouldn't have. A selection of three images stretched across James's desk—the men I'd killed at the strip club.

"Chief," I said, keeping my voice remarkably calm, considering, "tell me you are not making coasters out of dead sex traffickers."

"Keep your eyes on your own damn paper," James said, draping a tattoo-encrusted forearm across the images. "Didn't your momma raise you better than that?"

"James," Ann said, gathering the med kit up now that he'd stanched the bleeding, "don't bring Matthew's momma into this. Lord knows the poor woman did the best she could."

I probably should have felt offended, but there was no point. If I'd wanted a normal work environment, I'd have gone into real estate. For all his quirks, James was a damn good boss when the chips were down. Last time my ass had been in a sling, he and Frodo had both gone to the president on my behalf. That kind of loyalty wasn't easy to find.

With a nimbleness that belied her plump figure, Ann scooped up the pictures strewn across James's desk along with the X-Acto knife.

"You boys drink some coffee while I take these down to Thelma in imagery," Ann said. "And try not to spill any more blood. It took the custodians three visits to clean up last time. Must have been at least a pint of O negative."

I waited for Ann's lips to curve into a smile, but all she gave was a final disapproving frown before sweeping from the room in a flurry of skirts and Chanel perfume. Which meant that maybe her admonition hadn't been a joke at all. But before I could pursue that thought further, Frodo took the conversation in a different direction.

"Will you just ask her to marry you and get it over with?" Frodo said, settling into his favorite chair.

"The thought has crossed my mind," James said, reaching into his desk drawer for a spit cup and a tin of Copenhagen.

"Quit thinking and just do it," Frodo said. "You aren't getting any prettier. Matty—get me some coffee."

"Where's your service dog?"

"Holding down the rug in my apartment. And not any of that store-bought shit either. I know Chief has the Turkish blend somewhere."

I dutifully complied, heating the water in the kettle adjacent to the conference table and then pouring the steaming liquid into the Turkish coffee that Frodo loved. I thought about adding an ice cube to Frodo's so that the grounds wouldn't properly mix, but resisted the urge. Frodo might have been down one arm, but he was still a former Unit commando. The next pint of O negative splashed across the rug might be mine.

"All right," James said once we were seated, "where do we stand?"

And that was the million-dollar question for which I had no answer. At least no answer that James would like.

"I think we've hit a stopping point," I said, spinning my glass coffee mug on its coaster. "We turned Nazya over to Rawlings and his crew with the condition that Virginia gets to stay during the questioning. I don't think they'll get much more. Nazya doesn't know anything about who trafficked her."

"You said she recognized the Arab assassin," James said, and stuffed dip into his lip until his cheek resembled a chipmunk's. "Did anyone else seem familiar?"

I shook my head. "I showed her a picture of Charles, but no dice. I still don't know what he was doing at the strip club, and I've run out of ways to find out. I surprised Charles the first time. He won't get caught with his pants down again."

"What about your FBI friend?"

"I had to come clean with Rawlings about tracing Charles's phone."

"Why?" James said.

"This is a kinder, gentler Matty," Frodo said.

"Come on, Chief," I said. "It's the right thing to do. He stuck his neck out for me. We know that FBI Headquarters is running a close-hold CI investigation, but we still don't know the target. We're out of threads to pull."

"Maybe not quite yet," Frodo said, changing the video on the flat-screen TV from Al Jazeera to his DIA-issued iPhone. "A friend at NSA dug up something on the shooter you bagged in Austin, Matt. Sayid's son."

"Fantastic," I said, "but just out of curiosity, is your friend of the male or female persuasion?"

"What difference does that make?"

"You're not gonna answer?"

"Negative, Ghost Rider."

I smiled and let the matter drop. A couple of months ago, Frodo had let slip that he was seeing an NSA analyst. I'd been happy for him, but I'd known better than to push too hard. Like most commandos, Frodo had a string of failed relationships, and he was painfully private when it came to his love life. I was hoping to elicit a bit

more, but once he started quoting *Top Gun*, I knew not
to push further.

"So, what did this gender-unspecific but incredibly
attractive analyst discover?" I said.

"Matthew, let the boy be," James said.

"No worries, Chief," Frodo said, queuing up a video.
"This is how Matty acts when he's not getting any at
home."

That hit a little too close to the mark. Fortunately, a
series of thumbnail images depicting the shooter popped
up on the TV, giving me something else to think about.
The quality wasn't good, which meant that the photos
had probably been sifted from surveillance videos. Several showed frontal shots of the shooter's face, but most
were profiles.

"Where did these come from?" I said.

"Feeds from airport security cameras. Specifically,
Reagan, Istanbul, and Baghdad International."

"Baghdad was the originating airport?"

Frodo nodded. "That's the earliest we found him anyway. We scrapped the digital date-time stamps from the
various feeds in order to determine numerical order."

"Nice work," I said. "The new NSA facial-recognition
algorithms are fantastic, but I didn't realize we shared
that capability with the Turks or Iraqis."

"*Share* might be a tad generous."

"Oh," I said. "So your cute NSA analyst hacked into
the closed-circuit surveillance system of a NATO ally
without permission?"

"You can't handle the truth."

Top Gun and *A Few Good Men* in the same conversation. This mystery analyst really had Frodo rattled. I needed to make her acquaintance. Soon.

"What does this tell us that we didn't already know?" James said. "The shooter Matty bagged hopped on a plane in Baghdad. I'll go out on a limb and predict that the former Iraqi commandos who were with him did too. So what?"

"We've got a bit more than that, Chief," Frodo said. "I'd say that—"

"Wait," I said. "Spool it back."

"Spool what back?" James said.

"The video," I said. "Frodo, can you rewind?"

Frodo stabbed a button on his iPhone, and the video reversed. The TV showed a series of shots from outside of Baghdad International. Probably footage from at least three cameras stitched together, judging by the jerky transitions from frame to frame. Still, I'd seen something. . . .

"Stop," I said. "Go forward. Maybe five seconds. There. Can you enlarge the image at the bottom right of the screen?"

"So this is what it feels like to drive Miss Daisy," Frodo said. But he made the requested adjustment all the same.

The image filled the TV. The shooter was getting out of the backseat of a customized SUV. Nothing special. Nothing except that, for a fraction of a second, the person seated next to the shooter was visible. His thick black hair was neatly styled, and his obligatory beard was trimmed almost down to the skin. He could have been the Arabic equivalent of the guy in those Dos Equis commercials. The World's Most Interesting Man.

I'd thought I'd recovered from our last encounter.

I hadn't.

My major muscles groups began spasming. I grabbed my pants with both hands, trying to keep my arms from flailing.

"Matty?" Frodo said.

"Ann," James bellowed out the door. "Get a medic."

"I'm fine, I'm fine," I said through chattering teeth. "Just give me a second."

Closing my eyes, I reached for my mental playlist and found the opening guitar riff to "Even Flow." Pushing everything else away, I concentrated on following Stone Gossard's magical fingers note by breathtaking note. The first time through, nothing happened. But by the second, the spasms began to subside. As Eddie Vedder growled the opening lyrics on my third run through the song, the shaking stopped.

I opened my eyes to see Ann, Frodo, and James staring at me in silence. "I'm fine," I said again. "Really. This just happens sometimes."

For the first time since I'd known her, Ann Beaumont did not say a word. Instead, she looked at James, who gave a short nod. Bending down, she wrapped her arms around my shoulders and gave me a squeeze. Before I could say anything, she was gone, pulling the office door closed behind her.

"You're still getting the shakes?" Frodo said.

"Not as often," I said. "Only when something triggers them."

"Like him," James said, pointing a thick finger at the face in the center of the television.

"Like him," I said. "I don't even know his real name. I called him Mr. Suave in my after-action report."

"The guy who financed the splinter cell in Syria?" Frodo said. "That's him?"

"Yep," I said. "I'm sure of it. He got in my face while explaining how the chemical weapon he'd paid to develop would slowly turn me into a vegetable. We were almost nose to nose."

Frodo enlarged the picture again, took a screenshot of Mr. Suave's face, and dropped the image into a facial-recognition app. The software went to work, algorithms scouring every nook and cranny of his features before returning the verdict I'd somehow expected.

"Library's got nothing," Frodo said. "He's a ghost."

"If it's even the right guy," James said, and spit a muddy brown torrent into his white foam cup.

"It's him," I said, letting my irritation show.

"See it from my side," James said. "You were under a helluva lot of stress at the time. You saw this guy just once—"

"Twice," I said.

"Okay, twice. But for what? Ten minutes? After you saw him the first time, a squad of jihadis played soccer with your head. The second time, his terrorist buddies were about to slit the throat of the paramilitary officer you were supposed to rescue. That picture isn't even that great. I bet—"

"Chief, you ever been certain you were going to die?" I said. "Not the it-could-go-either-way thoughts you have when bullets are flying and things aren't looking so good. I'm talking about the dead-in-your-soul feeling that only comes from staring down the barrel of a gun. That instant when you know your time left on earth is measured in heartbeats. You ever been that certain you were about to die?"

James stared at me without speaking for a long moment. Then he gave a slow nod. "Once."

"Then you understand why I'm sure. It's him."

"All right," James said, setting his spit cup on the table. "Let's say it is. Maybe he had a hard-on for you and tried to help the son of his dead lieutenant settle the score. So what? Now the son's dead, just like the father. Your Mr. Suave got nothing. It's over."

"Maybe," I said, staring at the black-and-white image. "Or maybe he's waiting for a second shot."

"Why?" James said. "After his Austin op turned into a dumpster fire, he'd have to know he's on our radar. Why risk coming at you again?"

"I don't know," I said. "Figured I'd ask him that question face-to-face."

"The fuck you say?" James said.

"He's tried to punch my ticket twice—once on his home turf and once on mine. I'm not waiting around to see if the third time's the charm. I'm gonna go to Iraq, find him, and ask him some questions. Then I'm gonna put a bullet in his head."

"No, you're not," James said. "You still haven't recovered from your last op."

"I said I'm fine," I said.

"Son, I know you want to believe that. But believing something doesn't make it so. That shaking shit speaks for itself. You're in no condition to deploy. Besides, you're not the only rough man in this organization. You want to punch Mr. Suave's ticket? I can make that happen. But you aren't going to be the triggerman. You follow me?"

"Yep," I said.

"Matty, I know you want this. Bad. And I can sympathize. But I don't send my operators on one-way missions. Go home. Get some sleep. Tomorrow, you and Frodo do what you do. Crawl inside this douche bag's head. Track him down. I'll get him added to the kill list. By week's end, we'll be sending a Hellfire up his ass. Now, get out of here."

"Chief, I'm fine to finish the day. Really."

"I don't give a shit, Matthew. Until tomorrow morning, you're not welcome here. Go home."

I looked at Frodo for support, but for the first time, I could see he wasn't going to have my back. Not on this one. My little incident earlier must have looked worse than I thought.

Getting to my feet, I gave them both a smile I didn't feel and walked out. James's words rang in my ears as I shut the door.

Go home.

Love to. I just wasn't too sure where that was anymore.

TWENTY-TWO

pulled out of the DIA's parking lot, worked my way over to Malcolm X Avenue, and slid through the gate, just beating rush-hour traffic. My gut, the part of me that instinctively knew when a potential asset was ready to be pitched, was telling me James was wrong.

Mr. Suave was not a third-rate jihadi. He would not have funded an elaborate assassination attempt just to mollify an angry subordinate. During our second encounter in Syria, Mr. Suave had said he was a businessman. An unidealogical entrepreneur intent on profiting from the chaos engulfing Syria and Iraq.

But I believed he was more than that. He was also a survivor. Someone who'd thrived under the sadistic and vengeful rule of Saddam Hussein. Someone capable of turning to his advantage the anarchy that had run rampant in Iraq after the ill-thought-out US invasion. This was not the type of man who would just give up when he didn't succeed. If anything, his failure in Austin would make him more determined. A man who ran an empire spanning three countries could not afford to show fear.

In a culture in which generational wars were fought over perceived slights to honor, Mr. Suave was now more compelled than ever to finish the job he'd started. He would keep coming until he succeeded, and the next time, it might be Laila in a puddle of blood on a dirty Austin street instead of a hapless policeman.

No, this could end in just one of two ways—my death or his.

The thought of Laila made me want to call her. I loved the sound of my wife's voice. For security reasons, we never communicated while I was operational, but she faithfully left at least one voice message in our WhatsApp chat each day I was gone. Most of these messages were benign in nature—thoughts about a book she was reading, office gossip, a funny story she heard—but their effect was profound. Something about the texture and timbre of her voice helped fill the void Laila's absence created. I treasured listening to those cached voice messages on the long flights home.

When I was stateside, I called Laila at least once a day just to listen to her talk. But over the past several days, I hadn't phoned or even texted. My brain was in operational mode, so I'd stuffed Laila into the mental box I reserved for my normal life while overseas. But I wasn't overseas. In fact, nothing was stopping me from calling my wife at this exact moment. Nothing but the horrible way we'd left things after our aborted dinner.

I just want my husband back.

I was an idiot.

I'd pulled out my phone and was in the middle of dialing when it vibrated with an incoming call from an unknown number.

"Drake," I said, after thumbing the connect button.

"Matt, it's me."

Though I'd spoken to her over the phone less than a handful of times, her East Tennessee accent was unmistakable.

"Virginia," I said, "how are you?"

"I need to talk. Now. In person."

"Sure. Where?"

"Have you eaten?"

"Nope."

"Meet me at Ben's. I'll call ahead."

She hung up before I could reply. Apparently, Virginia had a lot on her mind. The feeling was mutual.

Ben's Steak House was a DC landmark. A place where important people gathered and an off-the-rack Brooks Brothers suit constituted casual wear; the men and women huddled in the restaurant's semiprivate booths preferred to shop at the trendy boutiques nestled along Connecticut Avenue. In my black fleece, boots, and jeans, I was a tad underdressed. Still, the brunette manning the hostess station offered me a warm smile. In a place flush with six-thousand-dollar hand-sewn suits, a pearly-snap shirt was a bit of a rarity.

"Howdy," the hostess said as I drew even with her station. Her accent was slight, but there if you knew to listen. You could take the girl out of Texas, but . . .

"A and M grad?" I said.

She nodded, her smile brightening.

"And here I thought we were going to be friends. Might as well get this out of the way—hook 'em, Horns."

Her smile became a mock frown. "Of the five guys who wear boots in this town, I meet the UT fan. Just my luck."

"Guilty," I said. "Went there for undergrad. Normally I wouldn't give an Aggie the time of day, but since we're probably the only Texans for miles, I'm willing to make an exception. How 'bout it?"

"Pleased to meet you," the woman said, sticking out her hand. "I'm Allie. Allie Mishler."

"Matt Drake. What's a girl like you doing in a place like this?"

"Penance," Allie said with a laugh. "I graduated in January with a journalism degree and had an internship lined up with a political magazine out here."

"But?"

"But it folded a week before Christmas."

"Sorry about that," I said.

Allie shrugged. "It's a kick in the teeth for sure, but I can't imagine what the staff's going through. Anyway, I'd already paid the deposit for my apartment, and I've got a little money saved up. Might as well give this city a shot. My blog's getting pretty good traffic. I'd love to parlay that into a full-time column somewhere. Until then, I'll work as a freelancer. I'm a journalist with a minor in poli sci. If I can't find a job here, I can't find one anywhere."

I nodded as I tried to sort through what exactly was happening. Allie was an attractive girl, but I was not in the habit of flirting with down-on-their-luck women ten years my junior. Then it hit me—Allie was only a little bit older than Nazya. And while Allie was pursuing her dreams, the Yazidi girl was doing her best just to piece her world back together. It never ceased to amaze me how terrible and wonderful life could be, all in the same instant.

"Sorry for rambling," Allie said, "but you're like a piece of home—even if you are a Longhorn. Do you have a reservation?"

"Yep. It's under Virginia, and please, don't apologize. In fact, give me the info for your blog. Journalism isn't my field, but this town is smaller than you'd think. I'm always happy to help out a fellow member of the Lone Star State."

"Texas forever," Allie said as she handed me a business card. "I post pieces once or twice a week. Now, enough about me. Your party's waiting."

Pocketing the card, I followed Allie to where Virginia was sitting in a dark corner. The perpetually sunny girl from East Tennessee looked anything but happy. Her normally clear blue eyes were puffy and red. Allie paused to ask if everything was all right, and Virginia assured her she was fine.

"What happened with Nazya?" I said after Allie disappeared with my drink order.

"What you'd expect," Virginia said, fiddling with her silverware. "She told her story to your FBI friends. Hearing it the first time at the safe house was bad enough. Listening as the agents debriefed her was even worse."

"I can imagine," I said, once again struck by the difference between Allie and Nazya. "I don't know how she's not huddled in a corner."

"I do," Virginia said, and took an enormous swallow from her mojito. "There's a second part. Something she didn't tell us before."

"What's that?"

"Nazya wasn't the only one kidnapped. The bastards also took her younger sister. She's desperate to save her."

"How old?"

"Fifteen."

I knew I'd regret asking the question, and now I had my just rewards. *Fifteen.* I had a fifteen-year-old niece named Elizabeth. She was a freshman in high school who ran track, dreamed of becoming a writer, and already shared my sister's unhealthy addiction to cowboy boots. The thought of blue-eyed, blond-haired Elizabeth in the hands of sex traffickers made my skin crawl.

"What'd the FBI agents say?" I said.

Virginia shrugged. "Nothing, really. The women interviewing her seemed sympathetic, but Nazya doesn't need sympathy. She needs someone to rescue her little sister."

"Which the FBI can't do," I said.

"Can't or won't?"

"Mostly can't. The FBI's constitutional authority begins and ends at our shorelines. There are FBI legal attachés, called legats, stationed overseas, but these agents don't have independent investigatory powers. Their job is to liaise with local law enforcement. Legats could help coordinate an investigation, but only if the host nation has the infrastructure and is willing to lead a search for Nazya's sister."

"Which Iraq isn't," Virginia said.

"Probably not. Between the rampant political corruption and continuing sectarian violence and Iran's ever-growing influence, Iraq is barely holding together. I doubt the Iraqi Federal Police are going to devote much time to one missing teenager. Especially when their nation's survival's at stake."

"So now what?" Virginia said.

I took a swallow of water before answering. I knew what Virginia was really asking, but I also lived in the real world. I'd learned long ago to divorce myself from the suffering I encountered on a daily basis. Civilization might have advanced by leaps and bounds in the last hundred years, but large swaths of the world were still medieval shitholes. These were the places I operated in. If I allowed myself to care about every injustice, I'd lose my sanity. So instead of answering Virginia's question, I asked one of my own. "Where's Nazya now?"

"In a Bureau safe house. When I left, she was trying to get ahold of her extended family. She has an older brother working in Turkey and an uncle still in Iraq. The FBI agents want her help finding the sex traffickers, but she's no pushover. When they wouldn't commit to helping her sister, Nazya's English dried up. But we both know the FBI isn't right for this job. Nazya needs someone who can go to Iraq and do what people with badges can't. Or won't."

And there it was. East Tennessee was nothing if not determined. I respected her grit, but thinking I could help was pure fantasy. It was time to let her know that.

"Listen," I said, "I know I promised you the chance to make a difference, but this isn't it. We don't know anything about Nazya's sister. Hell, we don't even know if she's still alive."

"Yes, we do," Virginia said, setting her iPhone on the table in front of me. "Nazya escaped her captors in Iraq twice. Each time she was able to collect more information about the organization holding her before she was recaptured. I won't tell you what the sex traffickers did to her each time they caught her, but I'm sure you can imagine. Anyway, she learned that the sex traffickers were using Facebook to sell the women they kidnap. Here's the page. This is her sister, Ferah. The post is only twenty-four hours old. Not only is Ferah still alive, but she's currently on the auction block."

I looked at the face staring back at me. Ferah's face. I couldn't save everyone. That was just the cold, hard fact. But I couldn't ignore the person in the picture either. Curly black hair framed a face caught midway between girl and woman. But her dark, vacant eyes ended any thoughts of girlish innocence. And then it wasn't Ferah I saw. It was Elizabeth.

Elizabeth with her crooked smile and stubborn sense

of right and wrong. Elizabeth the writer who already seemed to know there was more to Uncle Matt than met the eye. What would I do if Ferah's monsters had Elizabeth instead?

Anything.

Everything.

"Okay," I said, throwing a couple twenties on the table to settle the bill. "The Facebook information might change things. *Might*. But this isn't the movies. I can't go after Ferah with just a Facebook post. I need actionable intelligence, and we don't have any. Yet."

"But you've got an idea," Virginia said as we got to our feet. "Something that could help."

"Not something. But maybe someone."

TWENTY-THREE

Ever thought of calling first?"

"Does your momma call before she drops by?" I said, refusing to be intimidated by Frodo's less-than-friendly welcome.

"No," Frodo said. "That's why I put a GPS tracker on her Mustang."

"She still drives that old convertible? I thought you were gonna buy her a hybrid."

"I did. She leaves it in the garage. She thinks driving that gas guzzler is helping to make America energy independent."

"I love your mom," I said. "You gonna let us in or what? Virginia's getting cold."

At the mention of Virginia, Frodo's eyes grew bigger. He leaned around the half-open door of his town house and nodded at the chemist. "Sorry for being rude, but this really isn't a good time."

Virginia started to reply with what I'm sure would have been an apology and an offer to come back later. But before she could get the words out, another voice echoed from inside the apartment. A *feminine* voice.

"Frodo? Is everything all right?"

"Seems like this is the perfect time," I said, stepping into the doorway. "Invite us in before I make an ass of myself."

"Too late for that," Frodo said, but he opened the door all the same. "Come on in. But wipe your feet. Seamus just vacuumed."

"He vacuums?" I said.

"Unlike some people, my dog isn't a freeloading malcontent. He knows how to start the Roomba. Get in here. Virginia's shivering."

"Have the two of you considered couple's therapy?" Virginia said as she slipped past me.

"We tried," I said. "Frodo has trouble expressing his feelings."

A soft laugh that wasn't Virginia's greeted my reply. A pretty woman in her late twenties was standing in the kitchen holding a glass of red wine.

"You must be Matt," the woman said, smiling. "I'm Katherine."

"So good to meet you, Katherine. This is my colleague Virginia. I'd give you a hug, but Seamus is particular about what I touch."

At the sound of his name, the mutt opened his eyes and grumbled from somewhere deep in his chest. The murmur rattled my fillings. Katherine laughed again, a warm, pleasant sound that softened the edges of Frodo's decidedly masculine apartment. "I think I'm going to like you," Katherine said.

"You might want to reserve judgment until you find out why we're here," I said.

Seamus rumbled his agreement.

Ten minutes later, we were seated around Frodo's scarred coffee table, glasses of wine in the girls' hands while Frodo held a beer. Though it hadn't been stated outright, Katherine seemed to know what Frodo and I did for a living. This made me think that his mystery NSA analyst and Katherine were one and the same. Either way, the time for beating around the bush was over. If Frodo didn't want Katherine to be a part of our discussion, he'd let me know. The clock was ticking.

"I need help," I said after everyone was seated.

"Truer words have never been spoken," Frodo said.

"I'm serious, brother," I said. "Regardless of what James thinks, Mr. Suave isn't going to quit until one of us is dead. I can feel it."

"I'm not arguing, Matty," Frodo said, leaning forward in his chair, "but we've been down this road. While you were recuperating from your last solo op, I was trying to find something on this guy or his network. I came up empty. Like I said before, Mr. Suave is a ghost."

"Not anymore," I said, sliding Virginia's phone across the coffee table. "Take a look."

With undisguised reluctance, Frodo picked up the

phone and began to thumb through the images as Katherine peered over his shoulder.

"What am I seeing?" Frodo said.

"Facebook postings from the network of shitheads who kidnapped Nazya and smuggled her into the US along with the Iraqi commandos who tried to kill me," I said. "Mr. Suave's sex-trafficking network. Mr. Suave has Nazya's sister, Ferah. The girl's being auctioned as we speak."

"And you're gonna do what exactly?"

"Go to Iraq and rescue her. Then I'm going to find Mr. Suave and kill him. Simple, right?"

"The best plans are," Frodo said, handing the phone to Virginia. "But I still don't see enough intelligence to authorize an operation."

"Maybe not a kinetic capture or kill op," I said, "but certainly enough to start digging. And I don't mean sifting through paperwork here in the States. I'm talking about boots on the ground in Iraq to see what I can put together."

"Iraq's a big place," Frodo said.

"Agreed," I said. "That's why I need someone to trace these posts back to their digital roots and turn that info into actionable intelligence. Maybe someone who works at the NSA."

"Hold on," Frodo said, setting his beer on the coffee table. "If you want to chase a white whale, I'm not gonna stop you. But involving Katherine is crossing a line. What you're proposing is something extrajudicial. An outside job. People go to jail for this shit."

"Not necessarily," I said. "James gave us permission to pursue Mr. Suave. He just didn't want me in Iraq. Well, too damn bad. I'm going anyway. But that has nothing to do with Katherine. Put the request for NSA help through official channels. I don't care. Just get me something I can use once I'm in-country."

"Sounds reasonable," Katherine said.

"Baby, trust me," Frodo said, reaching toward Katherine. "With Matty things always *sound* reasonable. But they don't end up that way. He almost started World War Three last time he was overseas. Getting involved with him could kill your career."

"How old is this girl?" Katherine said, looking at Virginia.

"Fifteen," Virginia said, placing her wineglass on the table with shaking fingers. "Her sister says she loves horses. Had pictures of them all over her room. Now she's being held by monsters and auctioned off to the highest bidder."

"I'm in," Katherine said. "Official request or not, I'm in. How can I not be?"

"Great," I said. "I'll arrange my transportation into country, but I need cash. Frodo, unfreeze some operational accounts so I can draw on them. Katherine, Frodo's right—Iraq's a big place. I've got a network of assets in-country, but I need to know where to point them. Can you localize the sex traffickers' IP addresses?"

"On it," Katherine said.

"Great," I said. "I think that's it."

"Not quite," Virginia said. "I'm coming too."

"Not gonna happen," I said. "I—"

"Don't start," Virginia said, cutting me off. "This isn't a one-person job. Besides, you told me I'd get to do something that mattered. Something like this. I'm coming. End of discussion."

I looked at Frodo. After a long moment, he gave a slow nod.

"Okay," I said, turning to Virginia and Katherine. "Let's do this."

TWENTY-FOUR

MOSUL, IRAQ

If post–World War II boundaries had been drawn by a different hand, the city of Mosul might have become the crown jewel of the Middle East, perhaps even the Islamic world's equivalent to Tel Aviv. Mosul's lineage was both ancient and distinguished. Bisected by Iraq's most important waterway, the Tigris River, the sprawling metropolis occupies almost seventy square miles of potential. Home to the ruins of Nineveh, of Jonah-and-the-whale fame, Mosul is a trading city with easy access to Turkey, Syria, and Iran.

In ancient times, the city commanded the world's respect if not admiration. Now, after enduring decades of mismanagement under Saddam Hussein, horrible sectarian fighting during the US invasion, and occupation by ISIS, the would-be jewel of the Middle East was a cesspool in every sense of the word.

Stepping over the stream of foul-smelling raw sewage

flowing past what in happier times had been a sidewalk, I pulled open the passenger door of an idling Toyota Hilux and slipped inside. The compact truck roared into traffic with a seat-pressing acceleration that belied the vehicle's benign appearance. The Hilux, like its driver, was not what it seemed.

I knew, since I'd bought and paid for them both.

"My friend, we must stop meeting like this," Zain said. He offered me a handshake with a grip that was surprisingly strong. Though Zain was slight of stature, his body was hard, almost desiccated. As if the desert sun had long ago melted away any superfluous tissue, leaving behind only sinew and bone. He kept his eyes on the road as he shook my hand, driving like the seasoned smuggler he was. Only a fool took Mosul's traffic for granted.

My Syrian friend was many things, but a fool he was not.

"Inshallah," I said, switching to Arabic as I buckled my seat belt. "Much has happened in the last year. How have you been?"

Zain shrugged as he followed a second Hilux through an intersection. "As always, better than I should be, thanks to you. The information you provide is vital, especially with the Shias in Baghdad flirting with Iran. ISIS may no longer control Mosul, but that doesn't mean the city is safe. Thugs dressed in black, flying the Caliphate's flag, have given way to criminals and worse."

"Hezbollah?"

Zain nodded. "But those miscreants I can deal with. It's their masters who give me concern."

"The Iranian Quds Force is operating here? Openly?"

Another nod. "In the last several weeks, their presence has been blatant—checkpoints on the thoroughfares heading east and other nonsense. Officially, they are here to stop the violence from spreading to Iran."

"But unofficially?"

"The mullahs have been trying to expand their influence into Iraq since the butcher in Damascus asked them for help propping up his failing regime. What better way to provide that help than by securing a land bridge across the country separating them? But you did not come all this way to hear about my problems. What do you need?"

I paused before answering. A series of hazy cirrus clouds stretched across the all-encompassing azure sky like wisps of white hair. This was Iraq's wet season, and patches of green broke up the usually never-ending vista of brown as wheat and barley crops reached heavenward. With Mosul's population of close to one million, locating Mr. Suave, and by extension Ferah, wouldn't be easy.

But that was what I was here to do.

"I need to find two people," I said, "a man and a woman. A girl, really."

Switching driving hands from his right to his left, Zain reached into the leather messenger bag at his feet, withdrawing a cigar. After removing the cellophane casing, he slid the unlit stogie between his teeth and began to chew.

"Finding two people in a city this large is no small task," Zain said, working the cigar between his lips. "Tell me what you know. I will do what I can. But first, the items you requested are behind me."

Turning in my seat, I found a black nylon bag and pulled it into my lap. The heft alone was comforting. Unzipping the main pocket lifted my spirits even further. An assortment of ordnance and communications gear was nestled in custom-made mesh pockets. I selected a Glock, loaded the pistol, holstered it, and slid the rig into my waistband.

The feeling of relief was immediate. For the first time in fifteen hours, I was back in my element. Without logistical assistance from the DIA, traveling to Iraq had been difficult. Finding a way for Virginia and me to arrive in-country together had been impossible. For the initial leg of the trip, Frodo had secured us seats on a private Air Force jet heading to Turkey. But once we arrived, things got tricky.

Tradecraft dictates that clandestine operatives never infil on the same flight if at all possible. With the prevalence of artificial intelligence, foreign services have become adept at employing custom-designed algorithms to discover patterns in the vast amount of readily available open-source data. Patterns that revealed clandestine activity. With this in mind, we'd decided to come into country separately.

Since Virginia had never entered Iraq before, she was arriving via a commercial flight to Baghdad International in a couple of hours. I'd come in dark, taking a chartered flight into the still-nonoperational Mosul International

Airport. At least nonoperational for the Iraqi public. Due to its proximity to Turkey and Syria and its newly refurbished runway, quite a few unmarked planes were making regular stops at the airport, which was technically closed.

Once I'd secured passage into country, it had been a simple matter to make contact with Zain and arrange for him to pick me up. Though if the two Hilux trucks escorting us were any indication, nothing in Iraq was ever quite as simple as it seemed.

Zain ran one of the largest smuggling operations in this part of the world. Hell, probably in any part of the world. Prior to the Syrian civil war, he'd operated a successful and completely legal trucking company. But in the last decade, his organization had morphed into something a bit more nebulous. While he still moved legitimate goods through Turkey, Iraq, and Syria, the bulk of his business now involved smuggling arms and ammunition to the wide assortment of militias fighting against Assad.

Moving restricted material across three heavily guarded borders required a network of informants and people on the take that rivaled New York's Five Families. Zain had been one of the most successful recruitments I'd ever made. The intelligence his network provided was unrivaled, and I intended to put it to use getting Ferah out of Iraq while drawing a bull's-eye on Mr. Suave. Using her NSA tools, Katherine had been able to localize the Facebook IP addresses to Mosul. Now I needed Zain's help finding the man who didn't want to be found.

But first Zain needed to understand the risks.

"The man I'm looking for runs a large criminal enterprise," I said, paving the way for the next part of our conversation. "I need your help locating him. But before you say yes, I want you to know that this time things are different. When I asked for your assistance in Syria, I was trying to save one of my countrymen. Now, my actions might lead to the death of one of yours. This man is dangerous, Zain. Do you understand?"

Zain looked across the truck at me for an instant before returning his attention to the road. His expression had been strange—unreadable, even.

"Let us talk plainly, my friend," Zain said. "These never-ending wars have caused unimaginable suffering. And this is saying something. When it comes to suffering, we Arabs have both vivid imaginations and long memories. In any case, the war has also made me rich—powerful, even. Powerful men have a responsibility to use their authority wisely. *Inshallah* one day I will go back to being a simple truck driver. But I fear that day will be long in coming. Until then I will use what Allah has granted me wisely. Tell me what you need. If it is within my power, I will provide it."

I let out the breath I hadn't realized I'd been holding. Zain's recruitment had required more than just a simple pitch offering money in exchange for intelligence. By the time we'd met, Zain had already transitioned into the gray market and was reaping the financial benefits. More money wasn't going to grab his attention. Instead, I offered him the one thing he needed but couldn't buy—information.

In exchange for intelligence on ISIS and Assad's troop movements, I targeted Zain's logistical routes with an entire portfolio of intelligence, surveillance, and reconnaissance—or ISR—assets. He knew when bandits set up checkpoints intended to extort or outright murder his drivers and steal his cargo because I told him.

Without my help, Zain would have risen to the top of the smuggler heap eventually. With me in his corner, his ascendance had been meteoric. In return, he'd dedicated part of his vast logistical train to moving arms and equipment to the Syrian rebels while turning every one of his employees into a HUMINT collector. This arrangement had been hugely beneficial while I was in Syria, but it should have ended once I'd left.

It hadn't.

As September 11th had so aptly demonstrated, the intelligence community defaulted toward being reactive rather than proactive. I didn't intend to repeat this mistake with Zain. So even though the US had effectively washed its hands of Syria, I kept Zain's network active. I still pushed him information even though he was no longer an on-the-books asset.

My personal relationship with the smuggler aside, I'd believed that someday I'd need to use him operationally again. When that time came, I wanted him in my debt and ready to help. So far, that approach seemed to be bearing dividends, but the real test was coming.

Unaided by a foreign intelligence service, Mr. Suave had put together a complex operation that had nearly killed me. His professions to the contrary aside, my nemesis was no simple businessman or warlord. Going toe-to-toe with him would be the equivalent of declaring war on a sovereign nation. I wanted Zain to understand this before he agreed to help.

Once again, easier said than done.

I took out my cell phone and scrolled through the pictures until I found the screenshot of Ferah. "This girl is fifteen. Her name is Ferah, and she's about to be auctioned by sex traffickers. I'm not going to let that happen."

Zain exploded into a series of choice Arabic curses as he slammed his hand against the steering wheel. "I knew it. I knew it. Sooner or later I knew this would affect someone I cared about. It is to my great shame that I didn't fight this scourge before now. Once again, you are my conscience, Matthew."

"What do you know about the sex traffickers?" I said.

Zain tossed the cigar he'd been gnawing out the window before replying.

"The ISIS dogs started the practice of selling captured women and girls. Unfortunately, this was but one of the atrocities perpetrated by the Caliphate, but this aberration has outlived the black-clad imbeciles. Selling kidnapped women has become a profitable business. One of the local flesh traffickers actually tried to hire me to move his girls into Turkey. He was willing to pay handsomely."

"What did you say?"

Zain gave me another unreadable look. "I said nothing. Instead, I let my pistol do the talking. *Inshallah* the desert sands will never give up his worthless body."

I gave Zain's shoulder a squeeze, but he shrugged off my hand. "Do not think so highly of me because I exterminated this cockroach, Matthew. That should be the reaction of any reasonable man. But a good man would have done more. I have not bought, sold, or transported girls, but I have also not aided them. That makes me as much to blame as the *chelb* now rotting in the sand. What else do you know about this girl, this Ferah?"

"I know that this man runs the organization that took her." I switched to the augmented picture of Mr. Suave pieced together from the stolen airport security video. "Do you know him?"

Zain glanced at the phone and then gave a long sigh. "With you, Matthew, nothing is ever easy. Of course I know him. Who does not know the Devil?"

TWENTY-FIVE

The Devil?" I said.

I tried to sound nonchalant, but in my mind's eye, I saw Mr. Suave squatting in front of my broken body as he casually explained how the chemical weapon would devour my brain. He'd spoken in a matter-of-fact manner, as if giving me directions to the café down the street rather than discussing my death. I'd made an enemy or two over the course of my career. Hatred I could handle, but his total indifference terrified me.

"It isn't just a nickname," Zain said. "That is what he is. I've seen men kill for their country, or tribe, or god. But he is different. The Devil is motivated by power. Power and the money that comes with it."

"Who is he?"

Zain shook his head. "No one knows his true name. I've heard rumors that he was one of Saddam's generals. If so, he must not have been high-ranking. The truly important ones either followed their leader to the gallows or threw in with the Caliphate. But not the Devil."

"Then how do you know him?" I said.

"It's difficult to put into words," Zain said, reaching again for the messenger bag. "I've seen him only once, but I've known of him for many years. Much like you can't see the wind, but you can feel its effect. Things happened in my world—things shaped by unseen fingers. Certain organizations grew stronger while others faltered. The jihadis gave some towns a wide berth but ransacked others. The Russians targeted one tribe and left their neighbors untouched."

"That sounds very vague."

Zain shrugged. "It is the nature of things here. When order begins to supplant chaos, someone is managing the transition. Just because you can't see that person doesn't mean they're not there."

"Do you deal with the Devil?" I said.

Another shrug. "I deal with many people. Not directly with the Devil, but certainly his organization. What they do to the people who stand in their way makes the jihadis seem like schoolchildren. Are you sure there is no other path for you, Matthew?"

I paused before slowly shaking my head. "Sorry, my friend, but everything you've told me only confirms my suspicions. The Devil reached halfway across the world to get my attention. I don't think he's going to back down now."

"You're right," Zain said. "He won't. And for that, I'm sorry."

Something in Zain's voice started my spider senses tingling. My inner lizard had been trying to warn me, but I'd ignored it. Not because I'd doubted my instincts, but because I hadn't wanted to believe them. Zain had been my asset for more than three years. He'd risked his life for me. He was a friend. But as he'd been trying to tell me ever since I'd climbed into the Hilux, now things were different.

Even friendships fail in the face of the Devil.

I went for my Glock, but I was too late. The hand Zain had reached into the messenger bag now held a pistol instead of a cigar. I looked from the gaping barrel to Zain. His brown eyes were liquid, his expression torn.

But he pulled the trigger all the same.

TWENTY-SIX

I woke up in stages, my senses coming online one at a time. My sense of smell was first—musty staleness of enclosed spaces mixed with the sour odor of desperate men. Touch came next. The chill of a subterranean floor. The sandpaper-like texture of unfinished concrete. Sight arrived last and was the least revealing. The dimness of confinement coupled with drab walls and a prison cell's familiar steel bars.

I sat up, pushing myself out of the damp puddle in which I'd been lying. In the first good news of the day, it wasn't urine. But I wasn't lounging in a Jacuzzi either. Droplets of water dribbled down the wall in green streams, smelling of mold and corruption.

The room's mustiness seemed to be fogging my brain. I didn't know who I was, let alone how I'd gotten here. After several disconcerting seconds, my memory returned in patches like a paused movie beginning to play.

Zain.

Zain pointing a gun.

Zain pointing a gun and squeezing the trigger.

The image made me lurch, just like I had in the passenger seat. I reached for my chest, searching for blood-soaked fabric, but found nothing. Then I remembered the rest. Instead of the sharp *crack* of detonating gunpowder, I'd heard a spitting sound. Not the cough of a suppressor. More like the *pop* of an air pistol.

Or a tranquilizer gun.

Reaching beneath my sweat-slicked shirt, I found a welt where the dart had embedded its pointy head into my sternum. The skin was sore and warm to the touch, but my fingers came away blood free. In my surprise, I hadn't felt the dart's impact. I'd been too busy trying to process Zain's betrayal.

But whether I felt it or not, the tranquilizer dart had worked as advertised. One moment I'd been looking at the black fletching sprouting from my chest. The next the world had gone hazy. I remembered Zain saying something as the medication went to work, but his voice seemed to be coming from a long, long way away. I couldn't quite make out the words, but it sounded as though he was repeating the same thing over and over.

I'm sorry.

Or maybe that was just what I'd wanted to hear. Bottom line, I'd made a handler's most devastating mistake. I'd let myself believe that my relationship with Zain, the relationship between handler and asset, had become more than just transactional. I'd begun to believe we were friends.

And now that slip of sentimentality might have just cost me my life.

Closing my eyes, I wiped the grime from my face. The cell was just as dark when I opened them, but the dark outlines started to become recognizable in the damp gloom. A metal drain cover in the center of the sloped floor. Thick chains hanging from metal brackets drilled into a concrete ceiling. A coiled rubber hose fastened to a rusted spigot on the far wall.

I recognized what I saw and shuddered. These weren't instruments of confinement. They were implements of torture.

As if on cue, a series of overhead bulbs began to buzz, flooding my cell with light that was both harsh and somehow dirty. The bulbs hummed like a swarm of angry bees, and I squinted against the glare, eyeing my cell.

Bars covered a square window at the top of a metal door. The rest of the cell was as its shadow self had hinted—bare concrete walls meeting a rough concrete floor that sloped to a drain speckled with brown-tinged rust. The room was about two paces wide by three long. Big enough to curl into a fetal position, but much too small to completely stretch out.

I'd spent more time in places like this than I cared to admit, and my memories weren't exactly fond. I tried not to dwell on the blood-crusted manacles or the bits of gore clogging the drain cover. This was a place where bad things were done by bad people.

I didn't know what was in store, and trying to guess

was its own form of torture. Instead, I took inventory of my injuries, which, aside from the tender and bruised portion of my chest, were for once nonexistent.

Then I took deep, calming breaths.

I could not control what the men who held me would attempt, but I could control how I prepared for it. In some ways, this was analogous to waiting for the light above an aircraft's open doorway to change from red to green, signaling it was time to jump. Though I hated parachuting, most of my combat jumps had been relatively uneventful. For the few that hadn't been, no amount of prejump worrying would have changed the outcome. With this in mind, I closed my eyes, stretched my aching muscles, and waited for the invisible light to change from red to green.

I didn't have to wait long. With the shriek of rusted metal on metal, an unseen door opened. Then the sound of heavy footfalls echoed as someone descended a creaking staircase one step at a time. For better or worse, the light was now green.

Time to jump.

A prisoner and his captor are somewhat codependent. Unless your captors keep you bound hand and foot, at some point you start to cooperate with them. For instance, if you want to get fed, you do what they tell you. If the captors know their business, they establish this dependency early on, often with pain as a motivator.

After getting beaten enough times, or going without food or water long enough, even the most resistant prisoner breaks. Hollywood bullshit aside, everyone does.

It's what happens next that determines who survives and perhaps escapes and who becomes a mindless slug.

The invisible dog fence is a great example of this put into practice. After getting the shit shocked out of them a handful of times, most dogs accept the limits of their captivity. Oftentimes owners can even turn the electricity off because, after riding the lightning once or twice, the average dog never again tests the limits of his confinement.

He's been physiologically conditioned not to.

But every now and again, a dog takes the pain and still comes back for more. Equal parts stubborn and tough, that mongrel will eventually get free. Not because he's immune to the hurt, but because he's tenacious. Even after getting zapped ninety-nine times, the mutt still goes back to test the fence one more time. And that might be the one time the owner decided to save money on the electricity bill by shutting the fence off.

Is escaping a sure thing? Nope. Does it hurt like hell when the cattle prods underneath his collar light the dog's throat on fire? Yep. The truth is that the owner may never turn off the fence. But one thing's for sure: A dog that gives up has zero chance of ever visiting the pretty golden retriever next door.

Like I said, everyone breaks. It's what happens next that counts.

With that in mind, I got to my feet and shook out my

arms and legs. For whatever reason, my captors hadn't used the restraints hanging from the ceiling. I planned on taking advantage of that oversight. Maybe they wanted me to stare at the congealed blood on the shackles and piss myself. Or maybe they didn't take me for the fighting kind. Either way, they'd made a mistake. I wasn't the toughest guy around, but I was damn sure the most hardheaded.

One way or another, this dog wasn't staying put.

The steps grew louder, but I resisted the urge to peer through the bars at the top of the door. That would be a rookie mistake. If I were a jailer looking to establish dominance, I'd wait for my detainee to stick his head up to the bars, and then I'd crack him right in the nose.

No, I had a better idea.

The door to the cramped cell was hinged instead of sliding like the jail cells in the movies. That meant that it opened outward, which might just work to my advantage. The door was solid steel and therefore heavy. If the rest of my cell was any indication, the hinges were probably not well maintained. In fact, the damp air had most likely rusted them. This would make the door difficult to open.

Which meant my jailer would have to pull pretty hard.

Which in turn meant maybe I could give him a little help.

The footfalls were now right outside my cell. I waited for a moment, struck by indecision as I considered what might happen next. If it were me, I'd take a gander into the cell before opening the door, just in case my inmate was a hardheaded son of a bitch like yours truly. If that happened, my plan was dead on arrival. One look into the tiny confines would reveal my scheme even to the dumbest jailer.

On the other hand, I didn't have a plan B. I wasn't restrained now, but I knew that was too good to last. Besides, I'd heard only one set of footfalls. That meant I was one-on-one with my guard, which were probably the best odds I'd get.

Ever.

Hunching into the corner where the hinged side of the door met the wall, I watched the barred window, waiting to see if it darkened. I held my breath for a second and then heard the most glorious of sounds—a bolt-action lock turning.

Corroded tumblers groaned as metal scratched against metal. To me, the screeching sounded like the opening strains of "Ode to Joy." The door was about to swing open, and my numb-nuts jailer hadn't bothered to check the window. Maybe my captors figured the tranquilizer would still have me fast asleep. Or maybe this guy was at the bottom of the jihadi gene pool. I didn't care either way. All I knew was that I now had a five-in-fifty chance of getting past the invisible fence.

I wasn't going to waste it.

Crouching so that my shoulder was level with the midpart of the door, I coiled my muscles. I pictured how it would go—the door opening, me driving forward, shoulder punching into the metal like it was the final two-a-day football practice of the summer. With a bit of luck, the unexpected assistance from my side of the cell would slam the door outward into my captor's unsuspecting face. And if luck wasn't with me, well, it wasn't like the situation could somehow get worse. Yes, sir. I was positively giddy about my chances. Screw the five in fifty. I bet my odds were at least two in twenty.

With a final shriek, the lock disengaged, and the door inched open. I waited another heartbeat, allowing the solid steel to gain momentum as it started to swing.

Then I launched.

At first, things went exactly according to plan. I sprang out of my modified three-point stance, legs exploding outward, forearms piling into the door with a precision that would have made old Coach Nick Petrie proud. Truth be told, Coach Petrie liked a nip or two of whiskey with his lunch, so he wasn't always lucid by the end of practice. But if he'd been sober, Coach would have been turning cheetah flips at my superb form.

Except that as I was plowing the door open, I felt a disconcertingly small amount of resistance. Either Zain's tranquilizer dart had somehow given me superhuman strength, or smashing the cell's door into my stupid jailer's face wasn't going according to plan.

Probably because my stupid jailer wasn't quite so stupid.

As the door swung all the way open, I realized two things in rapid succession: One, my jailer must have yanked to get the door started and then stepped out of the way. Two, he'd stepped out of the way so that he could better aim the aerosol can now poking through the gap between the door and the frame.

The can hissed as its contents discharged. I clamped my mouth shut and held my breath, determined not to get knocked out again. I needn't have worried. At least about getting knocked out anyway. The can did not contain sleeping gas. What it did contain felt like liquid fire splashing over my eyes and nose. The noxious cloud ignited my mucous glands, constricted my airway, and generally made life rather unpleasant.

Pepper spray.

Fucking pepper spray.

Those who didn't know better might have been lulled into thinking that all aerosol-based skin irritants were created equal. That the tiny cans of Mace college girls carried on their key chains had the same chemical formulation as police-issue pepper spray. Or that what police used to subdue rambunctious crowds mirrored military-grade pepper spray.

This was not true. College-girl Mace was laughable. Police pepper spray was a bitch, but you could still fight through it. But military-grade pepper spray was a different animal altogether. It reached into your sinus cavities, clamped them shut, and then went to work transforming your mucous membranes into boiling cauldrons of lava. In non–tech speak, getting hit with military pepper spray felt like someone jamming molten forks into your eyeballs while an electrified boa constrictor tried to strangle you.

Except that the boa was on fire.

Hell, everything was on fire.

To paraphrase Frodo, the experience kind of sucked.

Once you've encountered military-grade pepper spray, you could never mistake it for anything else. Which is why I knew exactly what my supposedly dumb jailer had just used to fumigate my cell.

My eyes swelled shut within the first second, but I wasn't going to let a little inconvenience like that stop me. Besides, I didn't need to see just yet. I could hear the can of pepper spray hissing like a pissed-off cobra just to my right.

Lowering my head to protect my face from the stream of liquid napalm, I swung my fists up in a tight arc and leapt toward my attacker. As my feet left the floor, I briefly considered how stupid I'd look if I'd misjudged the distance and hit just air.

Then my angry knuckles found flesh.

Contact front.

While the stunt with the slowly opening door was pretty slick, my jailer still had a thing or two to learn about subduing prisoners. Or maybe he'd just never had a prisoner as batshit crazy as me. Either way, things were looking up. I probably had a one-in-ten shot of making it out alive, but those were the best odds I'd had all day.

One moment my jailer was hosing my luscious locks with pepper spray; the next I was spearing my scalp into his face while pounding his solar plexus with quick jabs. The results were delightful. I still couldn't see, but neither could he.

At least that was what I was assuming. Between the reassuring *crack* my forehead made against his nose, and the high-pitched squealing sound that started when I smothered his tear glands with my pepper-spray-lubed hair, he didn't seem to be having such a good day.

I could sympathize.

Fucking pepper spray.

My punch knocked him off-balance, and I hooked his leg with my heel and kicked backward. His knee popped as tendons and ligaments gave way to physics. He screamed, grabbing the leg, and I sent a ridge hand scything into his unprotected Adam's apple. The cartilage gave way, and he tumbled to the ground, where I kicked him in the head until he stopped moving.

Not exactly Bruce Lee smooth, but effective all the same.

Prying open my swollen eyelids, I got my first look around. Our tussle hadn't exactly been a master class in silent killing, and I was worried about what I'd find. But it wasn't what I saw that transformed the hopped-up adrenaline feeling I'd been riding into stomach-churning terror.

It was what I heard.

Clapping.

Not the tentative, embarrassed sort of applause that comes after a *Braveheart* speech falls short or even the restrained golf claps reserved for boardrooms. No, what I heard was the I-don't-give-a-fuck-who-hears-me kind of clap that drunk Patriots fans let loose on Super Bowl Sunday all over Boston.

Since I was pretty sure not even a Patriots fan would have hung out in a musty basement turned torture chamber, my new landlord had to be somewhere close by. And he was the kind of squirrelly that made my mother-in-law seem normal.

Pushing my eyelids farther apart, I turned toward the clapping only to feel the air leave my lungs in a rush. My tear-filled eyes burned like they'd been smeared with radioactive sand, but I still recognized the figure standing on the staircase leading to the basement.

Mr. Suave.

Or perhaps more fittingly—the Devil.

"That was quite the performance, Matthew," the Devil said, shouting over his own clapping. "Quite the performance indeed. I knew you wouldn't disappoint, but even I was taken aback by your pure unadulterated violence."

"Good," I said, "because what I'm about to do to you will make that look tame."

My voice sounded relatively calm, which was a miracle since my throat felt like I'd been gargling with shards of glass. But it wasn't the effects of the pepper spray I was fighting.

It was terror.

The last time I'd stood in front of this man, he'd calmly explained how he was going to kill me like we were talking about the weather. He was a sociopath, and I was stuck in his basement. And as every Tarantino fan knows, the problem with fighting in a basement is that you're fighting in a basement.

"Please, Matthew," the Devil said, shaking his head, "there's no need for bravado. We understand each other.

You and I have gazed into each other's souls. I know what you'd do if given the chance, but unlike my hapless associate, I won't provide you the opportunity."

He switched to rapid-fire Arabic before I could reply, too fast for me to follow. But I grasped the meaning all the same. Movement confirmed that I wasn't alone. Far from it. Four men materialized from the shadows. Solid men. Men who'd watched me beat their companion to death without so much as making a sound.

Just the sort of men the Devil would employ.

I leapt toward the Devil, thinking that if I could wrap my fingers around his thick throat, I'd at least have the pleasure of taking him with me. But I was much, much too slow. Twin pricks landed in the center of my back. Not a tranquilizer dart this time.

Something else.

I took exactly one more step before my limbs seized and every nerve in my body simultaneously screamed. Upon reflection, what I said earlier wasn't true. There was something I hated more than pepper spray.

Fucking Tasers.

TWENTY-SEVEN

It was the second bucket of water that got my attention. The first sluiced off without completely penetrating the mental fog induced by fifty thousand volts overloading my nervous system. Don't get me wrong: I'd been tased before. It's one of the many interrogation techniques you're "exposed to" during the Army's infamous Survival, Evasion, Resistance, and Escape, or SERE, program at scenic Fort Bragg, North Carolina.

However, even the hardened instructors who teach the resistance phase tase only in short bursts. Conversely, the Devil's acolytes had let the juice run until my brain decided to take a little break. I didn't pass out so much as I lost interest in reality for a bit. That said, nothing brings you back from an electricity-induced coma like a bucket of cold water. In fact, I might have described the experience as refreshingly bracing if my deadened nerves weren't still on vacation.

Actually, that wasn't quite true. The second bucket of water roused my slumbering nervous system with the subtlety of a foghorn. The water caught me full in the face, streaming through my hair and flushing dried pepper spray back into my eyes. I jerked upright as the pain scoured away any remaining confusion.

Fucking pepper spray.

"I'm awake," I said, sputtering, but not before getting drenched again. I tried to wipe the gunk from my face, but my hands and feet were handcuffed to a chair.

And who says jihadis don't learn from their mistakes?

My attempt at speech seemed to have the desired effect. Instead of yet another bucket of water, I heard the creak of a rusty nozzle. Then a stream of water blasted into my face. Sucking in a quick breath, I worked my head through the spray, trying to rinse away the foul chemicals.

I knew from experience that only an oily compound like dish soap could completely remove the noxious mixture, but this was better than nothing. After several seconds, my ad hoc shower stopped as the rusty faucet creaked again.

Shaking the moisture from my head and face like a soaked dog, I blew out a held breath and opened my eyes. The Devil sat across from me. He smiled as my blurry vision found him.

"Good," the Devil said. "You're back. My former associate went a bit overboard with the Taser. I was concerned he'd permanently damaged you."

"Former?" I said.

The Devil indicated a crumpled body slumped against the wall to my right with a wave. "I don't tolerate mistakes," the Devil said. "They're not good for business."

Once again I wondered just whom I was dealing with. As per the last time we met, the Devil was dressed casually in clothes that tastefully reflected his wealth. Handmade shoes of soft Italian leather. Western slacks and a tailored button-down shirt open at the throat. An outfit a stockbroker might wear to the country club for Sunday-morning brunch. Somehow, the attire looked at home on the Devil, even though we were huddled in a dingy torture chamber.

"Enough with the *Goodfellas* shtick," I said, trying to ignore the trembling in my right finger. "You're a two-bit thug, plain and simple. Your Santoni shoes and Tom Ford shirts look about as natural on you as lipstick on a pig. You might pretend otherwise, but you're no different from any other man I've put in the dirt. You'll go down just as easy."

Part of the art of surviving an interrogation was keeping the interrogator off-balance. I couldn't wrap my fingers around the Devil's windpipe, but if I could crawl inside his head and root around a bit, I might be able to turn things to my advantage. Let's face it: When the status quo was sitting chained to a chair half naked in an Iraqi dungeon, I really had nowhere to go but up.

Unfortunately, the Devil wasn't so accommodating.

"That's where you're wrong," the Devil said, leaning

forward, his meaty hands resting on his thighs. "I *am* different from anyone you've ever met. In fact, you're about to find out just how different."

"Fantastic," I said, shifting my weight to test the give on the chain securing me to the chair. "This sitting-in-the-basement shit is boring."

But instead of taking the bait, the Devil leaned back in his chair, crossed his arms, and smiled. "You're right, Matthew. The unnecessary delay my former associate caused has made me forget my manners. I haven't even explained why you're here."

The Devil held out his right hand, palm up, and one of his acolytes moved from where he'd been standing motionless against the wall. I gritted my teeth in preparation for another blast of pepper spray or an equally disagreeable session with the Taser. But it wasn't an implement of torture the bodyguard placed into the Devil's expectant hand.

It was an iPad.

The Devil took the device, tilted it so he could see, and smiled. "Ah, yes," he said, swiping an index finger across the screen, "this one should do nicely."

The Devil scooted closer, not near enough that we could touch, but close enough so that my weary eyes could see the device's black screen.

"What's that you Americans say?" the Devil said as another swipe brought the frozen video to life. "A picture's worth a thousand words? Well, then, this video should be quite valuable indeed."

I opened my mouth to give a smart-ass reply, but the

words died on my tongue as the video played. Once again, the Devil was full of surprises. The image was of a woman sitting at a café drinking coffee.

In the grand scale of evilness, this was pretty tame: no jihadis beheading a captive; no shots of chemical weapons employed on men, women, and children; not even a suicide bomber blowing himself and innocent civilians to bits. Just a woman sipping from a cardboard cup. All in all, not too horrible except for one tiny detail.

The woman in the video was Laila.

TWENTY-EIGHT

When it comes to surviving an interrogation, you can prepare yourself for many things. A video of your wife isn't one of them. One second I'd been plotting my escape; the next, the world's greenest eyes sucker punched me. The camera zoomed in, and Laila's face filled the screen. The resolution was so clear, I found myself reaching toward the image before handcuffs brought me up short.

For an instant I thought she could see me too. My lips were forming her name when the image froze. I took a breath, let it out. Took another. Exhaled.

Only then did I look from the iPad to the Devil holding it.

"You have no idea what you've just done," I said. The words surprised even me. Despite the jumble of emotions, and the hitching in my chest, my voice was calm, and my fingers had stopped twitching.

"You're wrong, Matthew. I know exactly what I've

done. Why else do you think your hands and feet are handcuffed to a chair bolted into concrete? I have nothing but the utmost respect for your abilities."

"Where is she?" I said in a dead voice.

"Exactly where you left her. The video was taken with a telephoto lens. She's completely safe. For now. Whether or not she remains that way is up to you. I will admit that the team watching her has nowhere near your skill. Then again, they don't need it. I'm certain your wife is quite extraordinary, but she is, after all, only a woman."

I wanted to rail against the Devil's casual dismissal of Laila, but Arab chauvinism aside, he was right. My wife was one of the most courageous people I knew, but she was an accountant. That was fine. She didn't need to be a barbarian. That was where I came in.

The Devil was a dead man walking.

"Let's get this over with," the Devil said, turning the iPad to face himself. "I can see that you're already considering solutions that are unhelpful. I need you to understand the seriousness of the situation. Hopefully, these photographs will make my case for me."

The Devil swiped the screen again and then doubled-tapped the center. "Yes, this will do," the Devil said before turning the device again so I could see it. "I know everything about you, Matthew, including the people you would instinctively run to for help. People like your former bodyguard, Frederick Tyler Cates, call sign Frodo."

Images flickered across the iPad in slide-show mode. Frodo hobbling past the DIA's main gate. Frodo walking to his apartment door.

"And let's not forget your boss, the indomitable James Scott Glass."

Now James was front and center. A distant shot of him leaving the gym. A closer one of him sitting at a restaurant table, a beer bottle pressed to his lips.

"And then there are these people. I know some of them are better friends than others, but I want you to know how extensively I've prepared."

The images changed in rapid fire, showing Rawlings, and Frodo's NSA girlfriend. Even my guitar teacher made the cut. And if the pictures had been the worst of what I saw, things still would have been manageable. Did I find it hard to believe that an Iraqi criminal had somehow penetrated my life and targeted my friends and co-workers? Yes. But at the end of the day, pictures were still just pictures. For all I knew, the Devil's team consisted of a couple of surveillance experts who'd snapped pictures before beating feet out of country.

But the series of images that came next put that thought to rest. The display changed from pictures to screenshots of e-mail accounts, text messages, contact lists, Google Maps printouts showing the locations of the cell phones belonging to my inner circle in real time. This shithead hadn't just penetrated my life; he'd broken it wide open. Anyone I'd thought of contacting was already compromised. And then, just to drive his point home, the screen centered on the location of a single cell phone.

Laila's.

Quite simply, what I was seeing was unbelievable.

"I must confess that you were not an easy nut to crack,

Matthew. I won't insult your intelligence by pretending that I know everything about you. You are, after all, a professional. Still, I need you to understand that I know enough. More than enough, actually. If you attempt to contact anyone in your life, I will know. And once I know, unpleasant things will happen to your very beautiful wife. Extremely unpleasant."

"I'm going to burn you to the ground." As before, the words tumbled out without conscious thought. Though I was seething, my voice was still emotionless. I wasn't posturing. I was stating a fact. The Devil was worm food.

"I know you believe that, Matthew, and I don't fault you. In your shoes I would feel the same way. But I am not in your shoes. I'm in mine. Listen to me when I tell you that I don't want to hurt your lovely Laila. I'm a businessman. Making an enemy of you would be very bad for business."

"Don't you think that ship has already sailed?"

The Devil shook his head. "No. You're angry right now, but you're still a professional. Moments like this are a hazard of your chosen vocation. But if you do what I ask, this will go away. Did it sting when Zain deceived you? I'm sure. But was it the first time an asset betrayed your trust? Or will it be the last? Of course not. Don't make this any harder than it has to be."

"What do you want?" I said.

"I want something that you are uniquely qualified to do."

"First you wanted to kill me, and now you want me to run an errand?" I said.

"You're right, Matthew," the Devil said, unbuttoning

his cuff links and rolling up his sleeves. "Deciding to kill you was premature. But surely you can see things from my perspective? For me, doing business depends on my reputation. A reputation you called into question by escaping from the terrorist cell I'd backed and destroying the chemical weapon I'd financed. Your actions caused my partners to doubt my ability to effectively manage my business, and doubt can be very dangerous."

"So you decided to kill me?" I said.

The Devil shrugged. "Killing you would have erased the blight on my reputation while allowing Sayid's son to prove his worth at the same time. But here again, you exceeded my expectations, Matthew. You eluded my team in Austin and tracked me here. You even did a fairly commendable job of escaping from your cell just now. No, a man like you is much too valuable to waste."

"Then what do you want?" I said.

"One step at a time, Matthew. One step at a time. I respect your abilities too much to tell you what I require now. Especially since you'd then have thirteen hours to consider your options."

"Thirteen hours?"

"Yes. I am a man of considerable means, but even I can't make the trip across the Atlantic pass faster. But I'm not a monster. I booked you a first-class ticket. Still, I'm getting ahead of myself. First, you need to clean up. Then you need to get to Baghdad International and catch a flight to Istanbul. You'll be given further instructions once you land."

"How?"

"One step at a time, Matthew. One step at a time."

TWENTY-NINE

"Turn here."

I obediently spun the wheel, directing our small sedan down a winding alley. Vendors clogged both sides of the street, hawking a variety of goods that would have given Walmart a run for its money. Pirated DVDs competed for space with freshly butchered meat. A rack of designer clothes stood next to a man selling genuine Persian rugs. So many merchants in such a confined space could have meant only one thing—an outpost manned by Americans had to be close by.

"Go. Drive."

The jackass in the passenger seat next to me wasn't much of a conversationalist. At first, I'd thought that was because he was the strong, silent type. Now I was beginning to realize that his English wasn't quite up to spec. If this were a normal drive through the greater metropolitan area of Mosul, I would have offered to switch languages. But I didn't. One, because I didn't want to let my chaperone in on the fact that I could sling Arabic with the best of them. Two, I wasn't really in the mood to make friends. I planned on killing this shithead.

Soon.

"Go!"

This time, my navigator punctuated his command by slapping me in the back of the head. It was an open-handed slap hard enough to get my attention, but not hard enough to do damage. Still, the blow was going to cost him. A moment ago, killing him would have been just a means to an end. But where I come from, one grown man doesn't slap another without consequences.

Dire consequences.

"Sorry," I said, easing off the gas. "People are everywhere. It's freaking me out. You know, performance anxiety."

My companion didn't so much as crack a smile, which confirmed my suspicions. I mean, who in the English-speaking world wouldn't have laughed at that joke? Instead, he pointed his Beretta at my head.

"Drive. Or die."

The pistol was a bit more compelling than his slap. I guess I could have pushed him even more, but sometimes discretion really is the better part of valor. Especially when you're minus a gun. Or a phone. Or anything I'd had on my person when I'd climbed into the car with Zain what seemed like days ago.

A man leading a camel stepped into the street, and I slammed on the brakes. The seat belt tightened across my shoulders. I turned toward my passenger only to find myself eye to eye with the Beretta.

"Keep your pants on," I said, threading my away around the animal. "I've never played chicken with a camel, but I think he'd probably win."

My captor kept the gun pointed at my temple for an uncomfortably long period of time. But after I edged past the camel and into the alley he'd indicated, he set the pistol in his lap.

"Drive," he said again.

Another slap, but his heart didn't seem to be in it. Or maybe he wasn't sure where his job description as my babysitter began and ended. Could he rough me up a bit if the situation dictated? Sure. But did he have permission to kill me? I didn't think so. Then again, thinking wasn't the same as knowing.

My problem was that the Devil hadn't laid his evil plans bare like a movie villain. Instead, he'd told me that the operation was going to progress in stages and that I would find out what I needed to know when I needed to know it. Then he'd given me a cell phone with instructions to keep it on my body at all times and sent me on my merry way. But not before making clear in no uncertain terms what would happen to Laila if I deviated from his instructions or attempted to contact my friends.

And I believed him.

But that was the only part of his story I believed. There was no scenario in which I did what he wanted and Laila and I both came through the experience scot-free. That wasn't how these things worked. The Devil needed

Laila alive as leverage over me for now, just like he needed me alive for whatever role I was to play in his master plan. But once I'd done my part, we'd fare no better than his associate who'd been too trigger-happy with the Taser. If I wanted to survive, I needed to stop playing defense and take the initiative.

I just wasn't sure how.

The opening sequence of one of my favorite Arnold Schwarzenegger movies came to mind. The one in which he plays a commando whose little girl has been kidnapped. After the dastardly deed is done, the bad guys leave one of their crew behind to negotiate with Arnold.

Big mistake.

Once Arnold realizes that the bad guy doesn't know where his daughter was taken, the future Terminator sends him to the afterlife with extreme prejudice. Then he gets about the business of finding his girl.

More than once, I'd considered just following Arnold's example.

Unfortunately, the Devil was a bit smarter than the average eighties bad guy. The phone I was carrying served as the Devil's eyes and ears. If the phone left my body or I deviated from the Devil's instructions, the guys watching Laila would go kinetic. On this topic, the Devil had laid out what would happen in exquisite detail. First, his men would snatch Laila. Then they'd video themselves raping and killing her.

An image of that potential horror flashed through my mind, and my right hand began to tremble. With considerable effort, I pushed the thought away, once again compartmentalizing Laila. Was I terrified at the thought of a hit team surveilling my wife? Sure. But I couldn't dwell on my terror—not now. Not while I was an ocean away with one of the Devil's lackeys keeping me company. Somehow, I needed to change the equation.

The alley gave way to a T intersection. I slowed the car and turned to my passenger.

"Which way?"

He pulled a phone from his shirt pocket with his left hand while still gripping the pistol with his right. After thumbing past a screen or two, he pointed left.

I turned the wheel and added gas.

This was new information. Either my babysitter didn't know where we were going, or he did but didn't know how to get there. Both of those scenarios lent themselves to certain possibilities.

We came to another intersection and I looked at my passenger.

"Well?"

"Yamiin," he said, pointing to the right.

I obediently accelerated, sending the little car zooming down a second side street that emptied into a four-lane thoroughfare. Easing into traffic, I merged the only way possible in Iraq—fearlessly and with liberal use of the horn.

Though I'd spent a good part of my adult life navigating the narrow thoroughfares that passed for streets in this part of world, practice did not make perfect. This was because driving in the Middle East was a bit like surfing a tsunami. Most of the time you were just along for the ride.

A chorus of horns behind me reached a deafening crescendo. Looking in my rearview mirror, I realized I wasn't the only American braving Iraqi traffic. The familiar boxy shape of an up-armored Humvee loomed about five car lengths back. The turret sported a dual-pintle mount outfitted with both an M249 SAW machine gun for antipersonnel and an Mk 19 40mm automatic grenade launcher for more persistent problems.

The gunner had her gloved hands wrapped around the M249, and she was swiveling the turret across her assigned field of fire with a veteran's practiced ease. I could see the outline of several other Hummers behind the lead vehicle, and the intermittent glimpses of their turrets showed them to be similarly outfitted. Whoever was leading this convoy was loaded for bear.

In that moment a horrible thought popped into my mind—what if our meeting wasn't random? What if this unsuspecting column of American soldiers had a role to play in the Devil's still-unspoken plan?

I slowly pressed down on the gas, opening a gap between me and the convoy. I stole a glance at my passenger as the distance widened. He was swiping his phone with one hand and holding the Beretta with the other. He either hadn't noticed the convoy or didn't care.

Both answers were fine with me.

Cutting off a pickup truck held together with baling wire and its driver's hopes and dreams, I edged into the lane closest to the median and further increased my speed. Looking into the rearview mirror a final time, I silently wished my brothers and sisters in arms safe travels.

But a flash of retina-burning white light let me know this was not to be.

The *boom* and corresponding blast jarred my fillings and smashed me against my seat belt half a second later. I slammed on the brakes as several *crunch*es happened in quick succession. The shock waves slammed our tiny sedan against its struts, threatening to overturn us.

I fought the wheel, straining to keep our vehicle on all four tires, even as my fight-or-flight response kicked in. Multiple command-triggered IEDs. This wasn't a simple insurgent gun and run. Multiple IEDs spoke to a certain level of sophistication as well as tactical patience. I was witnessing the opening salvos of a complex ambush.

I turned around in my seat as we came to a stop, looking through the rear window. A cloud of dense, oily black smoke obscured my view. Then a breeze pushed aside the billowing clouds, revealing the broken Hummer lying on its side, one run-flat tire slowly spinning. The turret gunner was gone, but someone was trying to push open the heavy passenger door from inside the vehicle.

Then the second phase of the ambush began.

The baritone *thump thump thump* of heavy machine gun fire echoed from a series of rolling hills to the left of the road. What had been barren soil moments before now held a trio of technicals—Toyota Hilux trucks modified to accept crew-served weapons. The truck nearest me had a machine gun mounted to a rack above the crew cab—a Russian-made DShK by the looks of it.

The heavy machine gun's spindly black barrel belied its ferocity. The weapon fired four-inch-long shells capable of punching through lightly armored ground vehicles and shredding helicopters that ventured too close.

It would wreak havoc on infantrymen in the open.

The gunner let loose another controlled burst of fire, walking green tracers across the broken Humvee. More than a few of the phosphorus-coated rounds lodged somewhere in the Hummer's exposed underside, and tongues of flames began licking at the rubber tires.

This was not good.

A fourth technical crested the hill about one hundred meters from my position. But this Hilux wasn't armed with anything as quaint as a machine gun. Instead, a long, narrow tube reminiscent of a skinny telephone pole sprouted from the back of the truck. As the driver backed the vehicle into position, two fighters oriented the recoilless rifle on the lead Hummer with the precise movements of a well-disciplined gun crew. Before my brain had time to fully process what I was seeing, the gun belched smoke, and the disabled Humvee erupted into flames.

Fuck me.

Things hadn't exactly been looking good for the home team before the 106mm antitank gun had arrived on the scene. Now any soldiers still alive had about as much of a chance of surviving as fish in a barrel.

"Drive! Drive! Drive!"

My passenger punctuated his screams with slaps to my head. These weren't so gentle. The thing of it was, he was right. Laila's life was on the line, and I would do anything to save her.

Absolutely anything.

And yet . . .

"Go!"

Another smack.

Putting the car into drive with my right hand, I simultaneously released the seat belt with my left. Then I floored it. The car lurched forward, tires squealing. The speedometer shot upward at an impressive rate for the old rattletrap. I waited for our speed to top forty. Then I took a deep breath, grabbed the steering wheel, locked both arms, and stomped on the brake.

The car skidded to a stop, whiplashing us against the seats. My legs and arms took most of the g-forces generated by the sudden deceleration, but my head still banged against the doorframe.

That was going to leave a mark.

My chaperone on the other hand had been wearing his seat belt. The restraint had worked as advertised, tightening across his torso, which meant that his arms were still locked in place.

But mine were not.

Torquing from the waist, I snapped a right jab into his temple. His head thudded against the window before rebounding into my left cross. I turned my shoulder into the punch, locking my elbow just as my fist crashed into his skull. The quick one-two wasn't enough to kill him, but the blows certainly rang his bell.

I scooped up the pistol, shoved the weapon into his face, and squeezed the trigger twice. Now, like Arnold, I was free to work the problem of recovering Laila on my terms.

The life-and-death struggle in our car went largely unnoticed by the surrounding traffic. Probably because the other drivers were too busy attempting to escape the still-active ambush behind them. Drivers were fleeing in every conceivable direction like cockroaches scattering from a sudden onslaught of light.

Slamming the car into reverse, I tucked the still-warm Beretta under my leg and joined the exodus. But instead of escaping, I pointed my rear bumper at the profile of the pickup truck with the long recoilless rifle and punched the accelerator.

Crazy? Maybe. But crazy or not, there was no way I was leaving fellow Americans in harm's way. Over the years, I'd sacrificed a good many things for this job.

Honor wasn't one of them.

THIRTY

Reacting to a near ambush was one of the first battle drills infantrymen mastered. The drill was both simple and effective. When caught in a kill zone, attack. Even so, I doubted that my wise instructors at the Infantry Officer Basic Course had this particular contingency in mind.

Steering in reverse at fifty miles per hour was an acquired skill, as my numerous contacts with other cars could attest. Still, the unintended impacts were bumper to side panel for the most part. This meant that while my speed abated temporarily, none of the glancing blows were stop-where-you-are crashes.

Besides, the drivers caught at the edge of a kill zone were remarkably forgiving. The ambushers were still raining lead down on the disabled convoy, and rounds were ricocheting in all directions. While none of the civilian vehicles had been intentionally targeted so far, no one seemed inclined to stop and exchange insurance information either.

Put another way, the scene on the roadway more resembled a demolition derby than commuters heading home after a hard day's work. Cars were bouncing off one another with the randomness of exploding popcorn kernels as traffic used any available avenue to get the hell out of Dodge.

For my purposes, the confusion was perfect. Even though I crunched off a few more bumpers than I would have liked, the overall pandemonium was flawless cover. With all the beeping horns, squealing tires, and metal-on-metal collisions, the fray of civilian vehicles didn't seem to be attracting the gun crew's attention. Instead, the ambushers were focused on killing Americans with ruthless efficiency.

Time to give them a taste of their own medicine.

After banging against a Toyota Land Cruiser, I shot off the pavement onto the sandy soil. The car's back end fishtailed on the loose gravel. I downshifted, hoping the front tires had enough purchase to launch me up the hill. If not, my little act of defiance would be about as short-lived as Custer's.

And just as successful.

The car's engine went from a whine to an all-out scream as the gerbils under the hood gave it all they had. Judging by my slow progress up the hill, that wasn't very much. If God wasn't outright laughing, He must have at least been smiling. After a heart-lurching moment, the front wheels caught, and I rocketed up the last section of hill before cresting the top. For the first time, I could see sky instead of just the sloping hill behind me.

Spinning the wheel one-handed, I centered the back bumper on the recoilless rifle and red-lined the engine. The car bounced across the hilltop, each pothole sending my head crashing into the ceiling. Even so, I was closing ground.

About half a second before impact, I suddenly had the urge to scream *ramming speed*, but didn't. Instead, I tucked my head below the seat, clamped my jaw shut, and braced for what I was certain would be a bone-jarring crash.

I was not disappointed.

One second I was huddled against the seat's sweat-soaked upholstery. The next I was pinballing between the steering wheel, dashboard, and door handle. For a moment or two, I thought the collision had dislodged both vehicles, sending my car tumbling downhill.

Then I realized that the tumbling was occurring only inside my throbbing head.

Disorientation—check.

Nausea—check.

Mother of all headaches—double check.

Hello, concussion.

Shaking my head in an effort to clear the cobwebs, I patted the floorboards until my fingers found the Beretta. Then it was time to go to work.

Opening my door, I slid out with the grace of a

drunken elephant. The world wasn't still spinning, but neither was it behaving. Turning my head, I dry heaved until a torrent of acidic bile rushed up my esophagus.

Maybe this line of work just wasn't for me.

Wrapping my left hand around the doorframe, I yanked myself upright, leading with the Beretta. I thumbed off the safety and stretched around the door, leaning heavily against the frame. I still didn't trust myself to walk, so hopefully I could take care of business from here.

The first thing I saw was encouraging in a macabre kind of way. One of the gun crewmen was sandwiched between my car's bumper and the truck's rear quarter panel. He was thrashing from side to side while coughing up blood, but his hands were empty. Since he clearly wasn't going anywhere, he could wait.

His partner had been luckier. Apparently, he'd been thrown clear during my kamikaze attack, because he came running around the front of the truck, screaming in Arabic. This did nothing for my headache. Nor did the Beretta's loud report as I put two rounds in his chest and one more in his head.

Then it was the first man's turn.

After that, my section of hillside was much quieter.

At least until the DShK put another controlled burst into the convoy. Green streaks slapped into the Hummers before the heavy bullets ricocheted, spinning into space like fireballs spit from a Roman candle.

My new vantage point offered a clear view of the entire convoy for the first time. What I saw wasn't good. Like the lead vehicle, the trail Humvee was nothing but billowing flames. However, a couple of the vehicles in the center of the group were still relatively intact. Two of them were Hummer gun trucks, but the third was different. Its roomier cab was designed to carry troops. Judging by the star-shaped black scorch marks, the vehicle had taken a hit from the recoilless rifle or an EFP near its drivetrain. The ordnance had disabled the vehicle, but the all-important crew quarters had escaped serious damage.

For now.

If I hadn't seen the precision with which the gun crew had employed the recoilless rifle firsthand, I would have thought this was the result of a lucky shot. Now I wasn't so sure. It was as if the attackers wanted the vehicle disabled rather than destroyed.

Why?

The answer to my unspoken question became clear a moment later. Soldiers dismounted from the other stricken vehicles and ran toward the disabled troop carrier, attempting to form an ad hoc perimeter. Someone important was inside. Someone the people running the ambush intended to capture.

The DShK lit into the unprotected soldiers, shredding the front rank and sending the survivors scattering. At the same time, the enemy fighters I'd seen dug in around the technical got to their feet and began bounding down the hillside. The DShK, along with a second machine gun mounted to the far truck, provided covering fire as the assault team moved.

Shit fire.

This was no ragtag band of Sunni extremists or a half-trained Shia militia. These were soldiers. Light infantrymen with obvious combat experience. Unless I did something fast, they would be on the troop carrier in seconds.

Every infantryman, from the most experienced Delta operator all the way down to the lowliest private in the 82nd Airborne, likes to think of himself as an unparalleled weapon. A weapon that could single-handedly fight and win a war without help from the Army's more cumbersome branches, like artillery or armor. And yet, when the shit hit the fan, every single one of those tough guys would admit that there was nothing quite so comforting as seeing an M1 Abrams main battle tank cresting a hillside.

Right about now I'd have given my left nut for a battery of 105mm howitzers on call, a platoon of Bradleys, or even a Stryker or two. But I didn't have any of those. What I did have was a Beretta pistol, two dead jihadis, and a recoilless rifle.

That would have to do.

Hopping onto the truck bed, I gave the recoilless rifle a quick once-over. While I'd never operated this variant before, we had something similar but smaller in the Ranger Regiment. That man-portable work of art was known as the Carl Gustaf. This vehicle-mounted version was much larger, but at the end of the day, a recoilless rifle was a recoilless rifle. I mean, let's face it: Infantry weapons were simple by design. This was partly because infantrymen were not bred to be rocket scientists and partly because the life expectancy of the average rifleman in combat was not terribly long.

Put more delicately, every member of an infantry platoon had at least a passing familiarity with each weapon the platoon employed. Just because you were a machine gunner today didn't mean you wouldn't become a mortarman tomorrow once bullets started flying and casualties started falling.

Hunkering down beside the long tube, I located the firing mechanism and verified that the breech was locked. This meant that the cannon was already loaded. Next, I checked that the traversing mechanism still worked by spinning the flywheel and watching the gun tube move accordingly. In a bit of luck, the force of the crash had canted the gun truck to the left, swinging the rifle's muzzle toward my intended target.

I put both hands on the metal flywheel and cranked as quickly as I could, but the barrel only inched along. Acutely aware of the ever-present *thump* from the two DShKs, I cranked harder, knowing I was in a race against time. After an eternity of cranking, the flywheel stopped. The traverse mechanism had hit its limit. I scrambled behind the gun and looked down the iron sights.

My plan had hit its first snag.

While my kamikaze attack had pushed the truck in the correct direction, the collision had also done a number on the gun's iron sights. The metal cross in the center of the sights was significantly tilted off axis. I'd have to do this the old-fashioned way.

Sighting down the length of the barrel, I found the technical with the mounted DShK.

The good news was that I seemed to be lined up in azimuth. The bad news was that the barrel looked a bit high. I located the wheel that controlled the gun's elevation and cranked down until the front sight post was centered on the DShK. Then I breathed a prayer, opened my mouth to equalize pressure against the coming concussion, and squeezed the trigger.

The ensuing backblast was ferocious. Like most Rangers, I had a love-hate relationship with the Gustaf. The ordnance it launched could reduce reinforced bunkers to clouds of dust like nobody's business, but that firepower came with a price. The explosion of gases propelling the shell down the Gustaf's rifled barrel smashed into your chest with the force of A-Rod swinging an aluminum bat. To ensure Gustaf gunners didn't permanently damage their hearts, each Ranger could fire the weapon only three times in a twenty-four-hour period.

At least in theory.

But with that theory or not, this vehicle-mounted variant put the Gustaf to shame. The report deafened me while the blast wave pounded against my fledgling concussion. I literally saw stars—an entire constellation's worth. My stomach heaved. I draped my head over the side and vomited onto the dead jihadi still pinned to the truck by my sedan's bumper. If I'm going to be honest, I found his predicament kind of funny. I mean, I'm sure the little fucker had given some thought to how his day might go, but I have to imagine that having his corpse puked on by a punch-drunk American probably hadn't made the list.

Hauling myself upright, I looked over the rifle barrel at the fruits of my labor. I smiled. At first. Orange flames covered the hillside as thick black smoke curled into the blue sky. And then my little celebration came to a screeching halt. The flames were coming from the Hilux beyond the one I'd targeted. My Kentucky windage had been a wee bit off. I'd put the first round over the DShK gunner and into the vehicle beside him.

Whoops.

And now the gunner was traversing his machine gun away from the convoy of disabled vehicles toward yours truly.

Double whoops.

I threw open the gun's breech, yanked out the hot shell, and sent the spent brass clattering over the tailgate. I scooped up a round from the ammo pile at my feet and fed it into the gun. The tank-killing projectile felt amazingly light to my adrenaline-soaked muscles, and I slammed the breech-locking mechanism closed with a bit more force than necessary. After grabbing the elevation flywheel, I began to turn just as the DShK cut loose.

On the off chance you haven't experienced it, getting shot at with a crew-served weapon is life-altering. One moment, I was certain I was about to send my jihadi friends to paradise. The next, slugs the size of golf balls were tearing sections from the pickup truck. Metal splinters whistled through the air as chunks of aluminum spun into space.

With rounds this big, there was no such thing as a grazing wound. A hit to an exposed limb meant instant amputation. A hit anywhere to the torso or head meant lights out.

Immediately.

I stretched out flat against the truck's bed, desperate to escape the lead hailstorm. But as much as I wanted to stay hunkered down, this would only prolong the inevitable. Hiding was dying. Rolling onto my back, I grabbed the elevation wheel and began to turn. I couldn't look down the barrel to see when I was on target, so instead I tried to remember how many turns I'd used before.

Ten?

Twenty?

I needed to drop the barrel about six inches, which was about half the distance I'd adjusted last time. If I fired over the DShK again, I was done. If I fired too low and hit the dirt short of the truck, I was done.

Like Goldilocks's porridge, this shot needed to be just right.

An unseen slap knocked my hand from the elevation wheel, sending pins and needles racing up my arm. For a moment, I thought a ricochet had taken my limb off at the elbow. Then I realized that it must have been the shock wave from a bullet crashing into the recoilless rifle's metal frame. How close had one of those Humvee-killing rounds come to my wrist?

Too close.

Stretching shaking hands back up to the cold steel, I cranked as metal splinters peppered my face and neck. Ten turns. That would have to do. But after reaching ten, I cranked the wheel one last time for the Airborne Ranger in the sky.

Then I squeezed the trigger.

Underneath the gun, the backblast was even worse. The shock wave crushed me against the truck, driving the breath from my lungs. I would have screamed if I'd had the air. Instead, my mouth just opened and closed like a beached guppy's. After a second or two, my chest quit spasming, and cool air flooded my lungs.

Rolling over, I vomited. Again. Then I grabbed hold of what was left of the truck bed and hoisted myself up, ignoring the jagged metal slicing my palms.

A glorious sight awaited. The second gun truck was engulfed in flames as secondary explosions sent unspent machine-gun rounds spiraling off in random directions. On the downward slope of the hill, the enemy assaulters had stopped their rush toward the troop carrier. Now they were retreating to the one remaining technical.

At first, I thought that I was the one who'd broken their morale. But two explosions erupting from the hillside one after the other put that notion to rest. As I watched, a third explosion shredded their ranks, blasting chunks of earth skyward. Then the remaining technical cartwheeled off the hill to the sound of more explosions.

Someone was engaging the enemy with precision fire. The pinpoint strikes were much too accurate to be artillery. The rounds had to be coming from somewhere else.

Scanning the sky, I found the source of the mayhem—a pair of A-10 fighters. As I stood up on wobbly legs to cheer, I realized two things in very short order. One, the flashes of light on the lead A-10's pylons meant another pair of rockets was heading toward a target. Two, only one target remained.

Me.

I sprinted the length of the truck bed and launched into space. In happier times, it might have been a beautiful swan dive. But today, the maneuver was significantly less graceful. More like a cross between a belly flop and a cannonball.

Fortunately, enthusiasm compensated for my lack of technique. I cleared the truck and the crest of the hill, sprawling down the incline toward the convoy. I had just enough time to consider how stupid I'd look if the pilot hadn't been aiming at me when the rockets hit.

This shock wave didn't just knock the wind out of me.

It knocked me out cold.

THIRTY-ONE

I came to my senses slowly, which was becoming an all-too-frequent experience. Once again, my hands and feet were secured. This time, there was the unmistakable feeling of plastic zip ties biting into my wrists. And I was hog-tied. Nothing says *bad day* quicker than waking up with your shoulders on fire and quads spasming because some jackass decided to tie your wrists to your ankles.

In fact, I might have given my new captor a piece of my mind if not for a couple of extenuating circumstances. And by *extenuating circumstances*, I mean the scratchy black hood covering my head. Not to mention the vibrating floor beneath my chest and the howling sound of turbine engines. I was in a helicopter, and helicopters were not conducive to talking.

Still, perhaps it was time to look on the bright side. I was alive. Also, I was on a helicopter, which probably meant I was back in friendly hands. Probably. Of course,

I was also hog-tied and hooded. This seemed to indicate that my newfound companions suspected that I'd had something to do with the ambush.

Suddenly, my position didn't seem all that enviable.

The American military is the best-disciplined fighting force in the world. Even so, it's still composed of fallible human beings. I know what it's like to stare at a captured prisoner while your friend's corpse is lying on a blood-soaked stretcher inches away. I remember thinking about how his pretty wife's face was going to crumple when the casualty-notification detail pulled into her driveway.

And that led to a dark place and even darker thoughts. Thoughts about how good it would feel to hurl the prisoner responsible for my fellow Ranger's death through the helicopter's open door. On that day, I'd resisted the urge to trade my soul for petty vengeance. But I'd still given the idea a good deal more thought than I cared to admit.

I struggled onto my side, intending to address my captors, but a kick to my ribs changed my mind.

"Stay still, motherfucker."

The speaker was shouting over the engines' roar, but I could still hear the deadly intent in his voice. I stopped moving, waiting for the pain in my ribs to subside. That's when I realized the constant pressure against my side was gone. The phone the Devil had strapped to my belt had been lost during the gunfight or had been taken from me while I was unconscious. Either way, this presented an opportunity.

But only if I acted quickly.

"I'm an American."

"I don't care if you're Brad Pitt. Move again, and I'll throw your ass out the door. You feel me?"

"I feel you, but I'm a DIA operative. I need to talk to the QRF leader. Is that you?"

I got another kick to the ribs for my trouble. This one was hard enough to roll me to my side.

"Maybe you didn't hear me. Your job is to lie there. Mine is to not chuck you into thin air. Right now you're making my job harder. I don't give a fuck who you are. Until we get back to the FOB, shut the fuck up."

That was all well and good, but the Devil had made it clear what would happen to Laila if I ditched the phone. The confusion surrounding the ambush might have bought me some breathing room, but I didn't know how much.

Either way, Laila's life was worth a hell of a lot more than a kick in the ribs.

I opened my mouth again, but before I could talk, an explosion rocked the helicopter. The floor lurched to the left, then angled sharply downward. The comforting whine of the engines turned to a nails-on-the-chalkboard screeching and then something even more terrifying.

Silence.

But silence on a battlefield never lasts long. In the space of a heartbeat or two, the void left by the engines' silence was filled with something else.

Screams.

THIRTY-TWO

slid across the helicopter's metal floor, the exposed rivet heads furrowing gashes into my chest and stomach. Riding in a helicopter without being strapped in can be a bit dicey during combat maneuvering. During a crash sequence, it's pretty close to a death sentence.

Something large and metal smashed into my face. My lip ruptured as the blow reverberated along my jaw. The floor shifted to the right, sending me tumbling into something else unyielding. This time, I took the impact on my shoulder. My arm went numb. I tried to curl into the fetal position, but my hog-tied hands and feet had other ideas.

More screams tore through the cabin, accompanied by the shriek of metal ripping away from metal. Smoke gagged me through the hood as the wet-sounding *thud*s of bodies pinballing around the helicopter's cabin filled the air. The sensations were coming too fast to differentiate.

The floor fell out from beneath me and then punched me in the face.

And the screams.

Always the screams.

Cursing competed with snatches of prayers. Voices rose in a crescendo of terror. More screams. I knew that when death came for me, it probably wouldn't be pleasant.

I just didn't think it would take this long.

The rotor blades began huffing, clawing for air. Then crumpling metal and breaking glass as the aircraft collided with the earth. I shot into space, and bounced twice against the ground before coming to rest in an awkward sprawl.

I was on my back, bound legs and hands beneath me. I couldn't see, but I could imagine what was happening easily enough. Flames reaching from the helicopter, scarlet fingers consuming everything they touched.

A staccato of *pops* was followed by a deep *whump* as the fuel cell detonated.

I rolled away from the inferno, trying to escape the unbearable heat.

Modern helicopters are marvels of technology. Redundant electrical systems, fly-by-wire controls, computer-assisted hovering, and the ability to traverse hundreds of miles and still hit a landing zone with a time on target of plus or minus thirty seconds.

But this technical innovation came at a steep price.

The composite materials that made the bird so fuel efficient off-gassed toxins when engulfed by flames, and the transmission's magnesium components burned at more than four thousand degrees Fahrenheit. Helicopters were all well and good when they were knifing through the air where they belonged, but God help you if they caught on fire. I'd once seen a Chinook take an RPG to the fuel tank during an insertion gone bad. After the five minutes I'd needed to reach the crash site, sheets of rolling flames had been the only thing left.

Another round of staccato *pop*s. This time, the noise seemed familiar, but I couldn't dedicate the mental energy to understand why. The fire had reached my clothes. I flopped on the ground, trying to smother the flames, as rocks bit into my skin.

Apparently, the inventor of *stop, drop, and roll* had never been hog-tied.

Thrashing against the soil, I screamed out my rage and terror. Seconds earlier, I'd been praying to live through the crash sequence. Now I was wishing I could take the prayer back. Maybe that's what Garth Brooks had meant by thanking God for unanswered prayers.

I screamed again as my pants ignited, and that was when I heard Arabic voices. It took a moment for my mind to render their words into English, but by then strong hands were beating against my arms and legs, smothering the fire. The relief was immediate. A heartbeat ago, I was on my way to dying a hideous death.

Now I was safe.

I sucked in a breath to offer my thanks, but couldn't

get the words past the lump in my chest. The surge of emotion was unexpected. I'd confronted death countless times before and had never choked. What the hell was wrong with me? I needed to get my shit together before my rescuers saw tears running down my face.

And then someone yanked the mask from my head. The cool air brought fresh tears as I coughed away soot and mucus. Once my vision finally cleared, I realized that old Garth had been right after all.

My rescuer wasn't a Special Forces operative or a fellow crash survivor. In fact, he wasn't American at all. Instead, I found myself face-to-face with a bearded man.

A bearded man with an empty missile launcher strapped to his back.

THIRTY-THREE

Brother—are you okay?"

The jihadi's dark eyes darted from my soot-covered face to my bound arms and legs. His features contorted with concern. "Can you speak?"

I could, but there was no way I could mimic his Iraqi accent. My Arabic was understandable, but I couldn't pass for a native. Clearing my throat, I spat and shook my head.

The jihadi let loose a string of curses as he drew a knife from his belt and sawed through my restraints with quick, practiced strokes.

"Come," my rescuer said, lifting me to my feet. "We must hurry. Surely Allah must have been smiling on you. You have quite a story. I know Bijan will want to hear it."

I nodded as the jihadi helped me toward an idling

technical. He was more right than he knew. I did have quite a story. Now I just needed to invent it.

The next thirty or so minutes passed about as uneventfully as you could expect, riding in the back of a Toyota Hilux with a bunch of wounded jihadis. From what I could gather, the battered and bloodied men strewn across the truck bed were the perpetrators of the convoy ambush. Some of them might even have had me to thank for their wounds, but I decided to keep that little nugget to myself.

Instead, I'd taken the plastic bottle of water someone had offered, uncapped it, and sloshed some around the inside my mouth. Then I'd spit the red-tinged liquid over the side of the truck. Next, I'd dumped some in my hands and washed the crust of equal parts soot, dust, and blood from my eyes. I'd thought that seeing clearly for the first time since the crash would be comforting.

I was wrong.

For most people, being on the receiving end of an A-10 rocket salvo would count as a bad day. Getting a helicopter shot out from under them *after* surviving an A-10 rocket salvo would be a very bad day. In fact, most people would assume that after enduring those two things back-to-back, they'd be due for a little good luck.

But they were not me.

I was in the number two vehicle in a caravan of technicals racing across the desert headed who in the hell knew where. I thought about asking the jihadi next to me, but he was too busy holding in the intestines trying to spill down the front of his pants. The guy next to him was doing the rapid, shallow breathing that usually means one's time on earth is almost over. The truck's fourth casualty was covered in shrapnel wounds that had just stopped bleeding.

In other words, he was already dead.

Weren't we the merry crew?

A large combat knife glittered from the dead jihadi's belt. I unsheathed the blade and cut away the charred remains of my pant legs. In the first good news of the day, the skin beneath had minimal blistering. First- and second-degree burns hurt like hell, but they aren't life-threatening or debilitating.

Score one for the home team.

With the knife still in my hand, I looked at the jihadi trying to hold his intestines together and considered my options. This dude was a dirtbag, no two ways about it. Between the convoy he and his buddies had ambushed and the helicopter they'd blown from the sky, he was definitely on my shit list. Also, now that I could devote some mental energy to the series of *pop*s I'd heard before the jihadi had rescued me, I understood their significance.

The fighters had been executing the crash survivors.

What I really wanted to do was slide the knife up to its hilt in between the jihadi's second and third ribs and smile as the blade plunged into his heart.

But I didn't.

Instead, I doubled the strips of cloth from my pants

on top of each other until I'd constructed a makeshift pressure bandage. Then I slid closer to him.

"Move your hands," I said in Arabic before succumbing to a coughing fit that sounded like chunks of rock grinding against one another.

The jihadi looked at me as if he didn't understand, but the fear in his eyes said otherwise. He knew he was dying. But he was also scared—terrified, really—about what he'd find once he moved his hands away from the gaping hole in his stomach.

"You must move your hands," I said again, showing him the bandages. "I can't stop the bleeding, but *inshallah* I might be able to slow it down. If not, you will die."

The man looked at me for a long moment and then slowly closed his eyes. When he opened them, he nodded.

He moved his trembling hands from the gaping wound, and I pushed his intestines back in as best I could. Next, I layered fabric over the wound, trying to ignore the familiar coppery smell of blood mixed with the fecal scent indicative of a perforated bowel. Coursing blood turned my hands sticky, but I bound the pressure bandage in place, tying it off with a square knot over his stomach.

Abdominal wounds are always horrible, but I'd never seen one this bad. In fact, he probably would have suffered less if I'd just given in to my earlier urge and slid the knife home. But I wasn't thinking about his comfort.

I was thinking about my survival.

"Will he live?"

The shouted question came from the Hilux's cab. The glass separating the cab from the truck bed had long since been removed or shattered. A fierce-looking man with a full beard and shaggy brown hair was yelling from inside.

I shook my head, holding up bloodstained hands. Hopefully the roar of the wind sweeping across the open truck bed would help to mask my poor Arabic, but I wasn't taking any chances.

"Do what you can," the man said. "We're almost there."

That was an interesting statement. As far as I could tell, we weren't almost anywhere. We were summiting a small hill, so I couldn't see what lay ahead of us, but the scenery to the left and right was hardly impressive. Flat, open desert. That was it. I turned back to see if my friend with the perforated bowel was still among the living when the passenger in the truck's cab pounded on the vehicle's frame to get my attention.

"Look," he said.

I followed his pointing finger as we crested the hill, and I did a double take. I'd been expecting one of two things: an isolated compound or a series of interconnected houses indicative of a small Iraqi village. Both had advantages and disadvantages. Remote compounds were easily defensible against an attacking ground force, but also extremely vulnerable to a couple of well-placed JDAMs.

Villages on the other hand were usually safe from air attack since American generals and politicians alike were averse to pictures of dead women and children on the nightly news. But the lumped-together structures made a stealthy approach by ground possible.

What greeted me on the reverse side of the slope was something else entirely. It was a mini outpost complete with HESCO barriers, guard towers, and controlled entry points. If the flag flying atop the bunker flanking the main gate had been the Stars and Stripes, I would have thought we were about to enter an American-controlled forward operating base, or FOB. But the flag wasn't red, white, or blue. It was green, white, and red. The colors of the world's only Shia-inspired theocracy.

Iran.

"Keep him alive," the man shouted, the wind tousling his thick hair. "The doctors inside will save him. You will see."

And that was what I was afraid of.

THIRTY-FOUR

The objective of war is to kill people, plain and simple. The advent of drones and precision weapons has mitigated some of the visceral nature of warfare. People can now sit in climate-controlled bunkers and rain down death without ever getting dirt beneath their fingernails. They don't have to smell the putrid stench of a gut wound or hear the screams of the dying. In some aspects, war was becoming a rather sanitary endeavor.

This was not that.

This was me in the back of a truck full of half-dead terrorists. Terrorists who'd killed my countrymen. Together, we were about to roll into a compound full of Iranian commandos who would love to chat with me while using sharp metal objects as conversation starters. In other words, it was me or them.

In that equation, *me* wins every day of the week.

Bending over my patient, I fussed over his bandages in

case the curly-haired guy in the truck was watching. Once I was sure that my back was blocking his view, I thrust the combat knife between the jihadi's ribs and twisted.

He shuddered once, gasped, and went still.

It was a cleaner death than he probably deserved, but I was not the judge or jury. I was simply the executioner. Without medical attention, he would have died in the next fifteen minutes. But if the Iranian surgeons were as shit hot as Curly believed, they might have been able to save him. Which meant that sooner or later, he'd start answering questions, and those answers would not match mine.

I couldn't allow that to happen.

Cold? Maybe. But life as a terrorist was a full-contact sport.

After wiping the blade on the dead jihadi's blood-soaked shirt, I slipped the weapon into my pants. Next I loosened his bandages and let the blood pool down the front of his trousers. Only then did I turn back to Curly.

"Hurry," I screamed. "He's bleeding out."

Curly looked at me, and his eyes widened. Then he turned back to the driver. The wind drowned out what he was saying, but it must have been a helluva speech. The truck surged forward, rocking me in the bed as we zoomed toward the compound's gate.

The guards manning the crew-served weapons out front moved to intercept us, but Curly beat them to the punch. Opening his door and standing half out of the cab while the truck was still moving, he screamed something in Farsi. Old Curly must have had some pull with the Iranians. The steel barrier cranked upward, and the guards waved us through.

To his credit, our driver didn't even slow down. Instead, he poured on the gas, and the truck accelerated through the compound's entrance, roaring past the guard station in a cloud of grit and engine exhaust. I took the opportunity to check the knife's positioning in my pants, ensuring it was secure and that the pointy end wasn't about to stab something important.

I might have been heading into a compound full of people who wanted to kill me, but that didn't mean I had to make their job any easier.

The driver took a quick left followed by a right, laying on his horn. Curly leaned out the window, shouting profanities in both Arabic and Farsi for good measure. I might not have been able to discuss the intricacies of the Shia sect of Islam with an Iranian in his own language, but I could curse with the best of them.

A final turn brought us within sight of a building with a red crescent painted on the side. Here again the driver poured on the speed as Curly slapped the truck's roof like he was whipping a horse down the final stretch of the Kentucky Derby. The whole thing might have been comical if we weren't closing on a rather solid structure at the better part of sixty miles an hour.

Just when I thought the driver planned to expedite the hospital's admissions paperwork by driving through the wall, he slammed on the brakes.

I tumbled across the truck bed until the cabin's forgiving steel frame gently arrested my forward motion.

This time, I managed to turtle before impact. My shoulders and arms took the brunt of the collision, but damn if I didn't bounce my head off the roll bars when we finally came to a stop. If I hadn't finished off the wounded jihadi before, he would have been good and dead now.

Thinking about the dead jihadi brought my scrambled brain back online. Trying to ignore the numbness radiating down my arm, I turned toward the dead man and retied his bandage. Then I pressed down with both hands as if I was keeping his intestines from spilling onto his shoes. This was the moment of truth. Either my half-baked idea would work, or I'd be the next one on the receiving end of a combat knife or two.

Fortunately, God heard my unspoken prayer. Or maybe He just wanted to see what I'd do next. Which made two of us. In any case, four men in scrubs came out the building's front door at a run, heading straight for me. As soon as I saw them, I started part two of my charade—CPR.

On a dead man.

As the trauma team rounded the back of the truck, they found me pounding away on the dead jihadi's chest like he was my best friend. I sold it for everything I was worth, compressing the dead man's chest like a maniac while screaming at him in Arabic.

Okay, I might have held a wee bit back. There was no way in hell I was doing rescue breathing on this dead asshole. I had no idea the places his mouth had been. My lips weren't going anywhere near his.

Even so, I was still covered in his blood up to my elbows. I straddled his dead body, administering chest compressions like I was George Clooney auditioning for *ER*. And my thespian debut must have worked. The trauma team rolled a gurney up to the truck bed.

Curly joined them, dropping the Hilux's tailgate. Grabbing my leg, he yelled something unintelligible, which I assumed roughly translated to *Get the fuck out of the way and let the professionals do their thing*.

A reasonable request, but reason and I had parted ways long ago.

The moment I stopped trying to save a dead man's life, Curly would be free to pepper me with questions. Questions that even Mr. Clooney with his famous theatrical skills would have a hard time answering. That meant I needed to stick with the dead jihadi for a little while longer. Finishing a compression, I rolled clear of his chest and knew what had to be done. As the medics hoisted the jihadi's limp body onto the gurney, I pinched off his nose, tilted back his head, and gave him a rescue breath.

I'd sucked on tailpipes that tasted better.

Seriously. If the horrific stomach wound hadn't killed him, I'm sure that whatever was decomposing in his mouth would have done the job. I gagged, choking back the vomit that wanted to rocket from my mouth just in time. Clearing my throat, I took stock of my options.

They were not pleasant.

On the positive side of things, the jihadi was now on the gurney and heading into the hospital. Unfortunately, this meant that the crowd of medics surrounding him was leaving me behind with Curly. I could not allow that to happen. I pushed my way to the moving gurney and gave the jihadi another rescue breath.

Sweet baby Jesus.

This time I did retch, but I managed not to throw up on my shoes. Even so, my performance let me follow the throng of medical personnel through the swinging doors and into the hospital proper. Victims often throw up into the mouths of the people rescue breathing for them. With this in mind, I was hoping that my puke session would help sell my performance. As I prepared to once again swap spit with a dead man, someone slapped me on the shoulder and pressed a bag valve mask into my hand.

Part of me wanted to weep with joy at the random stranger's kindness. The other half of me was consumed with a murderous rage at the thought that this device had been readily available the entire time I had been French-kissing the Elephant Man. Fitting the plastic across the jihadi's face, I began to bag him as one of the medics climbed onto the gurney and resumed chest compressions.

The trauma team seemed to know their jobs. If I hadn't stabbed him in the heart, he might have had a fighting chance. Unlike, say, the helicopter's crew and passengers he and his brethren had ruthlessly executed.

Reap the whirlwind, motherfucker.

Our little foursome was rapidly picking up new players as we rolled down the hospital's sparkling hallways. Additional men in scrubs joined the group, and it was starting to get downright crowded. Someone appeared at my shoulder, spoke words I didn't understand, and then reached past me to take over bagging the dead patient.

I took this as my cue.

Nodding my understanding, I stepped out of the way as the medical team pushed the gurney through another pair of swinging doors. As I'd hoped, my absence wasn't noticed. The noise and activity in the trauma room spiked as a team of dedicated medics worked to save a man long past saving. With a final look around to verify that I had indeed been forgotten, I eased past the corner and walked smack into Curly.

Son of a bitch.

He grabbed my shoulders as his brown eyes found mine. "Your friend. Did he make it?"

I shook my head.

"*Inshallah* he was martyred. I know the clerics say we should rejoice for those who are now in paradise, but I've never met a true warrior who took joy in the death of his brothers. Come. I have something that will ease your pain."

"Thank you, my brother," I said, "but I should get back. There is much to do."

"There's always much to do," Curly said, his fingers tightening around my arm. "But for now it can wait. Come."

This time the command wasn't a suggestion. I nodded, and Curly released my arm. He started back down the hallway, and I followed, considering my options. As usual they weren't particularly good. But they did beat lying dead on an operating table with a stab wound to the heart.

As Mom liked to say, sometimes happiness was just a matter of perspective.

THIRTY-FIVE

Curly wound through the maze of hallways with an ease suggesting he was a frequent visitor. This struck me as strange until I realized that the hospital was more than just a hospital. Within two or three hallways, the sterile surroundings gave way to something decidedly grimier. The lighting grew dimmer, the floor dirtier, and the people we passed more unkempt.

Not homeless person ratty per se, but definitely not the clean, scrub-wearing medical staff I'd seen earlier. In fact, the atmosphere began to remind me of a place I liked about as much as a hospital—prison.

My suspicions were confirmed when Curly took a final left into a dingy corridor bisected by a faded steel desk clearly past its prime. Behind the desk sat a man who'd also seen better days. He straightened his slouch at Curly's appearance, but his change in posture did nothing for his soiled uniform or unkempt, greasy hair. Curly shot a stream of Farsi at the man, who shrugged in response. A second, more forceful verbal barrage seemed to do the trick. The guard lumbered to his feet, unclipped a key ring from his belt, and handed it to Curly along with a clipboard.

Curly took the key ring, ignored the clipboard, and beckoned to me.

"I'm sorry for that *khar*," Curly said as he walked past the guard. "This world would be a better place if he'd strap on a suicide vest and martyr himself."

"You know him?" I said.

Curly nodded. "Too well, I'm afraid. He was wounded several months ago—a bullet graze to the leg, nothing more. Even so, he was sent here to recover. He's been recovering ever since. The Iranians took pity on him. Instead of being sent back to his unit, he guards an empty detention center."

"If it's empty, why do you need those?" I said, pointing to the key ring.

"It's not empty any longer," Curly said, a wolfish smile on his lips. "Come, come. This you will enjoy. I promise."

The little man quickened his pace until we'd reached a series of doors on either side of the hall. They weren't cell doors, but they looked sturdy enough. After passing three such doors, Curly paused at the fourth. He took a key from the key ring, and he inserted it into the shiny padlock that was securing a crossbar. With a twist of the key, the lock came loose. Grabbing the crossbar with both hands, Curly wrenched it open.

Then he turned to me.

"Go ahead," Curly said. "Take a look."

"At what?"

"At the reason your friend was martyred. What's inside won't bring him back, but it may help you find purpose in his death."

I stepped past Curly into the dimly lit room, my spider senses tingling.

I have a thing about sharing jail cells with homicidal terrorists. My last operation in Syria had landed me in just such a place. I'd made it out alive only because a troop of Delta assaulters breached the building moments before the jihadis holding me intended to livestream my execution. I'd lived, and the terrorists holding me hadn't.

But that didn't mean I'd gotten away scot-free.

The fingers on my right hand began to tremble.

"What is that?" Curly said, pointing to my hand as he stepped into the room beside me.

"Nothing," I said, clenching my fingers into fists. "What are we here to see?"

Curly looked from my spasming fist to my face. His brown eyes held something I wasn't expecting to see—compassion. Fortunately, he must have decided to play along with my ruse. Instead of asking a follow-up question, he pointed to a dark corner of the wall. "It's over there."

"What is?" I said, clasping my hands behind my back as I fought the tremors.

"The Jew."

I didn't quite follow what Curly was saying, but truth

be told, I wasn't really concentrating. The trembling had spread past my forearms, and spasms were now racking my shoulders. I hadn't had an episode this severe since . . . since that moment on a piss-soaked slab of concrete. The moment when I'd been convinced that my luck had finally run out.

Closing my eyes, I pictured my knockoff Gibson's worn neck. A week or two after I returned from Syria, Laila had surprised me with a high-end Baird acoustic. It was a magnificent instrument, way too much guitar for a strummer like me. But it was still my knockoff Gibson that I pictured in moments like this.

Stretching my fingers across imaginary frets, I started with a mournful E minor chord before sliding to a G. The G transitioned to a D before yielding a bright A. The haunting opening chords of John Anderson's "Seminole Wind" filled my mind, but the spasms continued.

This wasn't working.

"Brother—do you recognize him?"

Opening my eyes, I found Curly in the gloomy corner of the room holding someone by the hair. My teeth chattered. I didn't trust myself to speak, so I shook my head instead.

"Ah, the light in here is terrible," Curly said, reaching into his pocket. "How about now?"

He punctuated the question by activating a small flashlight. The beam caught the person he was holding full in the face, and I sucked in a breath in surprise. The features were black-and-blue, and the nose was pushed slightly off the center. But the person was recognizable all the same. Perhaps not to everyone, but certainly to me.

After all, spies made a habit of learning the faces of those who played the game. But in this incarnation, I wasn't a spy. I was a foreign-born jihadi. So rather than speak the man's name, I slowly shook my head.

"That's okay," Curly said. "I guess I shouldn't have expected you to. He's a Shin Bet agent. A bodyguard."

Curly was wrong. In the lexicon of espionage, agents are the people who are convinced to spy upon their countrymen. The people who do the convincing are known as case officers. If the beaten and bound man crumpled in the corner had been an operative for the Shin Bet, the nation of Israel's internal security force, that would have been his title. But he wasn't a bodyguard or even a member of the Shin Bet. His name was Benny Cohen, and he worked for an altogether different organization.

Benny was Mossad.

THIRTY-SIX

Most people hear the word *Mossad* and equate it with the CIA. This is accurate, after a fashion. But to really understand how the Israeli intelligence organization is an altogether different animal from its American counterpart, you have to understand the history behind the two organizations.

The CIA's heritage hearkened back to the Office of Strategic Services, or OSS, an organization conceived during World War II. This time of blood and fire certainly played a role in forging what would become the world's best-known intelligence agency, but the years following the CIA's 1947 founding were positively docile in comparison with the carnage endured by its predecessor. Don't get me wrong. Convincing men and women to spy against their own countries will never rank as one of the world's safest vocations. Some CIA officers did lose their lives during the Cold War, but these deaths were few and far between. Setting aside the Vietnam War, Agency casualties were almost nonexistent.

In fact, from the founding of the CIA until the war on terror began in earnest on September 11, 2001, only seventy CIA officers were killed in the line of duty. A sacrifice, to be certain, but when you considered that the Agency currently boasted more than twenty-one thousand employees, the chances of finishing out your career and collecting your government pension at age fifty-five were pretty good.

The Mossad had a very different lineage.

Unlike the United States, the modern state of Israel had neither natural barriers in the form of oceans nor friendly countries to act as a buffer against its enemies. In fact, Israel's geographical neighbors had tried on multiple occasions over the nation's short modern history to wipe it from the face of the earth.

During the Yom Kippur War, eight countries attacked Israel from all sides with thousands of armored vehicles, nearly overrunning the tiny country before the Israel Defense Forces counterattacked. Accordingly, Israel's intelligence service didn't have the luxury of playing by the good-old-boy rules the British and the Americans had adopted against the Soviet Union at the height of the Cold War.

No, the Israelis operated by a much simpler and more direct set of guiding principles best articulated by a statement from ancient Jewish law known as the Talmud: *If a man is coming to kill you, rise up and kill him first.*

Long before the Americans began to understand that

killing terrorists in their third-world dens was preferable to waiting for them to land on American soil, Israelis were sending squads of men and women all over the world. Known as *kidon* within the Mossad, these operatives had just one mission: kill the enemies of the state of Israel as if their very lives depended on doing so.

Because they did.

And the crumpled and beaten man on the floor in front of me was not just a high-ranking member of one of the world's most vicious and lethal intelligence agencies. He was director of the Special Operations Division. When it came time to let loose the *kidon* on Israel's enemies, Benny was the one who unchained their collars. Except that right about now, Benny didn't look like he was in charge of much of anything.

His right eye was swollen shut, and his left didn't look any better. His nose had been broken at least once, and rivulets of blood leaked from the corner of his mouth. Curly was holding Benny upright by strands of blood-matted hair, but the Israeli made no attempt to stand. I was guessing this was because he'd tried that already and had received a beating in response.

"He doesn't look like much of a bodyguard," I said, closing the distance to Benny.

Now that I was just an arm's length away, his injuries looked even more severe. Benny's right shoulder hung lower than the left, indicating that his clavicle was either broken or dislocated. His shackled feet were swollen, and his bare toes black-and-blue where they'd been stomped with thick-soled boots. His hands were cuffed in front of him, and two of the fingers on his left hand pointed off at odd angles.

"You mustn't judge a Jew by his appearance," Curly said, turning Benny's face first one way and then the other like he was showing off a freshly caught fish. "They may not look like much, but Shin Bet are worthy adversaries. Paradise is full of brothers who have underestimated these dogs."

As he spoke, Curly slapped Benny's face. The *crack* of flesh on flesh echoed through the small cell like a gunshot. Benny's head lolled back on his neck, drool snaking down his chin in ropy crimson lengths.

"Come on, Jew," Curly said, delivering another slap. "Wake up. We have questions."

This time, Benny's good eye fluttered as his brain tried to make sense of what his overloaded pain receptors were telling him.

"What's going to happen to him?" I said, hoping to spare Benny another slap with my question.

Curly shrugged. "I don't know—that's up to the Iranians. They were hoping to get an American general too, but that ambush failed. Still, in the right hands, a high-ranking Jew can be worth three Americans."

American generals. Interesting. So the Iranians, and by extension their proxy, Hezbollah, were conducting operations in Iraq. And not just ambushing American convoys with EFPs. I'd interrupted a full-on snatch mission—an effort to kidnap an American general from his convoy. That operation had failed, but the one against the Israeli had apparently succeeded.

Learning the itinerary and location of a high-ranking leader was no small intelligence feat. How had this information about not just one but two such officials from different nations been discovered? Maybe the more important question was, what was a Mossad officer doing in Iraq in the first place?

My brain raced, even as Curly fired a jab into Benny's solar plexus. Apparently, slaps weren't getting the job done. Time to move on to sterner stuff. Actually, it would have been nice if Benny had answered a question or two. There was more going on here than met the eye. Much more. And I was still playing catch-up.

Then again, maybe the opportunity to finally seize the initiative was sitting right in front of me if I was audacious enough to take it. As I'm sure Laila would attest, the list of my shortcomings was both long and not particularly distinguished. Fortunately, a lack of audacity wasn't among them.

As Curly reared back his fist for another strike, I snatched his wrist with one hand and drove the combat knife into the base of his skull with the other. The angle was wrong and the lighting poor, so I didn't sever the spinal cord right away. Instead, Curly's eyes bulged, and he struggled. He opened his mouth, but I transferred my grip, sealing his lips with my hand and smothering his cry.

Then I stabbed him in the neck again and again like a runaway sewing machine.

Anyone who says they prefer killing with a knife is either a liar or a psychopath. It's messy work under the best of conditions, and these were far from that. What I did to Curly wasn't enjoyable, but it was necessary. After several terrible seconds, it was done. Curly was dead, I was alive, and a new collection of gore graced the grimy floor.

After wiping the knife clean on Curly's pant leg, I slid it back into my pants before relieving the now-dead Hezbollah commander of his sidearm—a Glock 19. Curly and I couldn't be further apart on matters of ideology, but we shared the same taste in pistols. Perhaps there was a chance for peace in the Middle East after all. Press-checking the gun, I verified that a round was in the chamber, and then let the slide action forward.

With the pistol's comforting weight in my hand, I took a minute to take stock of things. They weren't good. I was covered in the blood of two dead jihadis and sharing cell space with a half-dead Mossad officer. While I was certain there was a punch line in there somewhere, my exhausted brain was having a hard time finding it. Even so, at least I'd bought myself a bit of breathing room.

Or at least that was what I thought for two glorious seconds. Then a pounding from outside the cell rattled the walls, ending my time of peaceful reflection. For a moment I was concerned about following proper prison etiquette. What was the polite thing to do—ask the knocker to enter or open the door myself? So many choices and so little time. In the end, the decision was made for me.

The cell's door swung open.

THIRTY-SEVEN

Now, if this had been a Michael Bay film, the slowly opening door would have revealed a stack of kitted-up Unit assaulters ready to help me escape. Hell, even if it had been a run-of-the-mill shoot-'em-up flick, an element of SEALs with gelled hair and designer sunglasses would have been on the other side.

Unfortunately, this was not a movie. The open door didn't reveal saviors from any military branch. Instead, I found myself face-to-face with the tubby Iranian guard and his ever-present clipboard.

Apparently, our surprise was mutual. The man's sleepy eyes grew alarmedly wide as he looked from me to Curly's body and back again. A particularly suave spy might have been able to defuse the situation with an artfully turned phrase or two. Unfortunately, suave is not my style. In moments like this, I revert to my Ranger pedigree as a blunt-force object. And that was fine, because a little blunt force goes a long way.

Hoisting Curly's limp body in front of me, I shoved the Glock into his back and pulled the trigger three times. In case you were wondering, a corpse does not make the best suppressor. But it will do in a pinch. The three slugs hit the Iranian in a remarkably tight grouping, considering the circumstances. The rounds punched through his solar plexus and breastbone, exiting in a spray of gore. The Iranian collapsed.

Now I had the blood of three dead jihadis on my clothes.

Dropping Curly's remains to the floor, I grabbed Sleepy by the feet and pulled him into the cell, which was now getting a bit crowded. Time to go. Popping my head out of the doorway, I did a quick peek down the hallway. Empty. Things were looking up.

And then Sleepy's radio started to squawk.

My unfortunate lack of suaveness aside, I am pretty good with languages. I speak decent Arabic and can get by in Pashto. Not enough to order a four-course meal, but I can coordinate an ambush with Afghan partners or tell my wife her eyes look pretty with that dress. At least that was what I thought I was saying. In any case, for reasons known only to the Almighty and Allah, Pashto and Farsi were distant cousins. So while I couldn't translate the words broadcasting from Curly's radio verbatim, I understood enough to know that the person on the other end wasn't happy.

Welcome to the club.

Grabbing the Mossad officer under the armpits, I hoisted him to his feet.

"Wakey, wakey, Benny," I said, dragging him toward the door. "Your rescue team is here."

So, calling myself a *team* might have been a bit of an exaggeration, but probably no more so than labeling what I was attempting a *rescue*. A misguided attempt at escape that more than likely would result in the deaths of us both was a much more apt description.

Then again, no one has ever accused case officers of being overly honest.

"Get your ass in gear, Benny," I said, straining against the spy's deadweight. "In case you haven't heard, Iranians aren't so fond of Jews."

Benny's eyes fluttered as we stumbled out the door, and his legs started to bear some of his weight. While I wanted to believe that my rousing speech had prompted the Israeli's newfound spirit of cooperation, it was just as likely that Curly hit like a girl. Either way, the Mossad officer was finally regaining his senses.

Benny mumbled in Hebrew as he propped himself against the wall with manacled hands.

"Couldn't agree more," I said, stooping down to scoop up the still-chattering radio and clip it to my belt. "But if you want to have a more substantive conversation, you need to switch to one of the three languages I speak. Okay, two and a half. My wife refuses to teach me how to swear in Pashto."

Benny gave his head a shake with the vigor of a dog

shedding water from his coat. Then his glassy eyes found mine.

"You're American?" Benny said.

"Of course," I said. "Who were you expecting? The French?"

"Can you uncuff me?" Benny said.

"No."

"Why not?"

"'Cause I didn't have time to grab the keys from the dead guard. Believe it or not, I didn't come here just to rescue you."

"Then why are you here?"

"To save the day, Benny. That's what Americans do. Can you walk?"

The Mossad officer closed his eyes as he swayed against the wall. But to his credit, he nodded.

"Good," I said. "Because Elvis is leaving the building."

Leaving Benny leaning against the wall, I edged down the hallway to the next intersection, leading with Curly's pistol. In the day's first bit of good news, the hallway was clear.

For now.

I ran back, grabbed Benny between the shoulder blades, and steered him down the hall with one hand while holding the Glock along the length of my leg with the other. If I had been in Benny's place, I would have been pretty happy to move from a cell crowded with dead men and covered with gore into a relatively empty hallway.

Unfortunately, the Israeli didn't seem to share my opinion.

"Where's the rest of your team?" Benny said, the words lisping past his battered lips.

"Outside," I said, pushing him down the hallway.

"How far?"

"About six thousand miles, give or take. I'm not exactly sure where we are, so the exact distance is a guess."

Benny mumbled something in Hebrew that I'm fairly certain translated to *Why the hell couldn't the Iranians have killed me when they had the chance?*

I understood how he felt. As Laila had reminded me on countless occasions, my humor was an acquired taste. Also, it became progressively more acquired the closer I came to death. Since our chances of getting out of this hospital turned prison were somewhere in the neighborhood between slim and none, I was probably about as funny as a corpse.

"I don't understand," Benny said, stumbling as his shackled feet tried to keep pace.

"That makes two of us, amigo. Here's the deal—I'm not sticking around, and I figured you probably didn't want to either. The jihadis seem to think you're a Shin Bet bodyguard, but I don't imagine that would have held up too much longer. Consider yourself lucky."

"This is luck?" Benny said.

"For sure. We might actually make it out of here."

"I find that unlikely."

"Fair enough. But I guarantee that if I'd left you in that cell, sooner or later someone would've discovered that you're not a Shin Bet anything."

This brought Benny up short. "You know who I am?" Benny said.

"Damn, son. Have you not been paying attention? I already told you I'm American. We know everything. Keep moving. My Farsi's for shit, but even I can tell that the gentleman on the radio is less than pleased."

As if on cue, the walkie-talkie blasted out another string of gibberish. And this gave me an idea.

"You speak Farsi?" I said, guiding Benny past Sleepy's now-abandoned desk.

"I'm Israeli," Benny said, glancing at me over his shoulder. "We know everything."

"No one likes a smart-ass. Is that a yes?"

"Yes."

"Good," I said, looking down the length of the still-deserted hall as I thought. "When I hold the radio to your lips, use your best scared-shitless Hezbollah accent to yell that the compound is being attacked."

"Which side?"

"I don't know. Pick a cardinal direction and go with it."

"You don't know where we are?" Benny said.

"I didn't exactly get a tour on the way in. Besides, you've got a three-in-four chance of getting this right. Try to be a little vague when you scream."

Benny let loose with another stream of Hebrew. I still didn't know what he was saying, but I had a sneaking suspicion his words weren't too complimentary to Americans. Or maybe just me. But that was okay. Perhaps this was the point in our relationship where we really started to bond. Kind of like Riggs and Murtaugh in *Lethal Weapon*.

"That's the plan?" Benny said, switching back to English. "I scream something vague in Farsi, and we hope for the best? That's it?"

So much for bonding.

"Pretty much. If you don't like it, your cell's that way. Shalom."

"Okay, okay. Give me the radio."

Pushing the transmit button, I held the radio to his lips, waited for Benny to start speaking, and then fired two shots down the empty hallway behind us. Benny shouted, and I released the transmit button.

"What was that?" Benny said, saliva frothing on his lips.

"I wasn't buying your performance," I said, "so I decided to help you sell it."

"You could have told me!"

"Nah—you seem like more of a method actor. Now, keep quiet for a sec."

I shoved the pistol down the back of my pants and then turned the radio's volume and squelch knobs to maximum. This time when I transmitted, a buzz of static greeted me. Locking the transmit button in place, I set the radio on the floor and then helped Benny down the hall.

Was it the best escape plan I'd ever hatched? Nope. But believe it or not, it actually wasn't the worst. Locking the radio into transmit mode was known as hot miking. By setting the radio to continuously broadcast, I'd essentially created a poor man's electronic jammer. Until the jihadis switched frequencies or located my radio, no one would be able to transmit. Hopefully, between the lack of radio communications and the confusion Benny's transmission had helped to create, we'd be able to slip out of the hospital-prison undetected.

Hopefully.

My battalion commander in the Ranger Regiment always said that hope was neither a method nor a combat multiplier. Then again, I was pretty sure he'd never tried to escape from an Iranian detention center with a shackled Mossad officer in tow. Come to think of it, maybe having Benny along for the ride wasn't so bad after all. Between us, we had two of the three Abrahamic faiths covered. All I needed was a Muslim to join the team. Then the Almighty would hear our desperate prayers on all three channels.

I thought about sharing this little insight with Benny, but didn't get the chance. Mainly because at that moment, three people rounded the corner, coming toward us.

For an instant, I'd thought that perhaps the Almighty had decided to cut me a break. Two of the three newcomers I knew, and one was even a Muslim. Then I realized that no, my relationship with the God of Abraham, Isaac, and Jacob was back to the status quo. He was either pissed or amused—most days I had a hard time telling which. My simple escape plan was about to get complicated. The Muslim in the group was Zain, and he had a gun.

A gun that was pointed at Virginia.

THIRTY-EIGHT

If I'd been a normal person, this would have been a fight-or-flight moment. Unfortunately, normal and I had parted ways long ago. So when I saw Zain, Virginia, and an Iranian Quds Force operative dressed in his fancy olive drab uniform, I had a shoot-or-don't-shoot moment instead. As in a do-I-think-I-can-put-a-bullet-into-two-bad-guys-before-they-put-a-bullet-into-me moment.

And this is where the calculus of the situation was not in my favor.

Anyone who knows anything about gunfights will tell you that action beats reaction every time. In this instance, Zain's action had begun the moment he saw me. His eyes had widened, and his index finger had begun taking the slack out of the pistol's trigger.

Since I'd been fiddling with the radio with both hands, my pistol was still in my pants. This meant that no matter how fast I was on the draw, Zain's action would beat my reaction. I could be mad about it, but in the end, my anger wouldn't change a thing. Physics was still physics.

So rather than go for my pistol, I tried something else.

Letting go of Benny, I raised both hands in the air, palms facing Zain, fingers spread. I was hoping that de-escalating would buy me time to somehow change the equation in my favor. But it turns out that my old commander was right—hope was neither a method nor a combat multiplier.

Zain fired his pistol.

And Virginia screamed.

Then the Quds Force operative slumped against the wall before sliding to the floor.

"My friend," Zain said, pointing his pistol downward as a smile stretched across his face. "It's good to see you."

"Pistol on the ground," I said, drawing the Glock from my pants. "Now."

This time I had action on my side. The Glock was locked out in front of me, the front sight post centered on Zain's head. I'd begun my trigger press as the pistol was coming onto target, and the slack was almost gone. The shot would break any second. For all intents and purposes, Zain was already dead.

He just didn't know it yet.

"Wait," Virginia said, stepping across my field of fire. "We're here to rescue you."

Few things piss me off more than someone stopping me from killing a person who needs killing. Then again, I was pretty sure that Virginia was still one of the good guys. At least she had been before I'd escaped from the Devil's henchman, broken up a Hezbollah ambush on an American convoy, survived a helicopter shootdown, and given mouth-to-mouth to a dead jihadi.

I'd been busy.

"There're only two of you, and one of you's wearing handcuffs," I said, pointing at Virginia's shackled wrists. "This doesn't look like much of a rescue."

Virginia said something in return, but Benny's hysterical laughter drowned out her reply.

So unprofessional.

"The handcuffs were part of our ruse," Zain said, handing Virginia a key he pulled from his pocket. "I needed a way to get her inside the compound. Who's your prisoner?"

"I found him in one of the cells," I said. "I figured he could use a lift."

"Ah, the Israeli," Zain said, nodding with approval. "Good thinking, my friend. He'll definitely be useful. Come, come. We don't have much time."

Reaching past Benny, I grabbed Virginia's sleeve and pulled her to the side, clearing my line of fire. "Zain," I said, pointing my pistol at the Syrian one-handed, "don't take this the wrong way, but you are at the top of my shit list. How did you know I was here?"

"Please, Matthew," Zain said, waving away my pistol like he was shooing off a bothersome fly. "It is my job to know things. First we leave, then we talk. Otherwise the diversion is wasted."

"Diversion?" I said.

At that moment a series of deep *whump*s echoed through the building as the walls shook and the lights flickered.

"Mortars," I said.

"Diversion," Zain said. "My men are shelling the compound."

"Interesting approach," I said as bits of plaster dust drifted down from the ceiling like snow. "How do they know they won't accidentally hit us?"

Zain shrugged. "I told them to pick a cardinal direction. There's a three-in-four chance they will miss. You must learn to trust Allah, my friend."

Once again Benny's laughter prevented me from replying. I'd heard that Israelis have a great sense of humor, but this was going too far. Maybe I could file an interagency complaint form later. To be fair, I wasn't all that sure there was going to *be* a later, but I'd burn that bridge when we came to it.

After freeing herself from the handcuffs, Virginia uncuffed Benny next. The Israeli smiled his thanks. He tried to take a step on his own and nearly collapsed.

"Easy there, Benny," I said, slipping his right arm over my left shoulder so I could keep my gun hand free. "Let me help."

I thought Benny was going to object, but he gave a quick nod instead. Given the severity of his wounds, I was amazed he was still standing. Even so, the adrenaline that had gotten him this far seemed to be rapidly fading. He wavered on his feet, and then Virginia slid beneath his other arm.

"Come, come," Zain said, beckoning us forward. "We don't have much time."

Another round of explosions shook the building, the detonations closer. The overhead lights extinguished, plunging the hall into darkness for a second before they flickered back to life.

"All right," I said, shifting my grip on Benny. "Lead the way."

Zain didn't need to be told twice. He took off down the hall, and Virginia and I did our best to follow.

THIRTY-NINE

Wait here," Zain said, bringing our ragtag band of misfits to a halt on the threshold of yet another T intersection.

Benny mumbled.

"Absolutely," I said, sliding past the Israeli as I edged up behind Zain to see what the holdup was.

"What did he say?" Virginia said.

"No idea," I said.

The Israeli had become increasingly lethargic as we'd wandered down the never-ending hallways, and he had taken to muttering in Hebrew. The strain of his injuries was definitely taking a toll, and he'd begun to hallucinate. He needed rest and a doctor's care, but I had no idea when we'd find either.

Sliding forward, I touched Zain on the shoulder. "Why'd we stop?"

"We must wait, my friend."

"For what?"

"The ending."

Zain's answer had an ominous ring that I didn't much care for. Before I could ask for clarification, Benny interrupted with another stream of Hebrew.

"If you want to curse, at least use a language I can understand," I said.

"Not cursing," Benny said. "Praying."

"Sounds reasonable to me," Virginia said, struggling under Benny's weight. "What do you think, Matt?"

"I'd like to understand what Zain meant by *the ending*," I said.

Zain switched to Arabic.

"The finish?" I said, translating on the fly.

"The finale," Benny said.

"Yes, finale," Zain said, pulling a cigar from his pocket and placing the unlit stogie in his mouth. "We must wait for the finale."

"Like at the end of a fireworks show?" I said.

"Yes. That."

Between Zain's passable English and my passable Arabic, our conversations were usually pretty straightforward. But every now and again, talking with him made me feel like a hamster running on an exercise wheel. Sometimes these points of confusion were genuine, and sometimes my asset hid behind linguistic ignorance because he didn't want to elaborate. I was preparing to dig into this particular misunderstanding but didn't get the chance. Mostly because at that moment, a bone-jarring blast hurled me into the far wall like a pinball launched from a rail gun.

The next several seconds were a bit touch and go. My ears were ringing, and the world seemed kind of fuzzy. When my eyes finally focused, I found myself blinking against the sudden onslaught of daylight. What moments before had been a solid cinder block wall now offered a breathtaking view of the rest of the compound.

"Fuck," Benny said from somewhere to my right. "Fuuuuuccccckkkkk."

I wanted to make a smart-ass comment about how the explosion had drastically improved Benny's English, but didn't. The traffic between my brain and my major muscle groups seemed a bit snarled. However, I took the now-familiar urge to vomit as a good sign. My brain might have been banged up, but it was still functioning. Grabbing hold of a chunk of wall, I pulled myself to my feet.

"Benny," I said, coughing through the cloud of choking dust.

"What?"

"Next time you get the urge to pray—don't."

"Fuuucccckkkk," Benny said, elegantly summing up the situation.

"Everybody else okay?" I said while I closed my eyes against the double images and painfully bright sun. "Virginia?"

"Here," Virginia said, her East Tennessee drawl thick enough to spread on biscuits. "What the hell was that?"

"Finale," Zain croaked.

Reaching down, I grabbed Virginia's hand and pulled her to her feet. Then I staggered across the rubble-strewn hallway like a drunken sailor toward Zain. Hooking the Syrian beneath his armpits, I hoisted him up. Half a dozen cuts were weeping blood, turning his face into abstract art, but the stone fragments seemed to have missed his eyes.

Maybe old Benny wasn't so bad at praying after all.

"Is there another finale?" I said, looking at the camp through the gaping hole in the wall. "Like, an encore?"

"No," Zain said, working his cigar out of the rubble and placing it back into his mouth. "Just one. My supply of cruise missiles was limited."

"Fantastic. Wait— Did you say *cruise missile*?"

"Yes—the American Tomahawk version. I acquired the warhead several months ago. This seemed like the right time to use it."

As usual, Zain's response provided more questions than answers. Small arms and even crew-served weapons were fairly easy to acquire, but a cruise missile's one-thousand-pound warhead wasn't on any arms trafficker's menu.

At least not until now.

Before I could ask a clarifying question or two, something caught my eye—a white ambulance with red trim. A crimson crescent graced the hood of the vehicle while twin red crosses were painted on the side panels. The red-and-white light bar on the roof was strobing, but the ambulance wasn't heading toward the front of the hospital.

It was racing toward us.

"Get ready, folks," I said. "We've got company."

"Not company," Zain said, craning his head around my shoulder. "Our rescue." Stepping past me into full view, he waved his arms over his head, and the ambulance flashed its brights in return.

"See?" Zain said. "Rescue."

As recognition signals went, flashing headlights and flailing arms weren't one of the techniques taught at the Farm. Then again, hanging out in the prison-hospital until one of the Quds Force operatives or Hezbollah fighters discovered us didn't seem like such a good idea either. I had no idea what had happened with Zain, but I'd take my chances with him over ending up in a cell with Benny any day.

Flashing headlights and flailing arms it was.

The ambulance slid to a stop in a cloud of dust, and two men dressed in scrubs hopped out. The driver ran to the back of the vehicle and opened the rear doors while the passenger sprinted over to Zain. The Syrian stopped him with a burst of Arabic and then pointed at Virginia. With a quick nod, the passenger scooped the chemist into his arms and carried her to the back of the ambulance. I expected a string of twangy curse words, but Virginia croaked a simple "Thank you" instead before sagging against the man's chest.

"Don't worry," I said as her eyes found mine. "Your first concussion is always your worst. It's all downhill after this."

Virginia didn't reply. Instead, she let a slender middle finger do the talking as the two men helped her inside the ambulance. I took the gesture as a sign that my favorite scientist was well on the road to recovery.

"Help," Benny said. "Please."

I turned toward the Israeli, but the smart-ass comment I'd prepared died on my lips. His right arm was hanging limp, and his pants were soaked in blood. After hoisting him into a fireman's carry, I jogged toward the ambulance.

Or at least tried to.

My head pounded in time with my steps like each footfall was rattling my brain inside my skull. I'd been dangerously close to exploding ordnance before, but never had the pleasure of experiencing the blast wave generated by a cruise missile's massive warhead.

Yet another item I could check off my bucket list.

I waited for the passenger and the driver to exit the rear of the ambulance before dumping the Mossad officer onto an empty stretcher. Then I helped Zain inside. Finally, it was my turn. I climbed into the blessedly cool interior and slammed the doors shut behind me. As soon as I was settled, Zain pounded on the partition separating us from the driver, and the vehicle surged forward.

We were all pretty banged up, but Benny was far and away the worst. He'd been in bad shape before, and the explosion hadn't exactly done wonders for his injuries. Rummaging through the cabinets built into the ambulance, I found a pair of trauma scissors and got to work on his pants. Since the Mossad officer was breathing without trouble, Triage 101 dictated that I needed to locate and stop the source of his bleeding before addressing any of Benny's other wounds.

After removing both pant legs, I found the problem. A piece of shrapnel had torn a gaping hole midway up

Benny's thigh. His femoral artery was untouched, but he was still bleeding like a stuck pig.

"Hey, Benny," I said, breaking open a packet of Quik-Clot gauze, "how you doing?" In situations like this, shock was often far more dangerous than the initial wound. Keeping the patient talking was one way to mitigate its effects.

"Benny," I said again as I stuffed the gauze into the wound and then wrapped the excess around his leg. "Can you hear me?"

"Unfortunately, yes."

His voice was slurred and his cadence sluggish. Shock was definitely setting in.

"Good," I said, grabbing Benny's hand and placing it on the gauze. "'Cause I need some help. Put pressure on this while I find a bandage. Also, would it have killed you to wear underwear today?"

"Sorry. I wasn't expecting visitors."

I found a pressure bandage and applied it directly over the gauze. The bleeding had already begun to slow as the clotting agent did its work, but I wasn't taking any chances. If the combined bandages didn't work, the next step was to tourniquet the leg. But first, I needed to push fluids to compensate for his blood loss.

Whoever had stocked the ambulance had done their job well. A series of IV kits was laid out on the shelf next to me. Choosing the nondislocated arm, I applied a tourniquet, readied the catheter, and promptly blew through the vein I was targeting.

"Shit," I said.

"Goddamn," Benny said, flinching as the needle bit through his skin. "Have you done this before?"

"On goats," I said. "But they didn't bitch as much. Also, they were a lot better hydrated. You should drink more water."

"I'll take that up with my Iranian jailers."

"Maybe angle the needle a bit," Virginia said. "That's how they do it on TV."

"Or don't push as hard," Zain said.

"Either of you want to do this?" I said, glaring at Zain and Virginia.

"Nope," Virginia said.

"You're doing a fine job," Zain said.

"Then shut the fuck up," I said, targeting another vein. This time, I slid the needle in like I'd been starting IVs my entire life. Ten seconds later I had the catheter taped down, the IV tubing attached, and saline flowing through the line.

Success.

"Tell me, Benny," I said, setting the valve controlling the fluid-flow rate to the maximum, "did you ever imagine that you'd end your captivity strapped half naked to a stretcher with your junk hanging out in the breeze?"

"No," the Israeli said. "I thought I'd be executed."

"Well, then you must be pretty happy with how things turned out."

"I'm not sure. The day's not over."

Truer words had never been spoken.

FORTY

So, now might be a good time to explain why you betrayed me to the Devil," I said, eyeing Zain. Once I'd finished with Benny, I'd taken a seat across from the smuggler, but not before drawing the Glock. It wasn't exactly pointed at Zain, but it wasn't exactly pointed away from him either. As Dad used to say, fool me twice, and I'm not a smart boy. Or maybe that had been Mom. Dad's folksy wisdom usually included an abstract reference to the pope.

"Good idea, my friend," Zain said. "We should be safe for at least the next fifteen minutes."

The thing about being a smart-ass is that it's damned hard to pull off when there's more than one in the crowd. Except in this case, I was fairly certain that Zain wasn't joking, which meant I had a different sort of problem altogether.

"Start talking," I said, reaching above my head to

grab one of the canvas handholds dangling from the ceiling.

Whatever our driver lacked in skill, he made up for with urgency. He'd been taking turns hard the entire time, but the last one felt like we'd been up on two wheels. I'd expected the first couple of minutes to be a bit hairy while we were still navigating the confines of the Iranian outpost. An outpost under mortar fire by Zain's men, I'll add. All things considered, this was actually a pretty good rescue.

So far.

But perhaps I needed to reserve judgment until I heard Zain's story.

"Certainly," Zain said, squaring his back against the ambulance's pitching wall like he was a tribal storyteller sitting around a campfire. "But where should I start? Before I shot you or after?"

"What?" Virginia said.

The Israeli gave a dry chuckle from his stretcher as if nothing really surprised him at this point.

I knew the feeling.

"So, I'm assuming Zain left out a couple of details when he met you at the airport," I said to Virginia.

"You could say that," Virginia said, pinning the smuggler to the wall with her glare. "He said that you were in trouble and needed our help."

"All true," Zain said.

"Except you didn't mention the part about selling me out to the Devil?" I said.

"How far is it to Tel Aviv?" Benny said, struggling upright. "I'm sure I could walk."

"You wouldn't make it ten feet," I said, pushing the Mossad officer back onto his stretcher before turning to Zain. "Why don't you start with why you made a bargain with the man who wanted to kill me? Seems like as good a place as any."

"Oh, that's simple," Zain said. "The Devil came to me with an offer—betray you or watch as he murdered my family."

"He has that kind of power?" I said. "Even over you?"

"Especially over me," Zain said, his thin features stretching into a mask of anger. "I might run the largest logistics network in Syria and Iraq, but I'm still just a simple smuggler. The Devil's influence extends far beyond just criminal enterprise. His tentacles reach from the slums of Aleppo to the Council of Representatives in Baghdad. His enforcers are former Iraqi commandos. His lunch guests are heads of state. The Devil doesn't negotiate with a man like me. He makes demands, and I follow them or suffer the consequences."

Zain actually shuddered when he finished speaking, and the gesture spoke volumes. My asset and onetime friend was an opportunist, but more than that, he was a survivor. A survivor who'd scratched out a living in the midst of one of the bloodiest civil wars in history. The horrors he'd witnessed were unimaginable, and he'd grown numb to threats in the process. Seeing friends and loved ones murdered tends to have that effect. But even a jaded veteran like Zain reacted viscerally to a threat from the Devil.

"Then why are you helping us now?" Virginia said.

Zain shrugged. "Technically, I fulfilled my end of the bargain. I delivered my friend Matthew into the Devil's hands."

"I doubt the Devil will see it that way," Virginia said.

Zain glanced at the chemist, but it was me his hard eyes found when he answered. "Maybe he won't," Zain said with another shrug. "But that does not change my responsibility."

"What responsibility?" I said.

Zain gave an exasperated sigh. "Matthew, I am not naive about the nature of our relationship. You are my handler. I am your agent, and I provide you intelligence. In turn, you provide things of value to my organization. We are businessmen, you and I."

"That's the same thing the Devil said," I said.

"The Devil is no more a businessman than Saddam Hussein was a diplomat," Zain said. "He is a barbarian, plain and simple. A barbarian willing to use any means necessary to achieve his goals."

"Forgive me," I said, "but from where I'm sitting, the difference between barbarian and businessman isn't always readily apparent."

"I understand why you might feel that way," Zain said. "But let me explain. I wasn't being completely truthful a minute ago, Matthew. Perhaps at one time we were just businessmen, but that is no longer the case. You've broken bread at my house. You've met my wife and held my children. These things matter. For an Arab, one thing will always come before profit, country, or even tribe. Family. I'm sorry for what you went through, but you must understand that I would never have left you with the Devil. You are family, Matthew. I don't betray my family."

"Then why hand me over in the first place?" I said.

"To buy time," Zain said.

"Time for what?" I said.

"Vengeance," Benny murmured from his stretcher.

"The Jew is right," Zain said, leaning forward to clasp my hands with his bony fingers. "An enemy has attacked my family. This must be met with vengeance. Blood and honor demand no less."

I looked at Zain while I turned his answer over in my mind, considering. What he said was believable, and his actions spoke even louder than his words. If not for him, I would still be trying to find my way out of the Iranian outpost with Benny in tow. And then there was Virginia. Zain certainly could have sweetened his deal with the Devil by tossing in Virginia, but he hadn't.

In any case, I needed him. I'd come here to rescue a fifteen-year-old girl and kill the Devil. I couldn't do either of those things without help. As Frodo had so succinctly stated, this was an outside job. A statement even more true now that the Devil had compromised my life back home. Even if I had a way to contact Frodo and Katherine for help, I couldn't risk it. Not until I understood how far the Devil had penetrated. And then there was Laila. The thought of my beautiful wife obliviously drinking a coffee as professional killers watched her every move turned my stomach into knots.

The way to protect Laila was simple—eliminate the Devil. But that was easier said than done. A man with the means and the reach to find me in Austin would not be easy to put down on his home turf. I needed help to kill the Devil.

I needed Zain.

"Okay, my friend," I said, extricating my hands from Zain's. "I accept your apology and welcome your assistance. After rescuing me, what did you plan to do next?"

Zain looked at me with a confused expression. "Next? There is no next. I am a smuggler, not a soldier, Matthew. Even so, I do know this—you are not a man to be trifled with. Setting you free is like uncaging a lion. My plan was to open your cage while trying not to get torn to pieces in the process. Tell me what you need, and I'll provide it."

His answer made sense. Though this part of the world boasted smartphones and Internet cafés, Western influence went only so far. Here, vendettas were still settled with the same ruthlessness that had made Zain's ancestors feared by empires the world over. By aiding me, Zain was doing the equivalent of slapping the Devil across the face with a leather glove and demanding satisfaction.

Except that in the Middle East, satisfaction mirrored a fight scene from *John Wick* more than a gentlemanly duel with pistols at ten paces. By rescuing me, Zain had just kicked off a blood feud with the Middle East's most notorious criminal. I could see why he wanted me to take the lead on what happened next.

"All right," I said as the truck made an abrupt turn to the left, "where are we headed now?"

"To one of my safe houses," Zain said. "It's well guarded, and my top lieutenants will be waiting for us."

"Why?" I said.

"To convene a war council. You are a deadly man, Matthew. But you cannot take on an army alone."

"I appreciate that, my friend," I said. "But before we meet your men, I'd like you to fill in some blanks. You said that the Devil came to you with an offer, correct?"

Zain nodded.

"So he knew I was coming to Iraq?"

Another nod.

"How?"

Zain shook his head. "Matthew, you are a brilliant spy, but sometimes you refuse to see what is right in front of you. The Devil knew that you were coming to Iraq the same way that Sayid was able to ambush you and Frodo as you tried to save your asset. Because someone told him."

In that moment, everything went fuzzy, as if I was looking at the world through the reflection of a fogged mirror. The ambient sounds faded to low murmurs while the ambulance's cramped cabin morphed into unrecognizable blobs of abstract art.

Part of me was aware that Zain's matter-of-fact statement had caused quite a stir. Questions were shouted, and Virginia was gesturing. Even Benny was diving into the mix. But I couldn't understand what they were saying. Or maybe I didn't want to. The implications of Zain's statement were rebounding inside my skull like the aftershocks from an earthquake.

Because someone told him.

In a flash, I was back in Syria with a semiconscious Frodo beside me. I could feel the throbbing where a bullet had torn through my leg. Taste the bitter metallic despair that came with knowing that Frodo and I would not survive the complex ambush that had ensnared us. An ambush initiated with an EFP that had disabled our Range Rover and amputated Frodo's left arm in a storm of blood and fire. We'd fled our vehicle only to be caught in a kill zone formed by two crew-served weapons and a squad of dismounted riflemen.

We were done.

I'd tried to call for the quick reaction force, or QRF, only to discover that my state-of-the-art software-driven radio had malfunctioned. As had Frodo's. A 7.62mm round through my leg had ended my attempt to carry Frodo to safety. Now, back-to-back with my critically injured friend, I was determined to honor my Ranger Regiment heritage and go out fighting.

Peering through the Trijicon 4x32 optic attached to my M4 rifle, I'd spotted a jihadi with a cell phone to his ear and a radio in his hand. Convinced that he was the one directing the ambush, I'd sighted on his exposed head and pulled the trigger. But even here, Syria was conspiring against me. An errant gust of wind had altered my shot's trajectory. Instead of blowing out the back of his head, I'd opened a bloody furrow down the side of his face.

Just my luck.

But the wounded jihadi hadn't ordered his squad of assaulters to bound toward us and finish the job. Instead, his men had broken contact and melted away just as a pair of Black Hawk Direct Action Penetrator gunships appeared on the horizon.

The rest was a blur of swirling dust and shouted commands. I remember the first gunship touching down, and medics running toward us. Everything else I saw through the haze that follows a morphine stick.

Zain's words prompted me to relive that scene from beginning to end, moment by moment, frame by frame. The scorching heat and eardrum-rupturing shriek as the EFP shredded the Range Rover. The iron tang of blood. The sour taste of fear. The horror of Frodo's injuries. The failure of our radios. The searing pain as a hundred-twenty-two-grain bullet punched through my leg. The sense of despair accompanying the realization that death was imminent.

Then the incredible relief when the DAPs appeared.

There.

In the moment between despair and salvation, I realized what I'd seen before but had never acknowledged. The image that had lurked in my subconscious agitating against my thoughts like a pebble in a shoe.

A cell phone.

Sayid had been talking on a cell phone.

To whom?

"Matthew!"

Startled, I realized that my fellow passengers were no longer quarrelling. In fact, they weren't even speaking. Instead, they were staring at me.

"Matthew!" Zain said again, grabbing my shoulder. "Are you here?"

"Yes," I said, still gathering my wits. "Sorry. What did you say?"

"I said that we've arrived at the safe house," Zain said, sliding back against the wall. "We're out of danger for the moment, but not for long. What now?"

"Easy," I said, getting to my feet and opening the ambulance's doors. "First, I find the Devil. Then I figure out who's been feeding him information."

"After that?" Zain said.

"After that, I'll kill them both," I said.

"Wait," Virginia said, grabbing my arm. "What about Nazya's sister? Are we leaving her with the sex traffickers?"

"Of course not," I said, climbing out of the ambulance, and then turning to lend Virginia a hand. "In fact, I think we can use Ferah to find the Devil."

"How?" Virginia said.

"We still have access to the Facebook page the Devil is using to auction her. It should lead us to him."

"But Zain just said someone has been feeding the Devil information. Someone who knew you were coming to Iraq. Aren't you worried that your reach back to Frodo is compromised?"

"I know it is," I said. "The Devil was pretty clear about that. He showed me encrypted text messages, transcriptions of conversations from my secure phone, pictures of Frodo, James, the whole gang. *Compromised* is too tame for what happened. We're so far burned, it makes what the FBI informants did to the Gambino crime family look like a bunch of teen gossip."

"Then how will we find Ferah?" Virginia said.

"We won't," I said. "Benny will."

FORTY-ONE

Virginia and Zain both turned to the Mossad officer, who was trying to hobble from the ambulance unassisted. For a moment, Benny seemed surprised at the sudden audience, but then he began to shake his head.

Violently.

"I have no idea what you're discussing, and I don't want to," the Israeli said, eventually giving in as two of Zain's men kept him from tumbling to the ground. "I appreciate your help, but kindly lend me a cell phone, and I will be on my way."

"Sorry, Benny," I said, shouldering his weight, "but we're going to need a favor first."

Benny frowned as if his battered brain was struggling to translate my words from English to Hebrew. Or more likely because what I was implying was a bit too over-the-top, even for me.

"So I'm a hostage now? Are you insane?"

"Of course not," I said with more than a little exasperation. "But I need your help. Desperately. Do you know why the Devil didn't just kill me?"

Benny shook his head.

"Because he wanted me to do a job for him. A job back in the US."

"What kind of job?" Benny said.

"He wouldn't say," I said, my stomach clenching as I relived the horror of those brief moments. "But he did tell me what would happen if I didn't complete his assignment. Or more precisely what would happen to my wife."

"He has your wife?" Virginia said.

"No. But he doesn't need to. He has a team surveilling her. He showed me pictures of her at her favorite coffee shop. In real time. And then he let me know how thoroughly he'd penetrated our organization, just in case I thought about reaching back to them for help. Then he gave me a phone I was supposed to keep on me at all times and assigned one of his thugs as my minder."

"Where're the phone and the minder now?" Virginia said.

"The minder's dead, and the phone burned up in a helicopter crash."

"Then the Devil thinks you're dead?" This time the question came from Zain.

"I'm not sure," I said. "But if he did, it would go a long way toward protecting my wife."

"I can help with that," Zain said. "My network will start rumors feeding faulty intelligence to the Devil's men. I'll make sure you're included in the casualty list from the convoy ambush. The Devil will eventually figure out the truth, but it will take him a day or two to separate fact from fiction."

I nodded, trying to look positive while I thought through the alternatives. If the Devil believed I was dead, he would have no reason to go after Laila. But if he suspected otherwise, my wife would pay the price.

In an instant, I was back at Taj's Place what seemed like a hundred years ago. The images came in rapid fire. The cream curve-hugging dress and silky brown skin. Midnight hair tumbling across bare shoulders. Green eyes shimmering with tears as she stood to leave.

I just want my husband back.

Her husband had been sitting right in front of her. Why hadn't I just told her that? Why had I let her walk away?

I just want my husband back.

Ripping myself back to the present, I focused on Benny. "My wife's life is in danger. To save her, I have to get to the Devil. The only way I can do that is to find where he's auctioning this girl."

I grabbed Virginia's phone and held it in front of Benny's face. "Her name is Ferah, and she's just fifteen. Fifteen, Benny. Help me find her."

"Why can't your NSA localize the website's IP address?" Benny said, looking away from the phone.

"Because someone close to me is feeding the Devil information," I said. "I don't know who, or how deeply he's penetrated my organization. I need your help. To put it more specifically, I need Unit 8200's help."

Benny glared at me, his eyes narrowing. Unit 8200 was Israel's answer to the NSA. While its existence wasn't denied, the organization wasn't exactly discussed in everyday conversation either.

"You don't know what you're asking," Benny said.

"Wrong," I said. "I know exactly what I'm asking. I'm asking for your assistance in a joint intelligence operation between the United States and the nation of Israel. An operation that will result in the death of a major destabilizing force in the Middle East."

"And what do I get out of this joint operation?" Benny said.

"Besides your life?" Virginia said. "Matt could have left you to rot."

"Easy now, Tennessee," I said, putting my hand on Virginia's arm. "This is just how Israelis negotiate. Don't take it personally. Besides, Benny's question is a fair one. If somebody asked me to authorize the NSA to run a collection against a foreign target, I'd want to know how it would help me too. Fair enough. But maybe I should start with a question—how exactly did you end up in that Iranian cell, Benny?"

The Mossad officer glared at me. But he didn't answer, which made me think I was on the right track.

"What's wrong?" I said. "Cat got your tongue? Okay, how about this? I'll make up a story, and you just listen, okay?"

Benny gave a small nod.

"Great," I said. "Here goes. In the short time I've been in-country, I couldn't help but notice how openly the Quds Force is operating. Usually the Iranians are content to stay out of the way while Hezbollah stirs up trouble for them. But not now. Hell, I wouldn't be surprised if the ambush on the American convoy I broke up had Quds Force members directing it. And that's pretty damn blatant since Tehran is about one thousand miles east of here. But you already knew about the Quds Force presence, didn't you, Benny?"

The Mossad officer didn't confirm my suspicions. But he didn't deny them either. Time to press forward.

"I have to think that the folks back in Jerusalem might have found all of this a wee bit disconcerting," I said. "In fact, I have a sneaking suspicion that Iranians on the ground in Iraq are also a wee bit disconcerting for the Iraqis. Especially the Sunni Muslim politicians in parliament who don't particularly want their country to become a de facto land bridge between Iran and Syria. I can't imagine it sits well with them to know that the Alawite sect exterminating Sunni rebels in Syria is being resupplied by Iran through Iraq. Enjoying the story so far?"

Another nod.

"Good, 'cause here's where it gets interesting. If I were in your shoes, I might fall back onto the old adage that the enemy of my enemy is my friend. I might even think it's worthwhile to travel covertly into Iraq to meet with a like-minded counterpart in the Iraqi National Intelligence Service. Except that something went wrong and instead of shaking hands with an Iraqi intelligence operative, you found yourself staring down the business end of an Iranian rifle. How'd I do?"

Benny stared at me for a beat, his face blank. Then he spoke. "What are you offering?"

"The Devil. You heard Zain describe him. His influence reaches from the slums of Aleppo to the halls of parliament. I don't think it's too much of a stretch to imagine that the man who employs former Iraqi commandos as his muscle probably had something to do with your blown operation. Help me find this girl and, by extension, the Devil. I'll bag him and give him to you."

"I thought you were going to kill him," Zain said.

I shrugged. "Let's just say that when it comes to killing, the Mossad's reputation precedes it. I have no reservations about your organization's ability and willingness to finish the job once I start it. Think about it—you get the Devil, his network, and the Hezbollah and Quds Force operatives on his payroll. Say yes, Benny. It's the best deal you're going to get."

Benny shook his head and mumbled another indecipherable phrase of Hebrew.

"What's that?"

"I said, give me a phone. Please."

"See?" I said, helping the spy up the steps to the safe house. "I knew we'd be friends."

FORTY-TWO

H ow does it taste?" Zain said, pushing another plate full of food toward me.

"Delicious," I said, forking a portion of meat into a warm pita and then taking a bite. "Simply delicious."

The meal was the first real one I'd had in twenty-four hours, and when it came to Middle Eastern hospitality, Zain didn't disappoint. After providing Benny with a phone, the smuggler had shown us to a table laden with dishes. The small feast had a sampling of everything that was good about Syrian cuisine—meze, kebab, kubbeh, desserts, and cups of strong dark coffee.

The smell was tantalizing, the meat straight from the grill, and the vegetables freshly harvested. And yet, contrary to what I'd told Zain, each bite had the culinary delight of sawdust. I ate to fill my stomach, nothing more. Perhaps because the whole of my attention was centered on the battered and bruised Israeli whispering into a cell phone.

The two men who had driven the rescue ambulance were smugglers like Zain, not medics. As such, the task of tending to Benny's injuries had fallen to me. As a Ranger, I'd audited parts of the thirty-six-week special operations combat medics course, but I was no medic. I could perform basic triage and trauma-mitigation tasks, but anything more complex was beyond my skill set. With Benny, I'd immobilized the bones I thought were broken, stopped the bleeding of his open wounds, and continued to push fluids. I'd given him low-level painkillers, but we'd mutually agreed to hold off administering anything stronger until he finished this phone call.

He was currently reclining on a couch in an adjacent room, his saline bag dangling from a field-expedient hanger I'd made using a light fixture. I'd moved him away from the community table, both so that he could conduct his conversation in private and so that he didn't have to watch as we ate. Until I was sure he didn't have internal injuries, he was on a saline diet.

But the right to privacy went only so far, especially when my wife's life balanced on the outcome of Benny's phone call. I was doing my best to eavesdrop, though Benny wasn't making my task any easier. He conducted the conversation in the guttural language of his people, as ancient as the desert sands surrounding Zain's spacious safe house. My Hebrew was rudimentary, to say the least, but like any case officer worth his salt, I was a dedicated student of body language.

Benny's was telling me plenty.

The intelligence officer had begun the call with an even cadence, no doubt providing identifying information and a code word to a very surprised Mossad phone operator. But once his bona fides had been established, Benny abandoned any pretense of normalcy. His Hebrew acquired a machine gun's staccato, ending with a crescendo that had Benny sitting up and yelling into the phone, despite his injuries.

After the better part of three minutes spent filling the airwaves with a constant stream of Hebrew, Benny paused, seemingly midsentence. For thirty long seconds, he remained frozen in place like an artist's model. Then he closed his eyes and eased onto his back. One hand ventured up to finger the splint I'd taped across his broken nose as he continued to listen in silence.

It was the silence that had turned Zain's delectable cuisine to ash. Shouting I could handle, but the deathly quiet from a man accustomed to giving orders was terrifying. Six thousand miles away, the woman I loved was at the mercy of a team of assassins. My plan to rescue her depended on cooperation from an Israeli who should have been at this moment rambunctiously planning his enemies' deaths.

Instead, he was as silent as a tomb.

Something was wrong. Very, very wrong.

With a final *ken*, Benny hung up the phone. Then he looked at me.

"There is a problem," the Israeli said, framing the words with a delicacy that was itself alarming.

"No kidding," Virginia said. "Perhaps you'd like to be more specific."

Another time, her sarcasm would have brought a smile to my face. But like the taste of Zain's magnificent food, the look on Benny's face turned any feeling of mirth to ash.

"The Iranians. They're pushing into Iraq."

"What?" I said. "More Hezbollah operatives?"

Benny slowly shook his head. "No. A Quds Force mechanized division. The Persians are going to war."

"Iran is invading Iraq?" I said.

"Yes," Benny said, "though they aren't terming it as such. Officially, the mechanized division is performing a peacekeeping mission. The Quds Force is assisting the Iraqi army by securing the resupply routes bridging Iran and Syria. But it's an invasion all the same. This is exactly what I was trying to prevent. I'm sorry about your wife— I really am. But Unit 8200 has more important taskings now."

"So that's it?" Virginia said, slamming her cup down on the table. "We save your life and get nothing but a thank-you in return?"

"No," Benny said, standing on unsteady feet, "you get the gratitude of the Mossad. That is not an insignificant thing."

Virginia leaned forward in her seat, ready to go another round, but my hand on her sleeve brought her up short.

"Let it go, East Tennessee," I said, squeezing her arm. "At the end of the day, Benny's first, middle, and last concern will always be the people of Israel. I'd have the same priorities in his position."

"No, you wouldn't," Virginia said.

Her statement lacked the emotion of her earlier outburst, but her matter-of-fact manner carried weight all the same. And the truth of it was, she was right. But that was neither here nor there. Benny's world had just turned upside down. Unless we were going to literally hold the Mossad operative hostage in exchange for his country's help, we were out of luck. Benny had called our bluff. I had enough shit going sideways at the moment. I wasn't about to add kidnapping Benny to the mix.

Besides, though Benny probably wasn't going to make my Christmas card list, I believed him when he said he owed me. In the business of espionage, having a high-ranking member of Israel's feared intelligence service in your debt was no small matter.

"No worries, Benny," I said, pushing away from the table to offer the Israeli a handshake. "Do what you need to do. If you need a lift somewhere, I'm sure Zain will oblige."

"No need," Benny said, giving us a weary smile. "I took the liberty of instructing my service to triangulate your phone. My compatriots should be arriving shortly."

As if on cue, the sound of rotor blades reverberated throughout the room. I looked at Zain, preparing to tell the smuggler to let his guards know that the incoming choppers were friendly, but my asset was already issuing commands to his subordinates in a steady stream of Arabic.

"Color me impressed, Benny," I said, helping the Mossad officer out to the building's courtyard. "Y'all had helicopters already pre-positioned. For a country of eight million, you have quite the operational reach."

"I've been missing for over a week," Benny said as a UH-60 Black Hawk did a low pass over the house before setting up an approach to the large courtyard. "Those helicopters were probably flown into country aboard C-130s within hours after I missed my first check-in. We don't leave people behind. Ever."

The Black Hawk touched down in a man-made storm of dust and grit. I put Benny's arm over my shoulder one last time to keep him upright, and to my surprise, he pulled me in for a hug.

"What I said about my gratitude wasn't just words," Benny said, yelling over the helicopter's twin turboshaft engines. "My service repays its debts."

Before I could reply, Benny ducked under the spinning rotor blades and climbed into the helicopter's cabin. With a roar of its turbine engines, the UH-60 leapt from the ground and thundered out of the compound, its wingman in trail.

"What now?" Virginia said, shading her eyes with her hand as she watched the helicopter fly out of sight.

"That's a good question," I said, heading back into the compound. "Benny flying the coop is a bitch, no two ways about it. Without him, I'm back to square one."

"What do you mean?" Virginia said.

Instead of answering her question, I turned to my asset and maybe friend. "Zain, I'm assuming that if your network put out some feelers, you could find the location of tonight's auction?"

The smuggler shrugged. "I believe so, yes. These *gawads* tend to advertise. The auction will allow men to purchase new slaves as well as trade in their current ones."

"Trade in?" Virginia said.

Zain nodded. "Yes. Most of the girls are exchanged numerous times. A man takes one home for a week, and when he tires of her, he sells his slave to someone else and buys another."

"Motherfuckers," Virginia said, her cream complexion flushing crimson.

"So finding the auction and by extension Ferah is doable," I said, thinking out loud, "but that's only half of the problem."

"What do you mean?" Virginia said.

"It's like this—rescuing Nazya's sister, while noble, does nothing to protect the next defenseless girl or the one after her. Zain, you said the Iraqi authorities have known about this sex-trafficking ring for some time. Why haven't the police done anything about it?"

"The Devil."

"Exactly. The key to all of this—Nazya, Ferah, Laila, the assassins trying to punch my ticket, the mole—all of it comes back to one man. The Devil. If we leave here without putting him in the ground, nothing will change. But without the NSA or Israel's Unit 8200, I don't see a way to get a lock on the Devil. He survived Saddam Hussein, the American invasion, the Iraqi civil war, and ISIS. He's a shadow. If he doesn't want to be found, he won't be."

"So maybe we make him come to us," Virginia said.

"How?"

"The same way you land any fish—by dangling something they really want in front of their nose."

"And that would be?"

"Me."

FORTY-THREE

Hang on," I said. "I must have misheard. For a second, I could have sworn you were suggesting we use you to bait a homicidal maniac."

"That's exactly what I'm suggesting," Virginia said.

"No."

"But you haven't even heard my plan."

"And I don't need to. The answer's still no."

"Why? Because I'm a girl and you think it's too dangerous?"

"Because you aren't a trained operative," I said. "Don't get me wrong. You're good at this. You're great at thinking on your feet, and I wouldn't have gotten this far without you. In fact, I think you have what it takes to be a case officer. But you aren't one yet. Not by a long shot."

"So this has nothing to do with the fact that I'm a woman and you want to protect me?"

"No."

Okay, so maybe Virginia's gender did play a small role in my calculus—I'd seen what those monsters had done to Nazya. I had no intention of letting East Tennessee get in the same zip code with a bunch of serial rapists, some of whom were convinced that their atrocities were sanctioned by Allah. But that didn't make my stated reason any less true. Virginia was not a trained operative, plain and simple.

"Well, that's funny," Virginia said, hands on her hips as her eyes bored into mine, "because me being a woman has everything to do with why I want in on this. Right now a fifteen-year-old girl is in the hands of the same beasts who gang-raped her sister. Fifteen. In a sane world she'd be practicing hairstyles with her friends. Instead she's about to be auctioned off as a sex slave."

"We'll get Ferah out," I said. "I promise."

"And I believe you," Virginia said, "but that's not good enough. Not anymore. You said it yourself—as long as the Devil's still breathing, she won't be the last fifteen-year-old at risk. I know you're worried about exposing me to more than I signed up for. I get it. Really I do. But I'm telling you that as a woman, as a human being, I won't be able to live with myself if I do nothing. I don't want to just rescue Ferah. I want to save all the girls. Every last one. To do that, we have to cut the head off this snake. We have to get to the Devil."

"I understand," I said, frustration coloring my words. "But I still don't get where you come in."

"That's because you're a man. A good man. But the

Devil isn't. I've heard how you described him—a business-man, not a jihadi. But more than that, he's a kingpin—a gangster. He wears handmade leather shoes and tailored shirts. It's not enough that he's successful. The Devil is into status. And what do you think is the ultimate status symbol for a piece-of-shit Arab sex trafficker?"

"A Western woman," Zain said from across the room.

"Exactly," Virginia said, turning to acknowledge his comment, "but not just any Western woman. Someone who looks completely different from the women here. Someone with blue eyes, auburn hair, and pale skin. Someone his friends would consider exotic. And do you know what would really get his rocks off?"

"An American woman," Zain answered.

"Bingo," Virginia said. "We land the Devil by baiting the hook with something he'll want as soon as he sees it—me. You said it yourself—Zain's men might find the auction's location, but we won't be sure the Devil will be there. Not unless I'm on the auction block."

"What if he sends someone else to bid for him?" I said.

Virginia smiled as she shook her head. "Not gonna happen. The Devil is a peacock. He isn't going to send an underling to take possession of his new toy. Not our guy. He'll show up to collect his American whore in person so that everyone can see. You know I'm right."

She was right, but that didn't mean I had to like it. On the surface, her plan had real merit. More than that, it was the only shot we had. The only shot Laila had. But just because Virginia's plan was sound didn't mean that my earlier objections were moot. I understood what she was saying, and I felt the veracity of her words in my bones. I even understood why she felt the way that she did. After all, Virginia was the one who'd heard Nazya's agonizing story firsthand.

But that didn't change the fact that Virginia wasn't qualified to do what she was proposing. She was a quick study and a steady hand, but at the end of the day, she was still a chemistry professor, not a spy. As much as she insisted otherwise, Virginia didn't understand what she was signing up for, not in the visceral, blood-in-the-dirt way that I did. If I went through with this, I was potentially exchanging one woman's life for another's— Virginia for Laila.

That was something I simply could not do.

"I'm sorry, Virginia," I said. "I really am. But I can't let you do this. I've been captured by the Devil twice. Each time I barely escaped with my life."

"But I'll have an advantage that you didn't," Virginia said.

"What?" I said.

"You. Look, you recruited me, remember? You said that I'd have the chance to do something that would light my blood on fire. Something that really mattered. We're talking about rescuing a fifteen-year-old girl from a bunch of monsters. I can't think of too many things that matter more than that. Truthfully, I'd do this by myself if I had to. But I don't have to because I've got you. The man who went head-to-head with the Devil twice and still came back for more. But this time the

Devil won't know you're coming. I'm not an operative—you're right about that. But I don't have to be. That's why you're here."

"You still don't get it," I said, shaking my head. Finding Zain's gaze, I directed my next comment at him. "Will you talk some sense into her?"

"I would," Zain said, "but I happen to believe she's right. Is what we're proposing risky? Yes. But in some ways, it's the perfect operation. Virginia just needs to be herself—a terrified woman about to be sold to a sex trafficker. And you just need to be yourself."

"Which is what?" I said.

"The sword of justice," Zain said. "If we do nothing, Ferah and countless girls like her will be lost. But more than that, the Devil, and the evil he represents, will continue to thrive. This isn't about you trusting Virginia, or even me, to do what must be done. No, I believe this is really about you trusting yourself, Matthew. This is who you are. This is what you do. Allah has placed an opportunity before us all. An opportunity to right some of the wrong that infects this place. We just need to be brave enough to seize it."

I looked from Zain's weather-beaten brown face to Virginia's creamy complexion. The two of them couldn't have been more different: a smuggler who'd eked out a living in this desert land, and a chemistry professor raised in the mountains of Tennessee. There was no reason why their paths should have ever intersected. None at all.

But here they were.

Here we were.

My relationship with God was complicated. Mom and Dad had done their best to inculcate me with their beliefs, but my childhood faith hadn't exactly weathered the transition to adulthood intact. The things I'd seen human beings do to one another since I'd left the sanctity of my boyhood home had left me questioning many things, my belief system included. It had been a long time since I'd even cracked the cover on the Bible Mom had tearfully given me when I'd headed off to college, but a fragment of a verse from the Book of Esther came to mind all the same.

And who knows but that you have come to your royal position for such a time as this?

Like Queen Esther, I found myself at the intersection of two paths. I could chalk Ferah up as yet another casualty to the horror that was the Middle East and try to get to the Devil a different way. Or I could risk everything, including the lives of the two people sitting across from me, in a desperate attempt to save her.

Maybe the fact that Virginia, Zain, and I were all sitting in a safe house in Iraq was due to something more than just coincidence. Maybe someone or something really did have a master plan.

A master plan that included such a time as this.

"All right," I said, looking from Zain to Virginia. "Let's roll."

FORTY-FOUR

The next several hours passed in a blur. Within minutes of my agreeing to Virginia's plan, Zain's men had converted the safe house's central meeting space into a makeshift tactical operations center, or TOC. A stream of workers carried in a large-screen TV, computers, maps of Mosul, and an assortment of Pelican cases. The TV went onto the wall and was quickly synced to the auction's Facebook page. The display showed pictures of the women currently for sale, their starting prices, and a clock counting down to the flesh market's inevitable conclusion. Maps were spread across hastily set-up card tables as Zain and his lieutenants annotated facilities with known ties to the Devil's organization with a precision that would have made a DIA analyst proud.

As they worked to provide me with a picture of the battlefield, I wandered over to the Pelican cases and started popping lids. Their contents should have surprised me, but somehow didn't. Maybe this was because I was becoming more jaded with each passing moment, or maybe nothing about Zain or his organization surprised me anymore.

After all, the man who'd engineered my prison break with a stolen American cruise missile surely wouldn't have had a problem acquiring a roomful of weapons and equipment. But not just any weapons and equipment. The kit nestled in the foam-lined Pelican cases would have been at home in a 5th Special Forces Group team room. Normally, I'd have been a bit disconcerted to find such high-tech gear in the hands of a Syrian smuggler.

Today, I was just happy to have the kit at my disposal.

"Anything else you need, Matthew?"

"Not right now," I said, turning my attention from the weapons and equipment to the smuggler who'd procured them. "I'm probably going to wish I hadn't asked this question, but where did these come from?" I pointed to the Pelican cases.

"Ahh," Zain said, following my finger, "they were provided by the Syrian Chief of Base. Your friend."

If I'd had any doubts before, it was becoming clearer by the moment that Charles Sinclair Robinson IV was not in any way, shape, or form my friend. Still, being an asshole was one thing, but providing CIA-specific equipment to a Syrian smuggler was out of character, even for Charles.

"He gave those to you?" I said, mentally inventorying the contents of the cases. Seeing next-generation body armor, top-of-the-line optics, and night-vision devices along with the tricked-out HKs with integrated suppressors in the hands of a Syrian was unusual. But the tech in the innocuous-looking plastic boxes took my apprehension to the next level. They held low-profile MBITR software-controlled radios—exactly like the ones that Frodo and I had been using while trying to rescue our asset and his family.

And they'd mysteriously failed just when we needed them the most.

"Not quite," Zain said. "These came from the stock the American provided to his asset."

"Sayid?"

"Yes."

"Then how did you get them?"

Zain shrugged. "One of Sayid's men liked to play dice. He wasn't very good at gambling and was even worse at managing his money. He ran up a substantial debt with some of my men, and when it came time to settle, he offered these in lieu of currency. I thought it was a fair trade."

"Why do I find it hard to believe that he just happened to be playing dice with one of your men?"

Another shrug, this time accompanied by a narrow smile. "Let's just say that I try to make the most of the opportunities Allah provides. My men have readied Virginia's profile. Would you care to see?"

I took one last look at the radios before turning back to Zain. Before this was all over, Charles and I would have a reckoning, no two ways about it. But first I had to rescue a girl and lure the Devil out of his lair without getting anyone else killed in the process. With that in view, my beef with Charles could wait.

"Okay," I said, turning to face the flat-screen, "show me what you've got."

Zain waved his hand, and a dozen shots of Virginia appeared on the TV. Invisible bands compressed my chest as I looked from image to image.

As instructed, the photography team had gone out of their way to ensure that Virginia couldn't be identified in the shots. None of the pictures featured a full view of her face, but it was her all the same. Here a tumbling of auburn hair. There a profile shot of a startling blue eye or an expanse of creamy white skin. Taken in total, the images were a mosaic of Virginia. Their incomplete nature somehow made her seem even more alluring.

We were actually doing this. I was putting Virginia on a sex trafficker's auction block.

What the hell am I thinking?

"Good, no?" Zain said, mistaking my disgusted silence for appreciation of his team's work.

I looked from the screen showing the auction site and the ticking clock to the images of Virginia. The faces of the other women about to be auctioned made my skin crawl, but they were similar to one another. Dark complexions, brown or black hair, and brown eyes. By contrast, the pictures featuring Virginia were the equivalent of a spotlight shining into a darkened room. She was going to stand out—that was for sure.

But would it be enough to land the Devil?

"Your photographer did good work," I said, not knowing what exactly to say.

"What do you think?" Virginia said, coming up behind me.

"I think this whole thing makes me want to vomit," I said.

"Join the club," Virginia said. "I'm not too keen on the plan either, but it's the best chance we've got."

I knew that she was right, but that didn't mean I had to like it. I was struggling to find something to say when Zain beat me to the punch.

"We can upload only one picture to the Facebook page," the Syrian said, chewing on his ever-present cigar. He stepped closer to the flat-screen, staring at each image. "Which?"

"That one," I said, pointing to the centermost image. The picture showed a quarter of Virginia's face, revealing a single shining blue eye framed by auburn curls. A dusting of freckles covered her cheek, like cinnamon sprinkled across a parchment of white. "No one sees that picture and walks away."

"I agree," Zain said. "Virginia?"

Virginia stared at me, her face flushing scarlet.

"What?" I said. "It's true. Okay, Zain. Put it up on the site. Start the bidding at double the asking price of the next-highest girl."

Zain gestured to one of his men. A moment later, Virginia's face popped onto the auction site. A collective silence fell as we waited for the first bid. After a full minute of waiting, the silence felt ominous. Finally, the first offer came in. And then another. And another. The dam broke as bids flowed in almost too fast to count. By the tenth, the highest bid was double the asking price. By the fifteenth, it was triple.

"We chummed the water," Virginia said, watching the dollars beside her icon click upward. "Now we just need the Devil to bite."

I nodded but didn't reply. I kept hearing one of my mom's favorite admonishments: *If you catch a tiger by the tail, you'd better hang on.* I had a feeling that the hard part wouldn't be getting the Devil to bite.

It would be surviving whatever came next.

FORTY-FIVE

M atthew. Matthew!"
I woke with a start, transitioning from sleep to wakefulness in an instant. Laila termed this ability my *instantaneous awakening*. She chalked it up to my being raised on a ranch, and she was half right. Much of the day-to-day work with animals had to be done before the sun came up, and my parents certainly weren't ones to tolerate a boy's request to sleep in when cows needed to be milked. But life on the desolate stretch of land my parents had optimistically called a ranch hadn't produced my instantaneous awakening.

I had combat to thank for that.

"I'm up, Zain. I'm up."

"I can see that, Matthew. But are you okay?"

I paused in the act of pulling on my boots, trying to understand what he meant. Though the room was dimly lit I could see Zain's face, but his expression offered no clues.

"Why do you ask?" I said.

Now his look of concern turned to one of embarrassment. "You were making noises in your sleep. Crying out."

His words prompted a flash of what I'd been dreaming. Like Zain's features, the details were elusive, but I remembered enough: women—girls, really. Lined up in rows, waiting. Their bodies covered by burkalike robes, their faces visible in abstract. Here an eye, there a pair of curved lips. I'd been running from girl to girl, trying to get them to follow me to safety. But my mouth couldn't form words, and my spectral hands passed right through them.

"I'm fine," I said, pushing the dream and the sense of hopelessness that had accompanied it away. "Just fine. Is it time?"

Zain shook his head. "Not yet. The others are still resting."

After watching Virginia's bids shoot through the roof, I'd started fleshing out a plan for the night's operation. It wasn't the stuff of which books were written.

Doctrinally, an operation like this should have had at least two separate teams. One to provide an outer cordon tasked with surveillance of the target and to act as a QRF if, or when, things went south. The smaller, inner team would be responsible for actions on the objective. In this case, those included identifying and rescuing Ferah and capturing or killing the Devil.

But even under these optimal conditions, the operation I was planning would still have been classified high-risk. And I didn't have optimal conditions. I had Syria's most well-connected smuggler and a chemistry professor. No one was going to be briefing this operation to West Point cadets once we were finished.

Still, I did have a card or two stacked in my favor. Zain's men had displayed impressive discipline while rescuing us from the Iranian outpost. One team had created a diversion with well-aimed mortar fire and the warhead from a retrofitted cruise missile, while the second had penetrated the compound and whisked us away. Rangers and Delta Force shooters they were not, but Zain's gang of smugglers was intelligent and could follow orders.

Wars had been won with less.

"How long till the auction goes live?" I said, pulling on my shirt.

"Three hours."

"Any movement on the possible sites?"

Zain shook his head, and I swore.

Everyone knew that Mosul had become a hotbed for sex traffickers. But once ISIS had been pushed out of the city, the flesh traders were no longer state sanctioned. When the Caliphate had still been in power, girls were actually brought to distribution sites and inventoried. Then their would-be rapists arrived and signed for the girls like they were checking out books from a library.

But that was then.

Now that Mosul was once again notionally under the control of the Iraqi government, the Devil had to be more discreet. Instead of using fixed locations, he kept his show on the road. He chose a different site for the flesh auction each time, and the location was announced via the same Facebook page potential buyers used to submit their bids.

To keep ahead of the Iraqi police, the Devil never revealed the location of the auction more than thirty minutes before it started. Assaulting an unreconnoitered objective with less than half an hour's prep would have been difficult for a Tier 1 unit, let alone Zain's band of merry men.

With this in mind, Zain and his lieutenants had identified a number of potential locations where the auction might be held and put them under surveillance. At last count we had eyes on half a dozen buildings in the hopes that our surveillance teams would pick up the preparatory activity that was bound to precede the auction. If the Facebook site was accurate, almost one hundred women were on the auction block. About half that many buyers had already submitted bids. Prepping a space for that kind of traffic wasn't going to happen in thirty minutes, but so far, our surveillance efforts had come up dry.

Time for plan B.

As if reading my mind, Zain said, "Thought you might want this." He handed me a cell phone along with a folded slip of paper.

"You sure he's got it?"

Zain adopted his best wounded-puppy-dog look, if a hardened Syrian smuggler could look like a wounded puppy.

"Matthew," Zain said, his dark eyes conveying the depths of his injured pride, "I run a network that moves thousands of tons of goods across the borders of three countries every day. I engineered and executed your rescue from an Iranian prison, a rescue worthy of your Charlie Force."

"I think you mean Delta," I said.

"Yes, yes. My point is that nothing moves in Iraq without my knowledge. Nothing. My men discovered the information you need. The question is, did you fulfill your end of the bargain?"

"We're about to find out," I said, accepting the phone.

I clicked into the device's contacts and tapped the single stored number. A moment later, the sound of a telephone ringing came through my earbuds. The phone rang twice, three times, then four as Zain stared at me with a look of studied indifference. This would not be a great start to our operation if my target failed to discover the phone I'd slipped into his pocket. No, that wasn't exactly true. I guess it would be more accurate to say that if the person on the other end of the line didn't answer, there would be no operation.

Zain still managed to look unconcerned, but I could tell the tension was getting to him too. He was chomping on his cigar like a dog worrying a steak bone. I was about to hang up and try again when the ringing ceased.

"Hello?"

"Benny," I said. "How was the helicopter ride?"

"Drake?"

"Yep."

"You planted this phone on me?"

"Sure did. Since you forgot to give me your business card before you left, it seemed like a good idea."

"I thought I was done with you," Benny said. "But you keep coming back. Like herpes."

"You wouldn't be the first to make that comparison," I said. "Now, as much as I'd like to chitchat, this is a business call."

"What kind of business?"

"The business of you showing me some gratitude for pulling your ass out of a jail cell. My momma says that it's impolite to remind someone that they owe you a favor, but here I am."

"Here you are. What do you need?"

"Unit 8200. I need them to lock down the Devil's phone."

"I think we've had this conversation. I am in your debt, but I can't do this for you. All of our ISR assets are focused on the Iranians."

"Then I need you to unfocus them," I said.

"Drake, I—"

"No, no. Hear me out. Since saving your life doesn't seem to carry a lot of weight, I'm prepared to sweeten the pot."

"How?"

"By giving you what you're looking for."

"And that would be . . . ?" Benny said.

"The location of the Iranian Quds Force cell that kidnapped you," I said, unfolding the paper Zain had slipped me to reveal his spidery handwriting. "My sources say that they killed your two bodyguards in the process. Maybe your life isn't important enough to retask Unit 8200, but how about getting a little payback for the two boys who died trying to protect you?"

I could almost feel Benny's anger radiating across the airwaves. The ominous silence was worse than his muttering Hebrew expletives. Was mentioning the deaths of his men a low blow? Yeah, probably. But a girl's life hung in the balance. The time for niceties had long since come and gone.

"You know where the terrorist cell is bedded down?" Benny said. "Right now?"

"Yep."

"Who's the cell leader?"

"Come on, Benny. You're insulting my intelligence."

"Who?"

I looked at the scrap of paper. "He goes by Bijan. Bijan Nuri. And he's a captain in the Quds Force. Does that ring a bell?"

Another beat of silence, then: "You have his location?"

"Eyes on him as we speak."

More silence, this time broken with a long sigh.

"Give me an hour."

"Benny, Benny, Benny. This is Unit 8200 we're talking about. They invented SIGINT while the rest of us knuckle draggers were still making chalk marks in alleys. Thirty minutes or I shop my tip to someone else."

"Who?"

"You think yours is the only intelligence service who'd

like a word with old Bijan? Thirty minutes, Benny. Don't be late."

I ended the call and handed the phone back to Zain.

"Will he do it?" Zain said.

"Yep."

"How do you know?"

"He's Mossad. They don't fuck around when it comes to dealing out payback. Kill a Jew, and they will track you to the ends of the earth. And the Iranians didn't kill just one. They were stupid enough to kill two. Israelis don't forgive, and they sure as hell don't forget."

"Sounds like someone else I know," Zain said before walking out of the room.

I thought about pushing back, but maybe being compared to a Mossad assassin wasn't the worst thing in the world.

Besides, as the Devil was about to discover, Zain was right.

FORTY-SIX

The call came thirty minutes later, almost to the second. I thought about ribbing Benny for coming so close to the deadline, but didn't. Maybe the signal-intercept guys at Unit 8200 were having an off day. Or more likely, maybe Benny had had to step on a couple of toes in order to bump my tasking to the front of the line. Either way, I was already sufficiently amped about finding the location of the auction site. I didn't need to tweak Benny.

Not too much anyway.

"I have the information," Benny said.

"I'm fine," I said. "Thanks for asking."

"Save the jokes. I've localized the phone, but you're not going to like what I've found."

"Try me," I said.

"He's in Syria."

"What?"

"You heard me."

"How can you be sure it's him?"

"We're sure," Benny said.

"You'll have to do better than that if you want the Iranians' location," I said.

Several moments of uncomfortable silence passed before Benny spoke. When he did, his voice was noticeably softer.

"We have certain *capabilities* that extend beyond just locating the phone," Benny said. "We have a positive ID on the man you seek. I swear it."

Now I was the one responsible for several moments of uncomfortable silence. Gaining positive ID on a high-value target, or HVT, was one of the most complicated aspects of a kill-or-capture mission. Localizing a phone was only part of the operational problem. Oftentimes a more daunting part was proving that the person holding the phone was actually the HVT. Voice intercepts were the most obvious way of confirming a person's identity, but using them required penetrating the phone *and* possessing a copy of the target's voice file to compare against.

We had neither.

A second method involved putting eyes on the target, either through physical surveillance or by way of a drone or strategically placed camera. Again, we had neither. This meant that the Israelis had a technological trick or two up their sleeves that they hadn't yet bothered to share with their American friends.

That wasn't exactly news since we had more than our fair share of tools, tactics, and procedures that we didn't exactly broadcast, for obvious reasons. Even so, *supposing* the Israelis had a way to identify the Devil solely off his cell phone number and *knowing* they did were two very different things. The number of lives riding on this operation was growing by the minute. So as much as I liked Benny Boy, I wasn't trusting my team to his word.

He was going to have to do better.

"Listen, Benny," I said, walking away from the hustle and bustle of our ad hoc TOC for a bit of privacy. "I'm not calling you a liar, but I do need something more concrete."

A slew of now-familiar-sounding Hebrew curses greeted my reply, and I waited patiently until the deluge slowed to a trickle. Once Benny finally ran out of words, and the ensuing silence grew too pronounced, he spoke.

"I'm texting you a video," Benny said.

My phone vibrated, announcing an incoming text. The quickness with which he'd sent it made me think that, as much as he pretended otherwise, my Mossad friend had already planned for this contingency. As Ronald Reagan famously said, *Trust but verify*.

I clicked on the file embedded in the text, and a video began to play. A video showing the Devil's unmistakable face. He was staring directly at the camera, his features scrunched up in concentration. The video was accompanied by the clicking sound recognizable by every human being over the age of six.

The Devil was texting, which meant that the Israelis had the ability to remotely compromise a phone's operating system using only its number. Very slick. But not as slick as learning that the Devil was at this very moment in Syria.

"Believe me now?" Benny said.

"Yep," I answered. "Give my compliments to the boys and girls in Unit 8200. They've developed a very neat toy."

My phone vibrated again as I received another text. This time, instead of a video, Benny had sent me a hyperlink.

"Click on the link," Benny said. "It will take you to a secure site. The interface is like Google Maps, except the flashing blue icon is the target phone."

"Nice," I said, clicking the link. Sure enough, my phone's browser opened a window, and there was the flashing blue icon, smack-dab in the middle of Syria— just like Benny had claimed.

"Save the flattery," Benny said. "You have what you want. Now give me what I need."

"I hate to do this to you, old buddy," I said, staring as the icon taunted me with every flash. "But my asking price just got a bit steeper. I need access to the contents of his phone."

"Not going to happen."

"Come on, Benny. Put yourself in my shoes. One more ask, and then we're even Steven. Scout's honor."

"No."

"Just a tiny bit of information."

"What?"

"Access the phone's call log and localize the number he's dialed the most times today."

"Believe it or not, I don't actually work for you."

"One more number, Benny. Then you can have your Iranians. After that, you'll never hear from me again. Promise."

This time my phone pinged before I'd even finished speaking. With an anxious finger I stabbed the link. A new browser window opened. The new flashing icon was centered in Mosul.

Hot damn.

"Here are the coordinates of the Iranians," I said, and read off the address Zain had provided. "Top floor of the building is a safe house. Bijan is inside. Good hunting."

"My debt is satisfied."

I thought about responding with something equally snippy, but didn't. Mostly because I'm way too mature for that, but also because Benny had already hung up.

That was okay. I knew where the Devil was and where he was heading. The rest of the operation would be a walk in the park.

Or something like that.

FORTY-SEVEN

The building that the Devil's underling was occupying wasn't just any building. It was a palace. Originally constructed by Saddam Hussein, the structure had played home to a revolving series of occupants since the dictator had been found cowering in a hole in the ground and later hanged.

First came the Americans, who were impressed with the palace's structural bones, but turned off by its gaudiness. A gold-plated commode sounded gangster enough, but was all sorts of impractical when it came to daily use. After the Americans, the building had been occupied by several bureaucrats and minor politicians. Then an enterprising businessman had purchased the palace and converted it into a nightclub.

According to Zain's local sources, the nightclub had been quite successful, right up until the black-clad ISIS jihadis had retaken Mosul from the feeble Iraqi army.

The zealots had swept into the city with a simple mandate: convert the inhabitants to their radical strain of Sunni Islam and eliminate any infidels.

Some people might have been intimidated by the scope of such a task, but not the ISIS foot soldiers. They were as fervent about their work as they were their faith. Two, since the acceptance criteria for their strain of Islam was stringent, while the qualifications for being an infidel were broad, it was often easier to just label someone an infidel and kill them. This was much more efficient than going through the time-consuming banality of a trial. After all, if the religious zealot administering the death sentences was wrong, and the victims really were Muslims, they'd still end up in paradise by Allah's side.

In other words, it was a win-win for everyone.

Needless to say, this variant of Islam wasn't terribly tolerant of the use of alcohol, tobacco, music, or anything particularly fun. As such, the palace-as-a-nightclub quickly morphed into something more fitting for an army of conquering jihadis: the palace-as-a-mosque. This version of the palace continued until the Kurds and Iraqis, backed by American airpower and special operations teams, drove ISIS from the city in a rain of blood and terror.

For a brief period following the jihadis' decimation, the palace had sat empty. But recently, the building had undergone renovations. No one was quite sure who had acquired the palace, only that he or she was well financed.

Extremely well financed.

For reasons unknown to the masons and the construction crews charged with building them, a series of perfectly level slabs of concrete reinforced with strips of rebar had been erected adjacent to the palace's entrance.

"What do you think they are?" Zain said, pointing to the symmetrically placed slabs as he looked at Google Earth images over my shoulder. "Foundations for outbuildings?"

"No," I said, feeling the pieces click together in my mind, "they're helipads."

"Helipads?" Zain said, scratching his chin. "Who needs to travel by helicopter?"

"Someone in Syria, I would imagine."

"So this is it?"

"It'd better be. This is where we're going."

The plan I'd developed was equal parts simple and complex. Simple because our objectives were straightforward: rescue Ferah and kill the Devil. The complex part extended to pretty much everything else.

"This thing is itchy as hell," Virginia said from behind me. "Half of me wants to round up every male at this flesh auction and sentence him to a life of wearing this shit at scenic Guantánamo Bay."

"And the other half?" I said.

"The other half thinks we should just put a bullet in their brains and be done."

I couldn't fault Virginia's reasoning, least of all because I agreed with her. The palace would be a target-rich environment. Unfortunately, I didn't have nearly enough resources to service all of them. Instead, I'd have to settle for saving Ferah and dealing with the biggest target of all: the Devil.

But as with all operations, the devil was in the details.

"Run it by me one more time," I said as our driver slowed, joining a long line of cars turning off the thoroughfare for the crushed-gravel road leading to the palace.

"Why?" Virginia said, shuffling closer so that she wouldn't have to yell. "Because you don't think I'll remember?"

"No. Because I don't think *I'll* remember."

"Seriously?"

"Of course not," I said, feeling the butterflies in my stomach that always came just before the start of an operation. "But I'm not into the whole keep-quiet-and-ponder-the-meaning-of-life shtick some guys do before a mission. Besides, I'm the mission commander, which means you have to do what I say. Start talking."

Virginia made a very unladylike gesture with her middle finger, but she began to speak.

"You're my pimp, so I stay close to you and keep my head down. At some point once we're inside, I'll be herded together with the other woman. When I find Ferah, I signal you."

"How many squeezes?"

"Three," Virginia said, holding up her right hand to reveal a thin leather glove covering her palm.

The glove looked like the kind of brace a doctor might prescribe if you spent too many hours hunched over a keyboard. In reality, the material held a pressure-activated switch that was linked via Bluetooth to a tiny transmitter sewn into the top of her burka. One of the many amazing pieces of tech in Zain's never-ending supply of Pelican cases.

"Good. And if you get into trouble?"

"I use my left hand."

This time Virginia punctuated her answer by clenching the fingers of her left hand into a fist and mashing down on the pressure switch in the second glove. In response, a tingling sensation ran the length of my left forearm as the tiny electrodes sewn into my sleeve sent out a continuously pulsating low-voltage signal.

I reset the device, flexing my fingers.

The configuration wasn't exactly NSA Suite B encrypted, but the wireless set allowed for voiceless communication, and the high-energy-density lithium batteries powering the miniature transmitters had more than enough juice to reach from one end of the palace to the other. More important, there would be no mistaking Virginia's duress signal. Once she tripped the transmitter on her left hand, I'd have a steady stream of invisible ants biting into my skin.

"What if you need to buy yourself time?" I said.

"Then I go for this," Virginia said, patting the small of her back, where a .38 snub-nose revolver was holstered. "Two to the chest, one to the head."

"If you need to use the pistol, don't worry about being fancy," I said, holding her gaze with my own. "Eliminate the immediate threat and hunker down. I will come for you."

"I know."

Though it was brief, I wasn't prepared for the depth Virginia's response communicated. Maybe it was because I'd never before gone into combat with a woman, or maybe there was something behind her eyes I wasn't prepared to address. Either way, Zain's voice echoing in my earbuds was a welcome interruption.

"Matthew, Matthew, can you hear me?"

I pointed toward my ear, signaling to Virginia that I had radio traffic, and then turned in my seat.

"Loud and clear, Zain," I said, staring at the red taillights of the car in front of me. "Go ahead, over."

Zain's response was a garbled, unintelligible mix of feedback and static. I heard my name again, but little else.

"Zain, I didn't understand your last. Say again, over."

This time the electronic noise was painfully loud. I fumbled for my cell phone, dialing back the volume on the miniature earbuds concealed deep within my ear canals. After several torturous seconds, silence returned. Thumbing the transmit button, I tried again.

"Zain, this is Matt. Say again, over."

Zain's response came through with perfect clarity, as if he were seated in the car next to me instead of an observation post a quarter of a mile distant.

"Matthew—we have trouble! Trouble!"

Zain was an exceptional source of intelligence, but a covert operative he was not. As such, I had to imagine his radio discipline was a little lacking. The urgency he voiced in the last transmission made the hair on the back of my neck stand up, but I wasn't all that concerned.

In the plan I had spliced together, Zain and his men were the outer cordon. Their job was to keep eyes on the objective and provide a diversion by assaulting the palace when I gave the signal. In other words, almost the exact roles they'd played exceedingly well at the Iranian hospital.

The palace sat nestled at the base of a set of rolling hills. Open fields surrounded the structure on three sides, while the Tigris River snaked by on the fourth. Zain was located at the summit of the nearest hill, approximately two hundred meters from the center of the palace. I was betting that Zain's elevated perch would allow him to maintain communication with both me and the breaching team as well as give an early warning if any unexpected visitors decided to crash the party.

As with any operation, I was expecting things to go wrong. That said, by my way of thinking, the real dangers to our team wouldn't begin until Virginia and I were actually inside the palace. Since the crushed-gravel road we'd just joined was a good hundred and fifty or so meters from the palace's gatehouse, we still had time to react if things went sideways. While I was concerned that something had spooked Zain, I wasn't overly worried.

At least not yet anyway.

And I continued to feel that way right up until my driver, Oliver, pulled through the double wrought iron gates set in the eight-foot-tall stone wall that separated the palace's outer grounds from its inner courtyard. A pair of guards with matching AK-47s slung across their chests played traffic cops at the gates, directing the steady stream of vehicles into ad hoc parking places.

Upon seeing us, one of the guards pointed to the right, and Oliver followed his instructions. It was only as our headlights played across what was waiting in the courtyard that I realized that Zain might not have been overreacting after all. We had trouble all right.

Trouble with a capital *T*.

FORTY-EIGHT

Well, shit," I said as Oliver swung our Land Rover toward the row of parked cars the guard had indicated.

"What?" Virginia said, her voice reflecting the anxiety in mine.

"Not now," I said, turning to Oliver instead. "Can you take a spot in the next row over?"

"Sorry, mate," Oliver said, edging our vehicle behind a parked car. "Too late."

Oliver had been the one addition to my original plan. In my version, only Virginia and I would have entered the palace, but Zain had made a compelling argument against that course of action. My hastily configured legend as a rich Eurotrash thug required that I incorporate a bodyguard into our retinue. And as Zain was quick to point out, no European worth his salt would entrust his life to an Arab gunman. Instead, Zain made a few calls and thirty minutes later, Oliver Wilson showed up at our doorstep.

Hailing from jolly old England, Oliver was in his mid-thirties, with close-cropped salt-and-pepper hair, pale eyes, a beard, and the weather-beaten face of a man who'd spent most of his life outdoors. A former Royal Marine, Oliver had four combat tours to his name, three of them in Iraq.

After coming down on orders for his fifth deployment, Oliver had promptly traded his green beret for a ball cap and a substantial raise. Like many special operations veterans, Oliver had decided to leave military service in favor of a well-compensated position in Iraq's thriving personal-protection industry. The company Oliver worked for had a number of legitimate contracts for Western diplomats, business executives, and minor government officials, but was also known for a willingness to accept more *creative* assignments.

Simply put, Oliver was a mercenary. While I didn't have anything against mercenaries in general, I tended to be a bit leery about putting my life in the hands of men who worked for the highest bidder. Then again, Oliver was an experienced shooter who spoke passable Arabic. Zain had used him to protect high-value shipments twice before and had given the former bootneck high marks.

In any case, I needed an extra man, and as the old saying went, beggars couldn't afford to be choosers.

"What's going on?" Virginia said, trying to edge her way between the seats for a better view.

"Stay back," I said, grabbing her shoulder and pushing her gently but firmly into her seat. "Party's started a little sooner than we thought. It's showtime."

I'd expected security to be tight—this was part of the plan. Virginia's profile had garnered more than a million in bids on the Facebook page alone, and that wasn't counting other social media platforms tied to the event.

Adding Virginia to the auction had completely changed its dynamics. This was no longer about just auctioning off hapless village girls who'd been kidnapped by criminals or ISIS murderers. Now the galleys were littered with European girls of all shapes and sizes. By their practiced poses, I had to guess that some of them were professionals, while others were clearly scared shitless.

The paragraph-long description under each girl was written in both Arabic and English. Clearly the clients for this particular soiree were high rollers, and the security presence reflected their status. Men with guns I was prepared for. Men with guns who were wearing the uniforms of the Iraqi Federal Police were a bit of a surprise.

"Do you think the police are here for some kind of raid?" Virginia said, ignoring my instructions to stay put by looking over my shoulder.

"I doubt it," Oliver said. "*Corruption* is still the word of the hour here. More than likely, they want a piece of the action."

"A bribe?" Virginia said.

"Or worse," I said. "They could be hired help."

"What do we do?" Virginia said as one of the policemen broke off from the group of partygoers he was questioning to head toward us.

"Stick with the plan," I said, including Oliver in my answer. "They haven't stopped anyone from entering the palace yet. We shouldn't be any different. Play your roles and everything will be fine."

"Promise?" Virginia said.

"Promise," I said.

Opening my door, I climbed out of the Land Rover, and Oliver did the same. I purposely turned away from the policeman as I waited for Oliver to interdict the Iraqi, as was befitting a man of my station. Except that the policeman didn't seem to be particularly impressed with my station. Ignoring Oliver's attempt to engage him in conversation, he grabbed my shoulder.

Or at least tried to.

As soon as I felt his fingers gather the fabric of my shirt, I spun toward him, locking his wrist with my right hand and barring his elbow with my left. I pivoted, the centrifugal force of my small circle exerting tremendous pressure on his locked joint. His head slammed into the metal doorframe before bouncing back like a soccer ball kicked against a concrete wall. And then Oliver joined the fun, snapping a straight jab into the policeman's temple.

The man crumpled, and that was that.

To his credit, the mercenary didn't hesitate. Reaching down, he grabbed the limp Iraqi by his belt and shirt collar. I opened the passenger door, and Oliver heaved the man inside, onto the seat next to Virginia, like he was tossing a bale of hay. Then he unsheathed a hidden knife with a *whisk* of leather on metal.

"No," I said, grabbing his wrist.

"No time to go soft, mate," Oliver said, looking back at me with cold eyes.

"Cuff him, gag him, and take his pistol," I said. "He might be a bad guy, or he might just be in the wrong place at the wrong time. Either way, we're not murderers."

Oliver held my gaze for a beat and then shrugged his wide shoulders. "You're the boss, mate."

The knife went back to wherever it came from, and Oliver climbed into the backseat alongside the policeman. While he carried out my instructions, I took a minute to see what, if any, commotion our little altercation had caused. Fortunately, the answer seemed to be very little.

The courtyard was lit with streams of lanterns reminiscent of a movie set for *Aladdin*, but the sun had disappeared, and the moon had not yet risen. Outside the shallow pools of orange light, darkness reigned. The clump of people with whom the policeman had been standing was gathered beneath the largest cluster of hanging lanterns. I was betting that their ruined night vision hadn't penetrated the shadows masking us.

So far, so good.

I heard the tailgate pop and then slam shut. A moment later Oliver joined me.

"He's gagged and cuffed. I put him in the back and locked his pistol in the glove box."

"Okay," I said, looking at Oliver. "You ready?"

Oliver gave a quick nod, which just served to remind

me how little I knew about the mercenary. If it had been Frodo watching my back, he would have responded with a quote from an eighties movie. Instead I got a nod and silence.

I guessed that would have to do.

"All right," I said. "Please, ask the lady to join us."

With another silent nod, Oliver walked to the other side of the Land Rover, opened the door, and pulled Virginia out none too gently by her arm. She had known this was coming, as had I, but the violence was still shocking. Virginia screamed, which was exactly in character, and Oliver responded by giving her an open-handed slap to the face.

The sound of flesh on flesh carried through the thin night air, and I ground my teeth. We'd all discussed the necessity to sell the act that Virginia was being trafficked, but slapping her across the face was a bit over-the-top. I tried to catch Oliver's gaze to express my displeasure, but his dead eyes refused to meet mine.

No matter. I was steadily adding to the Devil's butcher bill. Every hurt that Virginia suffered, every horror that had been endured by the girls on these premises, I would revisit on the Devil a thousandfold.

At least that was what I told myself as I followed Oliver and Virginia into the yawning, brightly lit gates of hell.

FORTY-NINE

"Sorry for the delay, sir. Would you care for a glass of champagne while you wait?"

I nodded and took the offered drink from a tuxedo-clad waiter, more to blend in with the crowd and give my hands something to do than anything else. Though from everything I'd seen so far, the champagne was probably worth sampling. I'd found myself in quite a few dark places over the years, and I'd imagined that infiltrating a sex-trafficking organization would rank as one of the worst. But so far, the experience had been rather benign. The atmosphere inside the palace resembled an exclusive Vegas nightclub more than it did a slavers' market.

After passing through an outer cordon of security stationed at the entrance to the palace, we reached a massive foyer, which could have encompassed my entire boyhood home with room to spare. The floor was marble, and the walls were paneled with cedar inlaid with gold. Glittering chandeliers hung from a black roof, their sparkling light resembling a galaxy of stars suspended against the night sky.

A bar ran the length of one side of the room while the other held a massive raised platform on which I assumed the auction would take place. The evening's patrons stood together in clumps, making small talk as scantily clad women knifed through the crowd, carrying trays laden with food, drinks, and drugs.

The air was thick with the scents of tobacco, hashish, pot, and incense along with several exotic smells I couldn't quite place. Soft music piped from hidden speakers competed with the sound of at least half a dozen languages. As I waited in the line snaking from the check-in desk, I heard bits of Russian, French, Spanish, and perhaps Mandarin along with Arabic and English.

I'd been expecting to see a gathering of local gangsters trafficking girls kidnapped from rural villages. Clearly, I'd underestimated the Devil once again. This was sex trafficking on a sophisticated, global scale.

"Hello, sir. Do you speak English?"

The question came from the man standing behind the check-in desk. Like everything else in the palace, his desk was understated but somehow still intimidating. It had been fashioned from a single piece of stone so dark that I would have thought it obsidian if not for the crisscrossing veins of sparkling silver.

Like his desk, the man behind it was dressed to impress but not overpower. Judging by its fit across his wide shoulders and narrow waist, the man's suit was obviously handmade. But the fabric's muted blacks and browns diluted rather than focused attention. Taken together, the man and the desk were impressive when viewed, but quickly forgotten when compared with the massive stage clearly meant to be the room's center of attention.

"Of course I speak English," I said, allowing just the right amount of disdain to slip into my German accent. Nothing says Eurotrash like German.

"Very good, sir. Will you be buying or selling tonight?"

"Selling. Unless of course the right something catches my eye."

The man behind the desk nodded as his fingers flew across a computer keyboard. "Yes, sir. Let's get your merchandise checked in first. Where is she?"

I snapped my fingers, and Oliver stepped from where he'd been standing behind me, Virginia in tow.

"What is her merchandise number?"

"Two eight nine," I said.

The man pursed his lips as he scrolled down his screen, then nodded. "Yes, I have her right here. Now, before you can check her in, I need to verify the merchandise."

"Verify?"

"Yes, sir," the man said with an apologetic shrug. "As you know, bidding has already begun. Before we accept her into stock, we need to confirm that she really is item two eight nine."

"And how will you do this?" I said, the irritation coloring my voice not entirely pretended.

"I assure you it's quite easy and causes no damage to the merchandise. We simply take a picture of her face, and then our algorithms compare her image with the image of item two eight nine."

"And if your algorithms decide they're not a match?"

"Then you are still more than welcome to sell your merchandise, but the bids for two eight nine will be negated. I'm sorry for the inconvenience, sir. But these are the rules."

"Fine, fine," I said. "Make it quick."

"Yes, sir," the man said, but his pleasant demeanor went through an abrupt change when he turned to address Oliver. "Bare her face, and make sure she stands still."

Yanking the *niqab* from her head, Oliver grabbed Virginia beneath the chin and turned her so that she was facing the camera.

"Good," the man said after clicking a series of buttons. "Now, if you'll just bear with me for a minute . . . Yes, the software confirms a match. We can now enter her into inventory."

The man clapped his hands, and two helpers appeared. "If your assistant will surrender the merchandise to my associates, we will take it from here. A retainer of ten percent of the current bid, or one hundred thousand dollars, will be credited to your account."

I reached into my suit jacket for my phone on the pretense of checking to see that the funds had transferred, while what I really wanted was an excuse to look at Virginia one last time. Our eyes met, and time seemed to stop. This was the moment of truth. We could have still walked out, and no one would have been the wiser. But once Virginia passed from Oliver to the two thugs, we were committed.

Her pale blue eyes bored into mine. She looked as terrified as I felt, but there was no sense of hesitation in her gaze. Only acceptance. I stared back long enough for her to give a barely perceptible nod. Then I withdrew my phone, consulted the balance of my newly established bank account, and confirmed that I was one hundred thousand dollars richer.

Then it was done.

"Okay," I said, slipping the phone back into my pocket. "We're all set."

"Very good, sir," the man said. "Here is your VIP lanyard. Enjoy your evening."

I nodded and turned away from his desk to find only Oliver remaining. The two men had vanished as silently as they'd appeared, taking Virginia with them.

All in all, I should have been happy. Other than the slight hiccup with the Iraqi policeman, everything was proceeding according to plan. And the policeman had been less of an issue than I'd imagined. I still didn't know what the police had been doing in the courtyard, but the Devil's men were providing security inside the venue. If members of the Iraqi Federal Police had realized one of their compatriots was missing, they weren't acting on the information.

Such was the reach of the Devil's power.

Yep, so far everything had happened exactly as I'd envisioned, which was in itself cause for concern. The Devil had been one step ahead of me since Austin. What were the odds that I'd figured out a way to one-up him now?

I didn't really want to know the answer to that question, but I had a feeling it was coming anyway.

FIFTY

What now?" Oliver said, looking from me to the crowd of buyers.

"We pay the kitchen staff a visit," I said with a confidence I didn't quite feel.

As per the instructions on the Facebook site, Oliver and I had both come unarmed. Or at least without guns. The carbon fiber blade Oliver had been ready to use on the Iraqi policeman still had to be on his body somewhere. The former Royal Marine had made a case for trying to conceal a pistol, but I'd vetoed the idea. The risk of getting barred from the party was just too great.

Rescuing Ferah and putting an end to the Devil depended on being able to get into the auction unmolested. Oliver swore up and down that the new composite-material pistol he'd acquired was undetectable, but I didn't think the risk was worth the reward.

Of course, just because I wasn't carrying now didn't

mean I intended to remain that way. No, I planned on having a gun in my waistband most ricky-tick. That was where Zain came in.

"They're in there," Oliver said, pointing to a service door at the far end of the room.

I nodded, but gestured for Oliver to wait as I reached into my pocket for the cell phone tethered to my miniature Bluetooth earbuds. Since we'd been surrounded by other partygoers from the parking lot until now, I hadn't tried to raise Zain since his last, aborted transmission. However, now that we were going to leave the proximity of the crowd, it made sense to try to check in with the smuggler. If nothing else, I wanted to ensure that his men and our weapons were where they needed to be.

"Zain, this is Matt. You copy, over?"

This time, not even the electronic noise I'd heard earlier accompanied my transmission. An unnerving silence was my only answer.

"Zain, this is Matt. Do you copy, over?"

Nothing.

"Can you hear me transmitting?" I said, turning to Oliver.

With a frown, the bearded man shook his head.

"You try."

Oliver reached into his right pocket before making a transmission that mirrored mine. I heard his voice because he was standing next to me, but my earbuds were silent.

"Anything?" I asked.

"No."

Turning so that my back shielded me from the rest of the room, I pulled out my cell phone and looked at the display. No bars, no Wi-Fi service, and the Bluetooth was off-line. I cycled the device off and on with the same results. I might as well have been transmitting from a Faraday cage.

Not good.

"See if you have cell service," I said, dropping the useless device back into my pocket.

Oliver pulled out his phone, fiddled with it, and then shook his head. "Bloody hell," Oliver said, looking from his phone to me, "no signal at all. What does that mean?"

"Must be a jammer close by," I said. "Military grade to be able to put out enough energy to blanket such a large area."

"Why jam the cell service?" Oliver said.

I shrugged. "That's the question. Could be the Devil doesn't want any of his guests contacting the outside world until the auction is over. Or it could be something else."

"Like what?"

"Like the operation's blown," I said. "Zain was trying to tell me something before his transmission cut out. Something about trouble."

"I thought he was warning us about the Iraqi policemen," Oliver said.

"Maybe. But did you think the policeman was hard to handle?"

"Not really."

"Me either," I said. "And I'd have to believe that Zain would come to the same conclusion. No, if the guy who engineered a prison break from a Quds Force installation was worried about something, I should be too."

"So what next?"

That was the million-dollar question. Rolling up my sleeve, I checked the receiver strapped to my arm to see if it was still synced with Virginia's transmitter. The tiny LED glowed a reassuring green, indicating that the devices were linked. Apparently, the frequency bands the jammer was blocking didn't overlap with the proprietary waveform our covert communications set used.

"Virginia's still good to go," I said. "She hasn't found Ferah yet, and she's not in trouble, so we don't abort. But we are going to take precautions."

"We still grabbing the weapons?" Oliver said.

I eyed the service door, considering. "Yes," I said, "but we're not going in blind."

I waited for a server to walk by, carrying an empty tray, and then snapped my fingers to get his attention.

"You there," I said in Arabic. "I have a request."

"Certainly," the waiter said. "Would you like something from the kitchen?"

"No. I wish to speak to the wine steward. Bring him to me. Immediately."

The waiter's eyes snapped from my face to the VIP medallion hanging from my neck and back again. "Of course, sir," the waiter said. "If you like, you're welcome to come with me so that you can view our wine selection firsthand."

"No, I would not like. I'm here to make a purchase, not tour the wine cellar. If you have a problem with my request, I can talk with the concierge."

"No problem at all, sir," the waiter said. "I'll be back with the wine steward shortly."

The wine steward in question, like several other members of the support staff, was one of Zain's men. Once again, my intrepid little smuggler had proven that he was worth his weight in gold—even if he did occasionally turn me into a pincushion for tranquilizer darts. Zain's solution for the inevitable security at the palace's entrance was to use support staff to smuggle in weapons. Weapons that would be made available to Oliver and me once we penetrated the outer cordon of security.

Like all good plans, Zain's idea was both simple and effective. As a major player in the criminal underworld, Zain had no trouble finding out who was providing support staff for the Devil's event once he knew its location. After that, it was only a matter of getting some of Zain's men hired on as well. Men who used catering cases outfitted with false bottoms to conceal the assault pack I'd requested.

Except that our simple plan now seemed to be unraveling at the seams a little more every second. With Zain's cryptic message still fresh in my mind, I had no intention of exchanging the safety provided by the crowd of potential buyers for the kitchen's tight confines.

If the Devil knew I was here, he'd want to remove me from the equation with minimal disruption to the event he'd spent untold amounts of time and money piecing together. The kitchen would offer a perfect opportunity to do just that. This was why I was bringing Zain's man to me instead of the other way around.

Across the room, the waiter disappeared behind the

swinging door leading to the kitchen as I tried to keep my ever-growing sense of unease at bay. Clandestine operations were tricky things. A good operative constantly navigated the razor's edge between heightened awareness and heightened stress. A healthy sense of distrust was essential to staying alive, but if left to fester, negative thoughts could quickly escalate into crippling terror. Terror that rendered an operative incapable of making decisions.

I was no more an expert at navigating these treacherous waters than any other spy. Still, over the years, I'd found a touchstone to bring things into perspective. My Glock. The absence of the comforting bulge in my waistband was profound. The sooner I got my hands on a pistol, the better.

"Boss? Hey, boss. You need to see this!"

Oliver grabbed my shoulder, giving it a shake.

"What?" I said, shrugging away his hand. The waiter had been inside for more than enough time to find the wine steward. If Zain's man didn't exit the kitchen door in the next minute or two, we had a problem.

"Look," Oliver said, grabbing my shoulder again.

I turned away from the door to face Oliver, and the irritation I felt at being interrupted vanished after I saw what had attracted his attention. At the opposite end of the cavernous room, the dormant stage lighting was coming to life, illuminating an elevated platform. A moment later, a spotlight mounted somewhere flared, casting a brilliant circle of light over the polished wood.

For a long second, the pool of light stood vacant.

And then the Devil entered from stage left.

"Fuck," I said, fumbling in my pocket for my cell phone. "Fuck, fuck, fuck."

Unfortunately, my cell phone, like my wife, was not impressed with harsh language. The jammer was still functioning as advertised. Oliver and I were completely cut off from the rest of our team.

"What now?" Oliver said.

"We call an audible," I said. "In fact, this is the best news I've had all day. I was starting to worry that the Devil wasn't going to leave Syria and, even if he did, that I wouldn't be able to find him in the crowd. But now he's done my work for me. That shithead should be shaking in his boots."

But the Devil did not seem to be shaking in his boots. In fact, he looked to be enjoying himself. Gazing out on the audience, he gave a broad smile as the spotlight warmed his bronze complexion and burnished his hair to a dark luster.

"Good evening, friends," the Devil said, overhead speakers sending his voice booming across the room. "And welcome. Those of you who know me know that I don't do anything in half measures. I assured you that tonight's party would fulfill your every desire. Have I kept my promise so far?"

An indecipherable murmur of voices answered. But if the Devil was bothered by the less-than-unanimous response, he didn't show it. Instead, his smile grew even wider.

"Yes, yes, I know. You're anxious to get to the bidding. I promise it will start momentarily. But before we begin, I wanted each and every one of you to know how much I value your business. I promised that this would be an event like no other, and I keep my promises. To set the tone for tonight, I want to begin the festivities with a gift. One lucky attendee will take home a present from me, free of charge. Bring her out."

The last sentence was delivered to someone offstage, and the crowd roared in response. My stomach churned from equal parts rage and disgust. My earlier speech to Virginia had been for my benefit as much as for hers. I couldn't save every oppressed and downtrodden person in this world. We would focus on Ferah and help any other girl we could, but there was a limit to what our team could accomplish.

Even so, what the Devil was about to do was particularly grotesque. He was giving away a woman as a door prize. While I couldn't save everyone, neither could I just stand and watch his twisted scheme unfold. Until I secured a weapon from Zain's man in the kitchen, I was as impotent as the would-be door prize. But I could at least mark the man who *won* the helpless woman and follow up with him later.

It wasn't much, but it was better than nothing.

And then two men dragged the door prize onstage, and everything changed. A murmur swept through the crowd as if suddenly tonight's patrons weren't quite so upset that the bidding hadn't started on time. In truth, I couldn't blame them.

My wife was an exceptionally beautiful woman.

FIFTY-ONE

I do not despair easily. As a company commander in the Ranger Regiment, and then as a DIA case officer, I'd experienced more bleak situations than most people navigate in a lifetime. I'd seen human depravity on a scale that could scarcely be imagined.

I'd helped medics place tiny form after tiny form into makeshift body bags after a suicide bomber had detonated his vest outside a school for girls in Kabul. I'd cradled a boy in my arms as his life bled away in a flood of crimson. I'd even been sitting next to Frodo when an EFP had transformed him from a world-class commando into a cripple.

I'd thought that I'd long since passed the point where the evil of this world surprised me.

I was wrong.

Seeing Laila onstage, her face streaked with tears, her luxurious black hair tangled, and her green eyes shimmering with terror, broke something deep within me. Here again, the Devil was one step ahead of me. Here again, he'd checkmated me before I'd moved my first piece.

This went beyond the squad of assassins who'd targeted me and killed an innocent cop in the process. Beyond even a monster who trafficked in the flesh of kidnapped girls. This was Laila—the woman who gave my life meaning. My wife was about to be raffled off as a door prize to a roomful of evil, lecherous men.

No.

The word seemed to come from everywhere and nowhere. From the very fiber of my being. From the essence of my soul.

No.

This was not going to happen.

Not today.

And that was when the muscles in my forearm began to twitch. At first, I chalked the sensation up to another attack of the shakes. A flare-up triggered by the stress of seeing my wife in the hands of a monster.

If only.

My affliction, while sometimes debilitating, was something I'd begun to learn how to manage. In fact, I'd already stretched my fingers into the opening chord of "Tequila Sunrise" when I realized that this sensation didn't feel anything like a typical episode. Rather than the dull numbness that usually accompanies the tremors, my forearm was on fire. Thousands of tiny unseen wasps were stinging the shit out of me.

Virginia.

Seeing Laila onstage had shaken me to the bone. I'd forgotten about everything and everyone else. Even the chemist from East Tennessee who'd gone into the lion's den to rescue a fifteen-year-old girl she'd never met. Once she found Ferah, Virginia would signal her success via the tiny transmitter hooked to the sensors on my right arm.

But the pins-and-needles sensation wasn't crawling down my right arm.

It was on my left.

Duress.

Virginia was in trouble, and she needed my help.

Help that I couldn't give.

FIFTY-TWO

What's wrong, mate?" Oliver said. "Cat got your tongue?"

I turned toward the mercenary only to find myself staring down a dark hole of indeterminate size. Though if I'd had to guess, I'd say it was about 9mm in diameter. Mainly because the hole was formed by a Glock 19's barrel.

"The thing I never understood about mercenaries," I said, looking from the pistol to Oliver, "is, why make all that money if you're not alive to spend it?"

"Fair enough," Oliver said. "But I'll do you one better. The thing I never understood about Yanks is why you still believe all that bollocks about liberty and justice for all."

"Well, maybe we should go have a pint," I said, taking

a step closer to the mercenary, "and talk through our differences like men."

"Love to, mate," Oliver said. "But not today. Now, stay where you are, or I'll be forced to kneecap you."

So apparently Oliver had instructions to take me alive. That was an interesting development.

"Come on, friend," I said, edging closer still. "It doesn't have to be this way. I don't know you, but I promise you this: I make a better friend than enemy."

"If only it were up to me," Oliver said, his dead eyes looking through me. "But you don't know the extent of the Devil's reach."

True enough. But I did know the extent of mine. I shot both hands out, sweeping the pistol barrel off-line with my right, while clamping the back of the pistol with my left. I felt the rear sight bite into my palm, and then I was twisting right, torquing my hips. Oliver's wrist broke with an audible *pop*.

Then the pistol was mine.

"I told you not to let him get close to you," said a voice to my right. A voice with an Irish accent.

I pivoted toward the sound, my pistol coming on-line only to freeze. I was nose to nose with the business end of a short-barreled tactical shotgun. Facing down Oliver's Glock had been a bit nerve-racking, but it didn't hold a candle to the shotgun's dark, imposing maw.

This was not a fight I was going to win.

As if to drive home this point, the unmistakable

sound of another shotgun's slide racking came from my left, a split second before an oval of cold steel pressed against the back of my head.

"That was very impressive," the Irishman said. "Truly it was. But trust me when I tell you this is over. Now. Place the pistol on the floor and walk toward the stage. Your wife is waiting."

FIFTY-THREE

A thousand scenarios flashed through my mind, each one more desperate than the last. The Devil held my wife's life in his hands, and I was pinned between two guys with sawed-off shotguns. My odds weren't great, but I had a feeling they wouldn't get any better once I got onstage. I had two choices—fight or die.

I chose to fight.

Or at least I would have if the Irishman hadn't fired his shotgun into my gut.

To say the pain was intense is a bit like saying that a nuclear blast is hot. The words might be true, but that doesn't mean the description is accurate. One second I was on my feet, trying to figure out how to kill these fuckers without getting myself or Laila whacked in the process. The next I was lying on the floor as my brain tried to figure out what had just happened.

In case you've never experienced it, the business end

of a sawed-off shotgun is loud. Eardrum-rupturing loud. So loud that I wasn't certain I would ever hear again. On any normal day, this might have been a cause for concern. But today, hearing was pretty far down on my hierarchy of needs. Instead, the sum of my attention was directed at the waves of pain radiating from my abdomen.

I opened my mouth, gasping for air, but my lungs didn't seem to be following instructions.

Everything from my breastbone to my belt buckle was on fire. Even my internal organs hurt, which until that moment I hadn't known was even possible. The world grayed around the edges as my vision tunneled toward blackness. I wish I could say that I gained some incredible insight about the meaning of life in those last few seconds, but I didn't. All I could think about was how damn much it hurt to die.

And then my lungs stopped spasming.

I drew a breath.

And another.

Which was strange because, while I am not a gun geek, I do know that a blast of buckshot at this range should have shredded my lungs. Come to think of it, my entire chest cavity should have been a gaping hole. But although it felt like someone had hit me with a sledge-hammer, my chest and abdomen still felt strangely connected.

Reaching toward the radiating pain's ground zero, my tentative fingers didn't find bits of tissue or bone shards. Instead, they touched canvas. Or, more accurately, the canvas cover of a flexible baton round, otherwise known as a beanbag round.

Well, son of a bitch. I was going to live.

"Smarts a bit, doesn't it?" the Irishman said, staring down at me with a smile. "I'm sorry about that. Truly I am. But I saw your eyes and knew the wheels were turning. And fer that, I'm proud of ya. Even so, I couldn't let things get out of hand, now, could I? Now, up ya go."

He pulled me to my feet, and pain shot the length of my body. If he hadn't been supporting me, I would have dropped to my knees. As it was, I vomited onto his shoes. An antipersonnel beanbag might have been a hell of a lot better than a load of double-aught buckshot, but my nervous system seemed to think that this was a distinction without a difference.

"Also, turnabout is fair play, wouldn't ya say? Me poor mate Oliver is going to have to learn to wank off left-handed until his wrist heals, isn't he?"

The Irishman's mention of Oliver made me remember the Glock. I dropped my head as I let out a groan, using the opportunity to search the floor for the weapon.

"Eyes up, laddie."

The Irishman poked me in the back with his shotgun. "You're a scrappy little bugger, aren't ya? Now, enough of this nonsense, or I'll have to ask me friend to hit ya with another beanbagger. This time in the testicles."

I turned to give the Irishman's friend a once-over, and did a double take. It was the same prick who'd been beating the shit out of Nazya in the strip club. The one who got away. And now that I saw him up close, I realized that I'd actually made his acquaintance even before the strip club—on the streets of Austin.

Well, son of a bitch.

Under normal circumstances this might have even been funny. I was standing in Saddam's palace after being gut-shot by a beanbag with an Irishman, a former Royal Marine, and an Iraqi commando turned assassin. But these weren't normal times, which for me was saying something.

While I was sure this would make a great story after a couple of beers, the shotgun's detonation had attracted the attention of every swinging dick in the palace. The crowd of would-be buyers, who had been body to body before, had now opened, clearing a path to the stage like Moses parting the Red Sea. Except instead of safety, something else waited on the far shore—the Devil and my wife. And they were both looking right at me.

"Matt," Laila said in a half sob, half hiccup. *"Maaaattt."*

That single word tore my heart in two. Anger, terror, and despair all welled up within me as the woman I loved called out my name. But it wasn't those dark things that ripped me apart. Anger, terror, and despair were old friends. No, it was the tiny ember burning from her impossibly green eyes that really crushed me. The way that she held herself erect even as tears streamed down her face.

It wasn't Laila's pain that nearly broke me. It was her hope. Hope rooted in just one thing—me. A hope that somehow everything would be all right just because I was here. But things weren't going to be all right.

Not even close.

FIFTY-FOUR

t's okay, baby," I said, locking eyes with Laila as if she and I were the only people in the crowded anteroom just off the main stage. As if we weren't surrounded by the Devil, his bodyguards, Oliver, and the sadistic Irishman. As if we were at our anniversary dinner back at Taj's Place instead of living the darkest moment of our lives.

"Everything's just fine," I said.

But everything wasn't fine. Not by a long shot.

Laila looked at me, her eyes glistening. She managed a single brave nod, but didn't speak. Maybe because she didn't trust her voice not to break. Or maybe because she was hoping this was just a nightmare and that she'd somehow wake up.

Either way, I was close enough to smell the warm, intoxicating scent of her skin. But it might as well have been miles rather than feet that separated us. The Devil's thick, hairy fingers were wrapped around Laila's slender biceps, and a shotgun was pressed againt my kidney.

Fine wasn't even in the same zip code.

apologize for the spectacle out there, Matthew," the Devil said as we walked down a dimly lit corridor, "but I needed to get the unpleasantness out of the way as quickly as possible. I'm sure you understand."

I was beginning to learn that the Devil had a gift for understatement. After his men had me fully in hand, the Devil had turned over the flesh auction to one of his acolytes and walked offstage. The jackass from the strip club pulled Laila along while a second bodyguard shadowed the Devil. The crowd surrounding me followed suit. Rough hands dragged me across the palace floor when I stumbled, which was often. The fresh bruises still forming on my abdomen made walking a bit of a chore.

There was also the matter of Oliver, who seemed less than thrilled with his newly broken wrist. Once we were off the stage and out of sight of the crowd, he expressed his displeasure through a sucker punch that caught me on the jaw. This was followed by a roundhouse to my temple that dropped me like a stone. The former Royal Marine then proceeded to stomp and kick me as I curled into the fetal position, trying to absorb his blows with my back and legs as opposed to my internal organs.

After a bit, the Irishman intervened and stopped the beating. The good news was that Oliver hadn't had the time to do any serious damage. The bad news was that he might have played forward for Manchester United before joining the military. One of his more inspired kicks had caught me squarely on the cheekbone. I still had all my teeth, but a couple were now kind of wobbly.

But worse than my injuries had been the sound of Laila's screams as she'd watched me take my lumps. For terrifying my wife, these men would pay with their lives.

Every last one of them.

"I feel obligated to say this once," I said, using the wall to push myself to my feet. "Let her go. Now."

The Devil smiled, revealing a row of perfectly even white teeth. "And if I do, then what? You'll let bygones be bygones?"

"No," I said, shaking my head. "But I'll give you a head start. Take your money and go to ground. Maybe I'll forget about you."

"Matthew, you still don't know what this is about, do you?"

"Last chance," I said. "Walk out of here now and live. Otherwise I swear to God that by the time I get through with you, there won't be enough left to feed the dogs."

I wasn't yelling, but there must have been something in my voice all the same. Though I could barely stand, the Irishman tightened his grip on my arm while the Devil's two bodyguards slid in front of their principal. Even Oliver got into the act, pointing the Glock at my forehead one-handed.

The Devil maintained his jovial grin, but something that looked like uncertainty slid into his eyes. Dad always said that one predator could recognize another. Maybe that was what the Devil saw. Or maybe it was something else. Something more primitive. Either way, I knew that in that instant I'd gotten to him. I'd rattled the Devil's chain.

And that was my mistake.

"Matthew, Matthew, Matthew," the Devil said, shaking his head. "For some reason, you still don't understand the lay of the land. But I have to say I admire your passion, even if it is wrongly placed."

Turning to the bodyguard on his right, the Devil let loose a rapid stream of Arabic. The words came too fast for me to translate. I got something about *her*, but then quit listening in favor of devoting my mental energy to figuring a way out of this mess.

Another mistake.

While I was in a mental twilight zone, one of the Devil's bodyguards crossed the hallway to a door set in the wall. Pulling it open, the man barked a command in what sounded like Farsi. A moment later, three men spilled from the room dragging a woman between them.

Virginia.

FIFTY-FIVE

M att," Virginia said as she saw me, "I'm sorry. I—"
Her sentence was cut short as the jackass from
the strip club backhanded her with the casual disregard
one might show a misbehaving dog. The blow rocked
Virginia, her hair billowing in a curtain of auburn. To
her credit, she didn't cry out, but her eyes filled with
tears as angry crimson marks erupted on her face.

I shifted my gaze from Virginia to the man who'd
struck her and then locked eyes with him.

"You're a fucking dead man." I paused between every
word, enunciating each syllable to ensure my Arabic was
flawless.

His brown eyes flashed. He opened his mouth to re-
spond, but the Devil didn't give him the chance.

"This posturing is both tiresome and time-consuming.
Allow me to speed things up," said the Devil.

The Devil reached toward Virginia as if to stroke her

cheek. She reflexively jerked away, opening space between her bruised skin and the Devil's probing fingers. Her terrified gaze found mine. I'd started to whisper something encouraging when I noticed the Devil's hand moving.

His other hand.

Light flickered across steel.

I ripped free of the Irishman's grasp, screaming a warning, but I was too late. A single shot rang out. The report amplified a thousandfold as it ricocheted off the stone walls and ceiling. One moment Virginia's eyes had been locked on mine. The next they were staring vacantly into space.

She slumped against the wall and then slowly slid to the ground.

I howled, stumbling toward her, trying to convince myself that what I'd just seen had not really happened. That the sassy girl from East Tennessee wasn't actually lying crumpled on the floor like a pile of discarded laundry.

"Motherfucker," I said, spittle flying from my lips as I turned from Virginia to the Devil. "Motherfucker, motherfucker!"

As smooth as silk, the Devil swung his pistol from Virginia to Laila. "Careful, Matthew. I'd hate to have to continue our lesson. But I will."

He pushed the stubby pistol into Laila's face, the barrel inches from her mound of black curls. I froze, my breath coming in ragged gasps. To her credit, my wife didn't say a word. Instead, she just stared at me, her striking green eyes unblinking.

Slowly, deliberately, I walked back from the edge of madness. Retribution would come, but not now. Not yet.

"What do you want?" I said, each word ripped from my soul.

"I want you to go to America and kill someone."

"Who?"

The Devil actually smiled. "That is the ironic part, Matthew. I want you to kill the man who has caused you so much pain—Charles Sinclair Robinson the Fourth."

"Charles?" I said, trying to wrap my mind around what the Devil was saying. "You want me to kill Charles? Why?"

"Because he's sloppy, and sloppy is bad for business."

"You have business with Charles?"

"That is not your concern," the Devil said. "Your concern should be your beautiful wife."

The Devil reached over to squeeze Laila's shoulder in an almost fatherly manner. "I made a mistake in our earlier arrangement. I've underestimated you, twice now. Once when I thought you would be more useful to me dead than alive. The second time when I entrusted your supervision to one of my associates. I won't make those mistakes again. These three gentlemen are Quds Force members and business partners. Your wife will remain their guest in the Islamic Republic of Iran until you've killed Mr. Robinson. Then and only then will she be allowed to leave. Are we clear?"

"Crystal," I said. "Let me say good-bye."

"Quickly," the Devil said.

I moved closer, and the Devil responded by shoving

his pistol into Laila's face, the barrel dimpling her cheek's soft skin.

"From there, if you please," the Devil said, his smile almost manic. "I've always heard that distance makes the heart grow fonder."

Turning to Laila, I tried to think of everything that I wanted to say. To tell her how much I loved her. That I was sorry. That I was a fool for letting her walk away that night in Austin. That our six years of marriage had been the happiest of my life.

But as usual, my wife beat me to the punch.

"You are my husband, Matthew Drake," Laila said, her eyes now dry, her voice steady. "*My* husband."

The emphasis on *my* was subtle, but I heard it all the same. I'd loved Laila before, but what I felt for her now was all-consuming.

"It will be okay," I said. "I promise."

"I know."

"All right," the Devil said, nodding to the Iranians holding Laila. "I think that's about enough. You know what you have to do, Matthew. Do it."

The Quds Force operatives, who'd moments ago escorted Virginia to her death, gathered around Laila. But they didn't have to drag her away. Instead, my wife walked with her head held high, as if the Iranian thugs were an honor guard rather than kidnappers. She crossed the narrow hallway with confident strides and passed through the now-open door without a backward glance.

"My, my," the Devil said as the door swung shut behind Laila. "She's quite a handful."

In spite of everything, I had to fight the urge to smile. The Devil was more right than he knew. Laila was a handful, but the trait seemed to run in our family. In an instant, our train wreck of an anniversary dinner came back to me as Laila's scent faded behind her.

I just want my husband back. When you find him, please let me know.

I'd come to Iraq to find a sex-trafficked girl, but I'd found someone else in the process. Me. And now, in our darkest hour, my wife wanted me to know that she saw me. That she saw the man I really was. The one with blood on his hands and vengeance in his heart. At this moment, Laila might have been walking through the valley of the shadow of death, but she feared no evil. Not because she was fearless, but because she knew in her heart I would come for her.

And she was right.

"Ready?" the Devil said, intruding into my thoughts.

I didn't answer right away. Instead, I took a long look at Virginia lying motionless on the ground, her black *niqab* now stained crimson. I looked at her face, at her half-lidded eyes staring into eternity. And then I burned every detail into my mind until the anger I'd fought to keep in check ignited. Rage surged through my veins like napalm, consuming everything in its path.

With my heart thundering and my fingers trembling in anticipation of the havoc they would wreak, I took a deep breath. And then another. I harnessed the wrath, bending it to my will like a wild mustang I was breaking to saddle. I needed the white-hot fury, but I also needed control. What had to be done next required cunning, not just anger-born strength.

The Devil would pay for his sins, but like the planning for any good ambush, his retribution needed to occur at a time and place of my choosing. Clenching my quivering fingers into fists, I took one last breath before looking deep into the eyes of a man who was already dead.

"I'm ready," I said.

As my gaze again found his, the Devil's ever-present smile soured. He took a step back while his hands fluttered as if warding off an imaginary blow.

I stood without moving.

Waiting.

Watching.

The Devil's face flushed, and he covered his embarrassment by snapping at my minders, "Why are you still standing there? Get him to the airport. We're on a timeline."

"Certainly," the Irishman said, pushing me toward the empty hallway. "Let's go, love, shall we?"

I let myself be herded toward the exit, but like Laila, I didn't bother to give the Devil a backward glance. Why bother?

The Devil was already dead.

FIFTY-SIX

There comes a time in any engagement when planning and strategy must yield to violence of action. When the potential energy created by rehearsals, operations orders, and precombat inspections becomes kinetic. The moment when you stop setting the conditions for the ambush and execute it instead.

My moment had just arrived.

After leaving the Devil and the corridor of death, we'd entered another winding hallway. The palace's maze of passages played havoc with my internal compass, but judging by the murmurs of raised voices ahead, we were moving closer to the room where the sex auction was being held, which in turn meant that with each step, I was moving farther away from Laila.

I had great faith in my ability to rescue my wife, but I was not Superman. If her three Quds Force captors were permitted to link up with the advancing Iranian army,

my ability to reclaim Laila without a troop of Unit assaulters backed up by a company of Rangers would be
close to zero. Since I had neither, I needed to act before
Laila's kidnappers spirited her away.

Which meant that the four men guarding me needed
to die.

Quickly.

The noise of the crowd swelled as we drew closer to
the door at the far end of the hallway, and I knew what
that noise represented. Hundreds of thugs and their
bodyguards, not to mention dozens more of the Devil's
private militia. In that room, I wouldn't stand a chance.

I needed to act.

Now.

I was outnumbered four to one, but the dimly lit narrow hallway forced my overconfident captors to move in
a rough single-file line. Even so, the situation wasn't exactly ideal. Then again, neither had been the weather at
Pointe du Hoc during the Normandy invasion.

Such was the life of a Ranger.

I closed my eyes, picturing the coming engagement as
if I had a God's-eye view of the battlefield. Four captors
walking single file with me stuck in the middle. Oliver
with his broken wrist in front, followed by the commando from the strip club, then me, then Commando
Two, with the Irishman bringing up the rear.

Last time I'd looked, the Irishman had been carrying
his sawed-off beanbag shotgun at the low-ready position.
Unlike the other minders, he was still expecting trouble.
And because of his attitude, my gut said that he was the

most dangerous one in the group. Ideally, I'd take him out of the equation first. But since he was trail in our little formation, that wasn't possible.

I'd have to improvise.

"What's your name, Irish?" I said, still following behind Commando One.

"Why do ye ask?"

"You look familiar to me."

"I very much doubt it."

"I'm a spy, Irish," I said. "And spies have a way with faces. We've never met. I'm sure of that. But I'm also sure I've seen your face before."

"So what, then?" the Irishman said. "We're to be friends now? Is that it?"

"Depends on you," I said. "I'm offering you a second chance. Right here. Right now."

"What? A second chance just for me? And why am I so special?"

"Because these monsters have already forfeited their souls. The Iraqis sell little girls into slavery. The Brit has dishonored his service and uniform for money. There's no hope for them. But there may be for you."

"Quiet," Commando Two said, poking me between the shoulder blades with his shotgun.

"Ah, lad," the Irishman said. "If you truly did recognize me, then ya'd understand you're just wasting your breath."

The doorway to the palace common area materialized out of the gloom, just steps away. That door was an inflection point. If we walked through it, my tactical advantage would be lost. But as we drew closer, the group would naturally bunch up as Oliver stopped to open it. Bunched-up targets meant it would be harder for my new friends to shoot me without hitting one another.

But if I waited too long and Oliver opened the door, reinforcements would come pouring through, further tilting the odds in an already lopsided melee.

"Nolan Burke," I said. "Former member of the Real IRA. Last seen in Northern Ireland in November of 2007 after an attack in which two policemen were killed. How am I doing so far?"

"Quiet, I said."

This time the bastard speared me in the left kidney with his shotgun. I nearly pissed myself as pain racked my still-sore abdomen.

"A bad bit of business that lot in Northern Ireland was," Nolan said. "A bad bit of business indeed. But if you know about that, then you should know that me soul is just as far gone as these others'."

"Maybe that's so," I said. "Maybe it isn't. There's only one way to know for sure."

And then the time for talking was over.

Oliver reached for the door handle, and the jackass from the strip club bunched up behind him. At the exact same moment, Commando Two lanced the shotgun into my other kidney. But this time, I was ready. Pushing through the pain, I spun the length of the barrel, deflecting it to the side even as I rocketed an elbow toward the commando's head.

I was going for his face.

I missed.

Rather than the pleasant bone-on-bone connection that happens when you shatter someone's jaw, I felt his windpipe give way in a pulpy squish. The commando dropped the shotgun, instinctively reaching for his throat. I snapped a thrust kick into his now-exposed chest, putting all my weight behind the movement. The space-creating blow lifted him off his feet, sending him crashing into Nolan.

Not what I'd been going for, but as Mom liked to say, when you have lemons, make a lemon-drop martini.

I scrambled for the shotgun, but a boot to my ribs convinced me I had other priorities. Commando One had joined the fight.

Folding around the foot in my stomach, I trapped the knee and wrenched the commando's leg to the side. I tried to find his back foot with my leg, intending to take him completely off his feet, but he stepped over my sweep and clocked me in the head with a straight jab.

The blow rang my bell, but I held on to his knee. Before he could follow up the jab with a cross, I swam my hand up his leg until I found testicles. Then I grabbed them and twisted, wrenching backward like I was pulling the starter cord on a lawn mower.

The big, tough commando who liked to rape teenage girls gave a decidedly untough-sounding scream as I did my best to separate his ball sack from his body. I followed up by slamming my shoulder into his solar plexus and then reached for his chin, intending to hip-throw him into a head dump.

I found his eyes instead.

Digging the fingers of one hand into what felt like half-congealed Jell-O, I hooked his eye sockets. He screamed and thrashed, but I kept digging even as I wormed my other hand up his shoulder until I cupped the nape of his neck. Then I torqued my hips, sending him over my shoulder. Using my hands as guides, I plowed him into the unforgiving floor headfirst, my body weight added to his.

The dull *thud* his skull made as it impacted the floor will stay with me for the rest of my days. Two of the Devil's men were now out of the fight.

Which unfortunately still left two more.

I caught motion to my left just in time to see Oliver pointing the Glock at my face, one-handed.

The key to fighting more than one person at a time lay in evening up the odds as soon as possible. I'd done pretty well in that arena, but still come up short. I thought about trying to talk my way out of this, but the look on Oliver's face said that he wasn't much interested in talking.

I screamed, trying to close the distance between us, but this time physics wasn't on my side. The pistol fired, and the report was loud enough that I thought my eardrums had burst, which was strange, because dead men don't usually care about burst eardrums. Then I realized that the report had sounded so incredibly loud because it had actually been two gunshots instead of one—a shotgun blast from behind me followed by Oliver's Glock.

And that made sense because Oliver was now lying on

his back, unmoving, with a beanbag-sized indent in his skull.

"Did you mean what you said, lad?" Nolan said from behind me. "About a second chance."

"I did," I said, turning to face the Irishman.

He still had his shotgun at low ready, but it wasn't exactly pointed at me. Of course, it wasn't exactly pointed away either, but I'd take what I could get.

"I can't guarantee what will happen," I said, "but I'll try to bring you in. I give you my word."

"I suppose that's all I can ask," Nolan said, lowering the shotgun. "Either way, I'd rather have you as a friend than an enemy. All right, then. Let's go find your wife."

FIFTY-SEVEN

They say that politics makes for strange bedfellows, and the battlefield is no exception. Even so, this was a first for me. In the almost decade I'd been making my living at the pointy end of the spear, I'd worked with everyone from Kurdish freedom fighters to Afghan warlords. I considered myself pretty open when it came to operational allies. Still, I'd never partnered with a former member of the IRA.

"This way," Nolan said, leading me past the sprawled bodies at a sprint. "We must move quickly."

In this, my new Irish friend and I were in violent agreement. I might have escaped the Devil's clutches unnoticed once, but he would make sure to keep better track of me this time. Sooner or later, he'd be expecting a check-in from his commando henchmen. When that didn't come, Laila would pay the price.

We must move quickly might just have been the understatement of the century.

"Where are we going?" I said as Nolan swung to the left, following a hallway that by my reckoning led to the opposite side of the palace from where we'd entered.

"With the ongoing Iranian offensive, the roads are too dangerous. The bodachs who have your wife will be using the helicopter."

"Helicopter?" I said.

"Yes. There are two outside."

Of course there were. We'd seen two helicopter pads on our Google Earth recon. It only made sense that two helicopters would occupy them. It also explained the Devil's sudden appearance after the Israelis had locked down his phone in Syria. I assumed that the Iranians weren't the only ones traveling by helicopter.

"Faster," I said to Nolan. "If Laila gets in a helicopter, we've lost her."

As if to give voice to my fears, the unmistakable whine of turbine engines spooling up filled the air. The helicopters. We weren't going to make it.

And then I had a thought.

Like all modern aircraft, helicopters relied on GPS to navigate. I was betting that the frequency bands that the satellite-based navigation signals utilized would probably also be affected by the Devil's military-grade jammer. This meant that for the helicopters to align their internal navigation systems prior to departure, the Devil would first need to switch off his jammer.

Digging my cell phone from my pocket, I looked at the display and nearly laughed with relief. The Wi-Fi band was still jammed, but I had cell service. I dialed Zain's number and held the device to my ear.

"Matthew?" Zain said. "Is that you?"

"Yes, it's me. I need—"

"It's a trap, Matthew. The Devil owns Oliver. He's waiting for you to—"

"I know, my friend. I know. The Devil found us."

"And you're still alive?"

"I am. Virginia is not."

"No! I—"

"Listen, my friend," I said. "I need your help. The Devil has my wife."

"Your wife?" Zain said.

"I don't have time to explain. Where are you?"

"Outside the building with my men. We're waiting in overwatch as planned."

"Can you see the helicopters?" I said. "They're on the red side."

"Helicopters? Why?"

"I think my wife is on one of them," I said.

"Stand by," Zain said. "I can't see the red side from here. We're moving."

Seventeen years of hitting target buildings in search of HVTs had taught the special operations community a thing or two about deconflicting fires and segmenting objectives. Rather than being designated by cardinal directions or *left* and *right*, the faces of a target building were now designated by color.

In this case, Zain and his men were set up to monitor the side of the building closest to the road, or the green side. In order to get a bead on the helipad, they'd need to maneuver to get line of sight on the red side, closest to the river.

Which would take time.

Time that Laila didn't have.

"We have the helipads in sight," Zain said, sounding out of breath. "Each is occupied by a single helicopter. The rotors of both helicopters are turning. What should we do?"

What indeed.

"Stand by," I said, sprinting to catch up with the Irishman, who was waiting for me next to the far door. "Does this go outside?" I said to Nolan. "To the helicopter pads?"

"Yes."

"How far to the helicopters?"

Nolan shrugged. "Maybe fifty meters?"

I paused, considering my options. As of this moment, I had to believe that the Devil was unaware of my escape. But if I popped out of the doorway like a jack-in-the-box, he might see me.

And then the jig would be up.

"Matthew," Zain said. "Both aircraft are preparing to take off. We have just seconds."

At that moment, a *boom* reverberated through the building, setting the overhead light swinging on its narrow cable.

I looked at the Irishman, and he had a dumbfounded

expression that mirrored mine. Whatever was happening now hadn't been on his agenda either.

"Zain," I said, mashing the transmit button on my cell, "what the fuck was that?"

"The Iraqi army has arrived. They're breaching the building."

"With what? Another one of your cruise missiles?"

"No, Matthew. A tank. A big one."

Holy hell. General Mattis famously said that when you know you're headed to a gunfight, you should bring all your friends with guns. While I agreed in principle, I also thought it best to make sure your friends didn't accidentally get shot in the back.

"Zain," I said, "is your diversion ready?"

"Of course. Do we fire on the gate now?"

"Change of plans," I said. "Does the gunner have line of sight to the helicopters?"

A pause that was much too long, and then: "Yes."

"Have him shift his aimpoint to the ground between them and stand by."

Nolan heard only my half of the conversation, but I could still tell by his incredulous look that he thought I'd lost my mind. Which was fair, because I wasn't really in a position to argue.

Still, two helicopters spinning up meant that two groups of people were leaving. Given what I knew about the Devil, I was betting that those two groups of people were probably traveling to two different destinations. After all, if the Devil intended to head to Iran, he could take Laila there himself.

Also, the Iraqi army was breaching his palace with a main battle tank. While I hadn't been an armor officer, it didn't take a genius to realize that an almost-fifty-ton tank didn't just sneak up on you.

If I had to guess, someone had tipped the Devil off and he'd decided that discretion was the better part of valor. He was abandoning his sex-trafficked girls and roomful of potential customers in order to ensure that he could live to fight another day. That meant that one of the helicopters held Laila and her Iranian captors, and the other the Devil, which in turn meant that one of those birds needed to be transformed into a ball of flames.

I just needed to figure out which was which.

"Matthew, the helicopters are lifting off."

I waited an agonizing second and then burst through the door, Nolan on my heels. As expected, I could hear the roar of turbine engines, but couldn't see the helicopters through the cloud of grit and sand generated by their rotor wash. This was good, because if I couldn't see the helicopters, their occupants shouldn't be able to see me.

In theory.

"Zain," I said, shouting over the shrieking engines, "do you know who's in what helicopter?"

"No, Matthew," Zain said. "What do you want us to do?"

"Are you with the man with the diversion device?"

"Yes."

"Put your hand on his shoulder. Make sure he doesn't fire until you give him the word. Understand?"

"Yes, yes, I understand. But which one? Which helicopter?"

Which indeed. Two helicopters with two very different passenger manifests. If I was right, one of them held Laila and one held the Devil.

That was a very big *if.*

The aircraft lifted together, clawing skyward as another *boom* rocked the palace. I'd attended several breaching courses during my time in the Ranger Regiment, and while I'd learned my share of field-expedient breaches, I'd never seen one that utilized the gun of a main battle tank.

First time for everything.

The dust cloud billowed, expanding outward like the aftershock from an IED. Then the helicopters popped out of the cloud. For a heart-stopping moment, they both flew eastward in formation. Then the trail aircraft broke to the left, heading west toward Syria, while the lead aircraft continued east.

East toward Iran and the advancing army.

I had my answer.

"Zain, target the aircraft heading west. I say again, target the aircraft breaking over the river. Confirm my last."

"Which helicopter, Matthew? Which one?"

Son of a bitch. I looked at Nolan and saw the shotgun he was holding.

"Do you have anything besides beanbag rounds for that?" I said.

"Slugs," Nolan said.

"Give them here."

Racking the shotgun's slide, I ejected the remaining beanbag rounds and then loaded six slugs.

"Zain," I said as I was loading, "you need to target the helicopter flying west. I say again, west. I will try to designate the direction with my shotgun. Look for the sparks."

I might as well have told Zain to look for Tinker Bell and follow her fairy dust toward the helicopter. With an M4 and tracer rounds, what I was suggesting might have been possible. A shotgun firing slugs had a range of about seventy-five meters. I had no chance of even reaching the helicopter, assuming Zain was even in a position to see me.

But I put the shotgun to my shoulder anyway and sighted down the barrel. I was still a Ranger, and Rangers didn't quit.

"The fuel cans," Nolan said, hitting me in the shoulder. "Shoot the fuel cans."

I looked from the Irishman to his outstretched finger and saw the pile of fuel cans next to the stack of generators providing power to the palace. Goddamn, but I was an idiot. Adjusting my aimpoint, I fired round after round into the fuel cans. The first two did nothing, but the third spun a can up in the air, trailing fuel behind it. Fuel that sprayed across the hot generators.

A second later, the vapor ignited in a satisfying *whoosh* that enveloped the generators.

"Zain, do you see the burning fuel cans?" I said.

"Yes! Yes!"

"Look above and find your target."

"Target acquired."

"Fire the device!"

The word *device* was a bit of a misnomer. During the planning phase of this goat rope of an operation, I'd told Zain we needed to have a diversion on standby. Not a Tomahawk-missile-level diversion, but something big enough to get the Devil's attention. With this in mind, I'd asked to see his weapons inventory, and after a little misdirection, Zain had grudgingly obliged.

One look into the warehouse he called an armory and I saw why. The gear he had "acquired" rivaled my company armory back in the Ranger Regiment. Most was Russian stock, which eased my conscience somewhat since that meant Zain hadn't been stealing *all* of the supplies I'd paid him to deliver to the Syrian freedom fighters.

However, he did have a healthy selection of American weapons, including several antitank missiles. The tube-launched, optically tracked, wire-guided—or TOW—missiles were nice if you could mount the launcher to a technical or a Humvee, but I was looking for something man-portable. Like the two boxes Zain had tried to steer me past. But one look at the nomenclature and I knew what was in them.

I'd asked him where he'd acquired this particular merchandise, but I might as well have been asking a fish why water was wet. Some things just were because they were.

A flash split the night sky to my right. A millisecond later, an ember of flame streaked overhead, trailing a cloud of noxious smoke and the particular *whoosh*ing sound a solid-propellant rocket engine makes in boost phase. I tracked the projectile's trajectory for the two seconds it took to intercept the helicopter.

Then there was a second, brighter flash of light, and the Devil was no more.

The explosion's rolling *boom* reached us a second later, like thunder after lightning, but by then done was done. Thanks to a Javelin antitank missile and a Syrian smuggler's gunnery skills, the Devil was now in hell with his namesake. Ordinarily, this would have been a time for high fives and fist bumps, but the second helicopter, the one containing my wife and her Iranian captors, was still heading eastward as fast as its jet engines could carry it.

The Devil might have been out of play, but Laila was still in danger.

"What now?" Nolan said, reading my mind.

"Now it's time to finish this."

FIFTY-EIGHT

To his credit, the Irishman didn't question the logic of my statement. He simply looked in the direction that the helicopter carrying Laila had disappeared, and then turned back to me.

"Then you're going to need wings," Nolan said. "Have ye got any?"

"Not yet," I said. "But I'm working on it."

Which was true, after a fashion. What was also true was that I didn't have a clue how I was going to get to Laila before she and the Quds Force men kidnapping her disappeared into the welcoming arms of the advancing Iranian army. Fortunately, my cell phone chose that moment to erupt, saving me from explaining to the Irishman how I was going to magically produce wings.

"Matthew?" Zain said. "Matthew? Did we hit the right one?"

"Good shooting, Zain," I said. "But now we need to get my wife. Do you have a helicopter?"

Ordinarily, I wouldn't have bothered to ask such a ridiculous question, but since the smuggler had managed to somehow appropriate a Javelin missile, I didn't think a helicopter was really too large a leap. Besides, nothing ventured, nothing gained.

"Sorry, Matthew. Not close by. I can get one in perhaps a day—does this help?"

No, it most certainly did not. But that wasn't Zain's problem; it was mine. So I pivoted.

"Don't worry about it. But can you meet me at the helipad with one of the assault packs? I'm a little light on weapons and equipment."

"Yes, Matthew. I'm coming."

The Irishman looked at me like I had horns growing from my forehead. "Ye've found wings now, then?" Nolan said.

"Not yet," I said, thumbing a new number into my cell phone. "But I've got a guardian angel."

At least I hoped I still had one. To be fair, he'd never let me down before. Then again, I'd never asked him to pull a fucking helicopter out of his magic hat. But what good were guardian angels if they couldn't do a little magic every now and then?

I tried to do the time-zone conversion while the phone rang, but gave up. He would answer. He always answered.

On the fifth ring, a familiar baritone came across the line. "Hello?"

"Frodo, it's me."

"Matty? Holy shit, brother. I knew you were going in dark, but what happened to the scheduled check-ins? It's been days."

"I'm in trouble," I said. "I don't have time to explain, but all comms are compromised. This line included. I need your help."

"Roger that," Frodo said, immediately transitioning to business. "Give me a SITREP and tell me what you need."

"Roger," I said. "SITREP as follows. Three Iranian Quds Force operatives have kidnapped Laila. They just departed my location in a Russian-made helicopter heading east. I believe they intend to link up with an IRGC mechanized division currently moving into Iraq. I need to interdict the helicopter before it reaches the division's frontline trace."

"Copy all," Frodo said. "I take it you need transportation?"

"That's affirm. Something fast. The helicopter's got a five-minute head start and counting. Stand by for my grid."

"Send it."

I read Frodo the GPS coordinates from my phone and then confirmed the alphanumeric sequence after Frodo repeated it back to me.

"Okay," Frodo said. "Be ready to roll. I'll call you with details on this line. Do you have a range and bearing to the helicopter?"

"Negative," I said. "But I will by the time you call back."

"Roger that," Frodo said. "Matty, verify one more time the precious cargo."

I closed my eyes for a moment, pushing back against the sudden wave of despair that threatened to overwhelm me. "Laila, brother," I said. "They've got Laila."

The line was quiet for a moment. Then Frodo spoke.

"I've got you, Matty," Frodo said. "Keep the faith and be ready. I'll bring the thunder."

I had to clear my throat before replying. Laila was still captive in a helicopter speeding east, but in that moment, I felt the narrative shift. Frodo was going to bring the thunder.

"Thank you, Frodo," I said. "Thank you."

"Consider it done. Out here."

I hung up the phone and turned to see the Irishman staring at me.

"You have some very interesting friends," Nolan said.

"He's not my friend," I said. "He's my brother."

"What now, then?" Nolan said.

"One more call," I said. Scrolling through the phone's list of recent calls, I found the one I wanted and dialed.

FIFTY-NINE

told you never to call me again. My debt is paid. We're even."

"I know," I said, turning away from Nolan for some privacy.

"Then why are we speaking?"

"Because now I need a favor," I said.

"No."

"Listen, Benny," I said, letting some of the rage boiling inside bubble through. "I know that normally we'd go back and forth like this was a Turkish bazaar, but I don't have time. I need your help, and you're going to give it, so let's just cut to the chase."

A long pause and then: "Are you sure you're not Israeli?"

"I'm not sure of a good many things, but on this matter I'm quite confident. Aren't you going to give me the price?"

"First the favor. Then the price."

A surge of irritation shot through me, but I forced my anger back into place. In the Middle East, this was the way things were done. Even between allies. Perhaps especially between allies.

"For argument's sake," I said, "can I assume that you have eyes on the Iranian frontline trace?"

"You can assume anything you want, but I'm not going to—"

"Benny."

"Yes, that would be a fair assumption," Benny said.

"Good, then I need you to pull one of your ISR assets off station and head west."

"Why?"

"Because I need you to locate a helicopter heading east. I believe it's trying to link up with the Iranian forward elements."

"Why?"

"The helicopter is carrying three Quds Force operatives." I paused for a moment, unsure how much to reveal. If Benny knew how urgently I needed the information, the cost would skyrocket. Then again, what was cost in comparison with Laila's life? At that moment, I would have provided Benny with the nuclear launch codes if I'd had them. Anything to get back my wife. "And my wife. The Iranians kidnapped my wife."

"Truly?" Benny said. "Those monsters have your wife?"

"Truly."

This time the Hebrew curses sounded strangely comforting.

"If I were able to locate this helicopter," Benny said, "what then?"

"Call me on this number and provide range and bearing to the aircraft."

"What will you do with this information?"

"Whatever it takes," I said.

Another pause, this one longer than the one before, then: "Let me see what I can do."

It occurred to me as the line went dead that Benny and I never had settled on a price. Then again, perhaps we didn't need to. Though we served different intelligence services, I had the sense that Benny was a good man.

At least that was what I was hoping.

SIXTY

ad—is that your ride?"

I looked from my phone to Nolan and then to where he was pointing. A black speck in the night sky was rapidly resolving into the discernible shape of an aircraft, though what kind of aircraft I wasn't quite sure. The speck was moving much too fast to be a helicopter. And then I saw the low-slung fuselage suspended between two oversized propellers, and the mystery was solved.

"That's it," I said, strobing the flashlight on my cell toward the Osprey. "Hang on to your shirt. The downdraft is a bitch."

The hybrid aircraft made the transition from plane to helicopter as its nacelles rotated upward, bringing the twin three-bladed proprotors from vertical to horizontal. The CV-22 bled off forward airspeed as it circled the palace, orienting into the wind before making a final approach to the now-vacated helipads. I turned my back to the aircraft's approach as, true to form, hurricane-force winds announced its arrival.

The snarling vortices generated by the six-thousand-horsepower engines smacked into my back like an invisible tidal wave, pelting me with all manner of grit and dirt and almost taking me off my feet in the process. After less than a second, every exposed inch of skin had been sandblasted by grime.

Then the tempest subsided.

"Holy shite," the Irishman said over a spasm of coughing. "You weren't kidding."

Wiping the tears from my eyes, I turned back to the Osprey to see the ramp lowered and the crew chief beckoning with a red-lens flashlight.

"I think that's my cue," I said, offering Nolan my hand. "I meant what I said. I'll do what I can to help you."

"And I believe you," Nolan said, returning my handshake. "But I think this gentleman wants to have a word with ye first."

Nolan pointed over my shoulder, and I turned to see Zain running up the gravel path leading to the helipads. The smuggler had an assault pack slung over his shoulder, a submachine gun in one hand, and his trusty AK-47 in the other.

"Here, Matthew," Zain said, passing me the submachine gun. "I figured you'd want something more precise than an AK. So I got you this."

This turned out to be an HK MP5 with an integrated

suppressor outfitted with an EOTech reflex sight and a two-point VTAC sling. Not the weapon to use for distance shooting, but for close-in work, there was nothing better.

"Magazines and a Glock are in here," Zain said, handing me the assault pack. "Let's go."

I took the assault pack but placed my hand on the Syrian's chest as he started toward the Osprey. "Thank you," I said. "But you're not coming."

"Your wife—," Zain said.

"Is my responsibility," I said. "I know you'd go with me if you could, but trust me—that crew chief isn't going to let you within fifty feet of his bird. I've got to do this alone."

For a moment, I thought Zain would argue. Instead, he just pulled me in for a hug. "Allah be with you, Matthew. Get her back from those monsters. We will find the girl Ferah. I was the one who tipped off the Army after I saw the corrupt police standing guard. With their help, *inshallah* we will save all the girls."

I nodded and grabbed the gear. I'd started hustling toward the clearly impatient crew chief when Zain gripped my arm.

"Wait, Matthew," Zain said. "I didn't have time to get you body armor. Take my chest rig instead."

I started to push the smuggler away, but found myself accepting the combination body armor and tactical harness. I told myself that it was a decision based purely on practicality. After all, there would probably be some more shooting before this was all over, and Zain's soft body armor offered a whole lot more ballistic protection than my filthy sport coat and shirt.

But I knew that wasn't the only reason. The truth was that I wanted something to remind me that I wasn't alone. That I still had friends, and that they had my back. Even if the best they could do in this moment was to offer me a sweat-stained tactical rig.

I slipped the rig over my shoulders, adjusted the Velcro straps, and cinched down the bindings. For not being an operator, Zain had done a respectable job assembling his kit. Miniature med pouch on the bottom left where it wouldn't interfere with a pistol holster, magazine pouches across the front, a small knife on the right, and several pockets filled with odds and ends along the sides.

In short, everything a growing boy needed to chase down the terrorists holding his wife.

"Thank you, my friend," I said, shouldering the assault kit. "For everything."

"Kill them," Zain said, gripping my free hand with both of his. "The men who took your wife, kill them all."

And with that, the Syrian turned back down the hill, disappearing into the night.

S o who are you exactly?"

The question was fair, but not one I intended to answer. At least not accurately. As a rule, spies tend to have a tenuous relationship with the truth, and I was no exception. But in this case, any deception on my part was more a function of survival than of subterfuge. After all, if I didn't tell the pilot the truth, then he didn't have to make the intellectual leap to believe it in all its absurdity.

Instead, I did what spies did best—deflected.

"What were your orders, Captain?" I said, adjusting the boom mike on the headset the crew chief had handed me so that the microphone rested just against my lips. Even in flight, a CV-22 Osprey was loud, and we were still sitting on the ground, though I hoped for not too much longer.

"My orders were to divert to this grid coordinate, pick you up, and provide whatever assistance you required."

"Perfect," I said. "Then get this thing in the air and start heading east."

"What's east?"

"A helicopter. We need to catch it."

"Then what?"

"Goddamn it," I said, not bothering to hide the tension knotting my stomach. "Were you unclear about anything I just said? Get us airborne and headed east before I reach down your throat and rip out your spine."

For a moment, I thought the Air Force pilot sitting in the left seat was going to argue. That would have been a mistake. But just as I was about to walk up the narrow passage separating the passenger compartment from the cockpit, the Osprey shot into the air like a homesick angel.

The sudden acceleration sent me sprawling across a pile of boxes the crew chief had stacked just to the right of the entrance ramp. I knew pilots could sometimes be divas, but this was some over-the-top bullshit.

"Pilot," I said, struggling back to my feet, "what the fuck is your call sign?"

"Hammer."

"Okay, Hammer. You're fired."

"What? You can't—"

"I can, and I just did. Copilot, what's your call sign?"

For a long moment no one spoke. Then a feminine voice answered, "Pom Pom."

"Pom Pom," I said. "Are you a good stick?"

"Yes, sir, I am."

"I'm not a sir. I'm Matt. And you are now the aircraft commander. Hammer, if you have a problem with that, get the fuck out of my airplane. I shit you not. Things are only going to get hairier from here. If you're not down with that, speak now. We'll land and put you off. I swear to Christ that if my orders are second-guessed again, I will get angry, and you will not enjoy that experience. Are we clear?"

"Yes, sir," Pom Pom said.

"It's Matt."

"Okay, Matt. What kind of helicopter are we looking for?"

"It was dark, but I think it was a civilian twin engine," I said.

"How long a head start does it have?" Pom Pom said.

I checked my watch. "Ten minutes."

"Okay. At our current airspeed, we should be intercepting in about fifteen mikes, but we don't have air-to-air radar. We can use our thermal-imaging system to help with the search, but without vectors, it's still going to be like trying to find a needle in a haystack."

"I'm working on it," I said. "What kind of call sign is Pom Pom anyway?"

The woman hesitated.

"Come on, Pom Pom," I said. "We're about to be in the shit together. Now is not the time to be shy."

"I was a competitive cheerleader in high school."

Okay, so I didn't see that one coming.

"Are you as good a pilot as you were a cheerleader?" I said.

"Better."

"Perfect. Here's the lowdown—that helicopter is carrying three Iranian Quds Force operatives and an American hostage. The hostage happens to be my wife. We have got to find the helicopter before it reaches the Iranian frontline trace. If we don't, she's gone. Are you picking up what I'm putting down?"

Another pause and then: "Yes, sir."

"Matt."

"Matt."

"Help me get my wife back, Pom Pom," I said. "Do some of that pilot shit."

"I love *Top Gun* as much as the next girl, but without vectors, we're going to fly right by your wife."

"I'll get you vectors."

"From where?" Pom Pom said.

"The Mossad, I hope."

"I'm sorry—did you just say the Mossad?"

"Hang on, Pom Pom," I said as the phone in my pocket began to vibrate. "I gotta take this call."

I slid the headset off without waiting for a response, clicked the answer button, and held the cell to my ear. "Drake."

I recognized Benny's voice, but his words were unintelligible over the aircraft's roar. I turned the phone's volume all the way up, but still couldn't make heads or tails of what my Israeli friend was saying.

"Benny," I said, barely hearing myself speak, "I can't hear you. I'm currently airborne on an eastwardly heading. I need you to text me the bearing and distance to the target helicopter. Bearing and distance. Out here."

Ending the call, I slid the headset back over my ears and then flipped the phone over, staring at the blank screen, willing a text message to appear. Then it hit me— the background noise had more than likely made my own instructions undecipherable. I thumbed in a quick text message repeating my instructions and sent it to the number that had just called.

A moment later a message appeared.

TRANSMISSION FAILURE

Fuck me running.

So apparently Benny's phone blocked unknown numbers. What in the actual hell? Did the Mossad have a problem with telemarketers? I screamed my frustration at the cabin's ceiling like a wolf howling its death cry.

Just one fucking break. That was all I was asking for. One fucking break.

The phone vibrated.

I looked at the screen, holding my breath.

BEARING 097 DEGREES. 10 KILOMETERS.

Hot damn. Maybe I ought to channel my inner wolf more often.

"Pom Pom, I've got the range and bearing," I said.

"Send it."

"Zero-nine-seven degrees. Ten kilometers."

"Roger, stand by."

I felt the aircraft tilt slightly to the right as my cheerleader turned aviator adjusted the Osprey's course. To my surprise, I found myself filling the empty space with prayer. And not just any prayer: the one my mother had prayed with me each night before bed when I was a child.

Our father who art in heaven, hallowed be thy name; thy kingdom come, thy will be done, on earth as it is in heaven . . .

I stopped there, not because I didn't remember the rest, but because that last part seemed strangely appropriate. Here I was, streaking through the heavens in the hopes of bringing Laila back to earth in one piece. I wasn't much of a theologian, but I seem to remember Jesus had once told his disciples that faith the size of a mustard seed could move mountains. Maybe that was a way of saying that people like me who didn't have much faith at all still had a shot at a miracle.

"Tally target, tally target. Two o'clock. One mile."

To my surprise, the voice belonged to Hammer. Maybe I'd been too harsh on the old boy earlier. Or maybe my last performance had him pretty convinced that I would dangle him out the back door by his entrails if he didn't find my wife. Either way, he had eyes on the helicopter.

"Tally," Pom Pom said, her voice resonating a calm I didn't feel. "Looks like they're about five hundred feet above ground level. We've got your helicopter. Now what?"

Now what, indeed.

SIXTY-ONE

'd been in my fair share of sticky situations. I'd been ambushed in Afghanistan, betrayed by a double agent to a terrorist organization in Syria, and caught in a cross fire between rival Shia and Sunni militias in Iraq. As the old-timers liked to say, I'd been in the shit. But what I've never been in was a CV-22 Osprey hurtling toward a helicopter holding three homicidal Quds Force operatives and my wife at a closure speed in excess of three hundred knots.

This was a new one, even for me.

"Matt—we're going to overtake them in ten seconds. In another five minutes, they'll be over the Iranian front-line trace. We're starting to get strobed by the air-defense systems embedded with the Iranians. What's the play?"

I wish I knew.

"What's our distance to the helicopter?" I said.

"About a five-hundred-meter slant range."

"Can they see us?"

"We're above and behind them, so I don't think so. But I can't be sure."

"Stay in their blind spot, but close to within one hundred meters."

"Roger that, but the clock's ticking."

I clamped my lips together, biting back the obnoxious reply lurking on the tip of my tongue. I couldn't be mad at Pom Pom. She was just doing her job. Now I needed to do mine.

Over the last several minutes, my eyes had started to adjust to the cabin's semidarkness. The pile of boxes I had tripped over during Hammer's passive-aggressive takeoff had slowly resolved into a series of familiar shapes—Pelican cases. Turning, I grabbed the crew chief by the shoulder and pointed toward the cases.

"What's in those?" I said.

He shrugged. "Beats the hell out of me, sir. We're supposed to be resupplying an Army ODA team. Or we were before we got the call to grab you."

Pelican cases destined for an Army Special Forces Operational Detachment Alpha, or A-team. Maybe I had faith as big as the proverbial mustard seed after all.

Nodding my thanks, I shuffled over to the boxes and popped open the top case. What was nestled in the foam cutouts looked like my Christmas and birthday presents all rolled into one. An HK G28 rifle. The sniper system was reliable, accurate, and fired the heavier 7.62mm round, ideal for Afghanistan's longer-engagement distances. It was also semiautomatic, which meant the shooter didn't have to manually cycle the bolt between each round—a necessity for the urban, target-rich environment of Iraq. For these reasons, the weapon had been Frodo's distance-shooting rifle of choice.

Even after he'd been detailed to serve as my bodyguard, Frodo had refused to let his hard-earned sniper skills slip away. As such, he'd insisted on spending time on thousand-meter-plus ranges whenever possible. And since he was no longer with his Joint Special Operations Command, or JSOC, brethren, the task of serving as his spotter fell to yours truly.

To be fair, I liked shooting as much as the next Ranger. Accordingly, Frodo switched off spotting duties with me frequently, taking the time to impart the mystical wisdom of long-distance shooting during the process. I'd always been pretty good with a rifle, but after five years with a level-one Unit sniper for a tutor, my skills had taken a decidedly more deadly turn.

Reaching into the Pelican case, I grabbed the upper receiver. A Schmidt & Bender scope was mounted to the Picatinny rail, indicating that the sniper who owned this long gun had already zeroed the optic. I turned back to the Pelican case and found a torque wrench prefit with a sprocket nestled next to the upper receiver's foam cutouts. After sliding the sprocket over the nuts attaching the scope, I tightened each down, ensuring the optic was securely mounted.

As I tightened the nuts, I noticed two blue paint markings on the upper receiver that corresponded to two additional markings on the Picatinny rail. This made me smile. It was an old sniper's trick. The markings ensured that the shooter remounted the optic to the exact same spot after each time the scope was removed so the rifle could be cleaned. Since the markings lined up perfectly, I was betting that the rifle had been zeroed to within an inch at a hundred meters.

I didn't know the mystery sniper's identity, but I had a feeling he and Frodo would have gotten along just fine.

I fit the upper and lower receivers together, the familiar weight comforting in my hands. The rifle certainly wasn't zeroed to my eye, but it should get the job done at one hundred meters or less. Now I just needed to figure out what in the hell I was going to shoot.

"Three minutes, Matt," Pom Pom said. "The antiaircraft radar strobes are pulsing more frequently. We need to get this show on the road."

Reaching into the Pelican case again, I grabbed two twenty-round magazines. I was preparing to slip one into my tactical vest when I noticed the rounds inside were tracers. Forget Frodo. I was going to give this sniper a hug if we ever met. Inserting the magazine into the magazine well, I pulled the rifle's charging handle to the rear and released it, watching as the bolt stripped a round from the magazine.

"Pom Pom," I said as I slid the second magazine into my chest rig, "did you ever fly helicopters?"

"No—fixed wing all the way."

"Hammer—what about you?"

"Nope."

Well, shit.

"No worries," I said, despite the fact that I was extremely worried. "Let me put this to you a different way: I need to bring down that helicopter without killing my wife. What would happen if I shot the fuel tank?"

"Bad idea," Pom Pom said. "A rifle bullet isn't going to cause the tank to explode, but most fuel cells are self-sealing. Besides, even if you do manage to puncture it, a rifle bullet isn't big enough to drain the fuel anywhere near fast enough. You need to get that helicopter on the ground. Now."

"What about the engine?" Hammer said.

"Come again?" I said.

"The engine. Even though that bird has two, most civilian models are underpowered. Take out one of the engines, and the pilot will have to land. Immediately."

"That's the spirit, Hammer," I said, extending the bipod mounted beneath the rifle's slim barrel. "I'm gonna take the shot from the starboard door, so I need you to come to an echelon-left formation. Put the helicopter at your two o'clock at a distance of one hundred meters. Then crab your nose to the left and hold her steady. That'll give me the widest firing arc."

"Wait," Pom Pom said. "It's not that easy. We'll need to rotate the engine nacelles up and out of the way so that you won't shoot through our proprotors. That means slowing down to about one hundred knots."

"Sounds like more pilot shit to me," I said, clipping myself to the airframe with a cargo strap the crew chief handed me. "Make it happen."

I knew what I was asking wasn't exactly easy, but

dwelling on the difficulty wouldn't bring us any closer to getting Laila back. The pilots needed to do what they did best. So did I. End of story. Every second spent talking instead of doing just got Laila and her captors one second closer to the advancing Iranian horde.

To their credit, the pilots didn't argue. Instead, they delved into a terse conversation among themselves and the Osprey's two crew chiefs to which I paid no attention. Not because I didn't care, but because I couldn't add anything of value. Instead, I hastily constructed a semistable shooting platform at the starboard door and began to breathe.

Distance shooting really was as much an art as a science, but a good portion of it came down to body mechanics. In other words, the shooter needed to hold as perfectly still as possible while pulling the trigger rearward as evenly as possible. Any unintended movement by the shooter imparted unwanted changes to the bullet's flight path. With this in mind, snipers paid an almost obsessive amount of attention to their respiration and heart rate.

Edging behind the rifle, I welded my cheek to the buttstock. Then I closed my eyes, imagining myself on the range with Frodo spotting over my shoulder. I blocked out everything, the rage, the terror, the heartache, everything but Frodo's steady baritone.

Count backward from five. Concentrate on slowing your breath with each number. Five . . .

I was dimly aware of the Osprey slowing as the nacelles rotated up, taking the proprotors with them.

. . . your arms and legs are floating. . . . Four . . . your jaw is soft. . . . Three . . .

One hundred knots' worth of cold night air poured in the open door, buffeting my shirt.

. . . your breathing is slow and even. . . . Two . . . the rifle is part of your body. . . . One . . .

Opening my eyes, I watched the night sky float past my optic. At first, I saw nothing but stars and empty space. Then the helicopter's shadowy outline swam into view.

"Tally target," I said, turning the circular knob mounted to the optic until a cherry red dot materialized in the center of the scope's etched lines. Without night-vision optics, I was going to have to do this the old-fashioned way. Using the red dot as a visual reference, I shifted my body until the crimson spot was centered on the glowing exhaust of the helicopter's left engine.

My stomach clenched as the helicopter rose and fell in my crosshairs. Too much motion. Little pockets of unseen turbulence were sending both aircraft bobbing up and down unpredictably. No way to get an accurate shot.

Remember—aim small, miss small.

Frodo's admonishment resonated. Dialing up the scope's magnification, I targeted a specific aspect of the engine exhaust—the right lower quadrant. The inherent motion was still there, but because I was focusing small, the ups and downs seemed less abrupt. Less random. I could compensate for this. I could make the shot.

"Range to target?" I said.

"Two hundred meters," Pom Pom said.

"Too far. Close to within one hundred, and then clear me hot."

"Roger. Stand by."

I could hear the tension in Pom Pom's voice, but I couldn't dwell on it. I had my own job to do.

The aircraft vibrated as Pom Pom fed more power to the engines. Then . . .

"Eighty-five meters," Pom Pom said. "Cleared hot. Cleared hot."

"Roger," I said, moving the fire selector switch from safe to single with my thumb. I placed the pad of my index finger on the trigger, waited for the natural pause between breaths, and began pressing the trigger rearward.

Slow is smooth. Smooth is fast. Fast is deadly.

"Matt—wait!"

Pom Pom's voice cut through my concentration with the subtlety of a submarine's dive Klaxon. I jerked my finger away from the trigger like I'd touched a hot stove.

"What?" I said.

"Make sure you fire straight up the rear of the engine exhaust. You don't want to accidentally clip the main rotor."

Oh, sweet baby Jesus.

"I have to shoot it straight up the ass end?" I said.

"Yes," Pom Pom said. "Otherwise you risk hitting the transmission, hydraulic pumps, or any of the other things that will transition the helicopter into a rock."

"Okay," I said. "Anything else I should worry about?"

"Yes, the radar strobes are no longer intermittent. We're out of time."

I adjusted my hold so that the bullet would transition straight through the helicopter's engine. Then I concentrated again on my breathing until I lost myself in the shooter's zen, repeating Frodo's mantra as I pressed the trigger rearward.

Slow is smooth. Smooth is fast. Fast is—

The shot broke, and the rifle kicked into my shoulder.

The crimson tracer arced through the sky, passing below the engine exhaust and into empty space.

Low.

Damn it.

Elevating my hold slightly, I started the shooting sequence again. The shot broke; the tracer passed through the exhaust.

Nothing changed.

What the actual fuck?

I fired five more times in rapid succession, each tracer disappearing into the glowing void. As the fifth shot broke, a ball of fire belched from the engine exhaust. For a moment or two, the helicopter continued flying normally. Then the nose dipped, and the aircraft started a ponderous descent, thick smoke trailing from its left engine.

"Got him," I said, tracking the helicopter's progress with my optic. "Got him, Pom Pom."

"Hell yeah!" Pom Pom said in her best cheerleader voice. "What next?"

"Follow it down."

SIXTY-TWO

Up until now, I'd thought I'd known a thing or two about terror. But I hadn't. Watching a helicopter carrying my wife plummet toward the desert floor was terror incarnate. I stared, my heart in my throat, as the helo slowly lost altitude. Then it flared and disappeared in a cloud of brown.

"Pom Pom," I said, "did you—"

"She's down safe, Matt," Pom Pom said. "Down safe."

Once again, the proverbial mustard seed had come through. Now it was time to transition to a role much more suited to me—the Angel of Death.

"You carrying fast ropes?" I said, turning to the closest crew chief.

"Roger, sir."

"Get one ready."

"The sixty or ninety?"

Sixty was on the tip of my tongue, but I stopped to

think. Fast roping looks cool. In fact, from a recruiting standpoint, fast roping ranks right up there with helo-casting or HAHO jumps for awesome pictures. After all, what's not to like about sliding down a rope beneath a hovering helicopter?

Everything is the answer you're looking for.

First off, I was terrified of heights in the soul-crushing, panic-inducing manner small children reserved for the unseen monsters lurking beneath their beds. But that was just the tip of the iceberg. Fast roping was hard on the body in a way that even parachuting wasn't. The average combat-loaded Ranger carries about eighty pounds of gear, counting his rucksack and weapon. But if you were one of the lucky few who got to hump specialty equipment like the radios, mortar base plates, or machine guns, that eighty pounds turned into one hundred plus pretty fast.

Now, imagine sliding down a rope with one hundred pounds on your back, using only your hands and feet for brakes. Suddenly it doesn't sound like quite so much fun, does it? That's why no Ranger has ever asked a crew chief for the ninety-foot rope. Ninety feet of rope means a third more time sliding for your life. This in turn means a third more friction on your hands as you try to slow your controlled fall.

Not to mention a third likelier chance of plummeting to your death.

But tonight things were different. For one, I wasn't combat loaded. Two, since I was outmanned at least three to one, four or five to one counting the pilots, I needed the element of surprise for as long as possible. So far, the Iranians didn't seem to know we were behind them. But that would all change if the CV-22 came to a hover and browned everything out.

"Pom Pom," I said, eyeing the thick lengths of rope, "will we get a dust cloud if we come to a hover at sixty feet?"

"Absolutely."

"What about ninety?"

"Probably. But it won't be nearly as noticeable."

Ninety it was.

"All right," I said, helping the crew chief drag the hefty rope bag to the edge of the platform, "here's how this is going to go. Come to a hover behind the helicopter. I'm going to fast rope out. Once I'm off the rope, pick up an orbit and give me some cover with your .50-cal ramp gun. Got it?"

"How do we know when to get you?" Pom Pom said.

"That'll be easy. As soon as you see me with my wife, come in hot. If any of those fuckers are still alive, smoke 'em."

"Roger that," Pom Pom said. "Coming to a hover. Ropes, ropes, ropes!"

The crew chief kicked the rope bag out the platform door. Next he leaned into space, checking to ensure the rope had made it all the way to the ground by verifying that the green IR chem light affixed to the end was horizontal, not vertical. Then he turned and slapped me on the shoulder.

"Go, go, go."

I cinched my VTAC sling tight, securing the HK to my back, and reached for the rope. This was when I encountered my first problem—I had no gloves.

"I need gloves," I yelled to the crew chief.

"What?"

"Gloves," I said, pointing at his hands.

"Shit," the crew chief said. "I don't have any for fast-roping. But you can have these."

He pulled off his Nomex aviator gloves and tossed them to me. I seated them with two quick yanks. Before I could think about the pain that would come next, I caught the rope, wrapped my feet around the length of bucking nylon, and slid into space.

SIXTY-THREE

A word about gloves. Not all are created equal. For instance, the gloves used to shield the hands of fast-roping Rangers were the equivalent size and thickness of welders' gloves. They weren't designed for dexterity. They were designed to keep the friction generated during the slide for life from blistering your hands.

In comparison, aviator gloves were designed to protect their wearer from a flash fire while still offering the nimbleness a pilot or a crew chief needed to action all the magical buttons and levers that kept their aircraft aloft. To put my dilemma in even simpler terms, I was grabbing a scalding pot while using a paper towel instead of a pot holder.

The results were just as predictable, not to mention unpleasant.

Even without a rucksack and extraneous gear to weigh me down, ninety feet on a rope was a long slide. About halfway down, I could feel heat radiating through my thin aviator gloves. By three-quarters, I was gritting my teeth against the pain. But it was still too much. With about fifteen feet to go, I had to choose between blistering my hands and stopping to allow the friction-generated heat to dissipate.

Option one meant potentially affecting my ability to shoot. Option two would cede the element of surprise. Neither option was good, so I did what Rangers always do in situations like this.

I improvised.

Clenching my jaw against the pain, I slid for another half a second, trying to shrink fifteen feet to somewhere north of eight. Then I let go.

And fell.

Next to my chute not opening, falling off a fast rope has always been one of my biggest nightmares. Then again, personal phobias tend to lose their potency when trained killers have the woman you love. I was in the air long enough to realize that I was falling, which in turn meant that I'd let go closer to twelve feet than eight.

Then I hit the ground.

I executed a PLF, or parachute landing fall, trying to dissipate some of the kinetic energy. Unfortunately, even the outstanding men and women who taught at the Army's airborne school couldn't have imagined this scenario. My knees were bent, but the jarring collision still sent a flash of pain the length of my spine. Based on previous experience, I'd just herniated a disc or three. But that rather unpleasant sensation quickly took a backseat to the feeling of red-hot nails punching through my kneecap. Apparently, my chosen landing zone was littered with stones, and my right knee had just found a rather large one.

Swearing, I stumbled to my feet, favoring my leg, as Pom Pom accelerated out of her hover, thundering away. The Iranian helicopter pilot had landed his bird in a field covered by knee-high scrub brush about three hundred yards away from two low hills bridged by a saddle. A road meandered to the left of the helicopter. The thoroughfare might have been paved once, but after more than a decade of nonstop fighting, the huge fissures crisscrossing the broken concrete were visible even by moonlight.

Pom Pom had done her work well, putting me down about fifty meters behind the stricken helicopter. Judging by the lack of noise, the pilots had killed the engines, but the main rotor was still turning, spindly blades drooping as the centrifugal force that stiffened them slowly bled away.

My plan, such as it was, centered around taking the Iranians by surprise, preferably while they were still bunched together near the helicopter. I'd done quite a bit of the precision shooting required for CQB. In the Ranger Regiment, my trusty M4 rifle was the weapon of choice for this task, but once I joined the DIA, much of the training favored MP5 variants due to their concealability and accuracy.

Even so, I'd never entered an engagement with such lopsided odds. Counting the pilots, I was outnumbered by as many as five to one, and I was operating at night.

The full moon provided decent illumination, but no-where near the tactical advantage I normally enjoyed when outfitted with night-vision goggles paired with an infrared laser mounted to my rifle.

And then there was the elephant in the room. Laila. Practicing stress shoots was all well and good, but seeing a loved one in your aiming reticle changed the equation. It had to. Even the most experienced operator was still a human being subject to human emotions. If putting a bullet into a bad guy holding a gun to your wife's head didn't give you a case of the jitters, you probably needed to talk to a shrink.

Or a divorce attorney.

All things considered, my current situation was less than ideal. On the other hand, I was alive and armed with a weapon accurate enough to drive nails. That would have to do.

Thumbing down the EOTech's brightness to try to save as much night vision as possible, I brought the HK to my shoulder and started toward the helicopter. As much as I tried to ignore it, the pain radiating from my knee forced me to limp, making my shooting platform decidedly less stable. The scarlet holographic circle pro-jected by the EOTech floated across the helicopter as I panned the HK left and right, searching for targets.

Having survived a helicopter hard landing a time or two myself, I could picture what was going on in the cockpit. First came the sense of euphoria at facing down gravity and living to tell the tale. Next was the realization that while you were alive, you were also stuck somewhere you did not want to be. Somewhere inhabited by people who wanted to kill you.

This revelation usually prompted two responses. First, the pilots would start working the radios in an attempt to get friendlies to the crash site. Next, any shooters on board would exit the downed bird and set up an ad hoc security perimeter.

By now the Iranians had had more than enough time to celebrate the fact that they were still alive. Any moment now the shooters should start egressing the aircraft. My plan was to put the HK's superb integrated suppressor to work by killing them as quickly and quietly as possible before they realized they had a predator in their midst.

I was about ten meters from the tail boom when I heard the squeak of metal on metal. Following the sound to the left, I saw the pilot and one of the passengers standing just outside the helicopter, staring skyward with the cabin's doors open. I could only guess that the helicopter's ambient noise had kept them from hearing the CV-22 loitering overhead, and now they were a bit perplexed.

I crouched on one knee, angling my muzzle line away from the fuselage to prevent any errant rounds from passing through the cabin, endangering Laila. Then I squeezed off a single shot into the passenger's head. Though incredibly accurate, the MP5's 9mm pistol rounds could be stopped by soft body armor, and I wasn't taking any chances.

The passenger collapsed, his AK-47 clattering to the ground beside him.

The pilot turned toward me, the weak green light spilling from inside the cockpit illuminating his confused expression. This time, I held the trigger down, putting a three-round burst into his chest.

Then there were two bodies on the ground.

So far, so good.

I stood and moved to the left, intending to get a better angle into the helicopter's interior, when a gun fired behind me. After the MP5's suppressed *pop*s, a pistol's unmuted discharge scared the shit out of me. But not as much as the sledgehammer that slammed into my back, squarely between my shoulder blades.

I stumbled, shifting my weight to my right leg, which promptly buckled. I tumbled to the ground, landing with the grace of a sumo wrestler on ice skates. After smacking my right shoulder, I rolled left, tracking the shooter's muzzle flash. No time to get a proper sight picture, so I shot from the hip. I squeezed the trigger twice, orienting the barrel onto target like I was pointing at the shooter with my left index finger. I walked the rounds from his crotch to his neck, and he flopped over backward.

Not the tightest shot grouping in the world, but once again, the MP5 had worked as advertised.

I pushed myself to my feet with my left hand, holding

the MP5 with my right. The throbbing between my shoulder blades flared with each breath, but it was the dull ache of deep bruising rather than the burning agony of a bullet wound.

Zain's body armor had just saved my life.

The *thump thump thump* of machine-gun fire reverberated from above and behind me, accompanied by the whine of ricocheting rounds. Spinning toward the sound, I saw a body torn to pieces lying in front of and to the left of the helicopter's nose.

Unlike his compatriot, this Quds Force operative had an AK-47 rifle in his lifeless hands. A 7.62mm round from which Zain's soft body armor would not have stopped. I owed Pom Pom's crew chief a case of beer once this was all over.

Four men dead meant one remaining.

Leading with the HK, I spied around the helicopter's open doors, clearing the cabin.

Empty.

Well, shit.

Hobbling past the helicopter's nose, I saw two figures backlit by moonlight about seventy-five meters away. The larger silhouette was dragging the smaller by her hair. As I stepped toward them, he jerked Laila between us and crouched behind her shoulder.

"Easy, Matthew," a familiar voice said. "You already have the death of one woman on your hands tonight. I'd hate for your wife to be number two."

The Devil. The fucking Devil. He must have switched helicopters. The little shit bag had more lives than a cat.

"Matt," Laila said, her voice breaking.

"Hush, baby," I said, panning the EOTech's holographic sight over Laila's shoulder. "It's almost over."

"Couldn't agree more, Matthew," the Devil said. "Put your weapon on the ground. Now."

The Osprey thundered overhead, turning lazy circles in the sky. Pom Pom's door gunner was pretty shit hot, but his .50-caliber machine gun was useless for an engagement like this. Saving Laila would require a precision shot from a precision shooter.

In other words, me.

"I'm not going to say this again," the Devil said. "Put your weapon on the ground."

"Or what?" I said, moving closer. "You'll kill her?"

I could hear the Devil, but I couldn't see him. The little bastard was crouching behind Laila, his head hidden by her hair. I could put a round over her shoulder, but that was an action of last resort. The HK was a close-in weapon, hell on wheels in the tight confines of urban warfare. It was not meant for a seventy-five-meter shot.

Not to mention that I was sure the Devil had a pistol buried in Laila's spine. A head shot, directly between the eyes, was the only guaranteed way to instantly incapacitate a gunman. Anything else risked the shooter's trigger finger spasming in death.

"Let her go," I said, shuffling closer still.

A shot rang out.

My heart stopped.

Not again. Please, Jesus. Not again.

Then Laila whimpered, and I could breathe.

"Last warning, Matthew," the Devil said. "The next shot will be in her kneecap. You're right. I can't kill her. But I can fill your pretty wife's arms and legs with holes until you tire of hearing her scream. Put down your weapon before I count to three."

If I dropped the HK, we were both dead. I'd have to take the shot.

"One."

I inhaled.

Exhaled.

Banished the image of Laila.

Forgot I even had a wife.

Or a swollen knee pulsing with every heartbeat.

Or a back spasming with every breath.

I forgot everything but the red dot floating over Laila's shoulder.

"Two."

I took another breath.

Exhaled.

Found the natural space between breaths.

Began to squeeze the trigger.

And then Pom Pom took matters into her own hands. Shrieking down from heaven like a falcon diving toward prey, the Osprey came to a twenty-foot hover. The eighty-knot rotor wash pummeled the Devil and Laila with gale-force winds. Laila stumbled backward, falling.

I saw my target.

The crimson dot found the Devil's face. I pulled the trigger. His head snapped backward. He fell to the ground. I staggered forward, firing twice more into his prone form.

Then it was over.

"Laila," I screamed, letting the VTAC sling catch the MP5 as I lurched toward her. "Laila!"

The Osprey had transitioned from a hover and was back circling overhead, but Laila had been knocked to the ground. She turned toward the sound of my voice as she struggled to her feet, midnight hair swirling in the wind. Moonlight washed across her face, and her heart-stopping green eyes found mine.

"Matt!"

I tried to run, but could manage only a drunken hobble. But not Laila. Legs pumping, raven hair billowing, she sprinted toward me.

"You came," Laila said, half speaking, half sobbing as she crashed into my chest. "You came for me."

"I'll always come for you," I said, crushing her to me. "I'm your husband."

I pressed my face into her hair, breathing her in with deep, gasping breaths. She wrapped herself around me, trembling in my arms. In that moment, everything was right with the world.

Absolutely everything.

And then that moment was gone.

A flash from the hillside split the darkness. I looked up to see a finger of flame shooting skyward, trailing a dirty cloud of gray like a comet's tail. The streak of fire bridged the distance to the loitering Osprey in less than a heart-beat, erupting under the aircraft's left engine with a thunderous boom.

At first, the CV-22 seemed to shrug off the impact, turning to the right, away from us, as oily smoke poured from the fuselage. Then everything changed. The stricken engine exploded, sending the three-bladed pro-protor spiraling into space in as many pieces. Flames engulfed the aircraft in billowing waves. Like an elk hamstrung by a pack of wolves, the Osprey seemed to stumble before slowly listing to the left. As the aircraft began to roll, it shuddered, then plummeted toward the unforgiving desert soil.

I tackled Laila, covering her body with my own, but the explosion as the CV-22 slammed into the ground still tossed us both into the air. Heat scorched my head and neck, and bits of metal and debris pinged off the stones next to me.

"What happened?" Laila said.

"Come on," I said, helping her to her feet. "We've got to go."

In that moment I was terrified, but terrified for the wrong reason. I was afraid Laila would ask where we were going, forcing me to tell her the truth. That I had no idea. None at all. The Osprey was now a cauldron of smoke and boiling fire. A pyre to the dead. With safety miles behind us and the Iranians just beyond the two hills, I dreaded hearing this unanswerable question from my wife's lips.

But there was another sound I should have been

dreading even more. The sound a high-velocity round makes when it impacts human flesh. One moment, Laila was facing me, her jade eyes boring into mine. The next, a dull *thump* came between us, followed by the rolling report of a Dragunov sniper rifle.

Then my wife collapsed to the ground, and my world collapsed with her.

SIXTY-FOUR

Laila," I screamed. "Laila!"

Blood washed over my hands in a crimson wave as her eyelashes fluttered.

"Matt?"

"Stay still, baby. Stay still."

A tiny portion of my mind realized that the angry buzzing sounds snapping past my head corresponded to the muzzle flashes on top of the hills in front of me. People were shooting at us. Probably the same people who had swatted the Osprey from the sky. But that didn't matter. Nothing mattered but the scarlet flood pouring over my fingertips.

"Laila? Can you hear me? You've got to keep talking."

Blood covered her torso. Spurting blood. Arterial blood. I ripped her shirt away, starting with her chest and moving out, fingers touching every inch of exposed skin, looking for the entry wound.

Nothing.

My heart shuddered as I swallowed a sob. The bullet hadn't passed through her chest cavity. Her lungs and heart were safe. Neck was untouched.

Where the fuck was the blood coming from?

With a start, I realized that there must not be an exit wound. The bullet was still lodged inside her. Rolling Laila over, I followed the same procedure, fingers probing skin as my breath came in shuddering gasps. Kidneys and liver untouched. No abdominal wound. No upper-chest wound.

What the fuck?

And then I saw it. High on the inside of her right arm. The bullet must have just clipped her brachial artery. Compressing the wound with one hand, I reached for Zain's med kit, unzipping it and scattering the contents on the ground beside me.

"Laila," I said, sorting through the mess one-handed, "can you hear me?"

She groaned, and I worked faster, sending packs of gauze, antiseptic wipes, and other odds and ends tumbling across the dirt until my fingers found what I sought—a tourniquet. Keeping pressure on the wound with my left hand, I slipped the tourniquet over her arm with my right, moving it as high up the limb as possible. Then I cinched down the Velcro band and began twisting the pencil-like rod attached to the tourniquet. Laila moaned as the unforgiving plastic bit into her skin, but I kept twisting and twisting, my heart shattering anew each time she groaned.

Finally, the bleeding stopped. Looping the Velcro back over the rod, I secured it in place. Laila murmured and her eyes fluttered, but she was alive. My wife was still alive.

For now.

In that instant, the sensations from the outside world I'd been ignoring came crashing back in. Muzzle flashes and rifle reports from the hillside and divots of sand erupting to either side of me. By luck, we'd fallen into a slight depression that was making it harder for the sharpshooters to achieve the correct angle. But the whine of bullets buzzing past my head let me know our luck wouldn't last long.

And then a buzzing of another sort demanded my attention. The buzzing of the cell phone in my pocket.

Squirming into the dirt beside Laila, I pulled the device from my pocket. Seven missed calls. *What in the hell?* I thumbed the answer button and held the phone to my ear.

"Drake."

"Matty, it's me."

"Frodo," I said. "Thank God. I'm in the shit, brother. I—"

"Matty, listen. We retasked a Global Hawk to monitor the Iranian advance. I've eyes on you right now. I got permission to launch the Apache QRF. Two gunships are inbound, but they're going to need a talk onto target. Can you do that?"

"How?"

"We're going to patch this cell through."

"That's possible?"

"It is now. The chief still swings a big stick when his boys are in harm's way. The technology to make this happen is beyond a knuckle dragger like me, but what I can tell you is that in about ten seconds you're going to be talking directly to the gunship pilots."

"Laila's hit," I said.

"How bad?"

"Not good. I've got her arm tourniqueted. The hemorrhaging has stopped, but she's lost a lot of blood. She's going into shock."

"Listen to Uncle Frodo. I've got two more Ospreys on the way. They're carrying a twelve-man A-team and their Iraqi partners. Use the Apaches to secure the LZ. Once you do that, I'll bring the Ospreys in and the Special Forces Eighteen-D medic will sort out Laila. Can you dig it?"

"I can dig it," I said.

"Good," Frodo said. "Now, fuck up some Iranians so we can get your wife home. Frodo out."

True to form, my best friend jumped off the line before I could thank him. But that was fine, because I knew the best way to express my gratitude was to follow his instructions.

Time to fuck up some Iranians.

SIXTY-FIVE

Any station this net, any station, this is Shock Zero-Nine, over."

It felt incredibly strange to hear a crackling radio transmission over my phone. But with rounds snapping by my head, and the geysers of dirt drawing ever closer, the gunship pilot's voice was also incredibly comforting.

"Shock Zero-Nine, this is Mustang Six," I said, my old call sign slipping off my lips. "I've got you loud and clear."

"Mustang Six, Shock Zero-Nine, have you the same. Shock Zero-Nine is a flight of two Apaches approximately thirty seconds out. Can you give me your grid coordinates and a quick SITREP?"

"Roger that, Zero-Nine. Stand by," I said, and placed the phone on the ground.

Controlling the Apaches would require my total and complete concentration. While I was directing the gunships' fire, my ability to check on Laila would be minimal. With this in mind, I verified that her tourniquet was still holding and that she wasn't hemorrhaging anywhere else. The bleeding was under control, but her skin felt clammy to the touch, and her respiration was increasing. She was going into shock, but there was nothing I could do.

Nothing but annihilate the men shooting at us as quickly as possible.

Scooting past Laila, I put my body between her and the volleys of small-arms fire raining down from the hillside. Then I laid the MP5 out in front of me. The little submachine gun had nowhere near the range required to hit back at our attackers, but judging by the changes in the position of their muzzle flashes, that might not be true for much longer.

The fighters on the top of the hill were still pouring suppressive fire across our position, keeping Laila and me pinned to the earth. But now I could see another series of flashes on the left side of the hill as a maneuvering group of riflemen bounded closer. The sprinkling of rounds kicking up dirt and debris to either side of me turned into a full-blown hailstorm as the overwatch team concentrated their fire and the maneuvering team found better angles for their own shots. Zain's chest rig jumped as a round tore through the shoulder strap.

We couldn't hold out for much longer.

"Zero-Nine, this is Six," I said. "Mustang Six is a two-man element taking fire from approximately fifteen to twenty dismounted fighters dug in on the hills two hundred meters to our twelve o'clock. I have one casualty, category urgent. A team of dismounts is bounding closer, and we are in danger of being overrun. Also, be advised that the fighters have MANPADS. I say again, the fighters have surface-to-air missiles. Stand by for grid, over."

I switched to the phone's GPS function and read off the string of alphanumeric characters that marked our position.

"Roger that, Mustang Six. Zero-Nine copies all. Hold on, son. The cavalry is coming. Shock Zero-Nine is thirty seconds out. I say again, we are thirty seconds out. Can you mark your position, over?"

"Zero-Nine, stand by," I said, kicking myself for not thinking of this contingency sooner.

As per any close-combat attack scenario, the gunship crews wanted to begin the engagement by verifying the position of friendly forces—in this case, Laila and me. To do this, the aviators needed a way to distinguish us from the bad guys. Usually this was done via an infrared strobe or a chem light, a glint tape, or a laser. Even a can of colored smoke or a brightly dyed VS-17 panel could get the job done.

But this wasn't my tactical vest; it was Zain's. And while the smuggler had saved Laila's life by outfitting his rig with a med kit, I had no reason to believe he carried anything I could use to mark my position. I knew that Zain had been in gunfights a time or two, but I doubted his experience extended to marking his position for a pair of Apache gunships.

I patted down his vest, searching for something. Anything. As I suspected, my Syrian friend didn't carry an IR strobe, a can of smoke, or even a chem light. But what he did have was his ever-present collection of cigars stuffed in a ziplock bag, and a lighter. Not exactly what I was hoping to find, but if Jesus managed to feed the five thousand with five loaves of bread and two fish, maybe a former Ranger could talk in a pair of Apaches using three Cohibas and a silver-plated Zippo.

"Shock, this is Mustang," I said, ripping open the ziplock bag. "I might have something that will work. You have thermals, correct?"

"That's affirm. Our targeting sight uses the infrared spectrum."

"Good. I'm marking my position with a cigar."

"Mustang, Shock. Did you say cigar, over?"

"Roger. I've got three of them."

"Okay, Mustang. We'll give it a try. Say when ready."

I stuck the three cigars between my lips and bit down. The bitter taste of tobacco flooded my mouth. I lit the ends with Zain's blowtorch of a lighter and sucked in a huge breath. The torrent of nicotine sent my head spinning, but instead of giving in to the urge to vomit, I lay back and began to puff. The night stars twinkled overhead as if laughing.

"Mustang Six, this is Shock. That's a negative on the cigars. Is there anything else you can use? Anything at all."

I tossed the cigars to the side as I gave in to a coughing fit. The helicopters were now close enough that I could hear the bass *whump* of their rotors, but without a way to let them know where I was, they might as well have been on the other side of the world. Next to me, the cigars hissed in the dirt.

I needed something easier for the Apache's thermal to see. Something hotter.

I needed a fire.

As I looked at the debris scattered in front of me, my eyes settled on the remnants of the medical kit. Sifting through the components, I saw a box of alcohol wipes. Ripping apart the cardboard, I found packets inside. Those would burn, but probably not any brighter than the cigars. I needed something with a bit more *oomph*.

Like a torch.

Tearing off my chest rig, I slipped out of my T-shirt and crumpled it into a ball. Then I broke open the alcohol wipes and wrapped them in the fabric. Finally, I lit the Zippo and touched the blue flame to an exposed corner of an alcohol wipe. The thin material ignited with a *whoosh*, burning my fingers in the process.

"Shock, this is Mustang. I just lit my fucking shirt on fire. Tell me you can see that, over."

The longest pause of my life and then: "Mustang, Shock. We've got it. I say again, we've got your position. Confirm bearing to targets."

Fucking pilots. I was lying in a shallow grave, bullets whizzing by my head, with my shirt on fire. And now he wanted an azimuth to target?

"Shock, negative on the bearing. I'll make this simple—

orient your attack run along the length of my body. Kill anything past my head, over."

"Mustang, Shock, roger all. Be advised—targets are danger close to your position. I say again, danger close. I'll need your initials to shoot."

"My initials?" I said.

"Roger, Mustang. This close, there's a good chance you're going to get hit by our volley. To make sure you understand the risk, we need the initials of your first and last name. We can't shoot danger close without them."

Fucking pilots.

"My initials are F.U. Now kill those fuckers!"

"Roger that. Standby, Mustang. Gun one is coming in hot."

At the words *coming in hot*, I contorted my body around Laila's, trying to shelter her from what was coming next, even though my efforts were probably futile. The Apache's 30mm chain gun fired bullets five inches in length equipped with shaped charges designed to penetrate two inches of rolled homogenous armor. If the pilot missed, the razor-edged shards would scythe through our bodies like they were butter.

But I held Laila tight all the same.

Light split the night sky in two as a jackhammer-like sound filled the air. And then the earth heaved upward, knocking the phone from my hand as the cannon rounds found their mark. A series of thunderclaps rolled across the ground as the shaped charges detonated, filling the air with whining bits of steel.

Laila moaned, and I held her tighter.

Then silence returned.

My body ached, my ears were ringing, and my knee throbbed from where I'd bounced off the ground. In other words, I was somehow still alive.

Peeking above the depression, I surveyed the carnage. Broken bodies and scattered limbs were everywhere. Absolute devastation. Some of the human debris was less than twenty meters from our little defilade. A moment more and the fighters would have overrun us, rendering the Apaches useless.

"Gun One, good hits," I said, picking up the phone from where it had fallen. "Gun Two, on Gun One."

"Gun Two, roger all. Inbound."

"What—," Laila began, but I didn't give her time to finish.

"Keep down," I said, pressing my body on top of hers again.

A split second later, the jackhammer raged overhead, and once again the earth vomited me skyward. This time, the incoming gunner must have been more certain about our position. He fired four or five bursts, giving new meaning to *bringing the thunder*. The cannon rounds detonated in a seemingly never-ending chain of explosions in front of me as expended brass from the hardworking cannon fell to either side of us like rain.

Then the gunship rocketed overhead.

Popping my head up, I was greeted with a scene from the apocalypse. Smoke, sulfur, human detritus, and the coppery stench of blood.

It was horrible.

It was wonderful.

"Good hits, Gun Two," I said, surveying the massacre. "Gun One—work over that ridgeline. The surface-to-air missiles came from that direction."

"Gun One, roger. Inbound."

Pairs of rockets streaked overhead, trailing tails of flame as they thundered through the sound barrier. Night became day on top of the ridgeline as the rockets' ten-pound high-explosive warheads detonated one after another. Gun 1 then added its cannon to the mix as the helicopter broke left, raking the hillside with flashbulb-like explosions.

No sooner had Gun 1 turned off target than Gun 2 took up the dance, bracketing the ridgeline in rocket and cannon fire. For a time, the Apaches worked without my help in a dance as beautiful as it was deadly. Then, after the sixth pass, the Angels of Death rested.

The world was quiet.

"Mustang, this is Shock. Targets have been neutralized, and the Ospreys are inbound, over."

"Roger that, Shock Zero-Nine. Thank you for the help. What's your name, over?"

"Darrin. Darrin Swan."

"You just saved my life, Darrin Swan," I said. "First round's on me."

"Roger all, Mustang Six. Happy to help."

Tossing down the phone, I reached for Laila and felt her pulse. It was fluttering much too rapidly, but she was hanging in there. At my touch, she slowly opened her eyes.

"Hi, baby," I said, stroking her ashen cheek. "Can you hear me?"

Her green eyes traveled across my filthy face and down my blood-streaked chest. Then she licked her lips and cleared her throat. "Baby, you look like shit."

Scooping her into my arms, I cradled my wife against my bare chest, rocking her back and forth as the first CV-22 touched down. A moment later, half a dozen figures materialized out of the gloom, one carrying an assault bag.

"Is this the patient?" the medic said, dropping to the ground beside his already-unzipped med bag.

"Yes," I said.

"How is she?"

"She's going to be fine," Laila said, squeezing my hand. "She has her husband back."

EPILOGUE

'd killed my share of men, but always on the field of battle, never in cold blood. I wasn't an assassin.

At least not until today.

Today, I'd traded my usual Glock 23 in for a 26. The "baby" Glock carried the same number of rounds, but was built for concealment rather than for accuracy. A pistol that fit perfectly in a woman's purse.

Or a killer's coat pocket.

For once, the DC winter weather was something worth enjoying. Though temperatures hovered in the high thirties, the cloudless blue sky and brilliant sunshine tricked you into feeling warmer. A promise made from this, the most self-important of cities, to its residents: that if they just suffered through a few more miserable weeks, spring would once again make the cherry trees flower.

Even here, on an isolated jogging path nestled deep in the woods, signs of spring were everywhere. The brook that paralleled the cracked asphalt jogging path bubbled and laughed as if grateful to finally be free from winter's icy grip. Squirrels chattered to one another from the treetops, and patches of black soil peeked through the melting snow.

All in all, it really was a beautiful day. One to be spent wandering the National Mall in hopes of seeing someone important or perhaps watching the majestic changing-of-the-guard ceremony at Arlington National Cemetery.

Or even running along a cracked asphalt jogging path deep in the woods.

To my right, I could hear the sound of footfalls just beyond where the path took a ninety-degree turn away from the creek and disappeared up a small hill into the woods. The foot strikes were not the haphazard slaps of a casual runner stretching his legs for a little late-afternoon exercise. No, the dull thuds of rubber against asphalt came with a metronome's precision. This was a runner with a capital *R*. A former collegiate athlete.

As the footfalls grew closer, I squatted at the edge of the path, fiddling with a shoelace that was already tied.

My windbreaker was two sizes too big, and a dark knit cap was pulled down low over my forehead and ears. I was wearing clothing that would conceal my recognizable build for the same reason that I'd chosen this particular section of path. Because I didn't want the person who was fast approaching to realize who was waiting for him.

Unzipping the windbreaker's side pocket, I gripped

the pistol with one gloved hand, keeping the other free at my side, all the while listening to the footfalls.

The footfalls of a man who wanted me dead.

For the first time, the man's cadence increased as he trotted down the hill. Then he made the ninety-degree turn and was hurtling toward me. His pace slowed as he saw my crouched form, the prehistoric part of his brain stem attempting to warn him.

But his lizard brain was much too late.

Standing in a rush, I exploded upward, grabbing his throat with one hand and shoving the Glock into his firm abs with the other.

"Hiya, Chuck," I said, looking into the startled eyes of Charles Sinclair Robinson IV. "Let's have us a little talk."

I hustled Charles off the path and into the woods as quickly as I could, frog-marching him with the Glock shoved into his kidney. Even so, by the time we'd walked ten meters, some of Charles's initial terror had given way to righteous indignation. He was already certain he could talk his way free.

But he was wrong.

"Drake," Charles said, turning toward me with his hands on his hips, "have you lost your mind?"

I let the Glock do the talking. Swinging the pistol in a tight arc, I caught him in the side of the head with the barrel before reversing to bring the plastic grip down on the bridge of his nose. Hard. Not with enough force to break his nose, but plenty to get his attention.

"Shut the fuck up," I said, grabbing him by the hair and screwing the pistol into his eye socket. "You will not speak again unless I give you permission. Nod if you understand."

Charles nodded.

"On your knees," I said, "and put your hands behind your back. Now."

I kept my grip on his hair as Charles complied, sliding behind him while pressing the Glock into the base of his neck.

"Here's what you need to understand," I said, yanking his head backward so that we were eye to eye. "I know everything. Every goddamn thing. I know about the money, the deal you had with Sayid, and what you did for the Devil. I know all. You are alive for one reason and one reason only. I want my cut. Do you understand? Speak."

"Yes," Charles said, trying to ease the pressure on his skull. "I understand."

"Excellent," I said. "Get on the ground. Facedown. Now."

"Why—," Charles said.

This time I hit him in the cheekbone. Maybe a little too hard. The front sight post snagged on his skin, opening a bloody furrow.

"All right, all right," Charles said, prostrating himself on the cold soil. "Jesus."

I reached into my pocket and grabbed a cell phone. I

opened up the appropriate app and dropped the device in front of Charles.

"You're going to transfer my share of the money to the bank account on the screen," I said. "Now. Speak."

"How do I know you won't kill me?" Charles said.

"You're right," I said, kicking Charles in the ribs. "You should be scared that I'll kill you. Terrified, really. But here's the thing, Chucky. You're a smart guy. I'm betting that your little business venture in Syria isn't the only one you've been eyeing. Shit, once you're the CIA Director, the sky's the limit. You'd make a better partner than a corpse. Transfer the money, Charles. Now. Seventy-five percent of your take."

Charles grabbed the phone, but his fingers weren't moving. Not yet, anyway. "How do I know this isn't a setup?"

This time I pictured Virginia lying in a pool of her own blood when I booted him in the ribs. At least one cracked. Maybe more. But who was counting?

"You really are a stupid motherfucker," I said once Charles had stopped moaning. "Look at the balance on my bank account. You think you were the only one skimming funds in Syria? This isn't a setup. I'm as dirty as you are. Just smarter. Now, transfer the fucking money."

Charles hesitated for another long second, and then his thumbs took on a life of their own. They stabbed the phone with reckless abandon for a minute or two. Then it was done.

"Here," Charles said, handing me the cell.

I took the device and looked at the screen. People say

that you can't assign a dollar amount to someone's life, but that just isn't true. The innocuous string of digits staring back at me represented the monetary value of my asset, his family, and Virginia. At least to Charles, anyway.

I slipped the phone back into my pocket and zipped it closed. Then I pushed the pistol into the top of Charles's skull, driving his face into the dirt.

"Listen up," I said. "If you've transferred a penny less than seventy-five percent of your take, I will pay you another visit. And when I do, it will make this little meeting look like a tea party. Understand? Speak."

"I understand," Charles said. "I understand!"

"Good," I said. "Now, I'm going to walk away. Keep your face in the fucking dirt until I'm gone. If you get up before then, I'll kneecap you. Nod if you understand."

Charles nodded, his head sliding back and forth in the snow.

"Fantastic," I said, walking slowly backward. "I'm glad we had this talk, Chucky. Good luck at the confirmation hearing."

Fifteen minutes later, I pulled open the passenger door of an unmarked Pontiac Grand Am and climbed inside. A blue cloud of cigarette smoke awaited.

"Did you burn through the entire pack while I was gone?" I said, unzipping my windbreaker.

"I told you," Agent Rawlings said. "I smoke when I'm nervous."

"You need therapy," I said, rolling down the window. "Did it come through?"

"Every goddamn word," Agent Rawlings said. "You're the best source I've ever run."

"You do not run me," I said, stripping the microphone and miniature transmitter from where Rawlings had taped them against my chest, "and I am no longer your source."

"You're gonna have to testify," Rawlings said.

"Bullshit," I said, tossing the listening device into his lap. "My part is done. Zain rescued the girls in Iraq, and Ferah and Nazya are reunited. One of the men who set all of this into motion is dead, and the other just transferred me a shitload of dirty money. You don't need me to testify. You already have more than enough to subpoena Charles's financials. I'd start here."

I activated the banking app and handed Rawlings the cell phone.

"Jesus," he said, his bushy eyebrows arching upward. "Stealing from the CIA pays well."

"That's not all Charles," I said. "It's also the account I used for the sex-trafficking auction. But tying Charles to the dirty money will certainly jump-start your investigation."

"Except there's the little matter of how you obtained this evidence," Rawlings said. "US attorneys aren't real fond of coercion."

"And I could give two shits," I said, glaring at Rawlings. "That motherfucker is lucky he's still breathing. He's the reason four of my people are dead and another's crippled. I would have been within my rights to put him in the ground."

"So why didn't you?" Rawlings said.

I took one deep breath and then another. "Here's the thing—I don't kill for money, and I don't get off on it. I do what needs to be done. That's it. I'm not a murderer. Not now. Not ever."

"Fair enough," Rawlings said, "but that still doesn't help me with my warrant."

"Maybe you ought to take a look at a blog run by a journalist named Allie Mishler," I said. "She's an investigative reporter. I heard she's got the scoop on Charles too."

I gave Rawlings the website's address, and he punched it into his phone.

"She sure does," Rawlings said. "That's a fantastic bit of reporting right there. You know what's even more fantastic? According to her byline, she's a Texas girl. What are the odds of that?"

"Tell me about the CI investigation," I said, "and I'll tell you about Allie."

"Nope," Rawlings said. "That's how I got into this shit show to begin with. I've still got more than enough to bring Charles in for questioning. Wanna tag along?"

"Rain check," I said, getting out of the car. "I've got dinner with my wife, and she hates it when I'm late."

ACKNOWLEDGMENTS

I hope you enjoyed reading *The Outside Man* as much as I enjoyed writing it. Actually, that's not true. As my good friend Nick Petrie, author of the Peter Ash novels, is never afraid to remind me, writing a book is hard. Writing two books borders on insanity. With that in mind, I'd like to thank some of the people who were brave enough to join me on this journey of madness.

I have the pleasure of writing for Berkley, and they really are the publishing dream team. Once again, editor extraordinaire Tom Colgan understood what I was trying to achieve and pushed me to go further. Publicist Loren Jaggers was great as always. Marketing guru Jin Yu really is a force of nature, as much at home planning and executing masterful marketing campaigns as she is helping hapless authors unlock their Facebook accounts. Seriously, Jin—it wasn't my fault!

Writing novels is not for the faint of heart. Fortunately for me, I have a built-in support group of like-minded lunatics in the form of fellow authors Nick Petrie, Bill Schweigart, and Graham Brown, along with our fearless agent, Barbara Poelle of the Irene Goodman Literary

Agency. I'd like to thank each of you for your humor and wisdom—I'm not sure which I valued more!

Speaking of Barbara, if you've never met her, you're in for a treat. She's smart, funny, and a fierce advocate for her authors. Thank you, Barbara, for always being in my corner.

Over the past several years of writing, I've been lucky enough to work with a stellar group of first readers. If you liked this book, then Erica Nichols, Tommy Ledbetter, Michelle Kime, and Bill Schweigart deserve a huge portion of the credit. If you didn't, it's probably because I didn't listen to their feedback closely enough!

I'd also like to thank Bill Schweigart and his lovely wife, Kate, for hosting me at their home numerous times so that Bill and I could talk through plot issues and drink beer. On a related note, if you haven't read Bill's first book, *The Beast of Barcroft*, you're missing out.

The kindness of the authors who write in the military/ political thriller genre is second only to the quality of their work. In particular, Matthew Betley, Sean Parnell, Joshua Hood, Simon Gervais, K.J. Howe, Anthony J. Tata, Laurie Chandlar, Jack Carr, Chris Hauty, Anne Wilson, Jeffrey Wilson, Brian Andrews, Kathleen Antrim, Mike Maden, Kyle Mills, Mark Greaney, and Brad Taylor all provided encouragement throughout the writing process.

Of these great folks, Mark Greaney and Brad Taylor were exceptionally kind. Mark selflessly used his platform to talk about my first novel, *Without Sanction*, and was more than willing to offer a rookie his thoughts on what it took to succeed in this business.

Likewise, Brad and Elaine Taylor took me under their wing, graciously providing invaluable lessons from their stellar writing career while going above and beyond to help me promote *Without Sanction*. Additionally, Brad traveled to Austin for my book launch party and was a stand-up guy when I told my dad he was really a SEAL. Sorry, Brad, but it was kind of funny!

In addition to the writers, this genre is also blessed to have some amazing reviewers and podcasters. Ryan Steck of The Real Book Spy fame and Slaven Tomasi of Lima Charlie Editing have both been exceptional advocates for my work. Additionally, the guys from *The Crew Reviews* podcast (Chris Albanese, Sean Cameron, Mike Houtz, and Eric Bishop) and Jason Piccolo from the *Protectors* podcast have all been immeasurably helpful.

As they did during *Without Sanction*, my cadre of subject-matter experts again generously provided me with answers to the numerous inane questions I encountered while writing *The Outside Man*. Specifically, former Army Ranger Brandon Cates offered valuable insight into why fast roping looks so much more fun than it actually is. By the same token, retired Sergeant Major Jason Beighley was kind enough to explain some of the intricacies of distance shooting in terms that even a former gun pilot could understand. As before, any technical inaccuracies are my responsibility, while anything that rang true is a testament to these fine folks.

On a serious note, *The Outside Man* deals with the horrific topic of sex trafficking. Much of my research into this horrible practice came from the heartbreaking book *The Last Girl*, written by Nadia Murad, herself a survivor of sex trafficking. If you want to understand this problem better, Nadia's book is a great place to start. If you want to do something to help, I'd humbly point you toward Imagine Goods (imaginegoods.com). Cofounded by my cousin, Michelle Kime, Imagine Goods exists to provide opportunities for empowerment through employment for survivors of trafficking. Ninety percent of Imagine Goods' artisans are survivors.

Once again, I'd be remiss if I didn't thank my long-time friend John Dixon. A fantastic writer in his own right, John has been my consigliere and confidant for the past decade. John, thank you for your wisdom and heartfelt advice. I couldn't have written this without you.

Finally, I'd like to thank my children, Will, Faith, and Kelia, and my wife, Angela. Without all of you, none of this would mean anything.

—DON

Turn the page for a taste of

HOSTILE INTENT

The new, electrifying Matt Drake thriller
Available in hardcover from Berkley in May 2022

AUSTIN, TEXAS

Four shots rang out in quick succession, the retort thunderously loud even through my Peltor hearing protection. I detested indoor shooting ranges with their close confines and dingy interiors. Some jackass with a hand cannon always seemed to be in the lane next to yours, and today was no exception. Whatever, shooting under crappy conditions was still shooting, and that beat the alternative.

Usually.

"What's he hitting?"

"Air," I said, eyeing the target adjacent mine. The crisp white paper overlaid with a bad-guy silhouette swung merrily beneath its metal hanger without a care in the world. I could see why. A scattering of holes graced the paper's edges, but the black target lines spiraling outward from the center were completely unbroken.

"You're kicking butt," I said, turning back to my own

lane and the woman sharing it. "Put another couple pairs center mass, and we'll call it a day."

"Already?" the woman said. "You must have other plans. Or something."

As a matter of fact, I did have other plans.

Or something.

But I knew better than to take the bait.

"Less talking. More shooting."

I gave the instructions in my no-nonsense firearms instructor's voice, and the woman responded accordingly. Settling into a shooter's stance, she adjusted her balance as she extended a 9mm Glock away from her chest in a two-handed grip. Her hips shifted as she transferred weight to the balls of her feet.

The movement was slight, but noticeable.

At least to me.

Then again, I do love my wife's hips.

I reached forward, touching Laila's back. "Remember to square your shoulders," I said, my fingertips pressing against smooth, silky skin.

My wife was an exquisitely beautiful woman. With a Pakistani father and Afghan mother, Laila was a melting pot of genes from one of the earth's most ethnically diverse territories. Modern-day Afghanistan and Pakistan had hosted countless foreign conquerors, and Laila's appearance reflected the region's collective influence. Her dark complexion and waves of midnight hair framed emerald eyes that still caused my heart to skip a beat.

This morning, she was wearing a simple white tank top paired with tight, faded jeans, and a ball cap embroidered with the Texas Gonzales flag. But there was nothing simple about the way the cream-colored shirt highlighted her almond skin or the thick black ponytail tumbling down her back.

On a normal day, the sight of my wife was distracting. Today, she was intoxicating.

"More coaching," Laila said. "Less touching." She adjusted her stance again, snugging her hips against mine. She squeezed off a pair of shots before I could reply, but she needn't have bothered.

I'd lost the capacity for speech.

Laila followed up her first aimed pair with a second, and then a third. The silhouette sported six new holes, all within the ten ring. The paper target was only five meters distant, but there was no doubt that Laila was getting the hang of this. I was a good coach, but she was a highly motivated student.

For good reason.

Her Glock's slide locked to the rear after the final shot. Laila ejected the spent magazine and placed it and the pistol onto the tray in front of her. Just like she'd been taught.

"How'd I do?" she said, facing me.

I could tell by the way her green eyes sparkled that she already knew the answer. Even so, she'd more than earned a compliment or two, and as her instructor, it was my job to give them.

"You did—"

The hand cannon erupted.

Again.

I jumped, and Laila shrieked.

A peal of male laughter greeted Laila's decidedly feminine exclamation, followed by an admonishment to "grow a pair."

Charming.

"Just a sec," I said. "I've got to take care of something."

"Where are you going?" Laila said, grabbing my biceps.

"Only be a minute," I said, smiling the smile that had melted the hearts of interrogators the world over.

"Matthew," Laila said.

Her green eyes were no longer sparkling. They were shimmering. This was a very important distinction. Sparkling eyes meant a happy wife. Shimmering ones were akin to the buzzing of a rattlesnake's rattle.

"Quick chat with our neighbors," I said. "Nothing more."

"You're a spy," Laila said. "You lie for a living."

She had me there.

"But never to you," I said. "Besides, lying's only a small part of the job. I mostly build bridges of cultural understanding."

"Bridges to nowhere," Laila said. Her tone was still less than pleased, but her eyes were no longer shimmering. This was important. A pissed-off wife meant that my "other plans" would amount to practicing my guitar.

Alone.

On the other hand, a happy wife meant that my

chances of getting lucky a second time today were at least fifty percent.

I'd toppled governments with worse odds.

"Right back," I said, and this time my smile wasn't forced.

I'd been operational for the last six weeks and had just flown back into country the previous evening. We were at the shooting range this morning because Laila wanted to practice, but I was hoping to help her out of that tank top afterward. No way was I going to let a couple of redneck jackwads mess that up.

Laila frowned, but she didn't ask me to stay.

Progress.

Sliding around the length of sheet metal diving our lane from the hand cannon, I introduced myself to the gentlemen occupying it.

"Y'all need help?" I said, smiling my second-best smile.

Only Laila got my first-best smile.

Laila and men who wanted to kill me.

My sudden appearance caught the shooters by surprise. My two new friends jumped at the sound of my voice. I thought that was kind of funny.

They did not.

"Help with what?" the one on the left said. He had the thick build of a former athlete whose frame now sported more fat than muscle. Judging by the smedium shirt stretched Saran Wrap–tight across his pudgy chest, he was in a bit of denial about his physical state.

"Great question," I said, still grinning ear to ear.

"From the looks of your target, you probably think I'm offering y'all shooting pointers. I'm not. I'm actually wondering if you need help with anatomy."

"Anatomy?"

This time the question came from the gentleman on the right, who looked as if he'd stepped from the pages of *Soldier of Fortune* magazine. Asolo boots, 5.11 pants, and a PFG shirt.

A regular tactical ninja.

"Yep," I said. "One of you geniuses just asked my wife to do something anatomically impossible. The way I figure it, y'all either need remedial schooling or were deliberately rude. Personally, I'm hoping for the schooling. Otherwise, I'll have to give you jackasses a tune-up. Believe me—no one wants to see that. Or you could just apologize, I guess. What's it gonna be, boys?"

The men sized me up before sharing a look. I understood. Don't get me wrong, at six feet and one hundred and eighty-five pounds, I wasn't physically insignificant. But neither was I Arnold Schwarzenegger. The 1980s Arnold Schwarzenegger, that is. Today's Arnold is still fit, but I could take him.

Probably.

In any case, I was sporting what Laila playfully termed my ragamuffin look. At least I hoped it was playful. My hair was long and my beard scruffy, but the Wrangler pearly snap shirt I was wearing framed the wide shoulders and broad back of a person for whom physical fitness was more than just a passing fancy. Put that all together, and I don't know what you get. But whatever it was didn't seem to be enough to convince Beefcake and Mr. Ninja to back down.

"Who the hell are you?" Beefcake said, folding his arms across his chest.

Now we were getting somewhere.

"Another great question," I said, my smile widening. "I'm—"

"Drake? Is there a Matt Drake here?"

The question came from behind me. I turned to see the man from the gun range's check-in counter holding open the door to the shooting lanes.

"I'm Drake," I said.

"Phone," the man said, "inside. Says he's your boss."

"I'm on vacation," I said.

"He said you'd say that. He also said to tell you that terrorists don't take vacations and neither do the people who hunt them. If you don't pick up the phone, he'll send the FBI. Again. Sorry—his words."

"Tell him I'm coming," I said. I waited a beat for the man to leave and for the heavy, soundproof door to close behind him. Then I turned back to Beefcake and Mr. Ninja.

"We're short on time, so I'll cut to the chase," I said. "You're going to apologize to my wife. Do it now, and we can all leave happy. Refuse, and I'll be forced to come find you *after* I finish putting another jihadi in the dirt. This will make me unhappy. I will express this unhappiness to you two next time we meet. So is it gonna to be now or later?"

They chose now.

Bridges to nowhere my ass.

Ready to find
your next great read?

Let us help.

Visit prh.com/nextread